2

FALLEN

A PRIDE & PREJUDICE VARIATION

JESSIE LEWIS

This is a work of fiction. Names, characters, businesses, places, events, locales, and incidents are either the products of the author's imagination or used in a fictitious manner. Any resemblance to actual persons, living or dead, or actual events is purely coincidental.

Edited by Kristi Rawley and Linda D'Orazio

Cover Design by Cloudcat Design

ISBN 978-1-951033-64-4 (ebook) and 978-1-951033-65-1 (paperback)

For every reader who ever yearned for a little more time with Jane Austen's Darcy and Elizabeth.

CONTENTS

Prologue

She stood on the other side of the door and listened to the rumble of voices beyond. None were raised, and neither were they likely to be, for it was not in either man's nature to rage. She wished they would speak up, though. She would hear for herself when one acknowledged she had saved him, and the other acknowledged he must now save her.

Something banged, and she jumped. An echoing ripple stirred deep inside her, but she ignored it and concentrated on the world outside her, for that one frightened her less. Someone had hammered a fist on a table. She was not surprised; it had never promised to be a convivial discussion, for everything had happened in the wrong order. What ought to have inspired relief, delight, and celebration had instead caused shock, outrage, and dismay, but that would all pass. In months and years to come, the order of events at the beginning would scarcely matter to anybody.

Carefully, she eased the door ajar by the smallest margin. She could see nothing but a sliver of the far wall, and she could hear nothing but the accentuated breathing of somebody who was extremely angry. Or perhaps it was that the air seemed to be thicker inside the chamber than out here, in the hallway. The weight of such a moment, making it difficult to catch one's breath.

"You cannot mean that."

"I assure you I do. I have never been more violently opposed to anything in my life."

Some of the heavy air must have leaked out through the crack, for she felt mired in it, suddenly. They were the right voices, but they were saying all the wrong things.

"You would not be so unscrupulous."

"Do not talk to me of scruples as though she overflows with them! Nothing you say will change my mind. I will not marry her."

The air was all gone, and coldness overtook her, as though she had fallen into icy water and was sinking into the blackness. The voices *were* raised now, but she could not hear them any better than when the door had been closed, for her ears were full of the thunderous beating of her terrified heart. Her stomach churned, as it was wont to do these days. He would not marry her. She was ruined. They were all ruined. The blackness closed in, and she hit the floor with a thud.

HE STOOD IN THE DOORWAY AND WATCHED HER CRAWL across the bed on her hands and knees while her sister attempted to calm her—or restrain her, he was not sure which.

"I do not want it!" she screamed. "Get it out of me, I do not want it!"

"How long has she been like this?"

"Since she felt the quickening," answered the man at his side.

She must have heard them talking, for she stopped railing and looked at him with a gasp. It had been some time since they were last in company, and he waited, without any anticipation of a happy reunion, to see how she would act. He was not particularly surprised when she let out an unearthly howl and launched herself off the bed towards him. He caught her by the wrists, preventing her from pounding her fists against him. She was weak, which was a worry.

"This is all your fault!" she screamed. "Why would you not have me? Look what you have reduced me to!"

Her appearance was shocking: her eyes rimmed with red and underscored with dark shadows, her complexion drawn and pallid. He felt a stirring of pity, for such she was: pitiable. He loosened his grip, only to tighten it again when he realised, with disgust, that she was attempting to snake her arms about his neck.

"'Tis not too late," she said feverishly. "I would make you an excellent wife."

"You can never be my wife." He was careful not to betray his revulsion lest it vex his companion, to whom he said, "She ought to be moved elsewhere."

She began to fight him again. "I do not wish to be sent away. I would go home!"

"You know that is not possible," said her sister, saving him the trouble.

All the fight left her; she wilted against him and emitted a long, desolate wail. "I do not want it. I do not want any of this. I do not deserve it."

He unceremoniously passed her back into the nearest pair of hands, fighting valiantly not to let his mouth curl into the sneer of disdain that lurked so closely beneath the surface of his composure. Had not she placed herself on such a high pedestal, she would never have had so far to fall. Unable to repress his feelings a moment longer, he turned on his heel and left.

1 Charming Neighbours

Elizabeth had removed only her bonnet and one glove when the door to her father's library swept open and he appeared, gesturing with some urgency for her to come inside. He closed it again almost before she was completely through.

"What on earth is the matter?" she enquired, laughing.

He put a finger to his lips. "Not so loud, Lizzy. Old Mrs Hanrahan is here, and until now, I have been giving an exceedingly convincing performance of someone who is not."

The pair exchanged grins, Elizabeth's broadening significantly when her father returned with exaggeratedly stealthy steps to his chair. She well understood his desire to remain out of the way of such a caller and could only pity her mother for being unable to do the same. Mrs Hanrahan rarely ventured out anymore—a circumstance to which nobody in the neighbourhood much objected, for she was a shrewish, unpleasant woman who never had anything interesting to say but always insisted on saying it at least ten times before she could be prevailed on to leave.

"She has been here since two o'clock," Mr Bennet informed her, "and every time another one of your sisters blunders into the room, it resets her to the beginning of her tale."

Elizabeth sat down opposite her father and smoothed a hand over her hair, windswept having lost her bonnet several times to sudden gusts on her walk. "I wonder what induced her to venture out from Hoxley."

"Your guess is as good as mine. But have no doubt, your mother will not allow us to remain ignorant for long."

Mrs Bennet did not disappoint. No sooner had Elizabeth set up the backgammon board and made her first move than her mother burst into the library in a welter of indignation. She narrowed her eyes upon discovering her second eldest child skulking within but was apparently too vexed at Mrs Hanrahan to waste any of her displeasure on Elizabeth. "Two hours! Two *hours* that odious woman has been here. Have you ever known anybody to take such a liberty?"

"Had you any other plans for the afternoon?" enquired her husband.

"I might have had. Not that Mrs Hanrahan had a care for it. Now my head aches, and I am certain I shall accomplish nothing for the rest of the day."

"In that case, I do not wonder at your pique. It was the height of presumption to think you required any assistance in achieving that end. Still, you may at least console yourself that half your afternoon has been given purpose, and the other half pretext."

"Purpose you call it? I see no purpose in wasting hours of one's time attending to the repeated complaints of a peevish, insensible woman."

"Perhaps you are right, but I hope not, for it would paint a very sorry picture of my existence."

"Did Mrs Hanrahan have anything of interest to say, Mama?" Elizabeth interjected, knowing as well as her father, though perhaps caring more, that her mother could only withstand so much provocation.

"Oh, nothing and nothing, as usual," Mrs Bennet replied. "Her roof is leaking, her ulcers have worsened, she is displeased with her new neighbours, her maid is stealing from her. Why come at all if only to repine? I have never known anybody take such pleasure in spreading misery wherever she goes."

"New neighbours?" said Mr Bennet. "What has she done with the old ones?"

Two spots of colour appeared on Mrs Bennet's cheeks and her mouth became so pinched it rendered her words stilted. "You know very well she has not done anything with them."

"With whom?" Elizabeth enquired. "I do not recall that there are any houses close enough to hers to call neighbours."

"You know the place, Lizzy," said her father. "The little cottage in the lea beyond the woods on the far side of Netherfield Park. Over towards Waterford."

"The one with no roof?" Her incredulity increased when it was confirmed to be the case. "I see why they must be a nuisance. Every word they say must go echoing across the valley to Hoxley."

"You are as tiresome as your father," cried Mrs Bennet. "The cottage was obviously refitted before they took up in it."

"By whom?" Elizabeth mused, wondering who would trouble themselves with such a dilapidated little house.

Mrs Bennet sighed impatiently. "I have not the slightest idea, and neither do I much care. Nobody who would live in a ramshackle hut in the middle of the woods is of the remotest interest to me. Why could not Mrs Hanrahan take more interest in her other neighbours? For Netherfield is but quarter or half a mile from Hoxley. Had she come with some pertinent information about Mr Bingley, then I should gladly have suffered a visit of two hours and considered the headache worthwhile."

"For what news were you hoping?" Elizabeth enquired. "Mr Bingley has not yet been in Hertfordshire a fortnight and already we have seen him at this month's assembly, once at his own house and once at ours, and we have twice dined in his company. Mrs Hanrahan hardly ever leaves home. I do not think she can know any more about him than we do."

"She might know whether Mrs Long has taken her nieces to call on him."

"I do not see how," said Mr Bennet. "Not even your voice will carry half a mile. I am quite sure Mrs Long's timid little squeak would not be audible at such a distance."

"I hope, if they have called, they received a warmer welcome than we did."

"Nonsense, Lizzy," her mother retorted. "Mr Bingley was as happy to see Jane when we called as he has been every time since. Need I remind you that he singled her out for *four* dances at the assembly?"

Elizabeth made no reply. Mr Bingley had, indeed, seemed pleased that Jane had called. His sisters, on the other hand, had received them with dismay that bordered on alarm, confirming her first impression of two ladies who considered themselves far superior to Hertfordshire society.

"And you know," said Mrs Bennet, undeterred, "Mr Bingley might have had other visitors come from Town who would have had to drive directly past Hoxley."

"Any newcomers must be an improvement on his present choice of friends, eh, Lizzy?"

Elizabeth met her father's gleeful expression with a wry smile. As well as his sisters, Mr Bingley's party consisted of his eldest sister's husband, Mr Hurst, and his oldest friend, Mr Darcy. Mr Hurst had yet to make much of an impression on anyone, being rather more interested in his cups than his company. Mr Darcy had set tongues wagging from the first moment he arrived at the Meryton Assembly rooms, first on account of his uncommon good looks, then the reports of his prodigious wealth, and finally his colossal pride, which, by the end of the evening, had proved objectionable enough to eclipse both his other, not inconsiderable, qualities. This superlative beginning notwithstanding, he had not truly covered himself in glory until the moment he refused an introduction to Elizabeth, declaring within full earshot that she was not handsome enough to tempt him, and that it would be a punishment to stand up with her. She had chosen to be diverted rather than vexed, for to be vexed was to afford him a victory, and she had no intention of allowing such a peacock anything even remotely resembling a triumph.

"There, you see?" said Mrs Bennet. "News of another, pleasanter houseguest than that horrid Mr Darcy would not be entirely unwelcome, would it? Though we can but hope that all Mr Bingley's friends have ten thousand a year."

"Mama, it makes no difference to me how many friends he has visiting, or how amiable any of them are, I am in no rush to find a husband. You must content yourself with the knowledge that Mr Bingley is agreeable enough for Jane."

"And rich enough for her mother," added Mr Bennet.

Mrs Bennet's eyes flashed. "I know it is all a fine joke to you, sir, but this house will not be ours forever, and you know very well I have not the means to support any of our girls on my own. Do not say I did not warn you if you depart this world before I, and they are all made homeless."

"I promise you, my dear, if I die first, I shall not say a word on the matter."

Suspecting her mother was nearing the limit of her composure, Elizabeth stood and reached for her arm. "Come, Mama, let me help you upstairs to lie down."

"Yes, it will be better if you lie down," said Mr Bennet to

his wife. "One cannot truly accomplish nothing until one is fully recumbent, preferably with five daughters and a maid in attendance to gratify one's every whim. Do take care not to groan too loudly though, for hysteria could so easily be mistaken for activity."

Elizabeth often wondered which had developed first: her mother's nervous disposition or her father's sarcastic humour, but she was certain they each were deeply indebted to the other for their proficiency in both.

2

No Harm in Waving

Saturday morning was so bright and warm that even Lydia was bestirred to leave the house and join all her sisters in calling on their Aunt Philips in Meryton. The nearest town to Longbourn village, Meryton was but a mile away. Nevertheless, Lydia exhausted her reserves by the time they reached the weir on the outskirts and began complaining loudly that her feet ached. Kitty soon joined in, and their combined protests grew so tiresome that, despite her fondness for walking, Elizabeth began to wish she had remained at home.

Relief came from an unexpected source. As they crossed the bridge, Lydia abruptly ceased her objections and pointed to something ahead of them. "What on earth is that?"

'That' turned out to be a scarlet coat, incongruously resplendent against the autumnal flora and dusty footpaths of Meryton's main thoroughfare. Its bearer disappeared around the corner; the Bennet ladies followed and were met with the remarkable sight of not one crimson-clad ensign, but an entire phalanx of them. Persuading them all to walk to town was suddenly the greatest idea Lydia had ever had, and she and Kitty danced ahead along the shopfronts, pointing out every handsome face and giggling over every young man too scrawny to properly fill his uniform.

Elizabeth edged around the crowd and herded her younger sisters in the direction of Mrs Philips's front door, persuading them to make haste with the shouted suggestion that they would have a better view from an upstairs window.

"They arrived this morning," her aunt said as she handed out plates of little biscuits to Elizabeth, Jane, and Mary, who had seated themselves with her at the table. "Though the officers came two days ago, apparently. Colonel Forster is in command of the unit, with Captain Carter as his second."

"I think that must be them, over there, by the pump," Kitty exclaimed excitedly from her station at the window.

"Lydia!" Elizabeth cried when her youngest sister leant dangerously far out over the sill and began waving indecorously in that direction.

"Oh, there is no harm in waving," said her aunt dismissively. "Let them have their fun. It will keep them occupied while Jane tells me all about Mr Bingley." As she spoke, she fixed her eldest niece with a probing look.

Jane opened her mouth, closed it again, blushed prettily, and yielded with a laugh. "I have not discovered anything of particular note, and neither have I attempted to. We talk about different things each time we meet—things relevant to the moment. I know he enjoys fishing and dislikes dogs that bark loudly. He does not like poetry, he does like dancing, and he once fell in a pond whilst pretending to catch a fairy for his sister."

Elizabeth laughed aloud at this and liked him even better than before—and she had been fairly well pleased with him already for inspiring her dearest sister's present glow of contentment with his marked attentions. Unlike her mother, she was not yet ready to speculate them into matrimony, but never had she known a person more deserving of happiness than Jane and seeing her thus was almost enough to make Mrs Bennet's relentless raptures on the subject bearable.

Mrs Philips was less impressed with Jane's findings, her face screwed up in an unflattering contortion of perplexity and vexation. "But does he have a house in London?"

The smile with which Jane had relayed all her other information faded. "I have not asked."

"No, of course not. But has not he mentioned it?"

"I think he said Mr Hurst has a house on Grosvenor Street."

This did not please Mrs Philips. "No townhouse *and* no estate. Even though Mrs Harrington heard that he inherited his father's fortune some six or seven years ago. Whatever is keeping him from settling down?"

"Perhaps he is searching for a place of which his sisters can approve," Elizabeth said. "In which case he is destined never to settle, for unless he means to buy St. James's, I doubt there is a place in the country that would satisfy them."

Jane looked as though she would object, but Mrs Philips pre-empted her. "They certainly seemed unimpressed at the assembly. And Mrs Long tells me they barely spoke to anyone but each other when they dined at Purvis Lodge." She nibbled her biscuit pensively. "It is exceedingly puzzling behaviour. They appear at once self-conscious and self-important."

There is a word for that, Elizabeth mused, but seeing Jane's delicate frown and suspecting it stemmed from a disinclination to think ill of Mr Bingley's relations, she kept to herself the thought that they were two of the vainest women she had ever met.

"They were barely acquainted with anybody on either of those two occasions," Jane demurred. "They were more likely just shy."

Elizabeth wrinkled her nose. With Miss Bingley's permanent expression of disdain, she rather thought not, but, "They are hardly young girls to be embarrassed in company," was as severe an observation as she dared make.

"Indeed not," said Mrs Philips. "Mrs Hurst is seven-and-twenty, I collect. Miss Bingley is slightly younger."

"Oh, I thought she was the older one," said Mary. "There is something about her that makes her seem more worldly."

"She certainly holds herself above everybody," Lydia said over her shoulder.

"Perhaps that is it," said Elizabeth in an attempt to soften her censure for Jane's sake. "She is farther away. It is merely a matter of perspective."

Jane indulged her with a smile but answered with typical generosity. "It would be unfair to judge Miss Bingley on her behaviour this week now that we know she has been unwell all along."

"What is this?" enquired Mrs Philips.

"She did not come with the rest of her party to dine at Mrs Robinson's last night," Elizabeth explained. "She has a cold, apparently," she added, attempting to keep the scepticism from her tone.

She need not have troubled herself, for Lydia, peeling herself away from the window and sitting heavily in a chair at the table, scoffed on her behalf. "A cold my eye! Her sister said she was not even ill."

In answer to her aunt's questioning look, but with an apologetic glance at Jane, Elizabeth explained, "When I expressed my hope that Miss Bingley was not *very* ill, Mr Bingley and Mrs Hurst gave conflicting answers. He said she had a bad cold, and her sister said she was only fatigued."

"It was hardly a surprising mix up," said Jane. "A sister is much better placed to comprehend a woman's complaints than her brother."

"True," said Mrs Philips with a nod. "But how did they explain the contradiction?"

"They never got the chance," Elizabeth answered. "Mr Darcy changed the subject." This she had noticed with no little amusement, for it was not the first time he had done as much. She had yet to decide his purpose on those occasions. Perhaps it was to divert the conversation to a subject of greater interest to him? Or possibly he could not countenance that anybody should forget his consequence and so inserted remarks into other people's conversations whenever he felt neglected.

"Oh, he spoke last night then?" said Mrs Philips. "That is an improvement, for he barely said a word at the assembly, except to slight you, Lizzy."

"They all spoke more last night, I thought," said Kitty, who had also left off waving from the window, which Elizabeth took to mean the militia had passed out of sight.

"I thought so too," said Mary. "Mrs Hurst spoke to me about playing the pianoforte for quarter of an hour after dinner."

"Aye," Elizabeth agreed. "She showed herself to be surprisingly good company out of her sister's shadow."

Jane evidently did not like this depiction; her brows drew together again. "You think it was Miss Bingley's absence that prompted Mrs Hurst to be more social?"

"It was a remarkable coincidence otherwise." Had her younger sisters not been present, Elizabeth would have pointed out that it was really no different to the way Kitty behaved whenever she was apart from Lydia. She settled for merely saying, "Miss Bingley is evidently the more assertive character."

"Mr Darcy was certainly more talkative in her absence," said Mary.

Elizabeth gave a snort of disdain. "A *little* more. Though why *he* should be more willing to speak when Miss Bingley is not present, I cannot imagine."

"Perhaps he does not like her either," said Lydia.

The suggestion diverted Elizabeth, for though Miss Bingley seemed eager to endorse Mr Darcy's every opinion, it was true that he never appeared particularly pleased by it. "Perhaps she likes *him* a tad too well, and he only dares relax when she is absent, lest he encourage her. Though, if that is the case, he ought not to be anxious, for he is just as unlikeable when he speaks as when he does not." Feeling suddenly that she had said too much on the subject of Mr Darcy, and before Jane could take it as a cue to switch from being Miss Bingley's advocate to his, Elizabeth asked whether she was looking forward to seeing Mr Bingley again at Lucas Lodge that evening.

"I am, very much."

"I hope he pays you all the attention you deserve, my dear," said Mrs Philips, patting Jane's hand. "You will have to tell me about it next time I see you. Lady Lucas was good enough to invite me, but I am expected at Mrs Norris's soiree. I had planned to be *indisposed* myself, for I heard Mrs Hanrahan was to be there, and I could not stomach her carping for an entire evening. But I have since received word that she has changed her mind, so now I shall go."

"According to Mr Fellowes, Mrs Hanrahan has a bad cold," Mary informed them.

"I heard Mrs Hanrahan sent a nasty letter to her mother, blaming her cold on the foul odours in their house," Lydia added. "She is a horrid old woman. No wonder nobody ever visits her."

"Mr Fellowes does," Mary pointed out.

"Only because it is his Christian duty to visit disobliging old women with no other friends," Lydia said, snorting at her own insult.

"That is fortunate for you then," replied Mary, "for it

means you will not be without visitors when you are grey-haired and infirm."

Elizabeth and Jane agreed it was probably a good time to take their sisters home. After a quick check to confirm the streets were empty once again, they thanked Mrs Philips for the refreshments and set out for Longbourn. About two hundred yards into the journey, Lydia recalled that from which the sight of a scarlet coat had distracted her and recommenced her protests with renewed zeal. Elizabeth put up with it as far as the other side of the bridge then decided she could withstand no more. She made her apologies to Jane and set off in the opposite direction to take advantage of the glorious sunshine with a much longer walk.

She wondered, as she crossed field after field at a quick pace, about the man her sister liked so well. Mr Bingley seemed such an amiable gentleman, it was unfathomable why he had chosen to surround himself with such disagreeable people. She supposed he could do little about his sisters, but his friendship with Mr Darcy was altogether more puzzling. Notwithstanding his obvious disdain for Hertfordshire society in general, Mr Darcy seemed to be particularly offended by his friend's enjoyment of it. The more Mr Bingley laughed and smiled, the more Mr Darcy seemed to resent it. Mr Bingley himself did not appear to mind, though Elizabeth was not convinced he had observed it, for he did not appear to have noticed *much* beyond the ethereal beauty of her older sister.

The distant sound of laughter caught her attention. Seeing no one either before or behind her, she clambered up onto the nearest stile to peer over the hedgerow. Beyond it, at the edge of a copse, walked a woman with her little girl. Childish laughter dipped in and out of earshot as the youngster dashed between the trees. She ducked into a thicket, followed by her mother, only to burst out farther down the track, leaving the woman within the grove shouting angrily for her to reveal herself. Elizabeth could not help but laugh; the child looked up, observed her watching, and waved merrily. She waved back until the woman shouted again, and the girl darted away along the treeline. Hoping the daring little mite would give her mother a decent chase, Elizabeth hopped down from the stile and carried on her way.

The encounter put her in mind of several other occasions of late that her laughter had drawn attention. More than once this past week, when she had been privately diverted by some folly or other, Mr Darcy had noticed. Though, unlike the sweet little girl in the field, he never looked happy about it; he only glared at her in contempt. Which, if he disdained mirth, was an imprudent tactic, for such supercilious nonsense was guaranteed only to divert her more. The next stile brought her out of the fields onto a more solid path and, with a laugh of delight, she broke into a run, soon outstripping the unsettling memory of Mr Darcy's penetrating stare.

3
Solitary Ramblings

"I STILL DO NOT SEE WHY WE COULD NOT ALL DINE AT Netherfield. I think it unpardonably uncivil to invite only one sister out of five. Imagine if somebody were to invite only one of them to dinner."

Elizabeth looked up from her work to where Lydia was draped across the sofa, picking idly at the fraying fabric on the arm. There was little point in explaining that she was likely to be overlooked for many more invitations if she did not learn a little decorum, for she would take no heed. "Only one of them attended Mrs Robinson's dinner," she said instead. "Depending on which one you snubbed, I am inclined to think there would be no hard feelings."

"Do not talk nonsense," said her mother. "Miss Bingley could hardly help being indisposed."

"Perhaps not." She returned to her work and added lightly, "She must have a strong constitution, though, for she seemed perfectly well recovered when we saw her at Lucas Lodge the next day."

"I thought she looked rather fatigued, as it happens."

"She must have been," said Lydia, "for she did not join in a single dance."

"She would not have danced anyway," said Mary. "Ladies and gentlemen of her consequence do not dance jigs and reels."

"Mr Darcy would have danced one, had not Lizzy refused him."

"Oh, yes! That was very well done, Lizzy," said Mrs Bennet proudly.

Mr Bennet lowered his book to peer at Elizabeth over the top, one eyebrow raised in question. Elizabeth smirked. "I shall not deny that declining was vastly satisfying, but it was not a complete victory. He only asked me because Sir William forced his hand. He could not have made the offer more reluctantly."

"I wonder that anyone can dislike dancing," Kitty said, frowning as though the very notion puzzled her beyond her powers of comprehension. "Surely, when Mr Bingley has his ball, Mr Darcy will not be able to evade the obligation?"

"Ooh, I had forgotten he said that!" cried Lydia. "A ball at Netherfield—only imagine!"

"Do not excite yourself, child," said Mr Bennet with a wink at Elizabeth. "They may very probably not invite you to that either."

The mere suggestion of being excluded threw Lydia into such a tumult of indignation that all talk of dancing was ended, though Elizabeth's thoughts lingered on the subject a little longer. Unlike Lydia, she did recall Mr Bingley, vexed that the Meryton Assembly had ended so early, declaring he would hold his own dance—and how exceedingly angry the pronouncement had appeared to make his friend. Despite being obliged to request the honour of her hand at Lucas Lodge, Mr Darcy's aversion to dancing had been confirmed in the same conversation when Sir William remarked on his disliking the amusement in general. In retrospect, Elizabeth began to regret refusing his grudging offer, for it seemed the greater punishment would have been to accept.

She did *not* regret challenging his practice of eavesdropping on her conversations, unable to think that he listened with any intention other than to disapprove and pleased to have shown herself beyond such intimidation. He had a satirical eye, and she had resolved to counter it with impertinence. All their dealings to date had convinced her this was the approach that his panoply of hubris was least prepared to withstand. Her success was difficult to determine—he had not seemed offended by her archness, but neither had he given up his disdainful scrutiny.

A gust of wind threw a noisy spattering of rain against the windows, so loudly that all the girls jumped, and even Mr Bennet frowned slightly. Only Mrs Bennet looked pleased. "I think it is getting heavier. What a lucky idea of mine to send Jane on horseback! There is no chance of them sending her home in this."

Elizabeth did not think it so very lucky. "I very much doubt that seeing Mr Bingley for half an hour tomorrow morning, in the same damp clothes as she wore today, and without Sanders to dress her hair, will be worth Jane's embarrassment."

"Better a little bit of embarrassment than a wasted opportunity," Mrs Bennet replied. "Have a little faith in your mother's schemes. It will all turn out for the best, just you wait and see."

ELIZABETH WAITED UNTIL PRECISELY TWO MINUTES TO NINE the next morning, when a servant arrived from Netherfield with a note from Jane informing them that she was suffering from a sore throat and a headache. Half an hour later, Elizabeth was more than halfway into the three miles to Netherfield, jumping over stiles and springing over puddles with impatient activity. She came to an abrupt halt upon rounding a hedgerow and almost colliding with a small girl running along the edge of the field. She had a dear little countenance, with a broad, unassuming smile that betrayed not a hint of concern at having met a complete stranger.

"Good morning," Elizabeth said, glancing about the field but seeing nobody else there. "Are you alone?"

The girl nodded proudly.

"Are you supposed to be alone?"

The girl shook her head, prouder still. "I have run away."

"I see. May I enquire why?"

She kept her head still this time but puffed up even further with pride until she veritably beamed with it. "I am exceedingly good at running."

Elizabeth could not help but grin. "Pray, what is your name?"

Her defiant expression softened into a pout that would have rivalled Lydia's best. "Miss Dunn, but please do not call me that. I do not like it at all, for I have not *done* anything. I like 'Anna' better."

"Very well, Anna. You may call me Lizzy."

As easily as that, she was returned to grinning merrily. "I wish Miss Paxton would call me Anna, but she says it is not ladylike."

"Miss Paxton?"

"The lady you saw chasing me yesterday. She never catches me. She is terrible at running."

Elizabeth frowned over this for a moment but soon comprehended her meaning. "It was you who waved at me!" Anna's broad smile confirmed it. "You made a merry picture, the pair of you. I had assumed Miss Paxton was your mother, though."

"She is my mother's cousin. I live with her in Persimmon Cottage. She does not like it, but I do, because it is near some woods that I know are magic, for I leave scraps out for the fairies every evening and they are gone every morning, though I have yet to see one."

"You have to be ever so quiet to see a fairy," Elizabeth told her solemnly. "They will not allow you to see them unless you are very, very still."

Anna nodded, wide-eyed, as though receiving sacred information. "I can be quiet for ages. I am not as good at being still, but I shall try my hardest."

Elizabeth smiled again, thoroughly endeared but, mindful of poor Miss Paxton, suggested that Anna return home to try the method directly. She had intended to offer to help her find her way back but had not the chance, for no sooner had she proposed the idea than Anna gave an excited squeal and ran back the way she had come. She seemed awfully young to be out walking by herself, but she was far from the smallest child Elizabeth had seen running unaccompanied about the countryside. This would have to do for reassurance, for it was all there was to be had. Keen not to delay seeing Jane any longer, she gave a shrug and carried on her way.

SHE WAS SHOWN INTO THE BREAKFAST PARLOUR UPON HER arrival at Netherfield, where she pretended not to notice the ladies' contemptuous gazes, which lingered on her bonnet, or perhaps her coat or shoes—whatever part of her dress it was that displeased them so. It was harder to ignore Mr Darcy's disapproval, for his severe gaze never wandered from her face. She had neither the time nor the inclination to challenge him, however, and enquired after Jane without giving any indication of having noticed he was there. She was made even less comfortable by the answer to her enquiry: her sister had slept ill, and though up, was very feverish and not well enough to leave her room.

"May I see her?"

"Why yes, of course," Miss Bingley replied, rising from the table and indicating that Elizabeth should follow her. This was an unexpected piece of civility; Elizabeth had anticipated being shown upstairs by a servant. Her surprise lasted only as long as it took to reach Jane's room, whereupon all other concerns paled to insignificance next to that which she felt upon first seeing her sister. Jane's head rested awkwardly in the corner of a winged chair, her brow glistened with perspiration and her eyes were glazed.

"Lizzy, you came!" That she was relieved to see her was clear, but so, too, was the weakness she betrayed when her outstretched arms wilted back into her lap before Elizabeth could reach them.

"Jane, you have been uncommonly reserved with the truth." She touched her sister's brow and confirmed a raging fever. "You said in your letter there was nothing much the matter with you other than a sore throat. Mama would have come herself had she known you were really ill."

"It was true when I wrote it." She gave a wan smile. "Mostly."

"We have sent for Mr Jones," Miss Bingley said from the doorway. "He ought to be here soon."

Elizabeth straightened to thank her, though she was hard pressed not to dissolve into laughter when she caught a glimpse of herself in a long dressing mirror. Her walk from Longbourn had rendered her complexion almost as feverish as Jane's, and her hair was so blowsy she resolved to retire that particular bonnet from use with immediate effect. *What a state in which to arrive before such a discriminating audience!* At least it would give Mr Darcy something new for which to despise her, for he had surely exhausted all other avenues of disappointment by now.

Miss Bingley inclined her head and excused herself to finish her breakfast. No sooner had she departed than Jane slumped further in her chair and said shakily, "Oh, Lizzy, it was awful!"

"Why, what happened?" Elizabeth dragged the chair from the dressing table over to sit next to Jane, taking up her hand and peering at her with the greatest concern.

"All was well until after dinner. Then I came over very warm and the room began to spin, and I had to admit that I did not feel up to riding home—and that meant I had to wait for the gentlemen to return from dining with the officers so I could be sent home in their carriage." She winced and rubbed her temple. "It must have appeared thoroughly contrived."

"But it could not be helped, Jane. And if they did think it a ruse last night, they cannot now, for you are clearly unwell."

"Perhaps, but at the time it seemed as though they were displeased—more so when Mr Bingley insisted that I remain here. Caroline looked most alarmed. Mr Darcy looked positively vexed."

Elizabeth pursed her lips, furious that he should have made poor Jane feel worse at such a moment. "I beg you would not concern yourself with what Mr Darcy thinks. It is not his house, and therefore his opinion of who stays here is of no consequence."

"I do not blame him for being angry," Jane said, squinting at her as though she were too bright to see properly. "To him, I could only have appeared to be one of two things—an unscrupulous opportunist or a genuine source of contagion."

"Or simply a vast inconvenience."

"But it is an inconvenience, is it not?" Her eyes slid fully closed. "Pray, do not come here ready to do battle, Lizzy. There is no need. Indeed, Caroline has been so very attentive,

I believe I must have mistaken her for piqued when actually she was only concerned."

If Elizabeth were to contradict Jane now, and admit her true opinion that Miss Bingley despised them both, she would be no better than Mr Darcy in making an unpleasant situation worse. "I can see you have been well looked after," she reassured her instead. "And I was received politely just now, so I think it is safe to assume there will be no battles today." She could not refrain from adding, "Though I do believe both Miss Bingley and Mrs Hurst will hold me in contempt forever for having walked so far by myself. You ought to have seen their horror when I arrived unaccompanied."

Jane's mouth widened into a fragile smile. Without opening her eyes, she said, "I expect that had more to do with the six inches of mud on your petticoat."

Elizabeth pivoted forward in her chair and lifted a foot to better inspect her hem. She stared open-mouthed for a moment, then burst into laughter at the dirty brown stains that would likely ruin what had been a perfectly good petticoat. "Oh Lord, I must have made quite an entrance."

"I am glad of it. You have made such an exhibition that my own must be quite forgotten by now."

Though Elizabeth was heartened to see Jane laugh, she did not like how it made her cough and was pleased when Miss Bingley returned with the apothecary. After a brief examination, he diagnosed a violent cold and gave the strict instruction that Jane must return to bed directly.

"Would not she be more comfortable in her own home?" enquired Miss Bingley with wide-eyed urgency.

"Miss Bennet is far too unwell to be moved," replied Mr Jones. "We must endeavour to get the better of this fever."

"We *absolutely* must," Miss Bingley agreed. "I beg you would do everything in your power to hasten her recovery."

Elizabeth was more inclined to believe she meant to

hasten Jane's removal from the house, but she had promised to fight no battles and so held her tongue, even when Miss Bingley enquired with very little patience how long Mr Jones thought Jane might be indisposed. His answer pleased nobody, but his promise to prepare some draughts saw him ushered enthusiastically from the room by everybody to attend to the task.

4
Greater Than the Sum of Its Parts

JANE'S FEVER PERSISTED THROUGHOUT THE DAY, AND Elizabeth did not once leave her side. The other ladies came and went—though they mostly went—and whenever present, were profuse in their sympathies. On one such occasion, Miss Bingley declared herself loath to observe anybody's suffering and condescended to mop Jane's brow. The intention had almost certainly been to exhibit her extraordinary compassion, but Elizabeth was unmoved. That Miss Bingley had shown herself capable of wielding a wet cloth did not compensate for the fact that she concluded the task with an enquiry as to whether Jane yet felt well enough to go home.

When Elizabeth had been at Netherfield above four hours, and the clock had received more pointed looks from its owners than it had hours on its face, she took up Jane's hand and whispered that it was time for her to go. Jane rolled her head towards her, her countenance showing as much alarm as her slack jaw and heavy eyelids permitted. "Oh no, Lizzy, do not leave me. I feel wretched."

"I shall come back first thing in the morning, but I really cannot stay any longer." Jane made a whimpering sound and clung weakly to her hand but was too polite to voice any further protest, which only made Elizabeth angry with those to whom her sister was deferring. Raising her voice slightly so as to be certain they heard from their seats, she added, "You must not be anxious. There is every reason to expect the attention you have received so far will continue. I am sure you will be attended throughout the night."

A pause, a sigh, and a palpable current of reluctance announced Miss Bingley's approach to Jane's bedside. "Of course, you must stay yourself, Miss Elizabeth. We would not be cruel enough to send you away when your sister is so unwell."

Jane's relief was as apparent as Miss Bingley's displeasure. There was little to be done about the latter, thus Elizabeth merely expressed her thanks and requested a pen and paper to send a note to Longbourn for her things. Both Bingley sisters left the room, and for a short time, Elizabeth read to Jane but stopped when it became clear her sister was too unwell to follow. She administered another spoonful of the draught Mr Jones had provided and then defied his strident advice and threw open the sash. The apothecary had been adamant that no fresh air be let into the room lest it exacerbate Jane's cold, but her sister and the room were both so hot that Elizabeth could not but think it would help reduce her fever.

She leant out over the sill and sucked in several deep breaths, then was arrested by a curious sight. On the far side of the garden, a tall figure in an elegant walking dress hastened away from the house along the path that led into the shrubbery. Elizabeth felt a pang of jealousy that Miss Bingley —for Miss Bingley it unmistakably was—should be free to walk out when she was confined to a stuffy sickroom. It was a fleeting sensation, immediately replaced with the vastly more diverting notion that she might have gone to Longbourn herself to fetch Elizabeth's things.

"What are you laughing about?" Jane enquired weakly.

"Nothing," she lied, sliding the window closed and returning to her side. "How are you feeling?"

"Awful," Jane answered with a doleful look and a small huff of laughter. "What a pitiful creature I am."

Elizabeth agreed with a broad grin and instructed her to try and sleep.

AT HALF-PAST SIX, ELIZABETH WAS CALLED FOR DINNER. Her empty stomach was the only part of her anticipating the occasion, and she dressed with little thought to anything other than being vaguely presentable. After ensuring Jane did not want for anything, she joined the others downstairs. Her arrival appeared to interrupt some manner of disagreement between Mr Bingley and his sister—the tone of their voices before she entered, and their sullen expressions afterwards, made it impossible to conclude otherwise—and for the briefest of moments there was an exceedingly awkward silence. Then Mr Darcy stepped forward and bowed formally. The claret stripes on his waistcoat, or maybe his black dinner jacket, made his eyes darker than usual, in an oddly disconcerting way.

"Good evening, Miss Bennet. May I enquire after your sister?"

She is not well enough to go home, so I beg you would cease asking! she thought, though she considered it more prudent to *say*, "I am afraid she is no better."

"I am sorry to hear that," said Mr Bingley. "Is there anything more that can be done for her?"

"Regrettably, I think not, sir. I hope, though, that you will not mind if I return to her immediately after dinner. She was resting very ill when I left her."

"But of course. Let us eat directly. The sooner we do, the

sooner you will be able to return upstairs." He offered his arm, and they filed out of the drawing room with the others.

Dinner was a restrained affair, which Elizabeth could not but think was due to her intrusion into the family setting. She did not trouble herself to talk much, for it seemed unlikely to be welcomed, and instead spent her time worrying about when Jane had last eaten anything.

"Is Nicholls unwell today, Caroline?" Mr Hurst said presently. "Every dish on the table is dismally bland."

"I had her cook something plainer," she answered. "I thought it might better suit Miss Eliza's tastes."

Mr Bingley banged his fork down on his plate and glared at his sister with uncommon rancour. Elizabeth was rather proud of herself for not laughing outright at Miss Bingley's prodigious indelicacy. Not many people of her acquaintance could so expertly fudge the veiling of a slight. She hid her smirk behind her glass and answered, "You are exceedingly thoughtful. The food is very much to my liking."

"Really?" said Mr Hurst, all astonishment. "You would not prefer a good ragout?"

"Ragout is too often over-seasoned in an attempt to make it greater than the sum of its parts. In my experience, anything that requires enhancement to make it palatable is likely to prove disappointing on closer inspection." Mr Hurst grunted and returned to his meal, shaking his head. After a brief glance at Mr Darcy, who looked on in grave silence, Elizabeth returned her attention to her meal.

"Does your sister enjoy any dish in particular?" Mr Bingley stammered. "I should be happy to have the cook prepare whatever will make her feel better."

"Thank you, sir. She is rather partial to plum cheese, but pray do not trouble your cook with it, for Jane has not much of an appetite at present."

Neither had Elizabeth, in truth, and her impatience to

return upstairs was making the time pass intolerably slowly. She sipped her wine and looked surreptitiously at the clock.

"You must be very worried about her," said Mr Darcy.

"I am." Had he seen her look? "Forgive me if I seem impatient, only she is rarely unwell."

"Not at all, it is entirely understandable. I sincerely hope you have the relief of seeing her soon recovered."

"Thank you," she replied, unsure why he should affect solicitude all of a sudden and unable to keep the suspicion from her tone.

"I am sure she will be better before we know it," said Miss Bingley sharply. "It is only a cold, after all."

Mr Darcy's countenance instantly regained its steely veneer—interesting to Elizabeth for the recognition that it must have been fleetingly absent. Mr Bingley fidgeted angrily in his seat, frowning at his sister. Whatever had been Miss Bingley's intention, Elizabeth did not imagine it was to attract everybody's disapprobation—and neither did she think the remark warranted it, for it was not dissimilar from Mrs Bennet's opinion of Jane's condition.

"I heard from Murrey this morning, Bingley," said Mr Darcy, abruptly commandeering the conversation once again. "He writes that he hopes to be back on his horse before the year is out."

"I cannot imagine that will end well," Mr Bingley replied. Noticing Elizabeth observing them, he added, "Mr Murrey is an acquaintance from Scarborough who had a nasty riding accident just before we left. He is a liability in a saddle and ought not to ride anywhere he can possibly walk."

"An affliction with which I can wholeheartedly sympathise," she replied.

"Indeed," said Miss Bingley. "How far was it you walked to get here this morning?"

"About three miles. How far did your walk this afternoon take you?"

The unctuous smile that had stretched Miss Bingley's lips thin moments before vanished. "Not far at all—I was merely taking some air after sitting for so long in Jane's room. I *much* prefer to ride, when I have the chance." Elizabeth gave no answer, and Miss Bingley was forced to look elsewhere for rescue. "As do you, Mr Darcy, if I am not greatly mistaken. You are excessively fond of riding, are you not?"

"I take great pleasure in it, yes."

"And excel at it, too."

Miss Bingley might as well have not spoken for all the notice Mr Darcy gave the compliment, neither thanking her nor refuting it—acting, in truth, as though he had not even heard it.

"I recall you asking Mr Goulding about his curricle," Elizabeth said, unable to resist drawing him out. "Do you own one?"

He confirmed very succinctly that he did.

"Most gentlemen of consequence do, Miss Eliza," Miss Bingley informed her. "Indeed, Charles, I urge you to consider purchasing one. They are quite *de rigueur* in the first circles."

By her side, Mrs Hurst nodded sagely. "Quite the thing."

"They are an efficient means of travel over short distances," Mr Darcy corrected them, adding, with an undecipherable look at Elizabeth, "I should not like to be accused of over-seasoning."

She smiled despite herself. "You never race it then?"

"Mr Darcy does not *race*. He is too sensible to drive at undue speed."

Miss Bingley's determination to know more about Mr Darcy than he did himself did not appear to be diverting him anywhere near as much as it was Elizabeth. She was sure she detected a flash of vexation in his countenance, though he did not allow it to show for long and answered collectedly. "If by 'race' you mean 'compete with another driver to arrive at a specified destination first', then the answer is no, Miss Bennet."

"Though, if you mean 'drive at undue speed', then the answer is most assuredly yes," Mr Bingley qualified with an impish expression.

"Indeed?"

"Oh! Certainly," Miss Bingley agreed, surprising nobody. "There is no keeping up with Mr Darcy in his curricle when he is not in a humour to dawdle."

There! Elizabeth triumphed, for Mr Darcy had unquestionably rolled his eyes and almost certainly clenched his jaw. Only when he transferred his angry glare from Miss Bingley to her did she realise she may have allowed a squeak of laughter to escape. She thought that an excellent moment to express a desire to check on Jane, and with Mr Bingley's hearty consent, she excused herself and ran upstairs. To her dismay, Jane had deteriorated further still. Thus, apart from an obligatory quarter of an hour in the drawing room later that evening, she spent the chief of the night in her sister's room, attending to her silently, and hoping against hope that her mother had been right to declare that people did not die of trifling colds.

5

Recurrent Encounters

ELIZABETH JUMPED OFF A STILE, DELIBERATELY AIMING FOR the centre of the large patch of mud on the other side of it, determined to make her boots and petticoat as dirty as possible and hoping that she would be seen by everyone when she returned to Netherfield later. If they must all despise her, she would not refrain from giving them sufficient cause.

Mrs Bennet had visited Netherfield, to assess for herself Jane's condition, and delivered a stunningly humiliating performance. She had revealed none of her capacity for compassion, having satisfied herself that Jane was not ill enough to require more than Elizabeth was already providing. Instead, she exhibited only the vaguest observance to propriety, acted on every improper impulse, and spoken aloud every small-minded thought that popped into her head.

Mr Bingley had gallantly forged past her every solecism with heroic ebullience, but his sisters had sniggered and sneered their way through the visit. Mr Darcy had stoically ignored Mrs Bennet's antagonism towards him, choosing not to entertain the argument she had attempted to have about the merits of country society over that of Town. To Elizabeth's mind, it would have been better had he expostulated, for then at least she might have challenged his infuriatingly superior air. Instead, he had said nothing, and she had been forced to suffer his contempt and her mother's folly in silence, with no defence against the indignity of either. Lydia had then plagued Mr Bingley until he agreed to keep his promise of holding a ball, which threw Miss Bingley and Mr Darcy into a furious round of urgent looks. And finally, Mr Jones had returned and declared Jane yet too unwell to be moved. This brought scowls to everybody's face except Mrs Bennet's, who had left for home, sans her two eldest daughters, beaming with delight.

The mud turned out to consist less of dirt than of water; Elizabeth's feet sank, her boots filled, and a rueful grin spread across her face. Not since she was eight years old had she jumped in a puddle with the purpose of disobliging someone else.

"Why are you laughing?"

She yelped and almost slipped over as she spun around to find the source of the question. She smiled when she saw little Anna Dunn standing on the stile from which she had just leapt. "I got my stockings wet," she answered, walking back to look into the field behind the girl. "Are you alone again?" When Anna nodded, Elizabeth gathered up her skirts, swung her legs back over the stile, and lowered herself to sit on the bottom step to speak to her gently but firmly. "Anna, it is a very good thing that you are good at running, but it is not quite such a good thing that you have run so far on your own. Miss Paxton must be very worried about you. I really think you ought to go back."

"But I do not wish to. There is nobody there. Not even the fairies speak to me."

"Do you and Miss Paxton live alone at the cottage then?"

Anna nodded. Cautiously, fearing an unhappy answer, Elizabeth enquired after her mother.

Anna sniffed and wiped her nose on her sleeve. "She lives up at the big house."

Elizabeth struggled to keep her countenance. "Netherfield?" She had half expected to discover that Anna was orphaned and was astonished by her mention of that place.

"Aye. She visits me when she can but is most often too busy, and I am not allowed to go there."

"No, I should imagine not." Elizabeth had never heard of a family to knowingly employ female servants with young dependants, and while she could imagine Mr Bingley being generous enough to allow it, his sisters were another matter entirely. "And your father?"

Anna's countenance contracted into a resolute frown and she shook her head sharply. "I am not allowed to speak of him. Everybody gets very angry if I do. Miss Paxton says it is because he refused to marry my mother."

Elizabeth's surprise was quickly replaced with compassion. Anna was such a sweet child—and evidently ignorant of the pitiful nature of her situation. She pushed herself to her feet and held out her hand. "Come. Your mother may not be able to visit often but imagine how dismayed she would be if she did, only to discover you missing. If you like, I could tell you some more tricks for spying on fairies on the way."

This was a proposition too enticing to refuse; Anna grabbed her hand and set off, leading Elizabeth back through the field whence she had come then off to the right. As promised, they talked as they walked, and in addition to the best methods for observing sprites, it was soon established that Anna was five-and-a-quarter years old, knew the Latin names of four types of butterflies, and preferred puppies to horses.

"I prefer most animals to horses," Elizabeth admitted. "I am particularly ill-disposed towards the one my sister rode here on Tuesday. The obstinate brute walked so slowly in the rain that she was soaked through and caught a violent cold."

"I had a cold last week!" Anna exclaimed, sounding rather more pleased about it than poor Jane.

"I am sorry to hear that. Were you very unwell?"

Anna chewed on her lip and shrugged. "I felt hot." She said it almost as a question, as though unsure whether feeling hot constituted being unwell. She perked up in the next moment, having apparently thought of something that better qualified her. "And my mother came to sit with me one evening, which she never usually does, so I think, maybe—" She stopped abruptly when her name was called from somewhere close by. She gasped and tugged her hand away from Elizabeth's. "That is Miss Paxton. I must go! I am not supposed to talk to anyone I do not know. Oh, she will be cross with me!"

"Go, then. Run along before she sees you," Elizabeth said, nudging her in the direction they had been headed. "She will not hear it from me that we ever met." As an afterthought, she called out in a stage whisper, "Good luck with the fairies!"

THE REFLECTIONS THIS ENCOUNTER PRODUCED OCCUPIED Elizabeth's mind to the exclusion of all else as she walked back to Netherfield, up the front steps, and through the front door, where she paused to hand her coat to the footman.

"I see you have been out walking again, Miss Bennet."

She looked up with a start. She was diverted not to have noticed Mr Darcy's approach—he was a difficult man to miss, being so very tall—but she was content to blame him for the oversight. It was grossly ungentlemanlike for a man to move about so stealthily. It denied one the opportunity for evasion. "I was in urgent need of some air and exercise," she replied. "There is nothing worse than to be confined within doors."

"You prefer being out of doors, do you?" he enquired, looking pointedly at her feet.

Elizabeth had forgotten her rebellious leap into a bog. The recollection of it, in conjunction with the good fortune of having returned to precisely the audience she had envisaged, brought a smile to her face. "That depends," she answered archly.

"On?"

"Who is inside." His fleeting look of surprise forced a small laugh from her lips. "Will you excuse me? I really must be getting back to Jane. I have been gone too long already."

"Of course." He bowed and walked away.

Smiling over his hasty escape, Elizabeth continued upstairs, where she discovered to her dismay that Jane's malaise persisted. The report of her meeting with Anna roused barely a glimmer of interest, and her complaints about Mrs Bennet's behaviour even less. Still preferring her sister's listless company to anybody else's in the house, she stayed by her side for the remainder of the day, leaving only to eat dinner and briefly show her face in the drawing room afterwards. She was profoundly pleased when Jane's fever finally broke much later that evening, whereupon both sisters were rewarded with their first decent night's sleep since they arrived at Netherfield.

JANE WAS IN FAR BETTER SPIRITS THE NEXT MORNING. An inventory of her symptoms revealed that most had diminished significantly, giving both sisters to hope that a corner had been turned in her recovery. It was agreed that, provided she felt up to it after another day of rest, she might come down for an hour after dinner—a prospect that cheered Elizabeth considerably.

"It is maddening that I should have been here all this time

yet not able to enjoy Mr Bingley's company for a second of it," Jane said from the chair in which she sat beneath two blankets. "You cannot know how it has plagued me, lying here wondering what I have been missing. Pray, tell me, what sort of things do they discuss?"

Elizabeth almost replied that she had not missed much at all but decided against it, suspecting it would occasion more consternation than comfort. "Whatever arises," she answered instead. "Last night there was a discussion about the relative values of inconstancy versus obstinacy. Mr Bingley, according to Mr Darcy, is too ready to yield to the persuasion of his friends, and unduly proud of the caprice this tendency betrays." She had to supress a smirk when Jane sat up straighter, visibly chafing at this depiction of her favourite.

"Was Mr Bingley offended?"

"Quite the reverse. He teased Mr Darcy about being ill-tempered and said he would not pay him half so much deference were he not so tall. He is an excellent sport, Jane. I like him very well indeed."

"I am pleased to hear you say so. I cannot reconcile myself to two friends so openly censuring one another for the sake of a debate, though. It seems too much like an argument to me."

"You are in accord with Mr Bingley then. He curtailed the conversation for precisely that reason." After a moment's reflection, Elizabeth added, "There is something singular about their friendship. I cannot put my finger on what it is exactly. They must enjoy one another's company, for why else would Mr Darcy be here, but they do not appear to agree on many things. And they are vastly different in temperament."

"You could say the same of us. It is not exceptional for two people of differing dispositions to get along."

"True. Perhaps it is nothing then. Only, Mr Darcy does occasionally seem angry with Mr Bingley. No, angry is the wrong word. Impatient? Oh, I do not know—but he gives the impression of observing him as though he might *become* cross at any moment. Not dissimilarly from how you and I watch Lydia, in fact, when we are attempting to ensure she does not make herself ridiculous."

Jane sighed. "Remember, you promised no battles. Not even with men who refuse to dance with you."

"I refused *him* again last night," Elizabeth replied, standing up and stretching. "He asked me to dance a reel, no doubt hoping I would say 'Yes' so he could despise my taste. I must credit him with the avoidance of any battle, though, for he was surprisingly gallant when I accused him of premeditated contempt and told him to despise me if he dared. Now, how do you propose we pass our time today? Shall I read to you from one of Mr Bingley's excellent books?"

Jane laughed—her first in a while that did not devolve into a cough. Elizabeth had begun to read several books supplied by the family over the last few days, but an admission made by Mr Bingley that his library was severely neglected had not been overstated, and both she and Jane had quickly tired of histories and political treaties. Yet, with little else to occupy them for the hours until dinner, it was agreed that Elizabeth would venture to the library in a last bid to see whether anything diverting could be found to read.

As she descended the stairs, another door opened somewhere below, and the sound of approaching voices trickled into earshot. An affected titter confirmed the identity of one of the speakers and convinced Elizabeth it was an encounter she could happily avoid. She ran down the remaining steps and sidled around the nearest door into an unlit antechamber. She clamped a hand over her mouth to smother a giggle. First jumping in puddles, now skulking in shadows—if she did not soon leave this place, she would not have two grains of good sense left to rub together.

"I am certain it is within your power to dissuade him," said

Miss Bingley as she approached on the other side of the door. "You have ever given him sound advice."

"As I did on this occasion," came the unmistakably sonorous reply that made Elizabeth doubly thankful to have evaded notice. "He disregarded it entirely. A ball cannot be avoided now."

Elizabeth peered through the open crack of the door to see Mr Darcy walk past, head bent in conversation with his fawning hostess, who then asked him whether he would care to join her on her walk. Elizabeth smiled wryly. For all the scornful looks she had received upon arriving on foot from Longbourn, it would seem Miss Bingley was quite the walker herself. Mr Darcy mumbled a reply that she could not hear, but she quite clearly saw him consent to the invitation with a nod. Which was curious, since she had begun to suspect that, regardless of Miss Bingley's best efforts, Mr Darcy disliked her intensely. They disappeared from view, and after waiting a moment or two for safety, she left her gloomy retreat and hastened in the opposite direction to the greater safety of the library.

A lengthy search thereof turned up nothing of interest. Large sections of the shelves were empty, and the rest seemed to be filled with whatever had been rejected by every self-respecting book seller in the county. To make Jane laugh, Elizabeth searched for the dreariest volume she could find and was prodigiously pleased to eventually discover *The General View of the Agriculture of the County of Hertford* by D. Walker, complete with illustration plates. Anticipating a few minutes of light-hearted fun, she swept out of the library, and walked directly into Mr Darcy. She let out a small grunt as the impact knocked her backwards, though she did not fall.

"Miss Bennet!" he exclaimed, seeming as stupefied as she by the misfortune of another encounter. "Forgive me, I was not looking where I was going."

She had not stumbled, because he had prevented it—something of which she only became aware when he removed his hand from her waist, leaving a distractingly cold area just below her ribs. "Nay, the fault was clearly mine, Mr Darcy." She said nothing more, for she had noticed the drift of his gaze towards the book tucked beneath her arm. She attempted to keep her countenance as he read the title, but when his surprise registered in the slight furrowing of his brow, she could not contain her amusement and hiccupped a small laugh. His head shot up, and he regarded her with unsettling penetration. Truly, she had never met anybody who took himself so seriously. "Did you enjoy your walk with Miss Bingley?" she enquired as a means of distraction.

After a flash of surprise, his countenance hardened into a glacial expression. His lips parted as though he would speak at least twice before he eventually committed to offering an apology for not having invited her or Mrs Hurst to join them.

"It was of no consequence to me, sir. You did not seem to be gone very long. I have probably walked the same distance searching for something passably entertaining to read in the library."

He made a small and distinctly sardonic noise. "Never has a better way of wasting one's time been invented than to search for a good book in Bingley's library."

"So I have discovered."

"Though it does boast several longwinded essays on agriculture, which, of course, are of interest to some."

Elizabeth schooled herself to solemnity but was privately captivated. Had the austere and illustrious Mr Darcy just made a joke? His expression remained inscrutable, but since it was more appealing to Elizabeth's playful nature that he should secretly be a great wit, she resolved instantly to expose him if she could. She pulled the book from beneath her arm and held it out with both hands before her. "My little bit of sport with Jane. She was adamant I would find something diverting to read if only I would look properly. I believe this will fulfil the requirement."

"I am sure *you* will find a way to make it entertaining."

Her resolve wavered; that savoured a lot less of wit and a lot more of scorn. "And what about you, sir? How have you been entertaining yourself with nothing to read?"

"I bring my own books whenever I visit Bingley."

"Do you? I wish I had known."

"I beg your pardon. It did not occur to me you might wish to borrow one."

"Of course not," she said, not even troubling herself to conceal her smile. "You were perfectly ready to believe me when I said I was not a great reader." She would not ordinarily have made any such admission, but on her first night at Netherfield, when she had picked up a book to avoid playing high at cards and Miss Bingley had made a barbed comment about her finding pleasure in nothing else, gainsaying her had been the only palatable recourse. She ought to have known it would provide Mr Darcy with another reason to despise her.

"No, indeed, madam," he replied. Looking at Walker's *General View*, he added, "Though, if your tastes run to an agrarian bent, it is unlikely you would have enjoyed anything of mine."

She tried and failed to discern whether he was teasing, but a laughing plea from Jane over the bannisters for her to make haste seemed to recall him to his purpose, relieving her of the trouble of trying to guess. He sent his regards to her sister and went on his way. Dismissing the glimmer of emotion in his eyes as a trick of the light, Elizabeth dashed up the stairs to delight her sister with an exceedingly silly reading of D. Walker's opening essay on the navigation courses of Hertfordshire.

6
Defects in Every Disposition

JANE DID INDEED FEEL STRONG ENOUGH TO VENTURE downstairs that evening. After another stilted dinner, Elizabeth ran to escort her, well wrapped against the cold, to the drawing room.

"Jane! What a relief to see you looking so well," Miss Bingley exclaimed. Elizabeth refrained from remarking that she might have relieved herself with the sight at any point that day, had she only troubled herself to walk upstairs.

"How unpleasant for you to have been so unwell," Mrs Hurst added. "And in a strange new place, too."

"I was fortunate in that regard," Jane replied. "Of course, I should have much preferred to be at home, not least to have avoided importuning you, but Netherfield does not feel so very new to me. Lizzy and I used to visit quite often when the Connellys lived here."

"Aye, one forgets that you have only lived here a few short weeks yourselves," Elizabeth added. "Has is yet begun to feel any less strange and new for you?"

"Less new, certainly," Miss Bingley replied.

"Is it very different from what you are used to?" Jane enquired, apparently not inclined to be vexed by this answer.

"Indeed, it is," replied Mrs Hurst. "There is a rather more sedate pace of life here than Town."

"I thought I had understood you were in Scarborough before you came here," said Elizabeth, unable to forget how both women had sneered at her mother's notions of country society.

"Mr Hurst and I have a house in Mayfair. My brother and sister do not always choose to join us there."

"You prefer the country, do you, Miss Bingley? I should not have expected that, given your many professions of admiration for fashionable society."

"My brother enjoys the country, Miss Eliza. Being unmarried, he requires that I keep house for him."

"That is not an inconsiderable sacrifice, if you would prefer to be in Town. You must be exceedingly fond of him."

"Of him, yes. Of all my family."

This was contrary to Elizabeth's every opinion of the lady, and the mix of unease and displeasure in Miss Bingley's countenance bade her tread with particular care. "And what is Scarborough like?" she enquired. "How does it compare to Meryton?"

"Remarkably well, as it happens. They are both small, nondescript country towns."

"In looks they are quite different, though," Mrs Hurst added. "Scarborough is obviously situated by the sea."

"Were you brave enough to sea-bathe?" Jane enquired.

"No, we never had the opportunity. Though it was not uncommon for a stray wave to turn a stroll along the beach into an unplanned paddle."

"That happened to me last summer," said Jane. "Do you remember, Lizzy?"

"I do! You were attempting to build a sandcastle with Matthew and Emily, and the tide rushed in behind you."

"We visited Weston with our aunt and uncle," Jane explained to their hosts. "Our cousins love the seaside. As do all children, I suppose."

There was an odd pause. Miss Bingley pursed her lips and looked at the fire. Mrs Hurst cleared her throat and enquired which uncle Jane meant, the one from Meryton or the one from Cheapside, satisfying Elizabeth that it was the allusion to their low connexions by which they were offended.

"My Uncle Gardiner, from London," Jane answered. "He is rather partial to sea-bathing and often takes my aunt and cousins to the coast."

"One of our acquaintance in Scarborough swam daily, do you recall, Caroline?" said Mrs Hurst.

"Yes, and always smelled vaguely of the sea as a consequence," Miss Bingley replied. "Which I confess amused me no end, since his name was Tench."

Jane laughed prettily. Elizabeth smiled, though privately she was, and continued to be for the next hour, confounded by Miss Bingley's manner. She was equal parts scorn and cordiality, flitting erratically between the two as though she had forgotten how to be properly agreeable or properly contemptuous and could maintain neither for very long. By the time the gentleman joined them, Elizabeth had made no further progress in comprehending her character, other than to decide that the lady herself was as much in the dark about it as she.

All her observations were overthrown at that point in any case, for everybody's behaviour altered completely upon the reintroduction of the opposite sex. Mrs Hurst, already firmly in her sister's shadow, slid obligingly back into her husband's as well—a penumbra so encompassing she seemed unable to escape it even when he stretched out on a sofa and went to sleep. Mr Bingley was delighted by Jane's presence and spoke of little else, and to few other people, for the remainder of the evening. Miss Bingley abandoned all autonomous thought and deferred it, comprehensively, to Mr Darcy. Everything he did was delightful to her; everything she said was for his delight; nothing either of them did or said delighted anybody as much as Elizabeth, who could scarcely keep her countenance as she watched them flatter and ignore each other respectively.

"I hope you will honour me with the first two dances," Mr Bingley said to Jane, sending a plume of sparks up the chimney as he stoked the fire for the fifth or sixth time. "Two dances *at least*. It has been too long since the Meryton Assembly. We must make up for lost time."

Mr Darcy looked up from his book. He did not comment, but he assumed that attitude Elizabeth had noticed was a habit of his, of watching his friend in anticipation of the need to intervene.

Miss Bingley took a more direct approach. "Charles, are you really serious in meditating a dance at Netherfield? I would advise you, before you determine on it, to consider the very great number of people it would bring to the house. There could easily be above one-hundred people in attendance."

"You are perfectly right, that is more people than I had anticipated," her brother replied. "I had better instruct Nicholls to begin making white soup directly."

"But Charles—"

"Mrs Hurst," said Mr Darcy. "Did I hear correctly that Lady Stone has commissioned a folly large enough to accommodate dances?"

"Why, yes," replied she. "Though it ought not to be difficult, since she never held a ball that more than a dozen couples attended."

"Was not it at one of her parties that Hurst attempted to waltz with a footman?" Mr Bingley said with a grin.

Mrs Hurst looked vastly unimpressed by the mention of it. Elizabeth glanced to observe Mr Darcy's opinion and was incredulous to discover that he had returned to reading his book. That he had redirected the conversation again was indisputable, but his object was anyone's guess. She was in no doubt that he was disinclined to attend a ball, but did he hope to prevent one being arranged by subverting every mention of it? Only her promise to Jane of no battles kept her from saying something exceedingly impertinent on the subject.

A battle can only be avoided for as long as there is no antagonism from either side, however, and as the evening wore on, more and more opportunities for engagement presented themselves until Elizabeth could resist no longer. "Tease him—laugh at him," she told Miss Bingley when asked how best to punish Mr Darcy for one of his satirical speeches.

Miss Bingley decried the very suggestion with comical affront, declaring that they would only expose themselves if they attempted to laugh without a subject.

"Mr Darcy is not to be laughed at!" cried Elizabeth, looking at the gentleman himself. "That is an uncommon advantage, and uncommon I hope it will continue, for it would be a great loss to me to have many such acquaintance. I dearly love a laugh."

She thought he nodded ever so slightly before replying with a small smile, "Miss Bingley has given me credit for more than can be. The wisest and the best of men may be rendered ridiculous by a person whose first object in life is a joke."

This is intended for me, Elizabeth thought, recalling his assertion that she could make a joke of even the most serious book. *He thinks I cannot be serious! Well, better that than to be incapable of laughing at anything!* "Certainly, there are such people, but I hope I am not one of them. I hope I never ridicule what is wise or good. Follies and nonsense, whims and inconsistencies do divert me, I own, and I laugh at them whenever I can. But these, I suppose, are precisely what you are without."

"It is not my experience that being wise or good makes one any less susceptible to folly. But I do my best to avoid those weaknesses that expose a strong understanding to ridicule."

"A valuable study—and one from which your friends are fortunate enough to benefit," she replied, thinking of his occasional habit of censoring Mr Bingley's conversation.

He shifted uneasily in his seat. "What is your meaning?"

"Only that such faultless behaviour must be a model for those around you."

"I have faults enough, Miss Bennet, but they are not, I hope, of understanding. My temper I dare not vouch for. It would perhaps be called resentful. I cannot forget the follies and vices of others so soon as I ought, nor their offences against myself—but as long as my own conduct is above reproach then the world can have no objection to my feelings."

"Moral rectitude is more important than true forgiveness in your opinion then?"

"Where forgiveness is impossible, morality must suffice."

"I suppose it must, if sanctimony can be considered superior to implacable resentment."

"It must, at least, be considered superior to irreverence."

"Do let us have a little music," cried Mrs Hurst in a strained voice. She made her way to the instrument—past her sister who had retired to a chair and looked rather ill—and began to play. Mr Darcy returned to his book, and Elizabeth, after noticing Jane's expression, was not sorry for it.

"Not everybody likes to debate the way you do, Lizzy," Jane whispered when they climbed the stairs to their rooms later.

Elizabeth scoffed. "I rather think Mr Darcy can withstand it. Besides, I should think it was a refreshing antidote to Miss Bingley's servility."

"A want of belligerence does not equate to servility. And Mr Darcy is Mr Bingley's guest. I hate to sound like Mama, but I beg you would remember where you are."

Elizabeth closed Jane's bedroom door behind them and helped her flagging sister to a chair. "Forgive me. I promised I would not argue. Though, I do not think my little tête-à-tête with Mr Darcy has done anything to lessen Mr Bingley's admiration for you."

Jane blushed and failed to hide her smile, which Elizabeth took as invitation to interrogate her about all that had passed between them as they whispered secretly by the fire, only relenting when the maid arrived to help Jane ready herself for bed.

Elizabeth wished her sister good night and left for her own room and was almost unsurprised to step directly into Mr Darcy's path on the landing. She gave a huff of incredulous laughter. Being under the same roof clearly made it more likely two people should run into each other, but it was a large house, and thrice in one day was excessive, verging on careless. "Mr Darcy. I beg your pardon."

"Not at all," he replied, stepping out of her way.

She walked past him but turned back at the last moment, and since he had not moved an inch and remained looking in her direction, this brought them face to face. "Jane believes I was too severe on you downstairs."

The dimness of the passage made it difficult to be certain, but it looked very much as though the corner of his mouth lifted into a smile. "Your sister shares Bingley's dislike of arguments, I take it."

"Jane does not argue with anybody if it can be avoided. She is altogether too sweet-tempered." She grinned ruefully, feeling suddenly like an errant child. "She is anxious that I might have incurred your disapprobation."

He looked at her intently. "I have already conceded that I dare not despise you, Miss Bennet. You may tell your sister she has no cause to be anxious. You are safe from me." He wished her goodnight and turned away, which was fortunate, for Elizabeth had no wish for him to observe the blush she could feel burning her cheeks as she hastened to her room.

THOUGH GENERALLY ABLE TO FIND HUMOUR IN MOST things, Elizabeth could not bring herself to be anything but vexed by her mother's blunt refusal to send the carriage the next morning. Determined to impose on the family not a moment longer than necessary, she persuaded Jane to appeal to Mr Bingley for the use of his. He, in turn, prevailed upon them to remain another day at Netherfield. Seeing that Jane dearly wished it, Elizabeth did not object. She could summon no enthusiasm for the walk Mr Bingley then proposed, however. The prospect of spending an hour or so making small talk with his sisters while he walked ahead with hers held no appeal whatsoever.

"I beg you would excuse me on this occasion, Jane. I should like to finish the piece I have been working on before we go home."

Jane regarded her searchingly—perhaps because it was the first time in Elizabeth's life that she had chosen embroidery above walking—but the lure of an hour on Mr Bingley's arm was too great to make her really curious. She left with the rest of the party, whereupon Elizabeth released a great sigh of consternation. She wondered briefly what to do and where to go but froze, her eyes wide in alarm, at the sound of a page turning. She bit her lips together. Finally, here was something at which she could laugh: it had somehow escaped her notice that Mr Darcy had not gone with the others. Among several of the disadvantages his presence posed, the most immediate was that she would now have to *actually* embroider for an hour.

She crossed the room to the sewing box. She could see him clearly now, seated in the opposite corner paying assiduous attention to one of his exclusive books. He neither looked at nor spoke to her. She returned the courtesy and set about her work, though it was too great a temptation not to occasionally glance to see whether he had fallen asleep. His eyes were open, however, and he turned the pages of his book like clockwork. Was this his method of sparing her from his disapprobation: to ignore her entirely? She laughed to herself, delighted by such nonsense, though after half an hour of it, the novelty had most certainly worn off. She put her work away, wished him good day, and quitted the room.

Without much purpose, she wandered the house until she reached her bedroom. There was nothing to do there either except lean against the window frame and stare jealously at the fields that lay between Netherfield and Longbourn. Her attention was caught by a movement in the shrubbery. She watched it, expecting to see a rabbit, but after another rustle, Miss Anna Dunn emerged and darted, laughing, across the lawn, her bonnet flapping behind her, held on only by its ribbon.

It could not be a good thing she was in full view of the house, but Elizabeth was loath to call out a warning lest it draw unnecessary attention. Her concern was rendered immaterial when Anna tripped on the edging stones that lined the drive and tumbled onto the gravel with a loud wail. She fumbled with the sash, intending to let Anna know she would come directly, but it was stuck fast—and it was too late anyway. Below, on the lawn, Mr Darcy appeared, striding towards the little girl with alarming purpose. Unable to prevent their meeting, Elizabeth could only watch in wretched suspense.

Whatever she had been expecting to see—angry hand gestures, Anna marched off the lawn—nothing could have surprised Elizabeth more than what she then observed. Upon reaching the child, Mr Darcy crouched down, removed a handkerchief from his pocket, and attended to her grazes. He said something that made Anna laugh—nay, made them *both* laugh. He stood, lifted her to her feet, and mimed brushing himself down; she copied him. He said something more serious, shaking his head as he did so; Anna hung her head, evidently admonished, though it seemed a gentle reprimand. Elizabeth was more amazed than ever when Mr Darcy returned to one knee, lifted Anna's chin with a finger, said something that returned a broad smile to her face, and tapped her playfully on the nose. With a small sideways nod, he dismissed her, and she ran, laughing once more, back the way she had come.

Elizabeth stepped back from the window so as not to be observed by Mr Darcy as he returned to the house. She lowered herself onto the edge of the bed, her mind awhirl, and there she remained, lost in thought, when Jane came looking for her.

"Ah, so you are in here. Mr Darcy said he did not know where you had gone. Is anything the matter?"

"No, not the matter. Though something is puzzling me exceedingly. Do you recall my telling you about the young girl I met out in one of the fields?" After a little prompting, Jane did recall, though her memory of the details was muddled.

"Her name is Anna Dunn. Her mother works here, at Netherfield."

"Her mother is in service? With so young a child? That is singular."

"Indeed it is, but that is not the point. The pertinent part is that she was here, just now, on the lawn." Elizabeth then related to her sister all that she had witnessed from the window.

"There, you see," Jane said when she was done. "He is not as terrible as you believed."

"I will not deny that in this, he acted with compassion—though, that just serves to give greater contrast to his behaviour towards everyone else."

Jane smiled the small, apologetic smile she saved for those rare occasions when she felt obliged to disagree with somebody. "I have never been as eager as you to condemn his general character simply because he was ill-tempered at one dance—though he was abominably rude to you. But I cannot say that I have ever felt any peculiar coldness from him. That he should be kind to a young child in distress does not strike me as so very odd."

Elizabeth did not argue. To do so would have been churlish, for whatever his faults, Mr Darcy was evidently not a monster. On the contrary, it would seem he was capable of some small acts of liberality, where it pleased him. *Gallantry, too,* she thought, recalling her encounter with him the previous evening. *And quite possibly humour, if I am not greatly mistaken, though he keeps that a well-guarded secret.* He nevertheless remained the proudest, most conceited person of her acquaintance. Indeed, the more she saw of him, the more contradictory his behaviour was revealed to be.

She agreed readily to Jane's suggestion that they join the rest of the party downstairs, for as Mr Darcy himself had said—to Mrs Bennet's vast displeasure—the confined and unvarying society of a country neighbourhood could in general supply but few deep, intricate characters. She would be foolish to waste any opportunity that arose to study one.

"THIS HAS, WITHOUT DOUBT, BEEN THE MOST ENJOYABLE day since we arrived in Hertfordshire," said Mr Bingley, tilting his glass in Jane's direction.

"Here, here!" agreed Mrs Hurst. "A perfect day—and with such glorious weather for the time of year."

"Perfect weather for sport," grumbled Mr Hurst around a mouthful of dinner. "A full day of it, and I might have stood a chance of catching up with Darcy. He is ahead of me by two-score-and-four."

"Indeed," Mr Bingley agreed, "but the grouse are not going anywhere, and my guests are." He grinned at Elizabeth and added, "My brother is fond of his sport."

"I am!" Mr Hurst said crossly. "Lord knows there is little else to do now that you have all taken against playing cards."

"We have not taken against cards," Miss Bingley corrected him. "But Mr Darcy indicated that he did not wish to play."

"Madam," said Mr Darcy, "you will very quickly make me the object of Hurst's contempt if you permanently banish every favourite diversion of his for which I express a momentary disinclination."

"Indeed you will," agreed the man himself. "I cannot comprehend why you should have been disinclined in the first place, Darcy. Loo is as good a way to pass an evening as any."

"For some."

"For you, until Thursday this week. You have never objected to it before."

"Do you propose by this, sir," Elizabeth interposed, "that because Mr Darcy enjoys playing loo, he may never pursue any other diversions? I do not think many people could adhere to such a notion."

Mr Hurst mumbled that he supposed not. Mr Darcy said nothing; he only looked briefly at Elizabeth, then back to his dinner.

Mr Bingley laughed unsympathetically. "If it makes you feel any better, Withers informed me yesterday that Netherfield has a pond over on the farthest boundary. How is that for a discovery, eh? It is all duckweed and algae at the moment, but you never know, there might be something worth catching beneath all that."

"Do not tell Darcy—he will empty it of fish as soon as look at it."

"By all means, have the pond to yourself, Hurst," said Mr Darcy. "I have no pressing desire to fish."

"Too kind, I am sure," Mr Hurst replied.

Elizabeth grinned widely. "Unless Mr Darcy's real purpose is to deny you *any* fish by professing himself disinclined to the sport in the hope that Miss Bingley will declare the pond off limits."

This was generally well received; Mr Bingley laughed heartily, Jane smiled enough for Elizabeth to be sure her impertinence was forgiven, and even Miss Bingley tittered graciously at her own expense. Mr Darcy only stared at Elizabeth darkly and said nothing, which did not surprise her one bit, for, continuing his theme from that morning, he had scarcely spoken ten words to her all afternoon.

"You are too cruel, Miss Eliza," Miss Bingley simpered. "Mr Darcy would never treat his friends so abominably. He is too generous by far."

Perhaps only because she was looking for it did Elizabeth see the flicker of vexation this produced on Mr Darcy's countenance.

"Even to his tenants and servants," his devoted advocate

continued, her flattery taking a truly arbitrary turn. "Which ought to be a model for you, Charles, when you do eventually buy a house."

"Yes, Caroline, I am well aware how faithfully you would have me imitate Darcy in all ways," Mr Bingley replied. "I assure you I am concentrating diligently on growing my legs another three inches, that I might equal him in stature as well as everything else."

"Does your father enjoy fishing, Miss Bennet?" said Mr Darcy to Jane.

Elizabeth wondered whether Mr Bingley were aware how often his conversations were arranged to better suit his friend.

"There is nowhere to fish at Longbourn, sir," Jane replied. "My great-grandfather had the pond filled in many years ago."

"That is a shame."

"It is," Elizabeth said, "though, as detailed in D. Walker's *General View of the Agriculture of Hertford*, there are copious rivers and streams in the county that might serve the keen angler."

Mr Darcy started to smile but visibly caught himself. Then he started to reply and stopped himself doing that, also. He resorted to looking at her in uncomfortable silence until Mr Hurst declared that the book sounded eminently informative and requested to borrow it. Elizabeth did her utmost to keep her composure, though with so much folly before her it was no easy task.

"Of course, with three lakes at Pemberley, Mr Darcy does not want for places to fish whenever he chooses," said Miss Bingley, leaning proprietarily towards him. Her compliment earned her nothing; Mr Darcy remained silent, exuding a studied air of indifference.

The same dismissive disdain with which he treats me! The sudden thought that he had identified her as a similar threat to his bachelorhood as Miss Bingley was so diverting that, try as she might, Elizabeth could not fully repress a laugh. It bubbled up and caught in her throat, obliging her to hastily cover her mouth with her napkin. It did not escape Mr Darcy's notice; he looked almost pained as he regarded her. She took pity on him and schooled herself to solemnity, though she could not but think it served him right. He ought never to have undertaken not to despise her if it was to be such a difficult promise to keep.

SERVICES WERE NOT UNTIL NINE THE NEXT MORNING, AND Elizabeth was awake, dressed, and roaming the park one last time by a quarter to eight. Since the day had come, at long last, to return home, she had chosen to explore the far side of the park one last time. She walked past Mr Bingley's pond—the discovery of which was not news to her, for she had used to sail boats on it when she was younger—and into a small copse of trees that clung obstinately to their rusting leaves. She plucked one that was no longer golden brown but skeletal and twisted it between her finger and thumb as she walked. She was glad to have done so when she espied Anna running along in front of a hedgerow in the distance, for she knew in an instant what to do with the gossamer frond. She waved energetically to attract attention, and Anna bounded towards her excitedly.

"Have you outrun Miss Paxton again?" Elizabeth enquired.

"She is not yet out of bed."

"So you have snuck out?" Anna nodded, and Elizabeth added in a tone of sisterly reproach, "I expect that is why you have no pelisse. Are not you cold?"

"No, ma'am, for I have been running!"

The pride with which Anna always spoke of running was vastly endearing, and Elizabeth wished she did not have to discourage her but could scarcely do otherwise. "It really is not safe for you to be out alone. Particularly if nobody knows where you are. You might get lost or hurt yourself, as you did up at the house yesterday."

Anna's nose wrinkled in puzzlement. "Did you see me?"

"Aye, from an upstairs window. I have been staying there with my sister Jane."

"Have you seen my mother while you have been there?"

"No, I do not believe so. But then, I have passed most of my time in my sister's room. She has been unwell, if you recall." She could not resist adding, "It seemed as though Mr Darcy—the gentleman who spoke to you on the lawn—was very kind."

"Oh, he was! I thought he would be more vexed."

"I confess, so did I. May I enquire what he said to you?"

Anna shrugged. "I think...that I should not be there and to go home?"

"And what was it he said that made you smile so, directly before you left?"

Anna's brow furrowed in thought for a moment before her smile returned to illuminate her countenance. "That I should see how fast I could run home." She ceased smiling and explained with the utmost gravity, "It made me smile because I like running."

Elizabeth assured her she knew. "Now, I am going to suggest very seriously that you do the same again. And before you pull that face, I have something special to give you. Open your hand. You must be exceedingly gentle." She placed the skeleton leaf on Anna's palm.

"What is it?"

"Well, it is difficult to be sure, but it looks very much like a fairy's wing, do not you think?"

Anna gasped; her eyes wide with wonder as she brought the leaf close to her face to examine it.

"You may keep it, as long as you promise me that you will go directly home and not run away again."

No promise was ever so readily or so hastily made, and Anna had soon disappeared between a gap in the hedgerow, her prize clutched carefully in her little fist. Elizabeth turned back to the house, pleased to have met with her new friend, but underwhelmed with the disappointingly reasonable answers she had received to her questions about Mr Darcy.

As though conscious of her frustrated studies, he kindly provided her with one last conundrum over which to puzzle. From her return to the house to the moment she and Jane left in Mr Bingley's carriage, he continued his determined campaign to say as few words to her as possible. He looked at her but rarely, chose not to join the rest of the party in waving off the carriage, and returned to the house immediately after services with only a curt bow as his good-bye. All of which made his decision to offer her his arm, escort her into services, and sit next to her throughout even harder to comprehend.

By the time the carriage reached Longbourn, Elizabeth had concluded that she must simply present a lesser danger than Miss Bingley. Seconds after disembarking, she forgot the matter entirely, distracted by Mrs Bennet's vociferous displeasure at their returning home early, underdressed against the cold, and still single.

8
New Acquaintances and Old Grievances

The parlour door closed, and all five Bennet sisters drooped in their seats, more than one of them groaning loudly.

"Lord, he is such a bore!"

"He is not easy company, Kitty," Jane agreed. "Though we must allow that he is not used to the society of so many women."

"At least he has stopped embarrassing you with his strange little compliments."

Elizabeth puffed out her cheeks and picked disconsolately at the trim of her sleeve. "That is because Mama has told him Jane will soon be engaged to Mr Bingley." Jane objected, but Elizabeth confirmed it was so. "And now he has transferred his attentions to me, though if he thinks *I* will marry him, he will be sorely disappointed."

"But you would be mistress of Longbourn," said Mary, frowning deeply.

"Even that would not be compensation enough!"

"I do not see why you should feel the need to be compensated. Our cousin is very respectable."

"His occupation is respectable, certainly, but clergyman or not, such a vain, obsequious man could never be truly esteemed."

"I would marry Mr Collins myself if he were as handsome as Mr Wickham," said Lydia with a sigh.

"It would be better to simply marry Mr Wickham," said Kitty. "Then your husband would be handsome *and* estimable."

Jane rolled her eyes at Elizabeth, and she smiled in return, though the idea was not without merit. She had known neither gentleman for longer than a day, but forced to choose, there really would be no contest. Mr Wickham, a friend and soon-to-be fellow officer of Mr Denny's, had been introduced to them in Meryton just now. He had met them with unaffected good cheer and conducted himself so charmingly it was impossible not to form an opinion immediately more favourable than that inspired by Mr Collins. A distant cousin and, as a consequence of Mr and Mrs Bennet's failure to produce a son, heir to Longbourn, *he* had arrived at Longbourn yesterday. His professed object was to rebuild a long-burnt familial bridge on the advice of his esteemed patroness, Lady Catherine de Bourgh. Any opportunity to acquaint himself with his future property was no doubt entirely incidental.

"I could marry him if I chose to," Lydia declared. "'Tis a shame our meeting just now was interrupted, else I would have had more time to work on him."

Elizabeth looked fondly at Jane. "I rather think *someone* did not mind the interruption. Particularly as Mr Bingley said he and his friend were on their way here with the express intention of asking after her."

"Indeed, that was a pleasant surprise," Jane replied with a coy smile. "Though I would have preferred that they *had* met us here, for we might have talked for longer then."

"We might have talked for longer *there* if Mr Darcy had not ridden off as he did," Mary observed.

"He probably recognised Mr Collins for the bore that he is and wished to avoid being trapped in conversation with him," said Kitty.

This brought the younger girls back to bemoaning their cousin's shortcomings and distracted them sufficiently that Elizabeth felt safe to speak quietly to Jane without their notice. "Did you happen to see what passed between Mr Wickham and Mr Darcy when they saw each other?"

Jane shook her head. "Why, was it remarkable?"

"I am not sure. Where Mr Darcy is concerned it is never easy to determine whether things are something or nothing. Only they did both appear affected, and I cannot but think they must be acquainted—and not on good terms."

"Did they acknowledge each other?"

"Aye, though barely—and then Mr Darcy rode away. That in itself is not out of character, for he often ignores people, but I have never seen him behave so poorly to Mr Bingley."

"Perhaps he thought it would be impolite to obtrude on the conversation we were already having with Mr Denny and Mr Wickham. In that light, one could consider Mr Bingley the uncivil one."

"True! Perhaps it *was* nothing then." Yet with every encounter, Elizabeth grew increasingly certain there was *something* more to know of Mr Darcy. His countenance gave little away, apart from those few occasions he let slip a smile at something she had said, or when he had laughed freely with Anna. She wished she had paid better attention to Mr Wickham during the meeting, for though his features were not as fine, they nevertheless boasted an openness that might have revealed more—but she had been chiefly looking at Mr Darcy.

"If it is anything imperative, we will find it out eventually," Jane said.

Feeling this was probably a gentle reproof not to pry, Elizabeth let the matter drop, and did not think about it again any more than three dozen times before bed.

As it happened, an opportunity to find out more presented itself sooner than she could have hoped. Some of the officers were engaged to dine with the Philipses the next day, and Mrs Philips had pressed Elizabeth, all her sisters, and her cousin to join them for supper afterwards. She was delighted to discover, upon her arrival, that Mr Wickham was in attendance. Though she spent the early part of the evening in impatient suspense, desperate to enquire about his history with Mr Darcy but knowing that delicacy prevented her from broaching the subject, she was not without other sources of gratification while she waited. Wickham, watched by every lady in the room, chose to sit with her, by which she could not fail to be flattered. His conversation, in contrast to Mr Darcy's determined silence, was vastly pleasing; he had much to say and said all of it with good humour and élan. His attentions, juxtaposed to Mr Collins's clumsy attempts, were exciting, and made her feel she must be of some importance to him. Yet he pleased her most when, without prompt from her, he mentioned the matter she most wished to discuss.

"Are you much acquainted with the gentlemen I saw you talking to in Meryton yesterday?"

"Only a little. They have not long been in the area."

Wickham nodded, his gaze fixed on his glass of wine, which he twisted back and forth on the table between them. "And how have they been received in the neighbourhood? Are they generally liked?"

"One of them is."

That earned her a full smile. "And the other?"

"The other...you may not hear spoken of quite so favourably. If I may be so bold, sir, I take it you are also acquainted with them both?"

"I have been connected with the Darcy family from my childhood. The Bingleys I know by association."

"Indeed! Are you here by design then, to see them?"

Wickham chuckled in a way that Elizabeth might have thought bitter had not his mouth, too well formed for resentment, made it seem otherwise. "Far from it. As you might have surmised from the cold manner of our meeting, Mr Darcy no longer welcomes my company."

"There are but few people whose company Mr Darcy enjoys, from what I have seen. I hope your plans will not be affected by his being in the neighbourhood."

"It would not be the first time he has driven me away, and ordinarily I might not object to going, for seeing him always gives me pain. But, as well as the inducement of obviously excellent society"—he leant forwards and regarded Elizabeth in a way that warmed her cheeks—"I must stay, for I have taken a commission in Colonel Forster's regiment. And since it seems Mr Darcy has taken a lease in the area, there is little to be done but suffer the occasional encounter."

"I am sorry to hear that will pain you, sir, but you are mistaken. It is Mr Bingley who has taken the lease on Netherfield Park. Mr Darcy may come and go at his convenience."

Wickham looked at her searchingly for a moment before his mouth twisted into a small but expressive smile. "Perhaps he will go, then, now that I am here. Though I doubt it. He is uncommonly devoted to his friend."

"Is he? I must say, that has not been my impression. I have recently stayed four days at Netherfield and most often Mr Darcy seems vexed by Mr Bingley."

"Mr Darcy is vexed by many things. He has a resentful disposition."

"This I can easily believe, for he has told me so himself." After so long meditating on Mr Darcy's character, Elizabeth supposed she ought to feel vindicated to hear somebody so well acquainted with him confirm it. Yet something undefinable prevented her from being satisfied. "I wonder, though," she said cautiously, "whether anyone can truly be all bad. Is not it possible that he has some element of good in him?"

"And, pray tell, what good has Mr Darcy done for you?"

"None for me!" she replied with a laugh. "He despises me quite as much as he does almost everybody else in Hertfordshire—but I cannot pretend that I have not seen him occasionally be solicitous to some."

"When it suits him, you mean? Aye, that sounds very like him. Pray, what did you see?"

"When I was at Netherfield recently, I saw him come to the rescue of a small child. A little girl—one of the servants' I believe, who really ought not to have been at the house—fell and hurt herself, and he went to her aid. There was no reason for him to go to her—the servants could easily have dealt with the situation, or she could have run home of her own volition, for she had only grazed her knees. But he went and was exceedingly gentle." She jumped when Wickham let out an abrupt bark of laughter.

"Well, well! I would never have credited it."

"Indeed. He is generally so disdainful. I have not been able to account for it."

"Mr Darcy does not want abilities, Miss Bennet. He can please where he chooses."

That he chose when to bestow his approbation, and when to withhold it, Elizabeth could also readily believe, for she had seen him consciously refrain from smiling at more than one of her own witticisms. *Evidently, I am not worth pleasing.*

She was, at least, in good company with Wickham. "It is very sad that he chooses not to please you, if you were once so close."

Wickham pulled a face of resigned sorrow. "His behaviour to myself has been scandalous—but I am afraid you will think me ill-mannered if I begin criticising your new friend, when you are determined to see the good in him."

She laughed aloud. "Mr Darcy and I are not friends, sir. I have seen him do one good thing, and had I my sister's temperament, that might be enough to convince me of his probity, but I am not as forbearing as Jane. And he has never shown me any particular consideration."

Wickham's enchanting little smile returned. "I shall tell you then, if only to prove that your temperament is not wanting—your opinion of Mr Darcy is wholly justified." He paused while there was a brief interruption from some of the other supper guests but afterwards continued in a conspiratorial tone. "His father, the late Mr Darcy, was my godfather, and excessively attached to me. I cannot do justice to his kindness. He bequeathed me the next presentation of the best living in his gift and a legacy of one-thousand pounds, but after his death, I was denied both."

"What? Why was his will disregarded?"

"I shall not lie to you, Miss Bennet. My godfather's attachment to me was so strong that at times he was more like a true father. As a consequence, very occasionally we argued, as all children do with their parents from time to time."

He paused, and Elizabeth encouraged him with a nod to continue. He could scarcely wish for a more understanding listener; arguments formed part of daily life at Longbourn, and none of her family loved each other any less for it.

He sighed and dipped his head dejectedly. "It is my greatest regret that in the days prior to his passing, we had one such altercation. Some trifling squabble so minor I can scarcely recall the foundation for it. Perhaps it was even my fault, for I was young, and the young are invariably imprudent. Tragically, he passed away very suddenly before we reconciled, and a lifetime of affection was undone in an instant. A man of honour could not have doubted the intention in the will, but his son asserted that I had forfeited all claim to it by my actions towards his father."

"Good heavens! Why did you not seek legal redress?"

"I refused to besmirch my godfather's good name. And, thanks to his son, I could not afford to."

"How abominable!" cried Elizabeth. "You ought to have been pitied for losing your godfather—your friend—at such a moment, not punished! What can have induced Mr Darcy to behave so cruelly?"

"A thorough, determined dislike of me was his motive—a dislike which I cannot but attribute in some measure to jealousy. Had the late Mr Darcy liked me less, his son might have borne with me better, but his father's uncommon attachment to me irritated him, I believe. I suspect he saw our disagreement as his opportunity to reclaim that preference which, in life, his father could never give him, and ruin me in his father's memory in perpetuity."

Elizabeth stared, appalled and—she could not deny—disappointed. For all his superiority, Mr Darcy's smile when he played with Anna had seemed to hold such promise, and she had been so determined to unearth something other than pride. "I had not thought him so bad as this," she said dispiritedly. "He deserves to be publicly disgraced."

"Oh, no!" cried Wickham, sitting forward and speaking with sudden urgency. "I beg you would say nothing of this to anyone." After a deep breath, he smiled and said more calmly, "Some time or other he will be disgraced—but it shall not be by me. Till I can forget his father, I can never expose *him*."

Elizabeth honoured him for such feelings and assured him

of her discretion. "He does not deserve such consideration. People ought to know what he is, for who is to say he would not turn against his new friends as he has his old one. Indeed, I am astonished at his intimacy with Mr Bingley. How can he, who is, I really believe, truly amiable, be in a friendship with such a man?"

"Mr Bingley *is* amiable, and that is precisely what makes him the perfect friend for Mr Darcy. One is so complying and the other so overbearing, they never have a problem one cannot scold the other out of in a day."

This was such a truthful depiction of the two men that Elizabeth could not help but laugh, which drew Lydia's notice.

"What are you laughing about with Mr Wickham, Lizzy? Would that you stop your chattering. You have kept him to yourself for too long now."

Wickham graciously took the blame and excused himself from Elizabeth to circulate Mrs Philips's parlour more widely. They had no further opportunity to talk before the evening drew to a close, though he caught her eye enough times to ensure that her cheeks retained a steady glow of complacency until the very end. Her mind was full of all she had heard, and while Mr Collins commandeered all conversation with his incessant moralising in the carriage home, Elizabeth privately replayed it all: Wickham's distressing tale; his sadness as he told it; the small, secret smile with which he occasionally regarded her; and—because she was even less able to account for it after all she had learnt—the inexplicable yet tantalising glimmer of compassion she had seen in the conceited and resentful Mr Darcy.

Differing Accounts

"WHAT ARE YOU DOING IN HERE?"

Elizabeth looked over her shoulder and smiled at Jane. "Getting some fresh air." It had been raining incessantly all day, preventing any escape outdoors. In desperation, she had retreated to the back parlour, thrown open the double doors to the garden, and pulled the love seat as close to the threshold as it could go without getting wet. She had been sitting there for the best part of an hour, swinging her feet in and out of the rain as she savoured the peace and quiet. She shuffled over to make room for Jane. "And stealing a moment away from Lydia and Kitty's squabbling over slippers and ribbon." This they had been doing relentlessly since Mr Bingley and his sisters came the day before to invite them all to the long-awaited Netherfield ball.

Jane wrapped her shawl more tightly around herself and sat down. "Do not begrudge them their excitement, Lizzy. 'Tis their first private dance. They are excessively excited."

"I was, too, until I was obliged to promise the first two dances to Mr Collins."

"That serves you right for provoking him. You ought not

to sport with people who have not the disposition to reciprocate."

"You are quite right. I have only myself to blame, and I shall suffer it with good grace—though I should much rather dance the first set with Mr Wickham."

After a pause and a shrewd look, Jane observed that Elizabeth seemed to like him very well.

"I confess I do."

"And do you feel any more reconciled to what he told you at Aunt Philips's?"

Elizabeth had, of course, relayed it all to Jane, for no promise to secrecy ever made was intended to exclude the confidence of a favourite sister. "No more, but no less either," she replied. "I am still inclined to believe he spoke the truth, for why would he admit that he argued with his godfather otherwise? He could have omitted that part completely and made himself infinitely more credible, but he even admitted the quarrel was his fault. In any case, it is not *he* who confounds me."

"Confounded is better than infuriated, which you were in a way to being yesterday. May I say that I am pleased you are not hastening to condemn Mr Darcy?"

Elizabeth rolled her head onto her shoulder to give her sister a wry look. "That is where we differ, Jane. You would find a way to think well of everybody involved. I am perfectly willing to accept that Mr Darcy has been hateful to Mr Wickham, for he has been hateful towards me from the first moment of our acquaintance."

"Lizzy, be fair," Jane said in a tone of gentle reproach. "He was uncivil at the assembly, but he has not really been ill-mannered since."

"You say that only because you slept through most of his incivility at Netherfield. He completely and deliberately ignored me on our last day there."

Jane shook her head and screwed her lips into an exasperated smirk. "I shall not argue, for I know I should be wasting my breath—but, if your mind is made up, what is it that yet confounds you?"

Elizabeth shrugged. "I hear such different accounts of him as puzzle me exceedingly. I am trying to make him out." She sat up and twisted in her seat to face Jane. "Speaking of character studies, it was charming how pleased Mr Bingley was to see you when he came yesterday."

"It was," Jane answered, bashful once more. "I wish he could have stayed a little longer, for if this rain continues, I shall not see him again before the ball."

"Yes, his sisters were in rather a hurry to leave—" She stopped talking, and they looked at each other in confusion, for a small commotion had started up out of sight in the garden. Much huffing, sighing, and shuffling of feet announced somebody's approach. In unison, they stood up and leant out of the door—just as Mr Collins trotted into sight, his hat held to his head with one hand and a soggy tome clutched to his side with the other.

"Mr Collins!" cried Jane. "Whatever are you doing out in the rain?"

Their cousin made a startled noise and dropped his book. When he bent to recover it, he lost his hat to the wet grass, then trod on it as he turned to see who had hailed him. Elizabeth and Jane stepped into the garden, one to retrieve his belongings from the ground and the other to guide him inside by the arm.

"Thank you, my dears! You are very kind."

"I did not know you had gone out," Elizabeth said as she helped him out of his wet coat.

"I set out to visit Mr Fellowes. I thought it would be prudent to introduce myself to the incumbent rector of what might one day be—" He closed his eyes and held up a hand.

"But it would not do for me to say too much on what the future may bring to Longbourn. Suffice to say that as a fellow clergyman, I felt it only right that I pay my respects. But I underestimated the fierceness of this rain. Never mind, I shall try again tomorrow, weather permitting."

"You are very good, sir," Jane said stiffly. Elizabeth clenched her teeth and said nothing.

"But I fear I interrupted your private conversation."

"You did." Waiting until a moment or two after the silence grew uncomfortable, Elizabeth added, "But you must not concern yourself. We were only discussing next week's ball."

"Ah, yes! What an occasion that promises to be. I am vastly anticipating our dance, Cousin Elizabeth."

"Excellent," she replied, noticing, because his unctuous grin permitted it, how many teeth he seemed to have crammed unevenly into his mouth. "I can scarcely wait."

He began brushing the grass off his hat. "It was gracious of Mr Bingley to extend the invitation to include me. I am excessively flattered—and not a little excited by the prospect of attending such a prestigious event with Mr Darcy of Pemberley."

Elizabeth glanced sceptically at Jane, who seemed equally perplexed. "Mr Darcy?"

"Why, yes. I am right, am I not—he is a guest of Mr Bingley's? I was sure that was the name I heard mentioned."

"Oh, you were correct about his name. We were only surprised by your enthusiasm."

He ceased brushing grass onto the carpet and regarded them both pityingly. "My dear cousins, I apologise. Of course you would not know, for you are perfectly sheltered from the world here. Mr Darcy is one of the most illustrious personages in the country."

Elizabeth raised an eyebrow. "Are you acquainted with the gentleman, sir, or did you come to this conclusion after he met us in the street on Tuesday and rode away without deigning to acknowledge us?"

Mr Collins opened his eyes wide. "*That* was Mr Darcy?"

"Yes, it was," said Elizabeth impatiently. "You will forgive my ignorance, sir, but what exactly is your connexion to him?"

"He is Lady Catherine's nephew. We have never actually been introduced, but I feel qualified to speak of him in the most favourable terms, for her ladyship speaks of him *very* highly and *very* often. I do believe she would esteem him equally were he not her nephew, for he is a most venerable gentleman, but her estimation must necessarily be greater since he is expected to marry her daughter."

"*Is* he?" said Elizabeth, attempting not to smile too broadly.

"He is, he is! I am surprised he has not mentioned it."

"We are none of us on such intimate terms with Mr Darcy as to discuss his marriage plans, sir. Though you are obviously very much in Lady Catherine's confidence if she discusses such things with you."

"Indeed!" he replied, puffing up with pride. "I flatter myself that I am a source of great comfort and companionship to her ladyship, as befits a man in my position."

"Allow me, in that case, to urge you to change out of those wet things, for she would surely be distraught were you to take a cold as poor Jane did last week."

Jane added her own encouragement by detailing some of her worst symptoms, and in short order they were relieved of their cousin's company.

"Poor Miss Bingley!" Elizabeth cried as soon as the door closed behind him.

"How so?"

"Mr Darcy is expected to marry his cousin! All Miss Bingley's attentions to him have been in vain!"

"You think she has set her cap at him?"

"Without a doubt! I have not heard him express an opinion yet upon which she has not hurled herself in zealous compliance. She looks to him for approbation of everything she says and does, though he never obliges her."

"I daresay she is only being polite. He is a man of significant consequence, do not forget—and her brother's oldest friend."

Elizabeth did not think for a moment it was *deference* that inspired Miss Bingley's officious attentions, but she thought it best not to press the matter. "It ought to be some comfort that Miss de Bourgh is unlikely to please him any more than she."

"And what do you know of what would please Mr Darcy?" Jane enquired, returning to the sofa.

Elizabeth leant with her forearms on the back of it. "Did not I relay to you the conversation we had at Netherfield about what talents a woman must possess in order to be called really accomplished?" When Jane shook her head, she explained, "To satisfy Mr Darcy's idea of the word, she must be able to sing, play, dance, draw, cover a screen, net a purse, paint a table, speak several languages, *and* read extensively."

Jane's frown gave away that she shared Elizabeth's doubt any such woman existed, but her words were more forgiving. "He ought to be pleased with Miss de Bourgh then, for Mr Collins described her as accomplished, handsome, and well-bred."

"Truly, Jane, only you could find praise in what Mr Collins said about the poor woman. He described her as being superior to the handsomest of her sex on account of her distinguished birth—which means she is not handsome at all—of too sickly a constitution to have achieved a single accomplishment, and too condescending to step down from her phaeton when she rides past his house. She sounds awful. Mr Darcy can only be marrying her to unite the estates."

"I suppose that is his prerogative." After a pause, Jane added, "Perhaps, if Lady Catherine talks of Miss de Bourgh marrying her cousin as often as Mr Collins suggests, that is where *he* got the idea."

"I beg you would not even joke! I cannot bear him." Elizabeth came back to sit next to her sister and reached for her hand. "*You* do not expect me to marry him, do you?"

"I do not! Forgive me, I did not mean to tease, but you need not make yourself anxious, for he cannot really mean to ask."

"But he does, Jane. He told Mama that was his purpose in coming to Longbourn."

"That was a joke, surely?"

"I wish it were, but as you have already pointed out, he has not the disposition to tease."

Jane began to look genuinely concerned. "But even if he does mean to ask the question eventually, surely he will wait to see whether he forms an attachment to one of us. He has only known us a few days!"

"You forget—Lady Catherine has instructed him to marry. He will not go back to Kent until he has secured himself a wife." She squeezed Jane's hand harder. "Pray, do not leave me alone with him. The best way to avoid the question is to avoid *him*. I shall have to make sure I am not caught with him on my own."

"You had better hope he does not propose during the first set on Tuesday then."

Elizabeth snatched back her hand and made a disgruntled noise that was made considerably less convincing by her laughter. "Jane Frances Bennet! Nobody in the world would believe me if I told them how cruel you can be sometimes."

10

A Report of a Most Alarming Nature

ELIZABETH TOOK PRODIGIOUS CARE OVER HER APPEARANCE on Tuesday evening, though not, she told herself, for any one's pleasure but her own. Which was just as well, for had she done so with any hope of pleasing Wickham, her endeavours would have been in vain. He had gone to Town on business, Mr Denny informed her upon arrival at Netherfield. The disappointment this occasioned, coupled with her sincere disinclination to be shackled to her cousin, meant Elizabeth was in a less than agreeable humour when the first set of the ball began. Her ill temper was rapidly exacerbated when her dancing partner began to speak, not with inane words of prearranged flattery as she had been anticipating, but on a subject no less vexing.

"I was in two minds as to whether we ought to dance at all," Mr Collins said as they set off into the first figure.

An auspicious beginning. "Is it my company that displeases you, sir, or my dancing?"

"Oh, my dear cousin, neither! It is my opinion of the occasion itself that has materially changed."

Elizabeth glanced around in search of what might have

distressed him but could see nothing untoward. The room was elegantly bedecked, the guests were all tastefully turned out, and the dance itself was being performed with proficiency and decorum rarely observed at the Meryton Assembly Rooms. She was obliged to wait for enlightenment until Mr Collins had promenaded around the set with Maria Lucas.

"I had not thought a ball of this kind could have any tendency to evil," he whispered on his return. "But I was mistaken, for it transpires that this is far from a respectable house."

She regarded him dubiously. "Dare I enquire what has brought you to this conclusion?"

"Not what, my dear, but who. I made it a point of civility to search out Mr Fellowes as soon as we arrived, since the rain prevented me from calling on him all week. In the course of our conversation, I enquired about the purview of his living."

It was Elizabeth's turn to circle the set with another dancer, and she performed it mechanically, too vexed by her cousin's unseemly attempt to discover the extent of his future tithes to take any pleasure in the dance.

"He informed me that the farthest parishioner he visits is Mrs Hanrahan at Hoxley House, not far from here," he said when she stood beside him once more. "He has visited her often of late, for she has been housebound with a cold." Another exchange of partners; another delay. "When he called on her yesterday—" A turn to the left. "She told him of some troubling goings-on at another nearby abode—" A turn to the right. "Persimmon Cottage."

Elizabeth almost lost her footing. *Anna's home!*

Mr Collins skipped towards her and away again, clapping his hands, whispering another few words each time he came near enough to be heard. "A woman and young child—have recently been installed there—and have been observed receiving regular visits from—a certain woman from this house."

They came to a halt and stood facing one another while the last few dancers completed the figure. Elizabeth reviled her cousin's look of superior satisfaction. She already thought him absurd, but to consider this an appropriate place for such a conversation, to be proud of having repeated it, was beyond stupid. "Making calls is hardly unusual, sir," she said quietly, and not very politely. "Perhaps they are relations."

"That is precisely what they are. The brazenness of situating a natural child—"

"Mr Collins!"

He stopped speaking, and a flush overspread his cheeks that remained until the very last note of the song. "I beg your pardon if I have offended you, Cousin Elizabeth," he said as he led her back to her seat.

She acknowledged him with a faint smile but after a moment, decided that was not enough. "Mr Collins, Mrs Hanrahan is a known gossip. I would caution you to give little credit to whatever tales her ennui has driven her to invent."

He recoiled slightly. "The report is not idle gossip. Mr Fellowes says he has good reason to believe—"

"Whatever Mr Fellowes believes he has discovered *became* gossip as soon as he repeated it to you."

"Nay, I must object. He confided the matter to me in the capacity of a fellow cleric."

"Then I daresay he expected you not to repeat it to *me*."

Mr Collins dropped her hand. "As my future wi—" He cleared his throat. "As my dearest cousin, I flattered myself that we might be more in accord on the subject."

"We are in accord on one point—that it would be scandalous were it to be made common knowledge, and that is a very good reason for not repeating it to anybody. Pray, consider what would become of the child were the mother publicly disgraced—a misfortune that would be all the more tragic if the report turned out to be false."

Mr Collins did not answer and instead startled her by abruptly folding himself almost to the floor in an absurdly low bow. Elizabeth stared at him in astonishment for less than a heartbeat before comprehending what must have induced the preposterous genuflection. "Good evening, Mr Darcy," she said before she had even turned to face him fully.

"Good evening, Miss Bennet," Mr Darcy replied sombrely.

Elizabeth wished he would not wear black, for it made his eyes significantly darker and his gaze even more disconcerting than usual. Or perhaps that was a result of his side whiskers, which had been trimmed since she last saw him and were now sharply defined along his cheekbones, accentuating the focus of his stare. Either way, she disliked the intensity with which he regarded her and was relieved when he looked away from her and down at her cousin.

"May I introduce my father's relation, Mr Collins," she said. "Mr Collins, this is—"

"Yes, yes, Mr Darcy! I am well aware, Cousin!" cried he. "The honour is all mine, sir. I am delighted to make your acquaintance—honoured and elated." He bowed again.

Mr Darcy's countenance took on a look of barely restrained incredulity at which Elizabeth could not help but smile. "I understand Mr Collins formed his excellent opinion of you based on the praise frequently bestowed in your favour by his patroness, Lady Catherine de Bourgh."

This was acknowledged with a mere grunt and a level stare, which, though unpardonably uncivil, had the arguably beneficial effect of making Mr Collins wither, pale, and ultimately scuttle away.

"Would you do me the honour of dancing the next with me, Miss Bennet?"

Elizabeth whipped her gaze back to Mr Darcy. His request

came so suddenly on the heels of her cousin's departure, and was so entirely unexpected, that she could think of no good reason to refuse. He thanked her, bowed, and walked away without another word. She exhaled heavily in frustration.

"I daresay you will find him very agreeable."

"Charlotte! Where were you when I needed you?"

"I have been dancing with Mr West."

"Not all week, surely?" She took her friend by the hand and pulled her through the crush to a quieter part of the house to appraise her of all that had transpired in the days since they last saw each other.

"So, Mr Collins is ridiculous and wishes to marry you, Mr Wickham is agreeable but gone astray, and Mr Darcy is worse than both of them put together, but you have agreed to dance with him anyway."

"Yes, that about sums it up."

"I had better not dance with Mr West again. You clearly ought not to be left alone."

Two ladies brushed past, almost knocking Charlotte's drink from her hand and forestalling any reply. Elizabeth stepped backwards, indicating with a nod the little alcove behind them. It was only as her friend was shuffling about, attempting to arrange her reticule, fan, drink and elbows into the tiny space, that she recognised the women. She put a finger to her lips and gestured for Charlotte to attend to their conversation.

"Where, Louisa? Show me!" growled Miss Bingley, twisting around in an attempt to look at something on the back of her gown.

"Here," replied Mrs Hurst, tugging at something on her sister's bodice. "The stitches have frayed."

"For heaven's sake! I told Dunn to stitch it twice."

"I think she has. It is just pulling. Why you insist on having everything made so tightly I do not know."

"You do know."

Mrs Hurst shook her head. "Do not make yourself anxious, Caroline, it is barely noticeable. And look—if I tuck this in here, it will be covered completely. There. Disaster averted."

Miss Bingley thanked her sister and they moved back into the crowd.

"They would not be happy to know we overheard that," Charlotte observed, stepping out of the alcove.

"No, indeed! Did you happen to catch the name of her maid?"

"I cannot say that I was paying much attention to that part, Lizzy. I was too busy trying not to make a sound. Why?"

"I shall have to tell you later," she replied, espying an approaching figure. "Wish me luck!"

"I shall not, because you do not need it." With more urgency, Charlotte added, "Lizzy, do not be a simpleton and allow your fancy for Wickham make you appear unpleasant in the eyes of a man of ten times his consequence."

"Ye of little faith," Elizabeth replied, at which point, Mr Darcy was upon them and she could only hope he did not see Charlotte roll her eyes and cross her fingers surreptitiously against her skirts as they passed in front of her to join the set.

"Do you talk by rule then, when you are dancing?" Mr Darcy enquired.

They had been going along for some time *without* talking before Elizabeth teased even this much out of him, and after an arch response and a sportive assessment of his taciturn disposition, into silence they fell once more. Why he had asked her to dance was a mystery. Perhaps it was because he had already laid the foundations of a steadfast antipathy with her, whereas any other person outside of his own party might be erroneously excited by his condescension into thinking they had aroused his interest. She turned away to hide a smile.

"May I enquire what amuses you?"

She grinned contritely at having been caught. "I am not at all convinced you would like to know."

"On the contrary. I would very much like to know."

"With a design to prove that my first object in life is a joke?"

"Not your first object," he replied, just as the dance began to draw them apart. "Though it would come a close second after your propensity to wilfully misunderstand people."

Caught off-guard, Elizabeth laughed when she would much rather not have. She watched him as they went down the line. Without any perceptible movement, his countenance seemed to have softened from inscrutable to something much more closely resembling complacency. *He considers that a hit!* Indeed, she conceded with a private smile that it probably was. "How fortunate that at least one of us is amenable to being ridiculed," she said to him when the dance next gave her the opportunity. She thought she saw a smile playing at the corners of his mouth, though he did not give in to it.

"I rest my case," he said. "It was not my intention to laugh at you."

"Perhaps not, but I should rather laugh at myself than not at all."

"You are not happy unless you are laughing at something?"

"That is an unsound correlation, sir. I am perfectly capable of being serious, but I am not made for ill humour. I am more often happy, and when I am happy, I laugh."

"I must conclude, then, that you did not derive any pleasure from your previous dance."

Something thrummed behind her breastbone at the

thought that he had been watching. "My cousin is an acquired taste. That I have yet to acquire."

"I thought I understood that you preferred to laugh at nonsense."

"And so I might have at any other time, but this evening he chose to vex me with an idle report that I did not find at all diverting. I was at pains to persuade him not to repeat it."

"I am exceedingly pleased to hear that you disapprove of gossip, Miss Bennet. It is the ruin of too many families."

The mention of ruined families recalled Elizabeth to Wickham's straitened circumstances, reminding her that she was supposed to be angry with Mr Darcy, and making her ashamed for having begun to enjoy herself. She felt compelled to redress the imbalance, and once they completed the next set of turns and stood facing each other again, she said, "When you met us in Meryton the other day, we had just been forming a new acquaintance."

The effect was immediate. A deeper shade of hauteur overspread Mr Darcy's features, and after an uncomfortably long pause, he said in a constrained manner, "I am encouraged by our conversation just now that I may safely leave the subject of Mr Wickham untouched."

The implication was clear: he suspected that Wickham would say something about him. He could not know how unfortunate his reference to her conversation with Mr Collins was. For though that gossip had been disagreeable, and though she had begged her cousin not to repeat it, the report of Anna's illegitimacy was ultimately true. The question remained, therefore, whether Mr Darcy wished her to distrust whatever Wickham told her, or simply not to repeat it to anybody.

"What congratulations will then flow in!"

Elizabeth started. She had been vaguely aware that Sir William had accosted them but was too engrossed in her private thoughts to have paid much heed to what he was saying. She regretted her inattention when she comprehended that his energetic proclamation had been meant for Jane and Mr Bingley, whom he was watching dance together. Mr Darcy was also regarding them, his expression distinctly less sanguine than Sir William's. Elizabeth bristled to see his displeasure, for one had to go considerably out of one's way to find a reason to object to Jane.

When Sir William received no response from either of them, he made his excuses and left, prompting Mr Darcy to collect himself and make a passably civil enquiry as to what books Elizabeth enjoyed reading. "Other than agricultural theses, of course," he added, smiling.

"I believe we have covered that topic, sir."

"We have begun it, but we have not exhausted it. Knowing you read widely is not the same as knowing what books you enjoy most."

"But you are much too late. You ought to have asked me that on my last day at Netherfield, instead of leaving me with nothing to do but embroider for half an hour."

"I do not see that I could be expected to know you were averse to the activity when you stated it as your intended pursuit."

"True, and had I known I would have to act on my words, I might have been better served to say that embroidery was not an engaging enough pursuit to tempt me and that it would be a punishment to sew another stitch." She flashed him a disarming smile. "But then I would have been obliged to trail around the garden at an invalid's pace for the next two hours, and that was more torture than I could bear when, left to my own devices, I could have walked home in one."

Her remark coincided with the end of the dance, giving her an excellent opportunity to demonstrate her proficiency in that area; after they had bowed and curtsied respectively, she turned and walked away.

"YOU LOOK VERY PLEASED WITH YOURSELF," SHE SAID WHEN she met with Jane in the supper room. Having just danced her second set with Mr Bingley, her sister glowed with more than just exercise. "I trust you are enjoying yourself?"

"Very much," Jane replied, but her expression soon turned serious. Turning away from the room and lowering her voice, she continued, "I asked Mr Bingley about Mr Wickham as you desired me to and, Lizzy, it is not as you suspected. Mr Darcy is not the reason he did not come this evening."

"What?"

"The reason Mr Wickham is not here is because Mr Bingley himself omitted him from the officers' invitation."

"Did he tell you why?"

"Not specifically, no, but—"

"Then Mr Darcy has obliged him to!"

"You did not allow me to finish. The mention of Mr Wickham brought Mr Bingley the closest I have seen him come to being genuinely vexed. He was most reluctant to discuss the matter, but he vouched emphatically for the conduct, probity, and honour of his friend and said Mr Wickham's coming into the country is a most insolent thing indeed."

This was the last thing Elizabeth had expected to hear. "Think you he has his own quarrel with Mr Wickham?"

"I only know that by his account, as well as his sister's, Mr Wickham is by no means a respectable young man. I am afraid he has been very imprudent and has deserved to lose Mr Darcy's regard."

"He has lost a good deal more than Mr Darcy's *regard*. What of the living he was denied?"

"Apparently he never took orders and therefore had no need of it."

"And what of the money he was bequeathed?"

"I did not press him on it, Lizzy. I know you wish to think well of Mr Wickham, but you would not like me to anger Mr Bingley by seeming to champion a gentleman with whom he is evidently on such bad terms, would you?"

"Certainly not." Indeed, had it occurred to Elizabeth that such questions might anger Mr Bingley, she would never have imposed on her sister to ask them. That they *had* angered the more commonly good-humoured gentleman was more than a little strange, but she resigned herself to being curious, for she had evidently heard all she could expect to on the matter from Mr Bingley and his friend.

Raucous laughter erupted behind them, followed by a loud and distinctive shriek. Elizabeth and Jane exchanged a weary look before heading to petition Lydia for the third or fourth time that evening to cease making herself ridiculous. After incurring another dose of their youngest sister's petulant wrath, they joined Mr Bingley at a table that was as far away from her as the supper room allowed. It seemed a successful plan until Mrs Bennet sat down next to them and emitted a stream of hysterical prognostications about all her daughters' imminent nuptials that made Lydia's conduct look exemplary by comparison. Elizabeth might have borne it slightly better had not Mr Darcy, followed by his loyal disciple, Miss Bingley, also seated themselves at the same table, as though to revel with superior glee in her relations' vulgarity. Her agonies multiplied as the minutes ticked by, peaking when Mary ensconced herself at the instrument and banged out a vastly unsuitable piece to the very best of her very limited ability.

"Why is Mary playing that awful dirge?"

Elizabeth closed her eyes and pretended that somebody

other than Kitty had spoken thus, and about somebody other than Mary.

"Sisters can be tiresome, can they not, Lizzy?" said Lady Lucas kindly, ignoring the fact that Mrs Bennet was still speaking to her, which did not matter because Mrs Bennet did not notice and continued regardless.

"On the whole, I should say their advantages outweigh their negatives," Elizabeth replied with a grateful smile, "but there are occasions that I could manage with one or two fewer."

"Lizzy, you will not fool Lady Lucas," said Jane, abandoning her tête-à-tête with Mr Bingley to join the conversation. "She has known us all our lives, remember. She is well aware who was the most troublesome Bennet sister when we were growing up."

This caused a small ripple of amusement among those sitting nearest—except Darcy, Elizabeth noticed. He continued impenetrably grave, no doubt as displeased by her childhood improprieties as he was by her present ones. "And you, sir?" she enquired pointedly. "Were you plagued by any brothers or sisters growing up?"

His eyes flicked to hers and he regarded her with a piercingly direct stare. "No, I was not."

"Ah...Darcy's mother sadly passed away when he was but a child," Bingley interposed uneasily. "I, on the other hand, grew up with two sisters, therefore I believe I can comprehend some of what you have suffered."

Elizabeth could scarcely keep from staring between the two gentlemen. For the first time that she could recall, *Bingley* had done the rescuing, directing the conversation away from Darcy if not with equal grace, then certainly with equal purpose. *This shines an entirely different light on their friendship,* she thought with wonder. *And throws into doubt Wickham's claim that one is overbearing and the other wholly compliant.*

It became apparent that she was rather too caught up in these reflections when Darcy looked in her direction again and frowned upon catching her staring at him. She looked away, embarrassed, and was further mortified when he rose from the table and excused himself. To her horror, he made it no more than two yards before Mr Collins accosted him. She strained to hear what her cousin said.

"Mr Darcy," he began. "Pray, excuse my presumption, but as the beneficiary of the best living in your aunt's gift, I feel it is acceptable, nay imperative, that I speak to you."

Elizabeth felt a frisson of alarm.

"Your aunt is a lady of particular rectitude and integrity," her cousin continued. "I am convinced there are few in the country who take such interest in the proper guidance of everybody connected to her, however distantly. But you, Mr Darcy, are as close to her ladyship as it is possible to be, and I feel, therefore, it is only right that I warn you—"

"Mr Collins!" Elizabeth hissed, sidling urgently between chairs to reach him.

"Cousin Elizabeth, please, I am speaking privately to Mr Darcy on a matter of some import."

Elizabeth threw a cursory look of apology in Darcy's direction. "I am sure it is very pressing, sir, only I wonder, is a ball the right place for private matters?"

Mr Collins frowned, doubting his clerical authority just long enough for Darcy to secure his escape with a stiff bow and a hasty departure. Elizabeth attached herself to her cousin's arm and tugged him towards the punch table. "Pray, tell me you were not about to repeat to Mr Darcy what you insinuated to me earlier?" she whispered when they were there.

"Indeed I was, for it is vital that he is warned what danger he is in."

"The only people in any danger from your calumny are

those who would be shunned by all of society were they to be exposed—and you."

"Me?"

"Aye." She splashed punch on her hand as she angrily filled a glass. "When I danced with Mr Darcy earlier this evening, he informed me that he despises idle reports. Do you think he would speak well of you to Lady Catherine if he discovered you had repeated unfounded and ruinous news under the roof of his oldest friend?"

"Well, I...I had not thought of it in quite those terms. But his reputation—"

"Mr Darcy does not need you to protect his reputation, sir. He has been managing these however-many years without your assistance." She took an unladylike swig of her punch and forced herself to be calm. "I think only of you, Cousin. It would be a great shame were your position jeopardised for the sake of one misplaced word."

The threat to his preferment eventually persuaded Mr Collins of the advantages of circumspection. To Elizabeth's dismay, it also appeared to persuade him she possessed the good sense and understanding he sought in his future partner in life. She spent the remainder of her evening listening to him advertise all the perquisites of his situation and racked up a debt of some magnitude to her friend Charlotte for her efforts to share the burden of his company.

She did not see Darcy again until she and her family awaited their carriage at the end of the evening. He appeared without warning and said not a word—only stood in simmering silence, glaring intermittently at Bingley, Mr Collins and, very occasionally, her. She did her best to ignore him, but his brooding presence was excessively disconcerting, and the way his lips parted each time she looked at him made her think he was considering addressing her. She had almost decided to speak to him herself when her mother filled the hall with an over-excited invitation for Bingley to dine at Longbourn.

Elizabeth closed her eyes and bit her lips together against a whimper of despair. When she opened them again, Darcy was looking directly ahead, and his mouth was clamped closed. She had never been so glad to hear a footman announce the readiness of her carriage. She was the first to climb aboard, where she squashed herself into the corner, squeezed her eyes shut, and passed the entire journey home wishing her evening away.

11 The Truth Will Always Out

ELIZABETH STRODE FURIOUSLY FROM THE FRONT DOOR AND out onto the lane, whereupon she broke into a run and dashed as fast as her skirts would allow for as far as her legs were able. No distance she could put between herself and the scene she had left behind was too great. Longbourn was in uproar; her two youngest sisters whispering and sniggering, her two eldest looking on with grave concern, her father chuckling disobligingly to himself, and her mother intermittently shrieking her displeasure and crooning her apologies to Mr Collins. That gentleman, it seemed, had taken their few frank exchanges at the ball the night before as proof that they were perfectly suited to be man and wife. In short, Mr Collins had proposed. Elizabeth looked forward to a time when she might be able to laugh at it. For now, angry exercise was all she had at her disposal to banish her woes.

Eventually, running slowed to walking and walking to meandering, until she came to a halt at a low stone wall with a view across the valley. She sat down heavily and let out all her breath in a loud and exasperated growl. Then she laughed to see the late autumn sun glinting off the stream at the bottom of the incline, for she wondered whether this particular tributary had featured in D. Walker's seminal book. Thinking of it called to mind a picture of Darcy outside the library at Netherfield, unsmiling and serious yet with a clandestine liveliness in his words and in his eyes—Elizabeth shook her head to dispel it. She had no wish to be reminded of the man who had passed the chief of the previous evening in contempt of her entire family.

She was almost grateful for the distraction of a noise, quiet at first but growing steadily louder, that sounded more and more like weeping. Clambering atop the wall to peer around, she immediately recognised a familiar figure walking through the long grass in the meadow behind her. Without hesitation, she hopped down off the wall and hastened over to crouch before her. "Anna, whatever is the matter?"

"Lizzy?" Anna wiped her eyes with her sleeve and stared as though Elizabeth were an apparition. The poor child looked utterly wretched, her clothes damp and muddy, and her countenance similarly besmirched.

"Are you lost?" Anna shook her head, and Elizabeth pressed, "You are a very long way from home. You promised me you would not run away again."

"'Tis not my home anymore. We have to leave."

Elizabeth's heart sank, suspecting that her best efforts to silence Mr Collins may not have been enough. "Has your mother lost her position?"

Anna wrinkled her nose. "I do not think so."

"Then why must you leave?"

"Mama says they are all going to London."

"Only Mr Bingley." Of this, Elizabeth was assured, for Mrs Bennet's invitation the night before had elicited the same information, along with a promise to join them for a family dinner upon his return. "And he is expected back on Friday."

"But Mama says the whole party is leaving to join him and

they are not coming back and they will close up the big house for good and I will not—" The remainder of her speech was lost to racking sobs.

Elizabeth pulled her into a hug and soothed her with such comforting noises as were always effective on her young cousins. Unable to conceive of a circumstance that would prompt Bingley to abandon Jane without explanation, she could only suppose Anna must be mistaken. Perhaps Miss Bingley meant to accompany her brother for the duration of his business. Indeed, that was likely, given her professed enjoyment of London society.

"I do not wish to go," Anna sobbed into Elizabeth's pelisse. "This is the nicest place we have ever lived. There are fairies!"

Elizabeth unwrapped the child from her arms and stroked her hair flat with the palms of her hands. "I assure you fairies live all over the country."

"But you do not! And you are my only friend."

"Oh, Anna. You will make friends wherever you go. But you really must stop running away like this. It is not safe. Come, let me walk you home."

Anna's face crumpled and she wept for another minute or two before Elizabeth's suggestion that she leave a farewell gift for the fairies lifted her spirits. They walked together, gathering feathers, teasels, and old man's beard into an eclectic bouquet, until they were close enough that Elizabeth trusted Anna to find her own way home. With the usual attentiveness of a five-year old, Anna's excitement to place her offering in 'the fairy spot' overrode all her previous angst, and she ran away with barely a backwards glance.

"I hope this will not be the last time we meet," Elizabeth called after her, but she received no response. She turned back toward Longbourn, hoping against hope that Anna, her mother, her mother's mistress, and *her* brother would all return to Netherfield soon. Yet the more she thought on it, the less likely it seemed that a short trip to London would require Miss Bingley's maid to permanently resettle her entire family in new lodgings.

She had come farther than she intended, and it took above an hour to reach home. When she did, she discovered her mother to be no less vexed than when she had left, and the rest of the day was spent listening to the litany of reasons why she was the most ungrateful, self-seeking of all Mrs Bennet's children. Mr Collins had found a new pursuit: poor Charlotte had arrived while Elizabeth was out, and her cousin had attached himself to her with an eagerness no doubt intended to pain everybody complicit in his rejection. Elizabeth sat silently through it all. Neither her mother's wrath nor her cousin's resentment troubled her nearly as much as what would become of Jane's heart if Bingley truly had gone forever.

FOUR-AND-TWENTY HOURS BROUGHT A FRAGILE CALM TO the household. Tempers were no less fraught, but Mrs Bennet had reduced her attacks on Elizabeth from vociferous laments to snide remarks. Mr Collins continued to avoid her whenever possible and ignore her whenever not, though he had, inexplicably, *not* gone home. Mrs Bennet more than once voiced the hope that he stayed to give Elizabeth time to change her mind. Elizabeth recognised he was far beyond any such generosity and suspected he meant to remind them that, with or without a connubial alliance, it would be his house eventually.

In the midst of so much unpleasantness, a walk to Meryton with her sisters and a fortuitous meeting with

Wickham proved an admirable distraction. He and Denny accompanied them back to Longbourn, and though Elizabeth had not forgotten Jane's warning, Wickham's easy charm and open manners, in stark contrast to Darcy's implacable reserve, soon reminded her why she had credited him with honesty to begin with.

"So tell me, Miss Elizabeth," he said to her as they walked. "How did you enjoy Mr Bingley's ball?"

"It had a few tolerable moments," she replied, drawing a chuckle from him. "I was sorry not to see you there. I understand you were not invited."

"Alas, I was not."

"I was shocked to learn of it. I did not think Mr Bingley capable of such ill will."

Wickham smiled enigmatically. "Will of any sort has never been a great Bingley trait. Mr Darcy, on the other hand, does not want for resolve. I suspect I have him to thank for my exclusion. I was not exaggerating when I said he does not like me."

"I do recall, though, that you do not care for his company much either."

"True, but I like yours, and I would certainly have tolerated his for the pleasure of dancing with you, had I been permitted."

Elizabeth felt the heat in her cheeks but did her best to maintain the appearance of composure as they arrived at the house and her father came out of his library to meet Wickham. Mrs Bennet did not come out of her bedroom, for she had not yet forgiven Elizabeth enough to be civil to any of her friends. There being only two officers to go around, the younger three girls soon ran off in search of more rewarding pursuits. As such, the conversation had begun to show real promise, until Mr Collins sidled into the room. He took up a perch on the sofa and surveyed the gathering with an air of offended pride, precipitating a lull in proceedings that persisted until they were interrupted a second time by the delivery of a letter for Jane.

It was from Netherfield and was opened immediately. Elizabeth watched her sister anxiously. She had said nothing of her conversation with Anna, having resolved that if, indeed, Bingley meant to forsake Jane, then he ought to tell her so himself. She regretted that decision intensely now that the news was in her sister's hands, and she had an audience as she read it. At length, Jane folded the letter away with an obvious effort to compose herself.

"What news, Cousin?" Mr Collins demanded, indifferent to her struggles.

Jane hesitated, visibly flustered. Elizabeth opened her mouth to assure her there was no need to reveal the contents of a private correspondence, but she was too late. With a trembling voice, Jane divulged that it was from Caroline Bingley. "The whole party have left Netherfield, and are on their way to Town, without any intention of coming back."

"That may well be for the best," said Mr Collins haughtily. After a short pause, during which everybody stared at him in bewilderment, he added, "His sister is, after all, a fallen woman."

Jane gasped loudly. Mr Denny choked out a barely permissible imprecation. Mr Bennet did not so much as grin, signifying perhaps the greatest degree of astonishment in the room. Elizabeth scarcely knew what to think, but in any case, was preoccupied watching Wickham, who was the only person present who did not appear surprised. The permanent smile that usually made his mouth so handsome had vanished, and he had paled significantly. Indeed, he looked almost exactly as he had the day he first encountered Darcy on the street in Meryton.

"You are mistaken, Mr Collins," Elizabeth said, feeling she

had no choice but to speak up. "The child is not Miss Bingley's but her maid's." A quick glance revealed Wickham to be watching the exchange intently.

"I must object, Cousin Elizabeth. Mr Fellowes—"

"Is not actually acquainted with any of those he is in such a rage to defame. Whereas I have stayed at Netherfield and can confirm that there is a child living nearby who goes by the same name as Miss Bingley's maid, who confirmed to me in person that her mother works at the house."

"Nay, I really think it is you who must be mistaken, Cousin—"

"Miss Elizabeth is not mistaken," interposed Wickham, whose smile and colour had both returned. He draped an elbow over the arm of the sofa and nonchalantly cocked his head. "The child belongs to the maid." When Mr Collins opened his mouth to object, he added, "You are aware of my connexion to the family of course—my godfather being Mr Darcy's late father?" Mr Collins's eyes widened; Wickham nodded, and continued, "We are not on such intimate terms these days, but in times gone by, we were close. I can reliably report, therefore, that Miss Dunn was Miss Bingley's maid when Mr Bingley senior died and has remained a favourite ever since—to the extent that she was allowed to remain in service even after she begot a natural child. I clearly recall Mr Darcy being appalled when Mr Bingley informed him of the arrangement."

"You are quite the font of knowledge, sir," opined Mr Bennet.

Wickham's easy smile broadened. "Ordinarily I would not have said anything, but I could not allow Mr Collins to continue under such an egregious misapprehension. Particularly when his patroness—Lady Catherine de Bourgh, I collect—is known to have a particular abhorrence of gossip."

"I am in your debt, sir," said Mr Collins breathily. "I thank you from the bottom of my heart for setting the matter straight and saving me from her ladyship's certain displeasure." Such was his perturbation that he did not add any of his usual pontification, and instead merely closed his mouth and stopped talking. As a result, there followed a rather awkward silence.

"Come, Denny," said Wickham, rising to his feet. "We have obtruded on these good people long enough. We ought to be going."

With a quick look at Jane that promised she would come back to her soon, Elizabeth followed the officers to the front of the house. "Might I have a brief word, Mr Wickham?"

He looked at Denny, who raised one eyebrow in a manner Elizabeth pretended not to comprehend and declared that he would walk back to his quarters alone. Wickham thanked him and turned back to Elizabeth. "How may I assist you?"

Aware that it was not quite proper they should talk alone, Elizabeth led him to a bench within full view of her father's library window and invited him to sit with her there. "I hope you will forgive my impertinence, sir, but I cannot allow this to pass without comment. Not when so much is at stake."

"You intrigue me. To what do you refer?"

"Miss Anna Dunn. Or should I say, Miss Anna Bingley. For she is Miss Bingley's daughter, is she not?"

Wickham froze for a moment, then gave a curt laugh and, to Elizabeth's dismay, nodded. "You are very astute, madam."

All the air emptied from Elizabeth's lungs at once. She had not truly expected him to confirm it. "Why then did you lie and tell everybody she was the maid's child?"

"I might ask you the same thing."

"I did not lie. That is who I believed she was until I saw your expression when it was mentioned. Then I began to suspect what you have just confirmed."

He smiled vaguely and shook his head at the ground. "Truth will always out in the end."

"But what *is* the truth?" Elizabeth cried. "Pray, sir, my sister is in a good way to being in love with Mr Bingley. She deserves to know if he is hiding something of this moment. I beg you would tell me what you know."

He turned an appraising look upon her. She withstood it until he acquiesced with a slight inclination of his head. "Very well. Though I can tell you no more than *you* already know—that Miss Bingley has a natural child."

Elizabeth attempted not to gasp, but the resulting drawn-out inhalation only made her sound more scandalised. "Then they have lied to us all."

"They have. They were unlikely to have been so well received otherwise."

"Oh, poor Jane! This is abominable! I see now why Mr Bingley did not want you at his ball—he was protecting his sister's scandalous secret! Do you know the history? Do you know who the father is?"

Wickham said nothing, only continued to regard her with his customary half-smile, and Elizabeth suddenly felt the impropriety of her questions. It was irrelevant in any case; she knew whoever it was had refused to marry Miss Bingley, thus the situation was the same regardless of whether he were a mill owner or a marquess. "Pardon me." She shook her head in a vain attempt to dislodge a more useful question from the clamour of angry accusations in her head. "Why have they kept that poor child in a tiny little cottage in the woods, away from anybody her own age?"

"That I cannot help you with. I heard occasional reports after she was first born, but my knowledge of the family has been rather wanting in recent years, as you can imagine. In truth, I assumed the girl would be placed with another family and disowned, as is common in their circles. I was exceedingly surprised when you revealed she was at Netherfield."

Elizabeth was so busy thinking that *this* must be the reason Miss Bingley always had her gowns stitched tightly—to conceal a mother's figure—that it was a moment before she realised the implication of what else Wickham had said. "I think you must be mistaken, sir. I did not mention the child to anybody but Jane."

"*Au contraire*, Miss Bennet. You told me Mr Darcy had gone to the aid of a young child and shown extraordinary compassion. I can assure you he would never behave thus towards a servant's child."

Elizabeth stared at him in disbelief. "Mr Darcy *knows* about this?"

Wickham looked at her in such an odd way that it made her doubt what she had asked until he finally answered with a nod. "Indeed, he feels a great sense of obligation to help them."

"I cannot imagine why. I have never known a man more preoccupied with his reputation. He cannot stand to be ridiculed or thought of as anything less than perfect. I should have thought he would have nothing to do with a family that was disgraced in the eyes of the world."

Wickham regarded her with a long, level look, as though he were weighing his words with the greatest of care. She supposed, in the circumstances, that was only right. "He has always taken care of them," he said presently. "Since they met, Mr Darcy has been like a brother to Mr Bingley. Which is useful, for he would never have kept this secret without Mr Darcy's assistance."

At last, Elizabeth comprehended Darcy's contempt for Miss Bingley. Whether he despised her for the position in which she had put her brother—his friend—or simply because she was ruined, was something only he could know. Yet whatever his feelings towards her might be, he had not abandoned the family. "Then he has been an incredibly good friend to them."

Wickham chuckled sardonically. "I believe I have said before that Mr Darcy can please where he chooses."

Elizabeth winced. "Forgive me. I forgot that he has been far from a great friend to you. But why do not you confront him with this knowledge? Why should you continue to keep this secret when he continues to withhold what is rightfully yours?"

Wickham dipped his head and rubbed at something on his uniform. When he looked up, he was still smiling, but rather more ruefully than before. "I find you are a very persuasive interrogator, Miss Bennet. I shall tell you, but you may not like my tale." He raised an eyebrow and waited for Elizabeth to nod her consent before he continued.

"While I was at university, I had something of an altercation with a fellow student. Nothing more than the sort of spat that is common between young men. Unfortunately for me, the other party happened to be the son of a very influential man, and his family were—and have been ever since—eager for retribution. I wrote, at the time, to Mr Darcy, requesting his assistance, which, to his credit, he gave. Unbeknownst to me, he kept the letter. When the Bingleys hit troubled waters some years later, I was reminded of its existence and told in no uncertain terms that if I revealed their secret, the letter would very quickly find its way into the hands of the family about whom it was written. There would be unpleasant consequences were that to happen—thus, I, too, find myself complicit in keeping Miss Bingley's ruin a secret."

Elizabeth was not often speechless, but there were few words—or perhaps too many—to articulate her incredulity. "He bribed you," she said feebly.

"Yes, he did."

She could not say why she felt so dismayed to learn this, or what prompted her to enquire, "Is it necessary for him to hold the letter over you in this way? Would you reveal the secret otherwise?"

Wickham looked away, squinting pensively into the distance as he considered his answer. "I might have done, at one time," he said at length. He looked back at her and smiled widely. "I think this whole tale can be taken as proof that I was reckless and imprudent in my youth. But much has changed since then. I would happily never see or speak of the Bingleys or Darcys again—though, I shall not deny that I should very much like my letter and my money."

Elizabeth pushed herself to her feet and set to pacing up and down in front of the bench, too agitated to remain still. "Is there no way you could speak to him—explain that you have improved? Surely he would listen?"

"You are aware of his resentful nature. Think you that is likely? But I have long reconciled myself to the stalemate in which he and I find ourselves. My present concern is that rumours of Miss Bingley's ruin have sprung up here, now, and there is a very real chance that if he hears of them, he will think they have come from me. In which case, the future of my letter would become infinitely less certain."

"That is why you supported my story about the maid?"

He nodded then leant forward and fixed her with a solemn expression. "I would be exceedingly grateful if you could persuade your cousin to say no more on the matter."

Elizabeth assured him she would impress upon Mr Collins the importance of keeping his counsel.

"Miss Lizzy?"

She turned to see the housekeeper at the front door. "Yes, Hill?"

"Your mother is asking for you, Miss."

"Tell her I shall come directly." To Wickham, Elizabeth said, "I had better go. I thank you sincerely for telling me all that you have, for it seems neither the Bingleys nor Mr Darcy were ever going to."

12

A Want of Proper Affection

ELIZABETH AND JANE HAD ALWAYS BEEN EXCEEDINGLY close. Having shared most of life's experiences, they had acquired a similar understanding of the world. What marked the difference between them was disposition. Whilst Elizabeth was quick-tempered, jumping from first impressions to laughing them off in rapid succession, Jane was steadier, preferring to be sure of her opinions before fixing on them, to not censure anybody hastily, and to find every person good and agreeable if she possibly could. Thus, they were both equally troubled by Wickham's disclosure, for there was no part at which Elizabeth could laugh, and Jane was struggling to find a single ounce of good.

"But can it be true?" Jane asked, and not for the first time.

"Can it be false?" Elizabeth replied.

They lapsed into silence again, having decided more than once already that there were enough facts in support of the story to make it distressingly plausible.

"We must commend Mr Bingley for the decision to keep his sister with him, at least," Jane said at length. "Plenty of men would have cast her off without a penny."

Elizabeth turned from looking out into the garden to looking at her sister. Jane was curled against her pillows, pale and withdrawn, and Elizabeth wished with all her being that Bingley had never come into Hertfordshire. He had, though, and nothing could be done to erase the mark he had left on her sister's heart. Thus, she said nothing in opposition to Jane's valiant attempts to paint his actions in a favourable light.

"And he has allowed her to keep her daughter with her," Jane continued. "Or at least nearby, which cannot be seen as anything but the most generous and compassionate kindness, knowing all that it endangers. He has undoubtedly saved her reputation at the risk of his own."

Elizabeth nodded and waited and was not surprised when eventually Jane ran out of positives.

"But I cannot bear to think how much he concealed from me, Lizzy. We spoke of so many things—and yet this he kept from me. He cannot have valued me at all."

Jane looked so forlorn that Elizabeth searched for something encouraging to give her a little heart. "I will say, now that I have had time to calm down a little, that he was in an unenviable position. It is not the sort of information with which one can introduce oneself. Yet at what point in an acquaintance does it become appropriate to divulge? Until he knew you, it was impossible to be sure you would not reveal his secret, or at least run a mile from an alliance. Angry though I am, I will concede that it is possible he intended to tell you once he was sure enough of your regard to believe you would accept if he proposed."

Jane smiled sadly. "Perhaps he never had any intention of telling me. It is easier to think that this has been an error of fancy on my part, for the deception appears far more innocuous if he never had any real affection for me."

"No, Jane! That is not possible. Nobody who has ever seen you together can doubt his affections."

"Then why has he left?"

"You do not know for certain that he has. Miss Bingley's letter speaks only of their going to London to enjoy more of the sights and entertainments she has missed for so long. Well, we can fill in there, 'since she was delivered of her daughter'. I expect Mr Bingley and Mr Darcy set her up here to be closer to Town, but it was not close enough to satisfy her. Add to that Mr Bingley's obvious affection for you, which must have made her more anxious than ever to get away, for we are not rich or grand enough for her liking. She would rather have him return to safeguarding her reputation while she carouses around Town. She has proved herself false in every way."

"If we thought alike of Miss Bingley, your representation of all this might make me quite easy. But I do not believe her friendship was false."

"Jane, she lied to you. And not just about a trifling little matter. She lied about having a child."

"Aye, she did, and I find that I do not blame her for it. The stigma attached to unmarried mothers is beyond anything I could bear. Even if she has managed to keep her secret safe, then she must yet live in constant fear of discovery and ruin—and not just for herself, but all her family. So no, I do not blame her for concealing it from me. What I cannot reconcile myself to, is how somebody of her character could have ended up in such a situation to begin with."

Elizabeth was sure that was because Jane's assessment of Miss Bingley's character was entirely wrong. She sighed and swung her legs down onto the floor so she could fully face her. "I believe we can rule out anything unspeakable, for Anna told me her father refused to marry Miss Bingley and that this was a point of contention in the family. In cases where there is no consent for intimacy, I imagine it is rarely expected or desired that marriage will follow."

"That is a comforting thought. I should not wish that on any woman."

"Nor I. It follows, though, that if Miss Bingley was put out that the father refused to marry her, then she must have been expecting that he would." She waited, but Jane seemed either unable or unwilling to conclude the argument herself, thus she continued, "There seem few alternatives than that she believed marriage would occur and acted precipitately."

Jane's eyes widened. "You think she pre-empted her vows?"

"Oh, Jane. We know she did. Else there would either be no child, or she would be married."

It was a moment or two before Jane replied with a sorrowful shake of her head. "In that case, I am extremely sorry for her."

"You are? *You* would not act so recklessly and put all your family at risk."

"No, I would not, but to be abandoned and left disgraced by a person she loved and believed would marry her is desperately cruel, and without doubt punishment enough for what may have been but one moment of imprudence. And as well as her disappointed hopes, she must carry the guilt of having made all her family suffer with her."

"This is a pitiful depiction indeed, but I must say, she did not seem particularly contrite. I am not sure I have ever met anybody who displayed less humility. Indeed, for somebody with such a glaring mistake in her past, she was unjustly superior."

"It is possible that she behaves self-importantly specifically to dispel all possible doubt as to her character."

It is also possible that despite all her mistakes, Miss Bingley still considers herself better than we are, she thought. *If only to emulate Darcy, who thinks the whole world is inferior to him.* Elizabeth kept this thought to herself and moved to sit next to Jane on the bed. "What cannot be denied is that Anna was not given away to an orphanage or another household. That she has been kept near to the family shows they must care for her, though why they have kept the poor dear in a cottage in the woods I do not know. Why not bring her into the house and own her as her daughter? Miss Bingley could have said she was widowed, or her husband was out of the country."

"She would have had to change her name for that."

"Oh yes. Well, why not say she was Mr and Mrs Hurst's daughter?"

"I understand they have only been married for two years."

"Have they indeed? I wonder whether Mr Hurst was informed of the situation before he married into the family—or if he even knows!"

Jane huffed a little laugh. "He must do. And it gives hope for Miss Bingley that if *he* was willing to marry into the family then *she* might yet find happiness with someone."

"There is always that hope," Elizabeth agreed. "Though despite her best efforts, I do not believe she will ever convince Mr Darcy that he will be the one."

Jane smiled and agreed that was very unlikely. "What think you to his part in this?"

That was a question Elizabeth was not ready to answer. Each time her thoughts veered anywhere near Darcy, she redirected them elsewhere, for his actions were the least comprehensible of everyone's. His behaviour ranged from jealous hypocrite to noble saviour, and on the rare occasions when she allowed herself to think of him, she was assaulted with either horrible pangs of disappointment or overwhelming feelings of incredulity. She preferred not to trouble herself. "I do not think of him at all," she replied. "I hope, when Mr

Bingley returns on Friday, he does not bring Mr Darcy back with him."

Jane smiled again but it was weak, and it did not last. She reached for Elizabeth's hand and took a deep breath. "I am not sure I want him to come back, Lizzy. I might not blame Miss Bingley, but the world certainly would. How could I justify exposing my own sisters to her ruin and disgrace?"

Elizabeth sighed likewise, desperately sad for her sister. "There is nothing to say her ruin would ever be exposed."

"I have no wish to gamble with my sisters' happiness. I should prefer not to be obliged to choose between theirs and my own."

Elizabeth would dearly have loved to tell Jane to follow her heart and marry wherever she chose, but they had three other sisters and wider family to consider, and she could not pretend she would not be similarly torn in the same position. There was little more she could offer in the way of comfort. They agreed between them that the matter ought to be kept secret, for Wickham's sake and Anna's. Elizabeth did not mention it, but she also privately resolved to do whatever she could to protect the Bingleys' secret lest it should one day become Jane's as well.

THE NEXT FEW DAYS WERE SPENT IN ANXIOUS TREPIDATION as every mention of the Bingleys brought renewed fear of the secret having been discovered. Yet Mr Collins showed hopeful signs of being permanently cured of idle talk, and Wickham had done what he could to bury the rumour within the officers' ranks. Thus, within a week, the only feelings stirred by the mention of the Netherfield party were everybody's increasing consternation that they had not yet returned, and Jane's increasing dread, confessed confidentially to Elizabeth, that they might.

The Bingleys' departure did little to diminish Mrs Bennet's resentment and was somehow added to the catalogue of misdeeds for which she constantly reproached Elizabeth. Nevertheless, no censure held a candle to the hostility that flowed from her when news arrived that Mr Collins had now become engaged to Charlotte Lucas.

In the fifteen years since Lydia's birth, it had been generally accepted in the Bennet household that Longbourn would eventually pass out of their immediate family. That this notion had been interrupted for the few days between Mr Collins's arrival and Elizabeth's refusal to marry him made very little difference to the expectations of most of them. For Mrs Bennet, however, that fleeting glimpse of hope had been enough to make this new loss as painful as if one of her own limbs, attached to her from birth, had been ripped away. That her home should now be entailed upon the daughter of Lady Lucas, the friend upon whom Mrs Bennet had most enjoyed looking down since she married the most eligible gentleman in the neighbourhood, was an injustice almost too great to bear.

Elizabeth received her mother's furious reproofs with far greater forbearance than she did the news itself, unable to accept that every objectionable aspect of the match that had so repulsed her was now indelibly fixed as the unavoidable future of her dearest friend.

"I see that you are displeased," Charlotte said to her at the first opportunity after the announcement was made. "But I have not the same opinion of marriage as you. I am not romantic. Neither am I beautiful, rich, or young. I would be foolish not to consider that life could be far worse if I do *not* marry, than if I marry Mr Collins."

Elizabeth gave a lopsided smile of commiseration, aware they would both know it for a lie if she demurred. Her smile soon disappeared when Charlotte continued.

"And when I think of Miss Bingley, well frankly it makes me envious. Her position allows her to behave promiscuously, cover up her sins, and live quite comfortably, enjoying the advantages of her rank and those of motherhood, all without judgment. Whilst I face the world's derision for my loneliness and spinsterhood. So no, I am not ashamed that I chose marriage, children, and security." Her voice dropped to a whisper. "Not ashamed at all."

"Charlotte," Elizabeth replied gently. "I am grieved to hear of your pain, and of course I comprehend your reasons—and wish you all the happiness in the world! Only...well, I am not sure what Mr Collins has told you, but Mr Wickham was quite adamant that it is Miss Bingley's *maid* who has a child."

"Yes, so Mr Collins said. But I find it exceedingly difficult to believe that Mr Wickham, or any man for that matter, should know all the particulars of the friend of a friend's lady's maid, let alone remember them five years after the fact. I tried to tell Mr Collins it was unlikely, but he—"

"I beg you would not correct him," Elizabeth interrupted, making Charlotte jump. "Forgive me for keeping this from you, but I gave my word I would not repeat it. Indeed, I am only repeating it now because not doing so might cause more harm than good." As succinctly as possible and with many pleas for secrecy, she relayed Wickham's story. Charlotte was every bit as astonished by it as *she* had been and was quite unable to account for some of the behaviour exhibited by those involved.

"So you see," Elizabeth concluded, "if my cousin mentions this to Lady Catherine, Mr Darcy is sure to find out and blame Mr Wickham. And if it all comes to light, then there will be no possibility of Jane ever marrying Mr Bingley. I know I ask much of you to go into a marriage withholding a truth from your husband, but I beg that you would allow Mr

Collins to continue in the belief that Anna is a servant's child."

"I can see why you are concerned," Charlotte replied in muted alarm. "Though you need not worry that Mr Collins will say anything. Mr Wickham's warning that Lady Catherine dislikes rumours has done what it was intended to do. *He* ought to be safe from suspicion. Whether Miss Bingley is as safe is another matter entirely, so I must ask, do you really think there is a chance Jane and Mr Bingley might still wed?"

Elizabeth could not say with any certainty that they might not, although the arrival of a second letter from Miss Bingley later that afternoon, whose very first sentence conveyed the assurance of their being all settled in London for the winter, made it seem rather doubtful.

13

Reminiscences and Resentment

Mr Collins was obliged to return to Hunsford the next day, yet the offer to return for another visit, extended before his engagement was announced, meant he did not long remain absent. Over the course of the next month, he went away, came back, and departed again, each time sending Mrs Bennet into an ever more pitiable state of nervous discontent. Elizabeth grew as impatient with Charlotte as with her cousin, for if she meant to go ahead with her preposterous scheme of marrying the most ridiculous man in the country, better that she get to the point instead of involving them all in the protracted and embarrassing spectacle of their courtship.

Far more welcome visitors were Mrs Bennet's brother, wife, and four children, who arrived to spend Christmas at Longbourn. Mrs Gardiner's steady presence was a coveted reprieve for Elizabeth, who greeted her with heartfelt pleasure as she stepped down from the carriage. Her four cousins followed their mother down the steps and filed out across the drive, stretching their legs after the long journey by racing across the lawn. Mr Gardiner strode playfully after them, encouraging the release of energy before they went into the house. Elizabeth looked on with an indulgent smile, though the scene she pictured in her mind differed from the one before her in two ways: the children were not her four cousins but one young girl, and the gentleman striding across the lawn was not her uncle but Darcy.

"And how are you, Lizzy? You look well."

Heat blossomed in her cheeks at the recognition of where her thoughts had gone. "Very well, I thank you. Though I have much to tell you."

The quantity of news had no bearing on the alacrity with which Elizabeth was able to impart it. Mrs Bennet's grievances occupied the first two hours of the Gardiners' visit, the Gardiners' own tidings another hour after that, and then there was dinner, followed by a long evening of merriment so agreeable that Mrs Bennet only twice remembered to scold Elizabeth for ruining all her hopes. It was not until the next day that the opportunity to talk privately to Mrs Gardiner presented itself, and then only because she alone was brave enough to volunteer to accompany Elizabeth on a walk. All the others refused on account of the bitter cold and the dusting of snow that had fallen overnight.

"You do not begrudge Miss Lucas the prospect of being mistress of Longbourn then?" asked Mrs Gardiner.

"Not at all," Elizabeth replied. "I never expected the position would be mine. I daresay it will make it easier, when the time comes, to know it will pass to a friend whom we can visit. But it will, I hope, be a long time before that happens, and until then, I do not believe her situation will be compensation enough for what she has given up. Nobody will convince me that she will ever be happy with my cousin."

"He does not sound a sensible man from what you have told me," her aunt agreed.

"Yet I have always considered Charlotte as one of the

most sensible people of my acquaintance. It is the most absurd decision for her to have made. Jane tells me I ought to make more allowance for difference of situation and temper, but I cannot allow for complete madness. I have quite given up on people, you know. Nobody is behaving as they ought to anymore."

"Your mother seems to be playing her part quite faithfully. I saw nothing in her theatricals that was not precisely as your uncle and I expected."

"True!" Elizabeth admitted, laughing. "The world truly would be adrift if Mama were not calling for her salts."

The conversation was paused while they went through a gate in single file. As Elizabeth latched it closed, Mrs Gardiner said behind her, "You refer to Mr Bingley, though, I suppose."

And his sister! thought Elizabeth as she considered the many people who had astonished or disappointed her of late. *And his friend.* She pushed away from the gate with a sigh. "I was convinced he would come back. Miss Bingley must have got her way."

"Yes—though I know not how much entertainment she will have in Town at this time of year. I am inclined to agree with you and think it a very thin excuse."

Elizabeth had not told Mrs Gardiner aught of Anna, the Bingleys' efforts to conceal her, or Darcy's having intimidated Wickham into silence. Living in London and being the wife of a tradesman, albeit a very successful one, had taught her aunt to be exceedingly conscious of rank and reputation. Revealing the secret to her would be the fastest way to ensure Jane never married Bingley. She had not, however, stinted on details of Miss Bingley's objectionable disdain for Hertfordshire society.

"I wonder, too," Mrs Gardiner continued, "how strong an inclination it can have been for Mr Bingley to be so easily talked out of it. I should be surprised if his sister was able to convince him he was not in love if he really was."

"She might not have succeeded alone, but you underestimate the influence his friend has over him. It was evident Mr Darcy did not approve of anything in Hertfordshire either, least of all anything called Bennet."

"In that case, I wonder what sort of husband Mr Bingley would have made. To be so irresolute, so careless of other people's feelings, is pitiful. Jane's disposition would not lend itself to such volatility in marriage. And I believe the same concern has occurred to her, for she professed to me that it would be just as well if he did not return."

"Oh yes," Elizabeth replied warmly, "Jane will tell you that she is perfectly resigned to his never coming back into the country, and that she will remember him fondly but not regret him at all. You must not listen to a word of it. I assure you she is wretched."

"That is regrettable, Lizzy, but it will pass a lot sooner than Miss Lucas's misery. A short, harmless flirtation and a fond memory is by far the better arrangement than a lifetime of unhappiness. I am sorry for her, though. For both of you. Between Mr Collins and Mr Bingley, you must have had quite enough of foolish young men."

They reached the end of the lane and Longbourn came into view. "Thank goodness!" Elizabeth exclaimed. "I can no longer feel my toes."

"It was you who wished to walk out," Mrs Gardiner replied laughingly. "You ought to have dressed better for it."

"I did not know you would be willing to walk so far."

"I did not know you had so much news."

Elizabeth grinned. "I have not told you all of it either. Not every acquaintance we have made these past few months has been disagreeable." As they went into the house and fumbled with numb fingers to unfasten their coats, she explained to her aunt that some of the officers of the recently arrived militia had proved to be much pleasanter neighbours than any of the party at Netherfield Park.

EVEN BETTER THAN DESCRIBING HIM TO HER AUNT, Elizabeth had the pleasure of introducing Wickham in person when he and several other officers joined them for dinner that evening. The conversation was easy, as always, for there was no ceremony to his address, and he spoke readily on whatever subject the ladies introduced. It was soon discovered that, to Mrs Gardiner, he had means of affording pleasure unconnected with his general powers when his association with the Bingleys, and therefore Darcy, came to her attention.

"You grew up at Pemberley?" she said with delight. "Before I married, I spent considerable time in that part of Derbyshire. I have friends there still—in Lambton."

"I know it well, madam, and remember it fondly, though I have been there but little since my godfather passed away."

"The late Mr Darcy," Elizabeth clarified for her aunt.

"Is that so?" she cried with great wonder. "Then you are fortunate indeed, sir, for I recall that he was a very fine gentleman by reputation."

"And in person, madam. A finer gentleman and kinder benefactor I could not imagine. Though I am predisposed to think so, for he was excessively fond of me and spent a good deal of time with me as I was growing up. Something for which the present Mr Darcy has never forgiven me."

Mrs Gardiner raised an eyebrow. "You do not get along, then? That is a shame."

"It might have been, had he turned out to be at all like his father. As it is, I do not consider myself much deprived. I prefer my society without bitterness or pride."

"Goodness! Have you a particular reason to think ill of him, or is this a condemnation of his general character?"

With surprisingly little prompting, Wickham launched into an account of what he had been denied from his godfather's will. He made no mention of Anna or the letter in Darcy's possession that bound him to secrecy on the matter—but his ready mention of everything else that Elizabeth had dutifully kept to herself for the past two months gave her pause. She supposed, however, that it must be gratifying to discuss his late godfather with somebody who had known him, if only very slightly.

"I am sorry for you, sir," said Mrs Gardiner, when she had heard it all. "I am trying to think whether I can recall anything of the present Mr Darcy's reputation from my time in the area, but I cannot say that I do, though there is no reason to suppose he should be any less proud than other young men of his rank. And I imagine losing his mother before he was out of leading strings deprived him of a measure of compassion that might have softened his temperament growing up."

"He was not quite that young, madam," Wickham corrected her. "He was ten when Lady Anne passed away."

Elizabeth thought immediately of the moment Darcy had left the supper table at the ball after a reference was made to his mother. She might not like him overmuch, but something yet tugged at her heart at the idea of any child losing his mother at so tender an age. "Do you know how she died?" she enquired, without really meaning to.

"It was an accident, was it not?" Mrs Gardiner said, looking at Wickham for confirmation.

"Yes," he replied. "Though I am not aware of all the particulars, for it was before my father's tenure at Pemberley, and it was never talked of in the family. My godfather never remarried. To some extent, that accounts for his affection towards me. My father was appointed steward not long after the accident, and he often said that my adventurous nature was a healthy distraction for a man in mourning."

"It must have been," Mrs Gardiner replied. "Which only makes it more tragic that his legacy to you was withheld. Being so close, you cannot have argued about anything so grievous as to warrant disinheritance."

Wickham's mouth curled into a small, forbearing smile. "I did not think so, madam, but others disagreed. Now pray, tell me, when you were in Lambton, did you ever eat at The Crown?"

The conversation turned to Mrs Gardiner's reminiscences of Lambton, delighting Elizabeth as much as any one for the glimpse it gave of her aunt before she married into the family, and they talked of nothing else until it came time for the officers to leave.

"You liked our Mr Wickham then, sister?" asked Mrs Bennet after they had gone.

"He seemed an agreeable young man," Mrs Gardiner replied.

"Was he?" Lydia said petulantly as she threw herself into an armchair. "Nobody would know, for Lizzy kept him to herself all evening."

"That was my fault, Lydia. It turns out we used to live in the same part of the country, and I was interrogating him about all the changes that have been made since I was last there."

"Nay, it was not your fault, Aunt. Lizzy always keeps Wickham to herself. Nobody ever gets to talk to him if she is there."

"I beg your pardon, Lydia," Elizabeth replied, pretending not to notice the manner in which Mrs Gardiner was regarding her. "I shall endeavour to say nothing to him the next time, and by all means you may spend the whole evening talking to him of lottery tickets and the fish you have won and the fish you have lost. I am sure he will find it scintillating."

Lydia scoffed dismissively. "Mr Wickham enjoys liveliness every bit as much as clever conversation. You are not the only person capable of pleasing him."

"I daresay less of your sister's cleverness would go a long way," said Mrs Bennet, who required very little in the way of invitation to renounce her second daughter's wilfulness. Elizabeth informed her mother that she was more than happy to comply and took herself and her objectionable wit off to bed.

14 Not the Sentimental Sort

The Gardiners' visit was rather too enjoyable for Elizabeth's liking; any less and it might not have flown by at such a pace. Adding to Elizabeth's reluctance to see them depart was the extra passenger they were taking with them. It had been suggested that a change of scenery might improve Jane's spirits, and Elizabeth was quite sure the scheme would prove a success. She was also without doubt of Longbourn being considerably less rational with her eldest sister gone, and she reflected as the trunks were loaded onto the carriage, that were she the sentimental sort, she might feel uncommonly dispirited to see them all go.

"We shall take good care of her," Mrs Gardiner said, taking her niece's arm and leading her away from the carriage and into the garden. "I only hope you will not miss her too terribly."

"Oh, you must not worry on my account. Mr Collins is due to return for the wedding in a few days so none of us shall want for conversation."

"I thought I understood that he was to stay at Lucas Lodge. I do not imagine you will see much of him."

"True, true. I shall have to content myself with Mr Wickham's society then."

"I am glad you mentioned him, for I have been meaning to talk to you about something." Mrs Gardiner's countenance took on a grave aspect. "You are a sensible girl, Lizzy. I trust that in this matter you will remain so and avoid forming a lasting attachment to him."

Elizabeth's attempt to rebuff any such suspicions were futile, and Mrs Gardiner repeated her plea, cautioning her niece to take care.

"You do not need to worry," Elizabeth insisted. "I have no objection to admitting I like him, but I am a very long way from being in love with him."

"That is reassuring, though partiality often finds a way to run into stronger sentiments without one noticing."

"Very well. I shall be on my guard against all imprudent affections. It vexes me that you must warn me at all, though. There would be no need if Mr Wickham had the fortune he ought to have had."

Mrs Gardiner stopped walking and touched Elizabeth's arm to ask that she face her. "You mistake me, Lizzy. Ordinarily I *would* warn you against so imprudent a match, but in this case, it is not his want of means that concerns me. It is that he seems rather more willing to bestow us all with charm than facts."

"I thought you liked him," Elizabeth said carefully, all too aware of what facts Wickham was concealing.

"He is very agreeable company, to be sure. But then, he invests a great deal of energy into ensuring we all think so. That is not the point—he is no different from most of the young men in England in that regard. What troubles me, is that he claims not to recall what he and his godfather argued about in their final moments together."

Elizabeth could not immediately think how to answer, for

she had been thinking of Anna and Wickham's concealment of her parentage, not this. "Is it so very strange?" she said in some confusion. "It was many years ago."

"Yet an eminently significant event. And one Mr Darcy has not forgiven. His memory must be clearer than Mr Wickham's."

"Mr Darcy *would* remember it—he has boasted to me himself of his resentful temper."

"It can be no more resentful than Mr Wickham's, or we should never have heard this tale of woe in the first place. People who are not bitter do not generally complain."

It galled Elizabeth to acknowledge that, of the two men, only Wickham ever had.

"I do not wish to pain you," her aunt continued. "I would only caution you against trusting everything he says. It is bad enough that I have one broken-hearted niece. I should hate to hear in a few weeks that I have two."

It was no hardship to give the assurance that she was not pained and easy to undertake that she would be more guarded in future, for she truly did not believe herself in love. They parted on the friendliest of terms, the only drawback being the undiminished sadness of separation that a difference of opinion might have lessened.

Living thirty miles away from her London relations, Elizabeth was used to not seeing them often. By the end of another week, their absence had once more returned to being familiar. She felt the loss of Jane's company much more keenly and was vastly cheered to receive her first letter from London.

My dearest Lizzy,

I hope you are keeping well, and that Mama is not punishing you still. I am settled into my room here at Gracechurch Street, which has been decorated since you and I last stayed and is pleasantly light and airy. My cousins have all been dears and shown me their favourite toys and their favourite walks in the park—indeed their favourites of everything. Their eagerness to please me is exceedingly sweet and matched only by my aunt and uncle's solicitude. I thank you for persuading me to come, for I know I shall enjoy my time here immensely. More so now that I have settled something for myself.

You know, as nobody else can, that recent events have troubled me greatly. On the subject of Mr Bingley, there is little to say. His situation is such that I cannot see any advantage in torturing myself with vain hopes, for even if he were to declare himself—well, we have discussed this. I shall not waste my uncle's ink repeating what you already know. His sister is a different matter. There is less cause to be wary of a friendship than a marriage; my family would be unconnected and therefore untouched in the event of any scandal. I see no reason, therefore, that she and I ought not to continue our acquaintance.

I can picture you reading this, and I imagine you have just leapt from your seat to pace up and down in anger, but pray do not be vexed. I am not a fool, and I recognise that I have been deceived, but I do not blame Miss Bingley; I pity her. It is for this reason that I called on her today. I hoped to somehow let it be known that I knew her secret and thought no less of her for it. I had no plan for how I would go about it, but in the end, it did not matter, for here we have been deceived again. Miss Bingley is not in Town. Mrs Hurst did not say where she was, only that she was staying with a friend in the country, though I think it safe to assume she is somewhere with her daughter.

This lie, more than all the others, makes me sorry for her. Her letter to me was so full of all the splendid entertainments she intended to pursue while she was here, with all her many friends. How desperately unhappy she must have been to write so effusively about things she wished to do but could not. And what pleasing affection it shows to have sacrificed those wishes in preference of remaining with her daughter.

I stayed for only ten minutes, for Mrs Hurst was going out. I asked her to pass on my regards to her sister, and I hope she will, for it might give Miss Bingley comfort to know that she has at least one friend in the world. It did not seem appropriate to send my regards to Mr Bingley, though I could not resist asking after him. He is well, but so much engaged with Mr Darcy that Mr and Mrs Hurst scarcely ever see him. Overall, I am pleased to have gone and anticipate that, after this more formal good-bye, my spirits will begin to improve. My next letter, I hope, will be happier, so I give you leave to cease worrying about me.

Elizabeth had stopped pacing when she read the part in which Jane teased her for doing so, but she started again now. She would never be able to view the world through the same trusting lens as her dearest sister. To her mind, Miss Bingley had evidently been involved in her brother's decision to leave and her not being with him in London did not excuse that deceit. As for Bingley having no time to spare for anyone but Darcy, she only hoped he was enjoying having his every dance partner canvassed for faults and his every conversation managed into tolerable parameters! She instantly felt guilty for thinking meanly of the man who had crouched before Anna and tapped her on the nose with such affection. Then she dismissed guilt in favour of indignation for having caught herself giving quarter to the man who so callously denied Wickham his legacy. Then she growled in vexation at always being spun in circles whenever she thought of Darcy at *all* and stormed from the room determined to do so no more.

WITH SO MANY VEXATIONS WEIGHING HER DOWN, THE DAYS dragged ever more slowly and, to worsen matters, Elizabeth was shedding company as though it was going out of fashion. Jane and the Gardiners were gone. Wickham had abruptly transferred his attentions to Miss King, an insipid girl whose greatest virtue was the recent death of an exceedingly rich uncle to whom she was the only heir.

Then came the time for Charlotte to leave, and despite Elizabeth's misgivings about the impending marriage, still she dreaded the loss of such an old and dear friend. On the day before her wedding, Charlotte came to Longbourn to say her farewells. Mrs Bennet received her reluctantly and made too many hateful remarks for Elizabeth to deflect every one. She was reduced to casting frequent apologetic glances at her friend until the visit came to an end.

"Charlotte, wait!" she cried, chasing after her down the stairs to give a friendlier good-bye. "I apologise for my mother. That was unpardonable."

"I understand," Charlotte replied with a weary smile. "I am sorry to have pained any of you."

"You have not pained *me*. Not in the least. I am anxious for your happiness, but as far as this house is concerned, I could not have wished for Longbourn to pass into better hands."

Charlotte took a deep breath and, to Elizabeth's vast surprise, let it out somewhat shakily. "That means a great deal to me, Eliza. Thank you."

"Then it was remiss of me not to have said it sooner, and I apologise for that, too."

Charlotte abruptly reached for her hands and launched

into an uncommonly sentimental plea for her to accompany her father and sister when they visited Hunsford in March. Though Elizabeth foresaw little pleasure in a visit with Mr Collins, she was by no means unaffected by her friend's distress and could not refuse. And even as she gave her word that she would go, other advantages came to mind that made it seem still less onerous. The chance to see for herself the woman to whom Darcy was purportedly engaged, for example. "I shall use the opportunity to try and discover whether Lady Catherine knows anything about her future son's clandestine gallantry towards the Bingleys," she added. "Without letting on that I know, of course."

Charlotte raised her eyebrows expressively. "I wondered whether you were still quite so keen to protect Mr Wickham's name, given that his attentions have wondered of late."

"You noticed too, did you?" she replied, grinning. "I should be a bitter creature indeed if I wished him ill simply because he pursued a match more likely to give him his independence."

"Aye," Charlotte replied somewhat coolly. "The pursuit of independence requires many people to put practicality above preference." She let the remark hang in the air just long enough for Elizabeth to feel the accusation in it before she added more gently, "I hope you will not mind my saying that I believe it may be for the best that you are no longer his favourite."

"Oh dear. Do you mean to warn me, as my aunt did, that he is not trustworthy?" She stopped laughing when her friend remained serious. "Come, Charlotte, you know what he is keeping secret—and why!"

"I know what he has told you, and I cannot help but think it odd."

"It is odd! The whole matter is exceedingly perverse."

"I mean his particular involvement. I have been thinking

about it, Eliza. He has been known to the Bingley family for many years. Mr Bingley despises him and singled him out to be excluded from his ball. Both he and his sister told Jane that he was not a respectable man. And when he came into the country, they moved away without explanation."

"That is all true, though I fail to take your meaning."

"My meaning is this—has not it occurred to you that Miss Bingley's child might be his?"

Elizabeth froze. 'He feels a great obligation to help them,' Wickham had said of Darcy, with that small, knowing smile of his. Of course he would, if his father's godson was responsible for Miss Bingley's fall from grace, but— "Surely not!" she said breathlessly. "He has admitted to being reckless when he was younger, but this is beyond...surely he would have exhibited some manner of shame, or embarrassment at least, upon seeing them?"

"I do not know that there is any truth to it," Charlotte said placatingly. "It was not my wish to cause you any distress in suggesting it. I only beg you would take care."

Though she could not believe it was necessary, she promised to be on her guard. Charlotte took her leave, the wedding took place, and Mr and Mrs Collins departed for Kent, leaving Elizabeth with even less society—and even more over which to puzzle.

WEEKS OF IDLENESS FOLLOWED, AND IDLENESS WAS something with which Elizabeth had never got on well. Her father's company offered some reprieve, his library even more. Occasional letters from Jane and Mrs Gardiner filled the odd half an hour with reading, generally followed by several hours worrying over her sister's unimproved spirits. Jane's many allusions to her time with Bingley convinced Elizabeth that her sister's affections had not diminished and brought continual reminders of her own confinement at Netherfield, which, in retrospect, seemed less tiresome than it had at the time. Indeed, there were plenty of times during the interminable weeks of February that she would have readily swapped the almost total want of intelligent conversation available at Longbourn for one decent argument with Darcy.

Of Wickham she saw but little. Charlotte's warning had shaken her, and on the subsequent few occasions they were in company she observed him, searching earnestly for proof of such a reprehensible shade in his character. His own acknowledgement to imprudence in his youth, his frank admission to having behaved poorly at University, and of deserving Darcy's suspicion at one time—not to mention his newfound interest in the recently enriched Miss King—made it impossible to overlook that he was not without fault. Even if he were not responsible for Miss Bingley's situation, Elizabeth could not but agree with Charlotte and Mrs Gardiner that it would be best not to pursue the acquaintance. Thus, she watched from afar as he directed his knowing smile at everybody, unsure of what she believed him capable, but congratulating herself on not having allowed herself to love him.

Only once before she departed for Hunsford did they happen to exchange more than mere civilities. In early March, two days before she was due to leave with Sir William and Maria Lucas, the Bennets attended a dinner at Lucas Lodge at which Elizabeth was seated next to Wickham. He displayed the same languid charm as always, making it impossible to tell whether he was outrageously self-assured or merely had naught to conceal. Unable to resist the temptation to discover more, Elizabeth said to him, "I travel to Hunsford later this week, sir. I shall finally have the chance to meet the indomitable Lady Catherine."

Wickham smiled slightly and did not look at all perturbed.

"You will enjoy that, I am sure, for she is nothing if not entertaining."

Elizabeth lowered her voice. "You are not going to remind me of my promise to keep your confidence?"

"I was not planning on it," he replied, equally quietly.

"You are remarkably confident that I shall not say anything that might reach Mr Darcy's ears."

The corner of his mouth lifted, and it looked far more like a sneer than a smile. "Your silence these past weeks has taught me to trust that you will keep your word."

"Aye, even when you switched your attentions to another," she replied, casting him a saucy grin and a raised eyebrow with the design of keeping the exchange friendly. "You are fortunate that I do not have a jealous temper."

He chuckled, though his smirk never reached the other corner of his mouth. "Come, come," he said in a low voice. "You do not want for understanding. You have no fortune of which to speak, and you are most certainly not in love with me. I credited you with comprehending that my circumstances, reduced as they are thanks to a certain gentleman, necessitate a certain amount of prudence, and trusted you would not be missish about it." He sipped his wine before continuing. "Besides, I do not flatter myself that you have kept this quiet for my benefit alone. You were already concealing the girl's existence before you discovered who she was. You evidently care what happens to her."

"And what about you, sir?" she asked warily. "Do you care what happens to her?"

"Oh, I care enormously. If she is exposed, then so shall I be, for Mr Darcy will not play caretaker to my letter for a moment longer than it profits him to keep it safe."

"Then you care about her only in so far as your reputations are entwined?" she whispered. "You have no deeper feelings here?"

"I have no pretension to deep feelings on this or any other matter," he replied, his smile never wavering. "I am not the sentimental sort."

"What are you discussing with Miss Elizabeth?" came a timorous enquiry from Miss King.

"Yes, tell us, Lizzy," added Lydia more loudly. "You look awfully serious."

Wickham answered that they were talking about Lady Catherine and that it was, indeed, a serious matter—and with that, all discussion of Anna came to an end. Whether by accident or design, no other opportunity to resume their talk presented itself before Mr Bennet called for his carriage at the end of the evening, and Elizabeth took her leave of all the officers for the last time before she went away.

Between Equals

THOUGH SHE HAD NOT INITIALLY RELISHED THE PROSPECT of a visit to Kent, Elizabeth's cares seemed to diminish the farther she travelled away from Meryton. As well as the relief of putting fifty miles between her and Wickham's secretive little smirk, she had the very great pleasure of spending the evening with Jane when she, Sir William, and Maria broke their journey for a night at the Gardiners' house in London. Notwithstanding her sister's lingering melancholy, the sisters were greatly cheered to be in each other's company once again, however briefly. And as she left London the next morning, Elizabeth had the unexpected happiness of an invitation to join her aunt and uncle on a tour of pleasure which they proposed taking in the summer. The destination was not yet decided, but the Lakes were suggested, and Elizabeth was all anticipation of such a delightful adventure. As Sir William's coach carried them into Kent, she was grown so impatient to impart her happy news to Charlotte that all her many objections to staying with Mr Collins were forgot.

They were soon remembered again. Marriage had lessened none of her cousin's eccentricities, and he seemed to have picked up a quantity of new ones in the intervening months. In his own home—which he was at great pains to remind Elizabeth could have been, but was not, hers—he talked uninterrupted, often over other people, and always with his mouth full at mealtimes. His sermons, practiced every evening after dinner in the parlour, comprised of interminable drivel with only the occasional inadvertent bit of nonsense by way of light relief. His raptures on the subject of Lady Catherine de Bourgh were unceasing. Everything he did, everywhere he went, every deed he undertook was ascribed to her munificence—or her superior benefaction, or her charitable superintendence of the estate, or the manner in which she sat in her pew on Sundays, or the colour of the gloves she wore on Thursdays.

Nothing, Elizabeth noted, was attributed to Charlotte's steady influence, though it was obvious to anyone who would trouble themselves to look for it. Her friend bore Mr Collins's folly with the patience of a saint, or—as she put it to Elizabeth one morning when they were alone—the patience of one whose marriage had brought her many perquisites to compensate for the inconvenience of the husband.

"I do not mind it," Charlotte said. "When one has grown up with a father as garrulous as mine, an occasionally fustian husband is not such a great adjustment. And I hope you will agree that this is a very comfortable house."

"It truly is," Elizabeth replied, looking at it over her shoulder as they walked between the rows of vegetables in the kitchen garden. "Quite picturesque, in fact. Have you sketched it yet?"

"I tried, but I have not produced anything that has done it justice. In truth, I have not had the time to spare. I find that between visits to the cottagers, summons to Rosings Park, and keeping house, I have little time left for such trifles as sketching."

Elizabeth plucked a sprig of rosemary and smelled it. "And that suits you very well, does it not, my practical friend?"

Charlotte smiled consciously. "It does."

"Had I known Hunsford was this idyllic, or this full of people who would benefit from a little of your good sense, I should not have worried nearly as much about you coming here."

"If you mean my husband, then I do believe that in time I might be able to temper his affectations and direct his zeal in more productive ways. If, however, you mean Lady Catherine—and I think you do—I cannot imagine I will have any influence on her, and neither is it right that I should. I am wholly unconnected to her other than by marriage to one of her rectors, and we are from vastly different spheres. She would not take direction from me even if I were to give it."

"A total want of connexion did not prevent her from remarking on my upbringing, education, and family," Elizabeth said, laughing at the memory of her first dinner at Rosings two days ago. "And who could argue, frankly, for she is the most obvious person to have an opinion on the matter. But I did not mean for you to begin directing her behaviour. Officiousness seems to be a family trait—I doubt it is in anyone's power to make either her ladyship or her nephew less overbearing. But you might, by example, teach others to be less afraid of her. You could begin with Miss de Bourgh."

Charlotte nodded pensively. "She does give the impression of being rather cowed by her mother. That could be easily resolved, though. If she were to marry and move away, Lady Catherine's influence would soon diminish."

"Aye, to be replaced by her husband's. You forget she is destined for her cousin, who is every bit as officious as his aunt."

"I rather think Mr Collins has overstated the nature of that alliance. Her ladyship clearly wishes for it, but Miss de

Bourgh is almost six-and-twenty and of a sickly constitution. If Mr Darcy intended to marry her, I imagine he would have got to it by now." Elizabeth laughed at her blunt appraisal of the situation, but Charlotte ignored her and instead enquired, "You believe him as bad as that, though, do you? I would have thought your opinion might have improved now that you know the reasons for his behaviour."

Elizabeth began plucking the leaves from her rosemary. "Even if all his motivations were honourable, it would not make him any less imperious. Granted, he has assisted the Bingleys, but he still looks down his nose at everybody else."

"He might be more respectful of his own relation, and one who is not embroiled in such a sordid affair."

"Undoubtedly, he would be, for he has the highest opinion of his own importance and his family cannot but benefit from the connexion. His conceit is infuriating. That he should treat the Bingleys with such generosity yet the whole of Meryton with so little! I do not mean to be the judge of whether they deserve his assistance—indeed, I am sure they do if Mr Wickham has been their ruin—but when you consider what Mr Darcy is overlooking to be a friend to them, it makes his behaviour towards the rest of us indefensible. My being poor was more disgusting to him than Miss Bingley's disgrace." Her sprig of rosemary was bare; she dropped it to the ground. Charlotte looked at it where it landed, then back at her, and Elizabeth did not much care for the little smile playing about her mouth.

"Miss Bingley's situation does not alter Mr Darcy's, Eliza. He is still a man of considerable consequence. He has a right to consider himself superior."

"In wealth and rank perhaps, but not in temperament, and certainly not in manners."

Charlotte threaded her arm through Elizabeth's and turned them along another path. "Speaking of manners, what of our other, more charming acquaintance? Did you have much contact with him before you left Longbourn?"

"Mr Wickham?" Elizabeth replied. "A little."

"And were you able to glean any hint of guilt on his part?"

"Not guilt, no. Whatever he may or may not have done, he exhibits no contrition for any of it. That is not to say that I believe him innocent either. There was something in his looks when I last spoke to him that made me doubt it. A cleverness that made all his professed troubles seem less pitiable."

"He never struck me as a particularly pitiable man. He was too self-assured. In that, he and Mr Darcy are more alike than either would wish to admit."

"They are not at all alike! Mr Darcy may be proud, but Mr Wickham is vain, and not even Jane could find an excuse for that."

Charlotte only smiled expressively and raised one eyebrow. Elizabeth's cheeks erupted with heat to have been caught defending Darcy—and far more emphatically than he deserved—and she was inordinately pleased when Maria came hurtling around the corner of the house, gesturing wildly.

"Charlotte! Eliza! Come quickly! Miss de Bourgh is at the gate!"

The heir to Rosings Park perched atop her phaeton with her trusty companion, Mrs Jenkins, by her side and looked down upon them with an expression that made her look as though she were about to sneeze. "Good day, Mrs Collins," she said in a voice that was at once tremulous and haughty. "I trust you are well?"

Charlotte answered that she was.

"And you, Miss Lucas?"

Maria squeaked and nodded, wide-eyed and reverential.

"And Miss Bennet. Are you well?"

"I am, thank you," Elizabeth answered. "As I hope you are?" A sharp look from Charlotte and a small harrumph of surprise from Mrs Jenkins warned her she may have spoken out of turn. Bewildered as to how, she waited for somebody to enlighten her.

"Nobody ever asks me whether I am well," said Miss de Bourgh. "They are always too afraid of the answer being negative."

"I see. Well, I sincerely hope for your sake the answer is favourable, though I admit, your driving about the estate in a phaeton rather inclined me to expect that it would be."

Miss de Bourgh raised her eyebrows slightly. "Your boldness at dinner was not a front then?"

"A front, madam?"

"Yes. An attempt to impress my mother."

"Indeed not. I assure you I was very much myself on Saturday."

"I thought as much. Your impertinence seemed too natural for it to be affected. I confess I was intrigued. I have never witnessed anybody address my mother in that manner before, other than my cousin Mr Darcy." A moment later she added, "What amuses you?"

Elizabeth had not realised she was smiling but had no qualms in admitting why. "'Tis the thought of Mr Darcy being impertinent. It does not seem very like him."

Miss de Bourgh leant forward, squinting as though she did not have the energy for a full frown. It was not nearly as effective as one of her cousin's stares. "Are you acquainted?" The prospect seemed to offend her much more than Elizabeth's insolence towards her mother.

"Aye," Elizabeth replied. "I met him in Hertfordshire last autumn."

"Oh yes, Mr Collins mentioned it." She sank back into her seat only to lean forward again, reanimated by a different offence. "You misunderstood me before. I did not mean to suggest that my cousin is impertinent. Darcy is frank, and frankness between equals can never be considered impertinent."

Elizabeth inclined her head.

Miss de Bourgh coughed, and Mrs Jenkins leapt into action, tugging blankets and shawls more snuggly about her and urging her to make haste and return home. Her charge nodded vaguely and waved her off. "You will see for yourself in a few weeks, Miss Bennet. He is coming to Rosings for Easter. You will see then what really impresses my mother."

Elizabeth smiled at the thought that the only way to impress Lady Catherine was likely to possess a vast estate, a colossal fortune, and to be engaged to her daughter—but it faded quickly as she became more and more distracted by the inexplicable fluttering in her stomach. She remained quiet while Charlotte and Maria bade farewell to their callers, and she had never been so pleased to see Mr Collins as when he appeared in the lane with Sir William, for his interrogation about precisely what Miss de Bourgh had said lasted just long enough for the unsettling feeling to pass.

16

Puzzling Gentlemen

The difference between life at Hunsford and Longbourn was stark enough that it took a little while for Elizabeth to acclimatise. Not being woken by the sound of Mary's regimental arpeggios, not falling asleep to Lydia and Kitty's squabbling, not passing all the hours in between listening to her mother's multifarious complaints had, initially, made her time in Kent seem somewhat staid. After two weeks, she had come to value the more tranquil pace of life. There was no doubt that after too much inaction she would wane into ennui, but for now, the company of her friend, two dinners at Rosings a week, the occasional letter from home, and an abundance of delightful walks were sufficient to keep her in spirits.

On this particular morning, she chose to walk along the sheltered path that edged an open grove on one side of the park. The place and the season were both so beautiful that every route thereabouts was pleasing to her, but this one had become her favourite upon walking there undisturbed for a fourth consecutive morning, for any path valued by none but herself was instantly dearer to her. The sun was trying its hardest to warm the spring day, but brisk air still pervaded the shade beneath the cover of the trees. Elizabeth did not mind; it kept her mind alert and steps lively, though her gloves were not quite thick enough to prevent her fingers feeling the chill as she read the letter from her father that had arrived that morning.

Her mother and sisters were in despair, he reported. The militia were leaving Meryton after Easter to join a training exercise at Basingstoke before going to Brighton for the summer. The news better pleased Elizabeth than her family. It meant Wickham would be gone before she returned home, and she would not have to trouble herself with the puzzle of his character ever again. *If only fortune would assist me so well in evading the other puzzling gentleman of my acquaintance, I should be entirely untroubled.* She shook her head free of the intrusive thought and returned to the letter from her father.

> *I hope Miss Lucas will not miss her father, but I for one am excessively pleased Sir William remained in Kent for but one week. With her husband and both daughters gone, Lady Lucas had taken to visiting Longbourn almost daily, which had been driving your mother distracted, convinced as she was that her friend sought only to make notes on the dimensions of all our rooms. She has called less often since her husband returned, though I always make sure to remark on the size of at least one fireplace or window when she does come, for your mother would be very dull without something to fire her up.*

Three pages of commentary on the silliness she had left behind, or perhaps her father's inimitable style of describing it, made her wistful enough to read the letter twice more as she made her way back to the parsonage, stopping only when she reached the front door. The housekeeper met her inside, fussing more than usual over taking her outdoor things from her.

"Whatever is the hurry?" Elizabeth said, laughing as the maid tugged her coat so urgently off her arms that she almost dropped her letter. "Am I late for something?"

Wallis looked at her dubiously. "Lady Catherine is here, ma'am. Did not you see her carriage?"

Elizabeth walked to the window and laughed to see Lady Catherine's equipage all but filling the lane. "I confess I was enjoying my letter too well," she replied, hastening to remove her scarf and bonnet. "Has she been here long?"

"No, ma'am, about five minutes. But the master was all in a pother that you were not at home."

"I can imagine!" With an apologetic smile and a quick glance in the hall mirror to ensure she was presentable, she hastened to the parlour.

If it had been up to Mr Collins, Elizabeth doubted her absence would have gone unadmonished, the affront to his patroness of not being perpetually at her beck and call unforgiveable in his eyes. Her ladyship was more bemused than affronted, however.

"Walking?" she enquired upon hearing the reason for Elizabeth's tardiness. "To where?"

"I had no particular destination in mind," Elizabeth replied, taking a seat and ignoring her cousin's furiously puckering top lip. It made him look like a nervous rabbit and was sure to make her laugh if she looked properly. "I was merely taking a little exercise, enjoying the view, and reading a letter I received this morning from home."

"All commendable pursuits," Lady Catherine replied, "but every one of them can and ought to be done within doors. It is the very purpose of windows and desks, though I suppose you cannot help the want of a long gallery in which to take your exercise."

"No indeed," Mr Collins said, "though the gallery at Rosings is truly remarkable. My cousin could not possibly choose to exercise anywhere else were she fortunate enough to have access to such an exquisite room. Not that I am suggesting your Ladyship allow such a thing. That was certainly not my meaning. Of course, no relation of mine would ever presume to aspire to such activity. Not that I am suggesting my cousin ought not to walk. It is, as you say, a commendable pursuit. But not under your Ladyship's roof. But not outdoors either—"

"What news did your letter bring from Hertfordshire, Eliza?" Charlotte enquired, rescuing her husband from arguing with himself any longer.

With a conspiratorial smile, Elizabeth relayed her father's report of the militia's departure and her family's dismay at the reduction in their society.

"Mr Bingley has not yet returned to Netherfield then?" enquired Maria before recalling her audience, glancing in horror at Lady Catherine as though anticipating a set down and sinking back into her seat with her lips clamped shut.

"Not yet," Elizabeth replied. "I do not believe he intends to return at all. I hope for my mother's sake he gives up the place so another family can take it and return a little variety to the neighbourhood."

"I know Mr Bingley," her Ladyship announced. Elizabeth was pleased for her; she might have suffered a forfeiture of confidence had they decided to discuss anything about which she was not an expert. "He has been a friend of my nephew for many years."

"Yes, so I understand." *She cannot know,* thought Elizabeth with certainty. *She would not mention them so blithely were she sensible of Miss Bingley's situation.*

"He will know what to do for the best with the house," her ladyship said with a decisive nod. "He is an acquaintance of Darcy's therefore he will not want for understanding. My nephew is an exceptionally discerning young man."

Thus, they were returned to Lady Catherine's favourite subject and Elizabeth relaxed, confident she would not be required to add anything further to the conversation, for it was a topic her ladyship could, and often did, carry alone for considerable time. She began to wonder whom Lady Catherine was attempting to impress with her panegyric. Mr Collins could scarcely venerate Darcy more than he already did, and her own opinion could be of no importance to such a woman. It ought to be for Miss de Bourgh's benefit, but she never came with her mother to the parsonage. That begged the question why not, and Elizabeth was hard pressed to keep from laughing at the thought that perhaps her ladyship did not much care for her over-precious daughter, and mayhap the reason she liked her nephew so well was because he was expected to take her away.

"He arrives this afternoon," Lady Catherine said, assisting Elizabeth greatly in her endeavour not to smile. *Today!* "And with him another of my nephews, Colonel Fitzwilliam. He is the younger son of my brother, the Earl of Matlock. It has been many months since I saw him or his brother. They are always so busy, my nephews, that I count myself fortunate if I receive one letter a quarter from each of them. Not Darcy, though. He is exceedingly diligent in his correspondence and never neglects to write to me at least once a fortnight."

Mr Collins had an opinion on letters that he thought it imperative he share with them, but for once, Elizabeth was not sorry for his prolixity. She was happy to let him talk while her mind raced to remember when next they were due to dine at Rosings, but she could not recall that they had any fixed engagements. That was well and good; it meant she would not be obliged to see Darcy until services on Easter Sunday at the earliest. Until she could avoid seeing him absolutely no longer, she would continue to ignore every thought of him that popped into her head—as she had done successfully with all the others thus far.

The next morning, Elizabeth wrote to her every relation. First her father, to whom she expressed her sympathies that neither she nor Jane were there to alleviate her mother's displeasure. Then Jane, to share the news of the militia's departure, in case her father had not written to her himself. Then Mrs Gardiner, to enquire about Jane. Then her mother, to commiserate with her many woes. All of this took almost an hour and left her no time to wonder what was occurring at Rosings, where Mr Collins had gone to pay his respects to Lady Catherine's newly arrived nephews, about which she was mildly curious—but not so much that it required she sit about thinking of nothing else. She had just taken out a fresh sheet of paper in preparation to write to Mary when Charlotte bustled into the room.

"Maria, Eliza! Mr Darcy and Colonel Fitzwilliam are coming back with Mr Collins! They are coming along the lane now!"

Maria jumped up from her chair and hastened to the window, exclaiming in surprise. Elizabeth calmly closed the inkwell and returned her blank sheet of paper to the drawer, wishing Charlotte had not entered the room in such a flurry, for then perhaps her heart would not have been set to racing so.

"I may thank you, Eliza, for this piece of civility," said Charlotte. "Mr Darcy would never have come so soon to wait upon me."

"I assure you it is not for me that he comes. Mr Darcy

dislikes me just as much as I do him, and—" The doorbell rang, and Elizabeth was forced to stop speaking to take a much-needed deep breath.

Mr Collins entered the room, followed by a gentleman who must be Colonel Fitzwilliam, followed by Darcy, who spared her only the most cursory of glances before turning to give a formal greeting to Charlotte. *Well,* thought Elizabeth, *there he is, in all his sartorially impeccable hauteur. The same in looks, the same in height. The same in charm.* Feeling unaccountably relieved, she laughed a little—a brief but distinct purr thrumming at the back of her throat. His eyes were on her in an instant, and she caught her breath; she had forgotten the intensity of his stare. The effect soon wore off, though, and was replaced with the almost insurmountable desire to poke out her tongue. For Charlotte's sake, she merely curtseyed to him without saying a word.

Colonel Fitzwilliam was introduced and discovered to be a most amiable man. He shared an obvious resemblance with his cousin, though he was not handsome in the way Darcy was. He smiled easily, though, and that gave him a different appeal. While Darcy said barely a word, the colonel spoke with ease. He seemed to know a good deal about Elizabeth and her family—information no doubt gleaned from his aunt, who would have wished to appear an authority on the matter.

"I understand you have four sisters back in Hertfordshire," he said to her at one point, after a discussion about Charlotte and Maria's brothers.

"I have four sisters but only three are at Longbourn," she answered. "My eldest has been in Town these three months." She could not resist saying to Darcy, "Have you never happened to see her there, sir?"

He seemed startled to have been addressed but, collecting himself, answered, "I have not been much in Town since I left Hertfordshire, Miss Bennet."

"Oh? I understood that you were much occupied with Mr Bingley there. Unless Mrs Hurst was mistaken." He frowned slightly so she added, "My sister called on her when she first arrived in London."

Darcy's mouth twisted into a rueful grimace. "She was not mistaken. I did spend some time with Bingley—only, not in Town."

Comprehension came to Elizabeth in a rush, and she felt a fool for having pressed him. He and Bingley must have been resettling Miss Bingley and Anna in a new location. Though she could not forgive any of them for abandoning Jane, she would never willingly say anything that might expose their secret.

"Somewhere nice, I hope," she said more temperately. Addressing the rest of the room, she went on, "Until two weeks ago, I would not have allowed that any county was as pleasant as Hertfordshire, but this part of Kent is fast becoming my favourite place to explore."

Colonel Fitzwilliam and Charlotte agreed in unison, and there followed a lively discussion of the best parts of Rosings Park while Mr Collins eulogised over the top of them both about the improvements Lady Catherine had made to the estate.

"I am not surprised to hear you have been exploring, Miss Bennet," said Darcy quietly.

Elizabeth turned to him with a sharp retort on her lips, vexed that he should have found something to criticise her for after all, but stilled when she met his gaze. He was smiling—not broadly, but so warmly it might have been described as proud. It reminded her very much of the way Anna smiled whenever she boasted of running.

Her hesitation seemed to give him a change of feeling, and his smile vanished. "I am pleased you like Rosings, madam," he said coolly. "It is a fine estate." He looked pointedly back to his cousin and said no more for the remainder of the visit, which ended after only another few minutes.

"Colonel Fitzwilliam is an agreeable gentleman," Charlotte said after they had gone. "And rather more talkative than his cousin."

"I wonder that Mr Darcy came at all," said Maria. "Why bother, if he did not mean to speak to anyone."

"Mr Darcy only speaks if he expects to amaze the whole room," Elizabeth remarked, although it was not strictly true, for the only person he had amazed on this visit was her. She exhaled angrily and returned to the desk to continue writing to all her sisters, determined to waste no more time puzzling over the infuriating man.

17

Improved Humours

The addition of new faces at Hunsford was opportune; two more visits from Colonel Fitzwilliam in the week following his arrival provided the perfect measure of liveliness to stave off the tedium Elizabeth feared might eventually set in otherwise. Of Darcy, his aunt, and his cousin Anne, there was no sign. They were evidently content with each other for company, which boded well for the time when such an arrangement was made official.

Though Colonel Fitzwilliam never said as much, Elizabeth fancied he found his relations' company underwhelming. His eagerness to converse whenever he called gave her to suspect that he had not the opportunity to do so as freely at Rosings. Fortunately for them all, he was erudite and good-humoured, and, unlike Mr Collins, never spoke for longer than any of them wished to listen. In some ways he reminded her of Wickham with his easy, often diverting conversation that posed little challenge to one's intellect and could be enjoyed at length with minimal effort. It was evident he did not want for understanding, though he clearly preferred to please people than to make them think.

Elizabeth reflected on this as she observed him sitting next to Darcy in church on Easter Sunday. It was the first time she had seen the latter since he called on Tuesday, and after a glut of the colonel's frequent smiles and easy manners, Darcy's taciturn disposition was markedly apparent. While they waited for Mr Collins to begin his sermon, Colonel Fitzwilliam talked to, and drew a grin from, every person in his immediate vicinity. Darcy sat mostly in silence, nodding occasionally to members of the congregation who paused to pay their respects, and even more infrequently talking to his aunt or cousins. The colonel did not desist when the service began and continued to whisper to his relations throughout. Elizabeth was intrigued to see that Darcy was not above enjoying his cousin's wit, but his smiles were discreet, and he earned none of the disapproving glares Lady Catherine directed at her more rebellious nephew.

It was while she was delighting in her ladyship's excessive ill humour that Elizabeth realised Darcy had noticed her watching them. She looked away hastily—then back again, unable to resist. He had returned his attention to Mr Collins, but she thought she could detect that he was smirking. She knew not what to make of it and was too curious not to steal another glance a moment later. But if it had been a smirk, it was gone now—his countenance returned to implacable solemnity. She resolved not to look at him again—and did not until the service was over, when she was obliged to join Charlotte in speaking to Lady Catherine. As they approached, Darcy leant to say something to his aunt that made her look up at him in surprise, but he said something else that seemed to appease her, whereupon she turned her attention to Charlotte.

"Your husband spoke well today, Mrs Collins. I am glad he took my advice and removed the passage about pigs."

"It was sound advice, your ladyship," Charlotte replied straight-faced, which impressed Elizabeth no end.

"Of course it was," said Lady Catherine. "Now, you have not dined with us all week. Join us at Rosings this evening. We will sit down at six. Pray tell Mr Collins I do not require him to come halfway through the afternoon as he has been in the habit of doing. We have my nephews for company at present. An hour before dinner will be acceptable."

Elizabeth looked sympathetically at her friend, knowing she would be thinking of the large and exorbitantly expensive leg of lamb already being prepared at the parsonage, but Charlotte accepted with typically phlegmatic grace. As they turned to leave, Elizabeth cast one last glance at Darcy, wondering whether his hasty whisper just now had been a request that his aunt extend the invitation to dinner. *How very like him that would be, to arrange matters to suit him regardless of what it cost anybody else.* She soon absolved him of officiousness on this occasion, however, for she could not conceive of a single reason why, after ignoring them all week, he should suddenly wish to dine with them.

DINNER AT ROSINGS WITH COLONEL FITZWILLIAM AND Darcy was not unlike dinner at Rosings without them, for Lady Catherine's dictatorial command of the conversation prevented talk straying onto subjects of interest to anyone but her. She impressed upon them all the prodigious good taste that her daughter had exhibited in approving this particular menu, informed her nephews that these were their favourite dishes, instructed Mr Collins that he was enjoying it even more than they for it was far better than he was used to, and would not permit it to be true that Maria did not like asparagus. With everybody's opinions under such strict regulation, dinner was a somewhat stilted affair.

Afterwards, when everyone had spread out about the drawing room and it was only in Lady Catherine's power to orchestrate one of the several conversations in the room, things became more interesting. Colonel Fitzwilliam wasted no time in commandeering Elizabeth's company, and for some time, entertained her with talk of all those topics denied them at dinner. She spared the odd glance for her friend, conscious that she not be abandoned to Lady Catherine without support, but she need not have worried. Charlotte was faring perfectly well, and far better than her husband, whose efforts to find a subject that pleased his patroness were growing ever more desperate.

It could not be helped, when looking at Charlotte, that Elizabeth should occasionally catch sight of Darcy. And whenever her gaze wandered in that direction, her enquiring mind took advantage of the opportunity to search for any hint of affection between him and Miss de Bourgh. There was little to go on between two such impassive individuals, but the more she observed, the more she began to suspect that Charlotte's supposition had been correct—the alliance was more aspired to than agreed upon. Towards the end of the evening—after Miss de Bourgh turned down a third invitation to join her two cousins and their guest at the pianoforte—Elizabeth decided that the only person in the room with any interest in the marriage could be Lady Catherine. Her daughter looked as interested in joining her intended's conversation as the stuffed bird on the mantlepiece—and equally as unperturbed by how uncommonly lively that conversation was becoming.

"You see!" Elizabeth said, laughing as another aria ended in a discordant jumble of notes and tangled fingers. "I told you I practise too little, and here is proof. But I have never been able to do what I see other ladies do and talk whilst I play. If you will keep requiring me to speak, I shall never get the end of a piece."

"Why has Miss Bennet stopped again?" Lady Catherine called from her chair. "This is most distracting."

"You sound like Darcy when he is shooting," said Colonel Fitzwilliam, ignoring his aunt as he had been doing most of the evening. "One word to him when he has a fowling piece in his hands, and he loses all notion of concentration and stops."

"That is the point," Darcy replied. "I do not shoot at anything if I cannot guarantee I shall shoot the *right* thing."

"That seems sensible to me," Elizabeth said. She looked from one cousin to the other. "How do *you* shoot, Colonel?"

"As though he is going into battle," Darcy answered. "Shouting and firing indiscriminately. It is terrifying." His face gave no hint of amusement whatsoever, and Elizabeth only gleaned that it was a tease from Fitzwilliam's broad grin and playful response.

"You are cruel indeed, Darcy. I made but one, trifling remark to Miss Bennet about your aversion to small talk—which was true, by the way—and you punish me by exposing me as a terrible aim."

"You are right," Darcy replied. "You only shot Sutcliffe once. The other bullet missed him completely. It is unfair to cavil."

"What?" Elizabeth cried, growing more amused by the moment. "Who is Mr Sutcliffe?"

"Lord Sutcliffe," Colonel Fitzwilliam corrected her. "My brother. And I did not shoot him—the bullet only grazed his left ear. And I was but six years old when the incident happened and have improved enough to make colonel since, whereas my cousin here is eight-and-twenty and is yet to acquire an iota of charm."

"Aye," said Elizabeth, "But I believe we have established that is not for want of ability. Mr Darcy said himself, he chooses not to perform to strangers."

Indeed, he *had* said that a little earlier in the evening when challenged about his behaviour in Meryton, and it had given her significant pause for thought. It was precisely as Wickham had said: Darcy unashamedly pleased where he chose. Yet, her reproof to him—that just as she could improve her piano playing by practising, so he could practise being more sociable—was turned on its head when he suggested that her choosing not to was equally recalcitrant. It was as expected that well-bred women should be accomplished and perform their talents in public as it was that well-bred gentlemen should converse easily in company, and neither she nor he felt obliged to comply. She would not like to admit to anyone that her inability to reason herself out of this unnerving affinity with Darcy was the true cause of her distraction at the instrument this evening.

"That makes you better than both of us," she continued to Colonel Fitzwilliam. "You took the trouble to correct your failing, which neither your cousin nor I have any intention of doing. Though I believe in some people's eyes, Mr Darcy's consequence greatly mitigates his reserve."

"As your singing does your playing."

Elizabeth looked at Darcy in astonishment, flustered at being unable to separate the joke from the compliment.

"Are you going to play something else, Miss Bennet?" called Lady Catherine. "My nephews did not ask you to sit at the instrument to make it look pretty."

Elizabeth took a deep breath and only allowed herself a little smile as she started playing again. She faltered almost immediately when Colonel Fitzwilliam muttered, "I did," though she laughed more at the way Darcy rolled his eyes than the colonel's piece of flattery. He so rarely showed what he was thinking that she took great pleasure in catching him when he let something slip, even if it was usually vexation.

"Do you come to Rosings often?" she enquired as she corrected her fingering and resumed playing.

"Not as often as Darcy," Colonel Fitzwilliam replied. "But then, he has always been the most dutiful cousin. Far more suited to the army than I, really."

Dutiful to his family, dutiful to his friends—no wonder he is so serious. He is all obligation and no pleasure.

"You have a proliferation of relatives, Fitzwilliam," said Darcy. "It would take all year to visit them any more frequently than you do. I have but few, therefore I do what I can for them."

"Aye, that you do," the colonel replied soberly. Perking up, he added, "Besides, I visit Lady Catherine more often than Anne visits my mother and father, so I ought to be considered tolerably obedient."

"More than tolerably, I should say. According to your cousin, you are by far the more complying nephew."

Darcy frowned in uncertainty as Colonel Fitzwilliam laughingly demanded to know what he had been saying.

"Your *other* cousin," Elizabeth clarified, glancing in Miss de Bourgh's direction, "assures me that the only other person alive who dares to be as impertinent to her mother as I apparently am, is Mr Darcy." She sent *him* a conspiratorial look then said to the colonel, "It is rather unjust that you should be considered the insubordinate one." It occurred to her too late that teasing such as this would draw attention to yet another likeness between her and Darcy, and she was almost glad when her ladyship interrupted to insult her playing again, for it excused her discomposure.

"You seem partial to simple melodies, Miss Bennet," Lady Catherine observed loudly. "You display a very quaint, country-minded taste with this sort of performance, but it will serve you ill in refined society."

This time when Darcy rolled his eyes, he very obviously meant for Elizabeth to see, and the triumph of not only having observed his reaction but being privy to it, manifested as a small flutter in her stomach. She considered attempting a more complex piece upon reaching the end of this one but was saved from the attempt by the announcement that her ladyship's carriage was ready to take her party home. Colonel Fitzwilliam and Darcy both came to see them off, and eventually Mr Collins ceased complimenting them long enough for the coachman to shut the carriage door and spur the horses into action.

"Thank you for playing for so long," Charlotte said. "I know you do not like to perform, but it pleased Lady Catherine."

"Did it?" Elizabeth replied, laughing doubtfully.

"Oh yes," said Mr Collins. "You must not take her remarks as criticism, my dear. Her ladyship only takes an interest in things of which she approves, so you may be assured that she enjoyed your performance, even if it was not faultless."

"What a relief," she replied. To Charlotte she smiled and added, "I did not mind in any case. I had a surprisingly agreeable evening."

"Yes, you did seem to be enjoying yourself. I even saw you smiling at Mr Darcy once or twice."

"He almost smiled at me once or twice, too. I think he may have had one too many glasses of wine at dinner."

"Perhaps he is more at liberty to enjoy himself here than in other places, where he has more responsibilities." Charlotte raised an eyebrow as she said this, and Elizabeth took her meaning. In Hertfordshire, Darcy had been burdened with assisting the Bingleys maintain their façade of respectability. Here, he was not only sans that concern, but sans the encumbrance of Miss Bingley's assiduous attentions. She giggled to herself at the juvenile thought, but something had improved his humour, and it was just as likely attributable to Miss Bingley as anybody else.

18

Wandering Too Near a Conversation

Elizabeth sighed with relief when Charlotte and Maria returned from their expedition to Hunsford. She had elected not to join them, for she was tired after their late return from Rosings the previous evening and had letters to write while they were out. She had enjoyed almost an hour of peace and quiet before receiving a most unexpected and, it transpired, uneasy visit, which she did not regret being interrupted.

"I am sorry we were longer than expected, Eliza. We—oh! Mr Darcy!" Charlotte shot Elizabeth an urgent look of enquiry. Elizabeth widened her eyes to express her equal bewilderment.

Darcy explained to Charlotte, as he had to Elizabeth, that he had believed all the ladies to be within when he called, and then fell silent. This had largely been the pattern to his entire visit—Elizabeth would make a comment, to which he would give a brief response and then cease talking until she thought of the next thing to say. After fifteen minutes of the same, she had used up all her reserves of innocuous observations and was content to leave her friend to find something to say. Charlotte obliged by thanking him for a pleasant evening at Rosings the day before.

"I believe it was your party that made the evening enjoyable, madam, but I am glad you found it so," Darcy replied.

After a brief hesitation, Charlotte sat down, prompting Maria to do the same. "I am sorry we were not here when you arrived. We would usually be at home at this time, but I had some unforeseen calls to make this morning."

"Were you able to see Mrs Grampion?" Elizabeth enquired.

"Yes, she was out of bed today—and exceedingly grateful for the lamb."

There was a pause, but Darcy said nothing, seemingly content to watch them talk.

"Um...did you finish your letters?" Charlotte enquired with a nervous glance in his direction.

"Yes, thank you," Elizabeth answered, now struggling not to laugh at the awkwardness of the situation. "Though, I decided against replying to Lydia. It would only encourage her to write again with more boasts of her good fortune, and I can only stand so much of other people's happiness before it begins to erode my own. She has mistaken me for Jane, who is always happiest when those around her are contented. I am a far more selfish creature and wish all the happiness for myself."

"It was very good of Mrs Forster to invite her. I am sure she will enjoy Brighton very well."

"I have no doubt," she said expressively. The news that Lydia had been invited to join Mrs Forster when the militia left Meryton was of grave concern to Elizabeth. She knew not whether Wickham was a cold-hearted seducer or merely a man with a vaguely chequered past, but his story was unlikely to be unique in a whole company of soldiers. Her youngest, most impressionable sister was the last person who ought to be sent off with them, but all she could do was write of her concerns to her father, which she had done in the strongest terms possible. "Speaking of visits," she said to Charlotte, "I hear your father is taking your mother to Bath."

"Yes, he is thinking of it. I do not know when, but I expect this summer."

Charlotte glanced at Darcy again, but Elizabeth was beyond caring for his comfort. If he wished to talk of anything more pertinent to his own interests, he could say it himself. "My mother is tied up with envy."

As though he had read her thoughts, Darcy abruptly stood up and said stiffly, "I have taken enough of your time, ladies. Pray, enjoy the rest of your day." Before any of them could reply, he bowed and left.

"What can be the meaning of this!" said Charlotte as soon as he was gone. "My dear Eliza, he must be in love with you, or he would never have called on us in this familiar way."

Elizabeth laughed. "Do you mean, with this inexplicable bit of logic, to ensure that I do not pine for my mother while I am away from her? Only she could conclude that a man who called only to sit in silence for fifteen minutes must be in love with me."

"He cannot have sat in complete silence for quarter of an hour."

"No, that is true. But he said nowhere near as much as Colonel Fitzwilliam does when he calls, and you have not accused him of being in love with me."

"But Colonel Fitzwilliam is generally more sociable. Mr Darcy has freely admitted disliking small talk, yet he came alone, without his cousin to carry the conversation. There is some logic, therefore, in concluding that he actively wished to talk to at least one person here."

"Well it cannot have been me, for he only said about ten words the whole time he was here." Indeed, Elizabeth was disappointed to find that Darcy had lost all the ease he displayed the previous night and had seemed much more like the man she had known in Hertfordshire—serious and reserved. "Perhaps he is in love with Maria and was devastated to discover her from home."

Maria looked petrified by the suggestion.

"Very well," Charlotte conceded with a smirk, "he is probably not in love. Perhaps he was struggling to find anything else to occupy him. Or perhaps he just wanted for a little conversation."

"Or he no longer wished to talk about whatever his aunt prescribed. The pair of them are quite ridiculous. One will not allow the conversation to wander away from her jurisdiction, the other will not wander anywhere near it unless he is absolutely obliged."

Charlotte inched forward to the edge of her seat. "And so what *did* you oblige him to talk about?"

"Whatever I could think of! This house, how far you are settled from your family, his aunt. The Bingleys."

Charlotte raised her eyebrows in surprise. Elizabeth stole a look at Maria and, seeing her all ears, was careful in what she said. "I mentioned how quickly they left last autumn."

"What did he say?"

"Very little—only that Mr Bingley is busy with his friends and might well give up Netherfield entirely as soon as any eligible purchase offers. He evidently did not wish to talk about it." She huffed a frustrated sigh. "But I think I rattled on too long and led the conversation to an end before he could say anything of interest."

"I am sure he was grateful for it. It is a topic about which I imagine he is exceedingly wary of saying too much."

"Aye, you are probably right. Still, 'tis done now, and we shall not have to trouble ourselves with worrying about it again for a while, for he took so little pleasure in this visit, he is unlikely to make another one soon."

In this, Elizabeth was quickly proved wrong. Darcy's call on Monday marked the beginning of more frequent visits to the parsonage from both him and his cousin. They called at various times of the morning, sometimes separately, sometimes together, and now and then accompanied by their aunt, but at no time did Darcy seem at ease. On the contrary, the more often he called, the less he seemed willing to say, though that was never a problem on those days when he called with Lady Catherine.

"You ought to have that tree at the front of the house removed, Mr Collins," her ladyship remarked on one such visit. "It blocks all the afternoon sun and obscures your view of Rosings."

"I had considered having it removed for that very reason," he replied, nodding vigorously. "And now that you mention it, I realise how long I have neglected the matter. I shall have Pierson look at it this very afternoon."

Elizabeth tried to hide her smile at poor Charlotte's exasperation. It was the third alteration to the house and garden to which her husband had committed to implementing before dinner, and she was growing discernibly more impatient with each one.

"Do not you think it provides invaluable privacy from the lane?" she enquired of her cousin.

"Privacy from whom?" Lady Catherine answered in his stead. "The only people who come along that lane are Anne and myself. No, you had much better get rid of it, sir."

Elizabeth sent her friend a look of sympathy and was pleased when Colonel Fitzwilliam spoke up. "I think it a very fine tree," he said. "It would ruin the look of the place if you took it down. Do not you agree, Darcy?"

Darcy did not answer. Elizabeth looked at him; he appeared to be attending to the conversation, for his gaze was fixed on that part of the room where Colonel Fitzwilliam and she were sitting, yet he made no reply.

"Darcy!" Colonel Fitzwilliam repeated, chuckling. "You are uncommonly stupid today, man. Liven up! My aunt was just telling Mr Collins he ought to remove that tree. I said he should leave it. What say you?"

Elizabeth had to smile at how utterly nonplussed Darcy looked by the question. He turned slowly to regard the tree over his shoulder, then back to the room, his expression a comical mix of disdain and bewilderment. "I have no opinion on the matter. Mr Collins may do as he chooses with his tree."

"And he has said he wishes to remove it," said Lady Catherine with a firm nod.

Seeing Charlotte looking rather hopeless, Elizabeth hastened to find something to say that might prevent her losing the last bastion of protection between her favourite retreat and the prying eyes of the passing nobility. "You may as well keep it, Mr Collins, for it will only shade the room during the summer, when a cool room is most desired anyway. All the other months of the year, it will have no foliage to speak of anyway."

"Then it will look bare and unsightly," Lady Catherine objected.

"Indeed it would!" agreed Mr Collins.

"Oh, I do not know. I have always thought trees are at their most beautiful when the leaves are resplendent in autumn colours. Or skeletal, like fairy wings."

No sooner had the words left her lips than she felt Darcy's eyes upon her, his intense stare hot on her cheek. A flurry of alarm swirled in her stomach when she comprehended the implications of what she had said, but she schooled herself to be more rational. If Darcy were aware that she and Anna were acquainted, he would surely have mentioned it. It was more likely Anna had shown him her 'fairy wing' without any mention of its provenance, and Darcy was only surprised by the coincidence. She dared not allow him to suspect what she knew, for though she no longer trusted Wickham, she had no wish to be the architect of his downfall by letting Darcy know he had broken his promise of silence. Ignoring his scrutiny as best she could, she continued to smile at Lady Catherine, who very obligingly took her to task over her opinion of winter foliage, giving her an excellent excuse not to say anything else for a time.

"Summer is a far superior time of year in general," her ladyship continued.

"I quite agree!" agreed Mr Collins, predictably.

"One requires fewer blankets and shawls when it is warm, and one's clothes have not the constant smell of firewood."

"I rather think you ought to get your chimneys looked at if your clothes smell of firewood, Aunt," said Colonel Fitzwilliam.

"There is nothing the matter with my chimneys."

"Quite the contrary! Rosings' chimneys are the finest in the county!" cried Mr Collins, revealing a heretofore uncelebrated knowledge of every smokestack in Kent that was, nevertheless, of no interest to any of the people he was hoping to impress. Lady Catherine ignored him entirely and turned to talk to Charlotte and Maria. Darcy did not appear to have heard him at all. With a wink at Elizabeth, Colonel Fitzwilliam leant towards Mr Collins and said, "If it is chimneys you appreciate, sir, you would like Pemberley very well. It has over a hundred."

"A hundred!" Mr Collins exclaimed, a hand on his chest and eyes round with wonder.

"Oh yes. Darcy had two installed in every room because he looks ridiculous in a shawl."

"What?" said Darcy irritably. "Pemberley does not have a hundred chimneys, Fitzwilliam. What are you about?"

"I am trying to get you to pay attention!" To Elizabeth, the colonel said, "I assure you, he is not usually this dull."

Elizabeth thought Darcy looked a little offended by this. Indeed, it was ungentlemanly of his cousin to tease him in front of people who were not his close acquaintances and, rather than join his cousin in laughing, she sent Darcy a small smile of encouragement. He did not smile back, but something altered in his demeanour—perhaps the infinitesimal softening of the line of his mouth or lowering of his shoulders as he exhaled slowly. Whatever it was, the overall impression was of his discomfort easing, and that was enough to assuage Elizabeth's guilt, as she later explained to Charlotte.

"I know you say he cannot be in love with you, Eliza," said her friend after the visit had ended, "but he certainly looks at you a great deal. And his cousin seemed to think he was peculiarly tongue-tied when he is not usually."

"I know, but it is not for the reason you think." Drawing her friend away from the others, Elizabeth said quietly, "I said something, without meaning to, that related to Miss Bingley's daughter—or could have, if one were aware of the connexion, which I had no idea he would be. It is a long story, but what I mean to say is, the distraction for which his cousin was teasing him was my fault—and not for any reason other than I said something that alarmed him greatly."

"Has your remark done any damage, do you think?"

"I hope not. Indeed, I believe not. He will not risk asking me what I know for the sake of one incidental remark about a dead leaf."

"Aye, you are right," interrupted Mr Collins, startling both ladies.

"About what, sir?"

"Dead leaves. We cannot have them if her ladyship disapproves. The tree must go."

"You would have to remove a good deal more than one tree to rid yourself of dead leaves, sir," replied Elizabeth. "Would not it be easier to sit with Lady Catherine in a different room next time she calls, so she is not reminded of the tree or any of its leaves, alive or dead?"

Charlotte seconded this plan and, with Elizabeth's assistance, spent the rest of the afternoon carefully steering her husband away from all the modifications Lady Catherine had suggested, leaving Elizabeth barely any time to dwell upon the way Darcy had looked at her when she smiled at him.

19

Wherefore the Woodpecker Laughs

THE MENTION OF ANNA RETURNED THE CHILD TO THE forefront of Elizabeth's mind. As she meandered along her favourite path the next morning, she fondly recalled their various meetings and wondered whether the spirited little girl had yet convinced herself of the presence of fairies in her new home. She would have loved this part of the world and this walk in particular, for the path beneath the canopy of these trees was flat, straight, wide, and secluded—perfect for illicit running. On a whim, Elizabeth sprang forward and ran as fast as she could towards the gate at the end of the track. The wind rushed at her face and snapped the ribbons of her bonnet about her ears, reminding her of when Anna had run onto the lawn at Netherfield and making her laugh with joy.

Her laughter turned to a squeal of surprise when the wind plucked her bonnet off her head and threw it away behind her. She came to a laughing, sliding halt and walked back to retrieve it. When she returned to the path, she shrieked yet more loudly, for there was somebody beyond the gate where there had not been moments before. Notwithstanding the bright daylight behind him that cast his face into shadow, she recognised the silhouette even before he began to speak.

"I beg your pardon if I startled you, madam. I was walking on another path and thought I heard a shout. Are you well?"

"Quite well, thank you, Mr Darcy."

"Miss Bennet!" He opened the gate and came towards her. "I could not see who it was in the shade. Is anything the matter?"

"Nothing at all." He was holding himself so ludicrously straight and speaking with such unnecessary ceremony that she was tempted to tell him she had been running, in a most undignified manner, and had been inspired to do so by the memory of his secret illegitimate ward. She did not think he would appreciate it overmuch, but the notion made her giggle a little.

He took two quick steps towards her but then seemed to change his mind and came up short, his hands behind his back. "I have myself just been walking up at the folly."

"There is a folly?"

"Yes. Should you like to see it? I could take you there now. You would appreciate the views."

She might well, but she would not appreciate another quarter of an hour or more of the same interminable taciturnity to which he had subjected her yesterday. "Thank you," she replied, "but I was about to turn back. Charlotte is expecting me."

"Of course. May I have the pleasure of escorting you?"

She could hardly refuse, and together they turned back to the parsonage, she silent because her hopes of a long, solitary walk had been dashed, and he, she presumed, because imposing aloofness was his favourite pastime. The farther they went without his saying anything, the more exasperated she became, privately ruing the misfortune of their having met at that precise moment and whatever misguided gallantry had obliged Darcy to offer his company when he so obviously did not wish to speak to her.

"This path is a favourite haunt of mine," she told him. "I walk this way most mornings." *There,* she thought, *you are safe now, sir. There is no chance we might happen across each other again.* Indeed, he looked uncommonly pleased with the information, smiling faintly but warmly in acknowledgement. A small eddy twisted up in Elizabeth's stomach. She blamed Darcy—if he smiled more often it would be less unnerving.

They walked on, the silence persisting long enough that it lost a little of its edge. Elizabeth began to think less of what was not being said and more of her surroundings. A robin hopped across the path in front of them; a rustle somewhere off to the right drew her eyes to the departing tail of a deer; the aroma of wild garlic ebbed and flowed between the trees on either side. It began to matter less that Darcy said little, particularly when, on those few occasions he did speak, he began pointing out things of interest: a vast fungus jutting out from an oak like a shelf; a tree, several feet back from the path, that he and his cousins had christened The Listening Post for the large ear-shaped hole in the trunk. When the unmistakable knocking of a woodpecker struck up, they both spun around, pointing at different parts of the canopy as they attempted to pinpoint the source.

"Perhaps there is more than one," Elizabeth whispered, laughingly.

Darcy laughed too, very lightly, but then stepped closer to her, leant forward to better align with her perspective, and pointed up at one tree in particular. The woodpecker was there, brilliant, iridescent green with bright red plumage on its crest.

Elizabeth watched it, fascinated, for some minutes as it hammered away at the trunk. "We had one in the garden at Longbourn once, but it was a black and white one." She naturally turned to face Darcy as she told him this but looked away hastily, suddenly conscious upon realising he was not watching the bird but her.

"The black and white ones are noisier," he replied, setting back off along the path. "But I have always preferred the green ones. When I was a boy, I thought they sounded as though they were laughing when they called to each other. I was always curious to know what amused them. I wished to be as happy as they seemed."

Elizabeth's childhood had been so full of chatter and laughter that this struck her as incredibly sad, yet he did not say it with any obvious melancholy, only unaffected earnestness. "I always think ducks sound as though they are laughing," she said with deliberate lightness, "but not in a way that makes me want to know what about. They seem peculiarly scornful creatures."

"Perhaps that is why your great-grandfather got rid of the pond."

She glanced at him; he was staring directly ahead with no hint of amusement in his countenance. She smiled to herself and said nothing. His way of saying witty things in complete seriousness was rather effective now that she was coming to recognise when he was at it. They fell back into silence and walked on, exchanging only a few further observances of the surrounding flora and fauna before they came to the turning that would take Elizabeth back to the parsonage. "I believe I can find my way from here, Mr Darcy."

He smiled again, and it flustered her no less than the previous time. "I do not doubt it, madam. Pray, enjoy the rest of your day." He bowed and carried on his way.

THE NEXT MORNING, AS SHE REACHED AND PASSED THE gate, Elizabeth thought what a good thing it was that Darcy had observed her caution and stayed away from her favourite path. She found, however, that she was not in as much of a humour for walking as usual and did not go farther than the other side of the grove before turning back towards the parsonage.

When she arrived back at the path beneath the trees, she discovered two things: Darcy had not heeded her after all, and she was not as sorry to see him as she had been yesterday. But then, contrary to all her expectations, his quiet, steady company had proved surprisingly tolerable; a refreshing alternative to her cousin's incessant pontificating and the bustle to which she was accustomed at home. That he had not expected her to entertain him, but seemed content to accompany her in companionable silence, had enabled her to still enjoy her reflections despite not being alone. Walking with him again would be no great imposition, and she accepted his offer to accompany her home with far less sullenness than last time.

They did not talk a great deal more, though his better knowledge of the area increased her pleasure of it, as he pointed out rare trees imported by his late uncle and views of distant landmarks she had previously overlooked. When eventually she returned to the parsonage, she was too late for breakfast, though it mattered not, for she had no appetite of which to speak.

ON WEDNESDAY MORNING, DARCY WAS WAITING FOR HER at the gate. "I should like to show you the folly. If it would please you."

"I should be very happy to see it," she replied and accepted his proffered arm. They walked along a path she had early on dismissed as less scenic than most others. After about a quarter of a mile, they reached a slight bend in the path and Darcy turned them towards a large shrub, behind which another path opened up before them.

"Oh! I missed this route entirely when I was exploring. I always go the other way."

"When Sir Lewis first had the folly installed, this was a far better kept path. But my aunt never liked the place—you cannot get to it by carriage—and it has fallen into disuse since his death. I ought to mention it to the steward but there seems little point when nobody visits it."

"I shall visit it, now I know of this path. But do not have it cleared on my account. I rather like the idea of a secret trail to a secluded folly."

Elizabeth was so intent on taking in her surroundings, she did not realise they had fallen back into silence until Darcy spoke again.

"Has your fondness for walking been gratified here in Kent?"

"Aye, very well indeed. The park is beautiful." She paused to unpick a clinging bramble from her pelisse. "And I have only got lost half a dozen times."

"You are remarkably intrepid, Miss Bennet. I do not know any other lady who would be unconcerned about getting lost in the woods."

"I can better manage a woodland path than all the passages and rooms in that place," she replied, pointing at Rosings, which could just be seen through the trees.

He nodded. "It has undergone many changes over time that have resulted in a less than intuitive arrangement of the rooms. Of course, it will not take a seasoned explorer such as yourself very long to familiarise yourself with it. Once you understand the layout of the upper floors, the lower ones will make much more sense."

"That is of little use to me, Mr Darcy. I am not so intrepid that I could sneak past the footmen and wander Lady Catherine's private rooms unchallenged."

"Not on this visit, no. Be careful here, it is slippery." He indicated to where the path narrowed and inclined steeply. Already flustered by his odd allusion to her being granted unrestricted access to Rosings in the future, Elizabeth grew more agitated still when it was necessary to let go of his arm to walk ahead, for she did not recall taking it. How long had they been walking arm in arm? Feeling herself colour deeply, she forged ahead up the slope.

On reaching the top, she forgot her discomfort entirely. The folly and the panorama surrounding it were beautiful. She had envisaged a vast, ornate construction, dominating the rise in consonance with all the de Bourgh family's other design choices. In fact, the folly was a dainty stone rotunda, with several stone benches, a sweet domed roof, and four pillars, three of which were draped with trailing wisteria. It looked as much like a fairy house as anything she had ever seen. "Anna would love it here!" she whispered to herself.

"Pardon?"

Elizabeth jumped; she had not realised Darcy was so close behind. "I was just...I thought...it is lovely."

He continued to look at her fixedly, though he did not appear angry. She wondered whether he had heard what she said and was pleased by it, but she was not about to risk endangering anybody by enquiring. Instead, she walked away to enjoy the view from the brow of the rise. "It is a spectacular vantage point. I confess, I had thought Kent was entirely flat."

"It is, compared to Derbyshire, but picturesque nevertheless."

"How close are we to the sea here?"

"About twenty miles."

"How far is it to France?"

"About seventy. Why?"

"I am only curious. I have never been this close to the continent."

"I do not think my aunt would like Rosings to be thought of as almost in enemy territory."

Elizabeth pulled a face of ambivalence as she reflected that it seemed a singularly accurate description—and was mortified to be caught at it. Darcy had walked just far enough ahead that when her silence bade him turn towards her, he met her eyes directly. She pressed her lips together against a laugh, anticipating his disapproving glare, but it never appeared.

"I believe she has been more used to consider Kent as The Garden of England," he replied, and the way his mouth moved as he said it made it seem as though he, too, was withholding a smile.

"People say all sorts of silly things to commend the places in which they live. Anyone who lives within forty miles of London will tell you they live in the Home Counties, as though anywhere north of Cambridgeshire is a foreign country. Mr Goulding is adamant that Cornwall is the Heart of England, but he grew up in Penzance, which I have always thought looked much more like England's Big Toe."

Darcy laughed—only a small, soft chuckle, but it rendered him so startlingly handsome that it distracted Elizabeth completely from what she was saying. Blinking away her surprise, she turned to stare fiercely at the panoramic.

"I shall always consider Derbyshire my home," he said. "I think you would like it very well."

"Well, you thought I would like this place, and you were right about that, so I daresay I would like Derbyshire, too." It was the first thing that came into her head, spoken hastily to cover her discomposure, but she wished she had said something that sounded less like one of Miss Bingley's panegyrics.

"I have been gone far longer than I told Charlotte I would be," she said abruptly. "I ought to be getting back."

He conceded with a small bow and no further comment, for which she was grateful. She rather resented his offering his hand at the top of the slope, however, for she disliked the implication that she required his assistance—until she slipped on the loose stones, at which point she laughed unrestrainedly at herself and thanked him for his foresight.

"You seem very close to Mrs Collins," he said when they were able to walk side by side again.

"Aye, she is a dear friend, and among the most level-headed of all my acquaintance, which I value greatly. Though, I have had occasion more recently to question her judgment."

Darcy's small smile satisfied her that he took her meaning. "She and Mr Collins seem happily settled, though."

"Aye, they are both delighted to be settled. Charlotte has the comfortable home to which she always aspired, and my cousin has finally been able to do something that pleased Lady Catherine. Whether they are quite as delighted with each other is less clear."

He smiled more widely at this but did not reply. He seemed deep in thought, and Elizabeth left him to it, pleased to have learnt the difference between his pensive silences and his disdainful ones. He appeared startled when she said good-bye at the turning to the parsonage and, if she was not mistaken, a little embarrassed by his absence of mind. She hoped her parting smile was assurance enough that she was not offended. Indeed, she was more inclined to wonder what he had been thinking.

ONE AFTERNOON, WHEN THEY RECEIVED NO CALLERS AT THE parsonage, and Mr Collins was loitering about making a nuisance of himself, Charlotte suggested that Elizabeth and Maria accompany her to visit some of the cottagers. Maria begged off, but Elizabeth readily agreed, and they set out with a basket of provisions each, to Hunsford village.

"I shall take you to see Mrs O'Neill first. She has just had her fourth baby, and I am sure she will not mind you holding him."

Elizabeth raised an eyebrow at her friend. "Is it really for my benefit that we are going somewhere we might cuddle a baby? It is not *I* who is newly married. Are you feeling clucky, Mrs Collins?" Charlotte blushed and Elizabeth gave her a playful nudge with her shoulder. "You will be blessed before you know it." Then, taking pity on her friend, she turned the conversation to other matters until they arrived.

Mrs O'Neill made no secret of her relief to receive visitors. She passed the squalling babe into Charlotte's arms before they had even passed the threshold and returned to chopping up carrots at her kitchen bench. Her other three children ran about under their feet, playing in that raucous manner that all small children do, drawing repeated angry remonstrations from their mother. Charlotte's attempt to enquire whether Mrs O'Neill was in good health was interrupted by a loud crash and a piercing scream and they all paused to look as one of the older children picked up the broken pieces of his wooden toy from the flagstones. He burst into tears, followed in quick succession by each of his younger siblings, and then his mother.

"Charlotte, why do not I take these three for a little walk while you talk to Mrs O'Neill?" Elizabeth suggested. The offer was quickly accepted and after helping with their coats, she shepherded them all out of the door. "Hold hands everybody. Now, which way shall we go?" She ought not to have asked, for it only encouraged them to begin squabbling. "If you are going to be troublesome, I shall make you walk backwards," she said with mock severity.

"That is easy," declared Peter, the eldest at seven years, turning around to prove it.

"I can do it, too," declared his younger sister, Sarah.

To Elizabeth's delight, Samuel, a little cherub of three years old, then tried to imitate his big brother and sister, resulting in a crab-like shuffle.

"Can you do it, Missus?" enquired Peter.

"I do not know. I think I might need your help." Thus, with Peter holding one of her hands, Sarah holding the other, and Samuel sidling along behind, Elizabeth and the three children set off, backwards, along the lane.

"Good day, Miss Bennet."

She whipped around. "Mr Darcy!" He was standing outside another cottage in the row with a gentleman she did not recognise, and was regarding her fixedly, though the glimmer in his eyes hinted at his being vastly diverted. "We were just going for a walk," she said airily, then staggered forwards a step as the children all huddled behind her legs, apparently less able to discern the amusement in Darcy's intent look. She bent to pick Samuel up and held him on her hip. "We thought we might as well go backwards as not, is that not right, little one?"

Samuel stuck his thumb in his mouth and nodded.

"Indeed," Darcy replied with a small lift of one eyebrow that nevertheless heightened Elizabeth's enjoyment of the children's game.

The other gentleman interrupted with an apology, explaining that he had another meeting to attend. For the sake of propriety, Darcy made a brief introduction to Lady Catherine's steward before dismissing him with a nod. To Elizabeth, he said "May I walk with you for a short distance? I am going the same way. If you *were* going this way. It was difficult to tell."

She grinned at his teasing. "Yes, if you wish." She set Samuel down and crouched to give all three children a new distraction. "What say you pick Mama some flowers to say sorry for making such a racket? Which of you can find the most?" They all spread out along the lane and she stood up, calling after them not to go too far.

"May I ask how you have acquired three children between yesterday and today?" Darcy enquired.

"They are Mrs O'Neill's." She pointed behind her to the family's cottage. "Mrs Collins is speaking to her. I am giving them a little peace and quiet."

"That is extremely good of you."

"It is no trouble. I am fond of children. I have four cousins about this age, and they are all sweet little things, always up to some mischief or other. The key is to keep them busy. An idle child is a disaster waiting to happen." Too late, she remembered Anna, so lonely that her only entertainment was running away from home—and too late, she recalled to whom she was talking. Wondering if his thoughts had gone in a similar direction, she glanced at Darcy, only to discover him regarding her with such intense concentration that she looked away again, breathless.

They walked on and presently fell back into easier conversation, stopping only when Peter returned to proudly present Elizabeth with a fistful of butchered daisies and a muddy feather. She thanked him sincerely. Sarah did much better, running back to them a few minutes later with a bright red poppy clutched in her hand. Samuel toddled up behind her holding up a dandelion that had gone to seed. When he took a deep breath to blow the seeds off the stalk and managed, instead, to suck most of them into his mouth, Elizabeth hastened, laughing, to his aid and told them all it was time to return home.

"I believe I shall have the pleasure of seeing you at Rosings for dinner this evening," Darcy said when she wished him good-bye.

"Yes, we have been summoned," she confirmed. "Lady Catherine intends to have the card tables out I understand. Which will be unfortunate for you, since you are disinclined to the activity."

"You know very well that is not true. I expressed a wish not to play on one occasion."

"I recall it well. Mr Hurst was most aggrieved."

He gave a small grunt of disdain. "Hurst brought that on himself by always insisting on playing high."

She laughed. "That cannot be a problem for you, sir."

"It is not." He held her gaze and her stomach did a strange little pirouette. "Good day, Miss Bennet," he said after a pause. "I shall look forward to seeing you again this evening."

Elizabeth watched the now familiar sight of Darcy's purposeful and dignified stride as he walked away. *Surely it cannot have been for me that he refused to play cards at Netherfield—*

he held me in utter contempt at the time! She shook her head. It was too long ago to remember properly and too unlikely an idea to warrant much attention. Instead, she took Samuel's little hand and turned all the children back towards home to give their mother her dubious collection of flowers.

Elizabeth was about to blow out her candle and climb into bed when there came a knock at her bedroom door.

"Would you like an extra blanket?" Charlotte called from the landing. "Maria has asked for one, and I have plenty to spare."

Elizabeth opened the door. "Thank you, I would. There is a definite chill in the air this evening."

"I think we all got chilled sitting in the carriage waiting for my husband to stop talking," Charlotte replied as she handed her the blanket. She looked at her searchingly for a few seconds before venturing, "Did you enjoy yourself this evening, Eliza?"

"Very much, thank you. What makes you ask? Did it seem otherwise?"

"You were just very quiet." With a furtive look over her shoulder, Charlotte ducked inside Elizabeth's room and closed the door. "I was worried Mr Collins had upset you."

Elizabeth screwed up her nose and thought hard about the many ridiculous things her cousin had said and done that day, but there were too many to narrow it down to one offence. "When?"

"As we left for Rosings, when he said you might as well not fuss over your hair any longer because it was more likely to please Lady Catherine if you kept it looking plain."

Elizabeth laughed with genuine pleasure, pleased Charlotte had repeated the absurd remark for she had not heard it the first time. She had, much to Mr Collins's displeasure, been too busy fussing with her hair in the hall mirror, uncommonly anxious that it should look well at dinner. "I confess I missed that."

Charlotte's face fell. "Oh! Then I have upset you for nothing!"

"Not at all. I hope I am more sensible than to worry over what Lady Catherine thinks of my hair."

"I am pleased to hear it. Though, if you were not upset, what made you so quiet?"

"I did not realise I was. Indeed, between my cousin, Lady Catherine, and Colonel Fitzwilliam, there is never a great deal of opportunity to say anything anyway." She had reflected on this over the course of the evening. Mr Collins's constant prattle and Lady Catherine's regular orations had long been a source of amusement and occasionally vague irritation. For the first time this evening, she had also begun to find Colonel Fitzwilliam's chatter a little tiresome. He was an exceedingly amiable gentleman but, more often than not, seemed to say the first thing that popped into his head merely to avoid any lengthy silence. This was worryingly akin to her mother's general approach to conversation and did not fill Elizabeth with any confidence in the value of what he said. "Far better only to speak when you have something of substance to say, do not you think?"

"I am not sure," Charlotte replied. "I know more than one person who might never open his mouth again if that were true." She bit her top lip—an old habit Elizabeth well knew meant she was hesitant to say whatever was on her mind—before adding, "Mr Darcy said even less than you this evening. I almost offered to swap tables at one point, for I thought you must be exasperated playing cards with a partner who never communicates his hand. But then you both seemed to do well enough."

Elizabeth grinned broadly. "We did, did we not? And he did communicate his hand, only more subtly than some of the other players managed. With looks, I suppose, and...oh, I do not know. I cannot say that I paid much attention to how we won so often. I just know that we did win, and it vexed her ladyship no end."

"You had an agreeable time then? Despite his barely saying anything to you."

"Well...yes. He might not have said much, but he did not ignore me."

"Oh no, he certainly did not do that. He scarcely stopped looking at you all evening."

Elizabeth began to feel a little warm. "That is hardly surprising. We were sitting opposite each other."

Charlotte narrowed her eyes. "Are you being deliberately obtuse, or do you really see nothing unusual in his behaviour towards you?"

"You really are beginning to sound like my mother, you know," she replied, laughing. "No, I do not see anything unusual in his behaviour. He goes for just as long now without speaking a word to me as he did in Hertfordshire, even when we are walking together. He has given me no reason to suspect his feelings for me are any different to what they were six months ago—and then, as you well know, he disdained my country ways and declared me not handsome enough for his liking."

Charlotte stared at her with a slightly amazed expression. "Do you and Mr Darcy often walk together?"

The heat spread to Elizabeth's cheeks and she floundered slightly before conceding that they had bumped into each other more than once on the same path.

"And you did not decide to walk on a different path after the first encounter?"

"It is my favourite," she replied with a shrug.

"Well," Charlotte said expressively. "I see I have been asking the wrong question. It is not whether Mr Darcy loves you but whether you love him."

Elizabeth laughed, and even to her ears it sounded a little shrill. "Charlotte, not even my mother could make the leap from occasionally walking with somebody to loving him."

"We both know that is not true. And besides, you did not just walk with him. You walked with him more than once, alone, and you kept it a secret, which you would not have done had not you enjoyed it. You would have come to me directly and complained that he had cut up your peace and ruined your walks. I knew you were distracted for some reason this evening. You are in love with him!"

The broader her friend's smile grew, the harder it was for Elizabeth to maintain hers. "Charlotte, I beg you would not tease me about this. I am not in love with Mr Darcy."

"And now I know that you are, because you have never asked me to stop teasing you about anything, the whole time I have known you."

"But you have never teased me about anything so serious before. I could never love him. He disdains all my friends and family, is almost certainly to blame, at least in part, for Jane's present misery, and has certainly never held me in any particular regard."

"Why has he been walking with you every day then?"

"I do not know! Probably for the same reason I have been walking with him—because we both enjoy walking and there is nothing else to do here—oh!" She stopped and twisted her hands together, grimacing contritely. "Oh, Charlotte, forgive me. I did not mean that. It is lovely here. It is just—I—"

Charlotte reached to squeeze her hand. "It is well, Eliza. I took no offence—and I am sorry for teasing you. I shall leave you to sleep now."

Her ready abandonment of the subject was even worse

than her pursuit of it, but Elizabeth could not contradict the implicit accusation without appearing to protest too much. Instead she said goodnight as light-heartedly as she could and closed the door behind Charlotte. Then, with admirable maturity, she threw herself onto her bed and buried her head beneath her pillow to muffle a loud groan.

The possibility of having formed an attachment to Darcy had never entered her head—and yet the moment Charlotte said the words, a heavy feeling of certainty had settled in her stomach, if not of love, then still of a decidedly powerful sentiment. She groaned again, more loudly. She did not love him. She *could not* love him. The oldest friend and co-conspirator of the man who had broken Jane's heart; a man hateful enough to deny his father's favourite his inheritance; a man who might walk with her in secret but would not deign to dance with her at a ball? *Never!* No, any feelings of warmth she might presently have for him were merely a consequence of his company being the least objectionable in a host of worse alternatives, coupled with Charlotte's determination to have at least one of them be in love with the other. Nothing more.

She slid the pillow off her head and sat up, feeling rather foolish for having flown into such a panic. It was not only unsurprising but sensible that one should learn to overlook a person's less admirable qualities and appreciate his better ones if one was to spend any significant time with him. And while she had reasons aplenty not to esteem Darcy, she was not short of knowledge that justified the lessening of her antipathy. She most certainly was not in love with him, but she did like—very much—what he had done to help protect Anna. She might not like his conceit, but she could respect the importance he placed upon his family. She might think him too reserved, but she appreciated that whatever he did say was well-informed and interesting. She might not approve of his pride, but she admired that he was not vain, despite having more reason than any other man of her acquaintance to be complacent about his looks. Despite one glance from him having the power to make her lose her place in a conversation. Despite his smile occasionally making her breathless.

She blew out the candle, extinguishing with it that train of thought, and rolled over to go to sleep, satisfied that she was perfectly safe from Mr Darcy.

21

Home Matters

To prove how indifferent she was to Darcy's company, Elizabeth set out later than usual for her walk the next morning, and in the opposite direction to the grove in which she usually met him. The small jolt of pleasure she received on seeing a gentleman approach through the trees was easily imputed to having become accustomed to walking in company. The fleeting hollow sensation that assailed her upon recognising Colonel Fitzwilliam was just as readily dismissed as hunger.

"Good morning, Miss Bennet," he greeted her. "This is a pleasant surprise. Had I known you favoured this path I should have walked here before today."

"I do not often come this way, as it happens. What brings you here this morning?"

"I have been making a tour of the park, as I generally do every year, and intend to close it with a call at the parsonage. Are you going much farther?"

"No, I should have turned in a moment. Is it unladylike to admit that I need something to eat?"

"It might be considered so by some, but not by me," he

replied with a grin. "You have heard the phrase, I am sure, that an army marches on its stomach. A good officer never ignores the demands of the appetite. Come! Allow me to escort you back for supplies." They turned and walked towards the parsonage together. "I hope you have enjoyed your time in Kent," he said as they went.

"I have, very much," Elizabeth replied. "I shall be sorry to leave."

"It is a lovely part of the country. Each time I return, I recall quite how fond of it I am. Which is fortunate, really, since Darcy has already postponed our departure once and seems of a mind to do so again."

The mention of that gentleman thoroughly discomposed her—and that, in turn, made her angry: at Charlotte, for putting ridiculous notions of love in her head; at herself, for being so easily affected; and at Darcy, for having such power over her. Feeling herself begin to redden, she said the first reproachful thing she could think of that would prove she was not in his thrall. "He is very fortunate you are so willing to be at his disposal. I do not know anybody who seems more to enjoy the power of telling people what to do, and where to go, and when, than Mr Darcy."

"He certainly has the means to go where he pleases, because he is rich," replied Colonel Fitzwilliam. "But he does not always have the advantage of choosing when."

"Oh yes," Elizabeth said drily. "I am sure he would much rather have stayed in Hertfordshire last autumn."

"I daresay the whole party would have preferred it after the expense and inconvenience of settling at Netherfield, but I understand an unforeseen development made it impossible."

Yes, she thought bitterly, *none of them could have foreseen that Bingley would fall in love with Jane. How disappointed they must all have been.* "You need not speak in riddles," she said indignantly. "I am well aware of the matter to which you refer."

He regarded her earnestly for a long moment before acknowledging it by inclining his head. "Darcy suspected you might know."

"Of his involvement? It was obvious to me, if not to some others. Mr Bingley would never have left of his own accord."

This seemed to surprise him. "Darcy's part in it is...regrettable. As is anybody's knowing about it. We had thought only Miss Bingley was suspected. I do not believe my cousin is aware of the extent of *your* cousin's knowledge of the matter."

"Mr Collins?"

"Yes. His name was mentioned in conjunction with every report that reached Darcy's or Bingley's ears in Hertfordshire. It was *his* industrious gossiping that eventually forced them to leave." After a pause, he added, "Not many people are as forbearing as you, Miss Bennet. There were others he told who were not likely to be as kind with this knowledge as you have been."

Elizabeth said nothing and continued walking, though her heart pounded and her mind raced. Colonel Fitzwilliam was not speaking of Bingley's affections for Jane, or Darcy's involvement in their separation—he was speaking of Anna! *And I have all but admitted what I know!* There was no use in pretending otherwise now. To admit they had been talking at cross purposes would only require Colonel Fitzwilliam to explain himself. "I am exceedingly sorry Mr Collins has caused so much trouble and distress," she said cautiously. "But I did not hear of this from him. Not at first anyway. I heard it from Anna." She dared not mention Wickham's name.

Fitzwilliam stopped in his tracks and turned to face her, all astonishment. "You have met her?"

"Pray, be not alarmed. It was quite by accident and nobody ever discovered it. She had run ahead of her companion, and I encouraged her to return, nothing more. She talked, as all five-year olds do, of home matters."

Colonel Fitzwilliam rubbed his eyebrow with a finger and exhaled heavily. "You know it all then? Miss Bingley's situation? Darcy's part in it?"

She nodded. "You may depend on my secrecy, sir."

"Your assurance is extremely welcome, madam—and, if I may, uncommonly liberal. I cannot think of many people who would have so willingly kept this secret or been so disinclined to condemn those responsible."

Elizabeth gave a lopsided smile and resumed walking. "I shall not pretend that I do not have an opinion of the matter —or of what the Bingleys' sudden departure cost certain members of my family. But I care very little for the world's opinion, and I have no desire to expose anybody to its general derision. Least of all an innocent young girl."

"My cousin would be delighted to hear you say that."

Elizabeth could not help but smile again at the memory of Darcy's affectionate encounter with Anna at Netherfield. "Mr Darcy is uncommonly kind to take such prodigious care of the Bingleys."

"He could scarcely have behaved otherwise in the circumstances. He is entirely too honourable not to assist with a situation so regrettably connected to him. He has done everything in his power to protect and provide for them."

This must be an allusion to Wickham, she thought. *So now I know the truth of it.* As preoccupied as she was with this revelation, she almost did not hear Colonel Fitzwilliam add, "Besides, Miss Darcy is too dear to him to leave her solely to the Bingleys' care."

It took a moment, and several reiterations in Elizabeth's mind, before the significance of this remark struck home. Then it stole the strength from her legs and caused her to stumble slightly before she regained her footing.

"Are you well?" The colonel enquired, laughing slightly as though he expected her to laugh with him.

"Yes, thank you," she lied. Her heart could not seem to catch up with itself; she felt alarmingly light-headed as it raced, double tempo, in her breast.

"Are you quite sure?" He had stopped laughing.

"A little faint, perhaps." She did her best to smile. "I told you I was hungry."

He chuckled, and when she did not immediately swoon, seemed content to take her word that all was well. *At least one of us is convinced.* After a moment, in a voice that did not sound like her own, she said, "Before I knew who she was, Anna told me her name was Miss Dunn."

"Ah, yes, Miss Bingley's maid. They used her name from the beginning so they could claim the child was hers if anyone grew too meddlesome. It helped that it also began with a D, of course, for it made a young child's occasional slips of the tongue more explicable."

"That makes sense," Elizabeth replied, though her words came out almost silently on account of her lungs being void of air.

Miss Darcy.

She was the greatest fool that ever lived. 'He refused to marry my mother'—so Anna had said of her father. In what possible circumstance would a man of Wickham's character and situation ever have refused to marry a woman as wealthy as Miss Bingley? What ever had made her think he might be Anna's father! The answer had been obvious from the outset, but she had been too blinded by Darcy's righteous probity to even consider the possibility. Anna was Darcy's natural child—named after his mother, no less! The image of him crouching to tap her on the nose was suddenly so painful it forced a small sob into her throat. She coughed it away, alarmed by the ferocity of her confusion and dismay.

"I beg your pardon, Miss Bennet," Colonel Fitzwilliam

said sombrely. "I have allowed myself to get carried away and say too much on an exceedingly delicate issue."

"Do not blame yourself, sir," she replied with forced lightness. "I believe we ended up on the subject more or less by accident."

"I have clearly made you uncomfortable, though. I do apologise."

"I do not think it is a matter with which anybody could be *comfortable*."

"Indeed. Let us talk of something else."

For the next few minutes, Elizabeth mumbled various distracted responses to the colonel's attempts at conversation but could scarcely conceal her relief when they reached the parsonage. She feigned composure for a further quarter of an hour while refreshments were served and eventually Fitzwilliam left them, but after five minutes of listening to Charlotte's plans for dinner, she could contain herself no longer. "Charlotte, forgive me, I must lie down."

"Why yes, of course. Are you unwell?"

"No. I do not know. Maybe. Pray excuse me." She heard Charlotte follow her at first, but once she reached the stairs, her friend remained at the bottom. Only after she turned a corner out of sight did Elizabeth allow her poise to crumble. Her next breath came out as a shaky sob, and tears distorted the landing as she dashed along it to her room. She swung the door shut and pressed her forehead to the back of it.

Miss Darcy!

"She is his," she whispered, and felt the tears begin to fall. The implications were too vast to comprehend, though they all flew at her with equal force, jabbing at her thoughts, attempting to win her notice. Why had he refused to marry? Did he mean to wed his cousin after all—was Rosings a greater prize than his own child? Why, then, had he spent so much time following Miss Bingley about the country, setting her up in various homes, and staying with her under the same roof? A swell of nausea accompanied the realisation that they may very well still be lovers. Nausea turned to burning indignation that he had so carelessly and cruelly engaged *her* heart enough that she cared. For she did care. There was no denying it; the pain in her chest that had begun on the walk and not relented since was too piercing to have been caused by anything other than love.

The agitation and tears this discovery occasioned brought on a headache that confined her to her room until Mr Collins knocked to remind her of their engagement to drink tea at Rosings. There was no possibility of her attending her cousins there. Indeed, she knew not how she would ever face Darcy again, but for today at least, evasion was her only recourse. Charlotte, seeing she was really unwell, did not press her to go, and with very little attention paid to her husband's displeasure, bustled everybody else out of the house, leaving Elizabeth alone but for her aching head and broken heart.

22 Indelibly Jarred

WHEN THEY WERE GONE, AND HER PACING WITHIN DOORS had not alleviated any of her distress, Elizabeth almost settled on going out for another walk. Rain and the unwillingness to be reminded of her recent time spent with Darcy put pay to the idea, increasing her feeling of helplessness. She reviled her own discomposure. The revelation ought not to have affected her in any way other than to confirm what she already knew but had allowed herself to forget—that Darcy considered himself above everyone, beyond society's judgment, and exempt from the usual constraints of human decency. She wished she could laugh at such a deficiency in his character—one that several months ago would have vastly gratified her desire to think ill of him—but it was too late. She had seen, comprehended, and come to admire too much not to be utterly undone with disappointment and dismay.

She was roused from these pitiful reflections by the sound of the doorbell, and her spirits were thrown into utter disarray when she saw Darcy himself walk into the room.

"I hope you are feeling better," he began immediately.

"Mrs Collins informed us you had a headache, but I hope it is nothing serious."

"I am well," she answered with forced civility.

He sat down for a few moments then stood up again. Elizabeth was unsurprised by his uneasiness, in no doubt he had come to discuss Anna, for Colonel Fitzwilliam must have conveyed to him that she knew of his concealment. She would not make his excuses for him and refused to say a word as he walked about the room. After a silence of several minutes, he came towards her in an agitated manner and thus began—

"In vain have I struggled. It will not do. My feelings will not be repressed. You must allow me to tell you how ardently I admire and love you."

Elizabeth stared, coloured, despaired, and was silent. She had not supposed anything could hurt more deeply than the revelation that Darcy was the most dishonourable man of her acquaintance, and she was in love with him; that he should return her affections was too painful to bear.

Her silence proved sufficient encouragement for him to continue. "For many months now, I have fought against what can only be considered a highly imprudent attachment, but when you did not arrive with the rest of the party at Rosings, my disappointment was such that I could fool myself no longer. A fool I must truly be, for I have come to depend on you entirely for my own happiness and am desolate whenever I am apart from you."

He must have seen something in her countenance that gave him pause, for his brow furrowed and his tone lost some of its fervour. "I see you are surprised. Indeed, the very impediments that you must be wondering at my having overlooked are what prevented me from declaring myself sooner. But you may be assured, I am reconciled to every obstacle to the match. Your family's situation is regrettable and will, inevitably, attract attention I could well do without, but that cannot be helped. My family and friends are unlikely to support the union—the disparity between our relative situations is so great there will always be opposition to it—but if I can overcome such objections, then others cannot long continue to think of it as a degradation. The inferiority of your connexions will cease to be a concern to anyone who has the pleasure of knowing you. I myself could count the time in days or hours that it took my feelings to jump from indifference to passionate admiration." He stepped closer. "You are in my thoughts at every hour of the day—when I wake, when I eat, when I sleep. I am gone mad with feelings that, despite all my endeavours, I have been unable to conquer, and I beg you would put an end to my struggles and agree to be my wife."

He stopped speaking and, from the knowing smile that played about his lips, seemed poised to accept her answer with immediate pleasure. It only exacerbated Elizabeth's agony, for she had no wish to pain him, but his words could not be unsaid, and he had broken her heart into so many pieces she could not hold them all together in her hands. "How dare you?" she whispered.

Darcy's smile vanished. A look of confusion and hurt flitted across his features but was replaced almost instantly with a more severe hauteur than she had ever seen on him before. "Excuse me?"

"How dare you vilify my situation when your own is so egregiously wanting." He blanched but made no reply, and she hurled her next words at him, furious at the cowardice he displayed in making her be the one to broach the matter. "I know your secret, sir!"

"I am aware of that."

Her chest contracted painfully. "You do not deny it?"

He shook his head. "I cannot."

"Then were you hoping it would not come up?"

"Of course not. I planned to explain it in full, but I thought it more important to tell you my feelings first."

"You have done very well in that case, for you could not have made your feelings any clearer. My connexions are deplorable, and I am unworthy of your admiration or hand in marriage." She took a deep, shuddering breath, fighting to maintain her composure—an endeavour made significantly trickier when, rather than deny it, Darcy frowned in apparent confusion.

"If you know my situation, you must comprehend my need to avoid anything that would draw attention to it. Marrying someone whose condition in life is so decidedly beneath my own is scarcely likely to *evade* notice. The want of connexion would be an even greater evil to me than to Bingley, and only the utmost force of passion persuaded me to put aside those objections that I took such pains to point out to him."

Elizabeth sat back in her chair, aghast. "I suspected you were involved in his decision to go. I never imagined it was because you feared his attachment to my sister might expose *you* to ridicule!"

"Him too! Towards Bingley I have been kinder than to myself."

"Have you? He is the least to blame in all this, excepting Anna herself, yet you have denied him happiness with a woman who in every way would have suited his disposition. With the motivation of protecting your own reputation, you have separated him from my sister, involving them both in misery of the acutest kind."

He had the audacity to shake his head. "I never saw your sister display any sign of regard for my friend strong enough to convince me his happiness with her would be assured."

"Perhaps that is because, despite your opinion of my family, Jane is too genteel to reveal her deepest sentiments to anybody as unconnected to her as you."

"Your superior knowledge of your sister must cast doubt on my judgment of her affections, but not all your relations are so demure. Forgive me if I offend you by speaking plainly, madam, but you cannot deny the total want of propriety so frequently, so almost uniformly betrayed by your mother, by your three younger sisters, and occasionally even by your father."

Elizabeth gave a wordless cry. "Yet none of *them* is concealing a natural child from the world."

Darcy showed no contrition. Rather, he seemed to grow angrier with every objection Elizabeth put forward, as though it vexed him that she would not be scolded into agreeing with his reasoning. "True, but if you consider *that* such a reprehensible stain on *my* situation, I cannot but wonder why you are in such a rage to upbraid me for separating Bingley from your sister?"

"It is hardly the same! But in any case, it ought to have been their choice to make, not yours. You took shameless advantage of Mr Bingley's obvious dependence on your judgment, and you convinced him to act against his will because *you* are afraid of being disgraced. But you could have avoided all threat of ruin—Mr Bingley could have married where he chose—had you only acted properly to begin with and married Miss Bingley."

Darcy's expression betrayed his greatest bewilderment yet. "You must see that is impossible."

"No, I cannot see that, when you have stooped so low as to offer for me, and I must be considered a far more inferior choice by all the connexions you are so desperate to impress."

"I did not—that is not what I—I did not stoop to offering for you, Elizabeth. The situation of your mother's relations, your family's general conduct, may not be ideal, but I thought I had made clear that I am reconciled to all the obstacles which initially opposed my inclination."

"How exceedingly magnanimous of you, Mr Darcy. Are you proposing, with this prodigious piece of civility, that my family's want of consequence is a greater evil than an illegitimate child?"

"No, of course not, but the existence of one demands caution in regard to the other."

"Your reasonableness on this subject is absurd! You may apply as many arguments as you choose to justify the situation, but there is more at stake here than reason can defend." She pressed a palm to her sternum in a vain attempt to alleviate the hollowness there and said breathlessly, "How could you ask this of me?"

He stepped backwards, his shoulders slumped, his entire demeanour that of defeat. "Forgive me. I thought in you I had found somebody who would understand. Somebody who would neither judge nor blame me. Somebody who could learn to cherish Anna as I do."

"Then I wonder what sort of woman you must take me for. You are right—our families are very different, and here is proof. Circumstances such as these might be condoned in your world, which you have so eloquently and emphatically extolled as superior to mine. But in the sphere in which I grew up, I can assure you, this sort of thing is by no means acceptable. Anna is illegitimate. What you are asking of me is unfair—think of *my* family's reputation, think of *my* sensibilities to always be reminded of...what you consider proper behaviour. How could I respect you?"

"Good God! I would never treat you in that way, and I most certainly do not consider it proper behaviour." He paused to run a hand over his face. Then he shook his head and said more calmly, "Forgive me, Miss Bennet. I did not consider how this would appear to you, but I beg you would believe that I would never—"

"Nay, forgive *me*, sir, but how could I ever trust you?"

He inhaled deeply and held it for a long time before breathing out through his nose, his jaw clenched. "Am I to be indelibly tarred with this brush then?" he enquired at last. "Am I to be thus rejected, are my hopes of happiness to be thus denied, because of Miss Bingley's past scheming?"

Elizabeth's mouth fell open, her heart intolerably heavy with disillusionment. "Surely you do not mean to lay all the blame for this at Miss Bingley's door. Even with my limited comprehension of the matter, I do not believe she can have ended up a mother on her own." She was rewarded for this observation with more glowering silence, which she took it upon herself to fill. "But it is not merely this affair for which you seem to have eschewed all culpability. What of Mr Wickham? On that subject what can you have to say? Under what misrepresentation can you here impose on others? Or will you deny that you have withheld the advantages which you must know to have been designed for him?"

"Wickham does not deserve any of the advantages he believes he is owed by my father," he replied, his voice dripping with bitterness.

"Is he also underserving of his liberty? Or can you justify still holding him to account with a letter that would see him cruelly punished for a mistake he made many years ago?"

"Yes, I can justify it very easily. His past behaviour has been reprehensible."

"Well, he is demonstrably not alone in that! But though he has improved since, you will not relinquish either his letter or his legacy, thus he is prevented from building a new and better life. Nobody should hold that much power over another person."

Darcy was glaring at the nearby table-top with alarming vehemence and almost bared his teeth when he said, with glacial severity, "The man is not worth your concern."

Elizabeth felt herself growing angrier with every moment.

"You would dictate who is worthy of my concern? You, who have disdained every person I hold dear in Hertfordshire—who have treated the happiness of your oldest friend with contempt—who have allowed your cousin to continue in the hope of your marrying her but have blithely proposed to me as though her feelings mean nothing—who have blamed Miss Bingley for every unwelcome consequence of a mistake that was never hers alone—and who claims to cherish the innocent young child whom you have hidden away her whole life like a dirty secret. I believe I shall judge for myself who is worthy of my concern, Mr Darcy, for you are not the paragon of discernment you believe yourself to be. You live by a different set of rules, where it is acceptable to think meanly of everybody outside your own circle, while you behave as you please without censure. It is arrogant—arrogant and conceited, and I thought you were better than this—" Without warning, Elizabeth's anger turned to wretchedness, and her attempt to blink away unbidden tears pushed one or two of them over her lashes to roll down her cheeks. "But I was wrong."

"You have said quite enough, madam," Darcy said stiffly. "I perfectly comprehend your feelings and have now only to be ashamed of what my own have been. Forgive me for having taken up so much of your time and accept my best wishes for your health and happiness."

With these words he hastily left the room, and Elizabeth heard him the next moment open the front door and quit the house. She remained standing for a heartbeat or two longer, staring at the tree that blocked the path along which he must be walking away. When she comprehended there was nothing to be done to bring him back or return him to the man she had believed him to be when she awoke that morning, she succumbed to the weakness in her legs, sat down, and cried.

Elizabeth slept little that night, and what respite she received was curtailed by painfully bright sunlight pouring through her open curtains the next morning. A moment of blissful amnesia just after waking lasted only as long as it took her to blink the glare away. Then her memories of all that had been said and felt the day before came crashing back with merciless clarity. She had no tears left to cry and climbed out of bed in a numb stupor.

"Heavens, are you ill?" Charlotte cried when Elizabeth entered the parlour. She hastened to her side and felt her brow for a fever. "Shall I call for the apothecary?"

"There is nothing the matter with me, I merely slept ill," Elizabeth replied. With a small smile she added, "I did not think I looked quite that shocking."

"I beg your pardon—you do not. Only exceedingly pale. Here, have some tea and toast. It will brighten you up."

Elizabeth obliged her, though she had no desire to either eat or drink.

"Is there anything in particular that kept you awake all night? Can I help in any way?"

She smiled sadly and shook her head. No amount of talking would change the situation; Anna could not be reasoned away. In any case, to explain what she had learnt about Darcy would inevitably reveal to her astute friend the extent of her feelings for him, for the discovery would not otherwise have cost her a moment's sleep. She had much rather never acknowledge her errant and unwanted attachment. Having sprung up from nowhere, it could not take long to fade again and would do so sooner if it was not dwelt upon.

"Will you be sorry to see the gentlemen leave this week?" Charlotte enquired rather indelicately. Elizabeth refused to be drawn and answered as indifferently as she could that though they had provided a pleasant addition to the party at Rosings, she had been content before they arrived and had no doubt that she would be content after they were gone.

"Do you think you will see either of them again at Netherfield?"

"I doubt it."

"It is only that Colonel Fitzwilliam seemed to imply last night that he might see you again soon. I wondered whether he meant to visit Mr Bingley at Netherfield with his cousin, but perhaps he hopes to see you in London."

Elizabeth stared at the table. Had Darcy informed his cousin of his intention to propose? She could only imagine the contemptuous words that must have been directed at her by both gentlemen when Darcy returned from the parsonage rejected and reproached. She did not imagine a man such as he was very often refused what he desired, and even less frequently admonished for desiring it. She laughed very slightly at having been the one to do it, but it came out tremulously, teetering on the brink of turning into a sob, and she felt a rising panic at the uncommon fragility of her spirits. She put her cup down on the table and stood up before agitation could get the better of her. "I hope you will excuse me,

Charlotte. I am in great need of some fresh air. Would you mind terribly if we talked later on?"

Assured by Charlotte that they had no engagements that day, Elizabeth fetched her coat and all but ran out of the door.

SHE DARED NOT WALK ANY OF THE PATHS ON WHICH SHE had previously met Darcy or his cousin and instead turned up the lane that led her farther from the turnpike road. She walked swiftly, but not fast enough to outrun her memories of yesterday, which hounded her along the path, stirring her indignation to match the fury of her steps. It was difficult to countenance quite how reprehensible Darcy had shown himself to be. She used to think his pride was the worst of it—pride that was now revealed to be staggeringly hypocritical—but the true defects of his character evidently ran far deeper. She could scarcely believe the indifference with which he had dismissed his responsibility towards Miss Bingley. To judge her unworthy of him when he had been the means of ruining her was the cruellest form of conceit. To have condemned Anna to a life marred by prejudice, disadvantage, and a want of all the privilege to which he had claim, all whilst professing to care for her—it was unfathomably callous. Her breath came faster as she stormed along the path, recalling the contempt, the pride, almost, with which he had admitted separating Bingley from Jane, and the venom with which he had renounced any regret for his dealings with Wickham.

Wickham! She was ashamed to think of the readiness with which she had laid these charges at *his* door. She perfectly remembered everything that passed in conversation between them, and she was struck anew by the significance of the omissions in his tale that had always troubled her. They were not, as she had supposed, prevarications regarding his own culpability, but Darcy's, which he was prohibited from discussing on pain of being ruined himself by the publication of his letter.

She came up short and put a palm to her forehead. *The letter! I have revealed that I know about it!* She wished rather than believed it would not provoke Darcy to punish Wickham by releasing it, but her estimation of his character was in such tatters she hardly knew what to expect of him. *How could I have been so wretchedly blind?* She slowed to a weary meander, unwilling to acknowledge the answer. Yet, for all her anger, there was still a terrible hollowness inside her that would not abate, and which she could not define: a feeling of disappointment—a feeling of loss. She supposed she was grieving the man she had believed Darcy to be. She did not think she would ever forgive him for making her love him.

Her stomach knotted when she caught a glimpse of a gentleman through the trees. He was moving in her direction, and, fearful of it being Darcy, Elizabeth retreated directly. But the person who advanced was now near enough to see her, and stepping forward with eagerness, pronounced her name. She had turned away, but on hearing herself called in a voice that proved it to be someone other than Darcy, she waited for him to catch up.

"Good morning, Cousin Elizabeth," Mr Collins wheezed as he huffed and puffed his way to her side. "I am just come from the village. I see you, too, are headed home. Let us walk together."

It was a better alternative to having only regrets for company, and she turned to walk with him.

"I flatter myself that you are enjoying your time with us," he said when he had caught his breath. "Mrs Collins and I keep a very comfortable home."

"You do indeed, sir."

He hummed his satisfaction through a tight-lipped grin. "You have seen, I suppose, how content Mrs Collins is with her new situation. Though we live humbly, our connexion with the de Bourgh family gives us claim to such superior society as must gratify any young lady. Mrs Collins is, I know, very pleased with the attention she receives from her ladyship, and the standing it affords her within the parish."

Elizabeth nodded. *This is meant for me,* she thought. *I am to repent for refusing him, and Charlotte's contentment is to be my punishment.* Rather than allowing it to injure her, she embraced the opportunity to distract herself and indulged Mr Collins all the way home with talk of his fine choice of wife and her eminently sensible choice of situation. The slight improvement in her spirits this afforded was quashed instantly when Maria greeted them at the front door with the news that they had narrowly missed Colonel Fitzwilliam and Mr Darcy.

"They called to take their leave," she told them excitedly. "They are returning to London today, which cannot have pleased Lady Catherine, for she said yesterday that they meant to stay for another week. Mr Darcy stayed for only a few minutes, but Colonel Fitzwilliam sat with us for at least an hour hoping for you to return. He almost resolved to walk after you until you could be found."

The hollowness in Elizabeth's chest expanded a little more, vexing her no end. She ought to be pleased never to see Darcy again and despised the wretchedness the news of his departure produced.

"Would that you had come to find *me*!" cried Mr Collins. "Whatever will they think of my not having been here to say good-bye!"

"They will think you are hard-working and worthy of the position bestowed upon you by their aunt," Charlotte replied, but it was no good. Mr Collins snatched his hat back from the maid and marched out of the door. Elizabeth would not have been surprised had he chased Darcy's carriage all the way to London if it meant he could pay his respects, but in the end, he got no farther than Rosings. This they all learnt when he returned a short time later to inform them that Lady Catherine was most put out by her nephews' sudden departure and had insisted they join her for dinner to make up for the deprivation.

"THEY WOULD NOT HAVE LEFT SO SUDDENLY IN THE NORMAL course of things, but Darcy had urgent business in London. And he was most displeased by it, too, I could tell, for he was very dull—very dull indeed—when it came time to leave. Fitzwilliam was in better spirits, though still sorry to go. I have told them both to return as soon as may be, for there is no purpose depriving themselves if they are happiest here."

Elizabeth watched Lady Catherine from her seat in the corner of the sofa and wondered whether she had any idea of the imbroglio in which Darcy was involved. Throughout dinner she had been attempting to decide, without any success. She transferred her observations to Miss de Bourgh, cocooned beneath a profusion of blankets next to the fire, and wondered how much *she* knew of her cousin's history. The woman said so very little it was difficult to guess what her opinion of anything might be, but Elizabeth knew she thought well of Darcy, since she had complimented him on his frankness. *Has he been frank with you about this?* Perhaps that was why they had never married: because she would not have him either. *Or was it that he wished to spare you the indignity he had no scruple in asking me to bear?*

And that it would have been the gravest of indignities was irrefutable. For the past five or more years, Darcy had accompanied Miss Bingley up and down the country, setting her up in this establishment or that, to all intents and purposes treating her as though she were his mistress. What did he mean to do with her after he married—continue as before?

Would he have his wife be the next Georgiana Cavendish, bringing up children that were not her own and sharing her home with his lovers? *And he claimed to admire me!* It was difficult for Elizabeth to credit any declaration of regard from a man who meant to subject her to perpetual shame and mortification.

"You are excessively dull this evening, Miss Bennet," said Lady Catherine. "Are you sickening for something?"

"I have a slight headache, madam, nothing more."

"That is the second headache in as many days. Are you eating properly?"

"I believe so."

"Good. One of my tenants has been struck down with an affliction that the apothecary believes has been brought on by too unvaried a diet, and I assure you it was apathy and not a want of means that brought it on. A dislike of vegetables is no excuse to neglect oneself, and now he is unable to work his farm. I might have been forced to evict him had not Darcy visited him this week and made a better arrangement. That is very like my nephew. He always insists on doing the best he can for people."

A satirical huff of laughter was past her lips before Elizabeth knew it was coming. She covered it quickly with a cough, but was convinced by this that Lady Catherine, for all her resolve to be an authority on everyone's business, did not know that her precious nephew had begot an illegitimate child on a woman whom he would not deign to marry. Certainly, her ladyship could not know in what contempt Darcy held her hopes for his marrying her daughter. "Mr Darcy is all goodness," she said, unable to produce a smile.

Lady Catherine narrowed her eyes slightly, though whether it was because she detected Elizabeth's sarcasm or was concerned by her cough was unclear. Elizabeth could think of nothing to say and could not have said it anyway for she was fast losing an already tenuous grip on her composure. The silence stretched long until Mr Collins launched into the breach with a monologue of such sycophantic excess that even Lady Catherine appeared slightly nauseated by it. The energy with which he apologised for Elizabeth's incivility was equal only to that with which he expressed his displeasure in the carriage on the way home. She bore it with as much humility as she could muster for Charlotte's sake but excused herself to bed as soon as they arrived home. There she comforted herself by re-reading the latest letter from her uncle, confirming that he would send his man to meet Maria and her at Bromley on Saturday. Hunsford had lost all its charm and it was consolation to know that one week would see her returned to friendlier faces—Jane's chief among them.

24

Stubborn Hearts

Elizabeth crouched to look at the snail crawling over the small, chubby hand of the rather dirty five-year old before her. "That is a very handsome snail. Does he have a name?"

"'Tis a girl, and her name is Princess Phoebe."

"Oh well, in that case..." She curtseyed, drawing a giggle from her young cousin, who then ran back to join her siblings.

Elizabeth watched her go, savouring the joy of being returned to her family. Never in her life had she suffered such a distressing barrage of feelings as she had endured these past weeks. Outrage and affront had slowly given way to simmering indignation, but she had been unable to overcome anything beyond that, for her heart simply refused to relinquish its interest in the affair. Had she felt less, she could have laughed herself out of any concern for Darcy's sordid past some time ago. As it was, disillusionment and heartache had taken up permanent residence beneath her breastbone, flaring up constantly to tinge all her other emotions with sadness.

She felt it now, as she watched Emily pick the snail off her hand and try to attach it to her youngest brother's face, and she pressed a hand to her chest to try to quash the unpleasant sensation. She ought to have called out for her cousin to desist, but she was momentarily paralysed by a sudden influx of unbidden and overwhelming reminiscences of Anna. She, too, was a sweet, spirited little thing, with deeply endearing innocence and a streak of adventurousness of which Elizabeth heartily approved. *Could I have loved her, as Darcy wished me to?* If she had proved to be half as delightful as any of her cousins then, regardless of her feelings for either parent, it would have been the work of a moment to love her completely.

"What was that my little terror had in her hand?" Mrs Gardiner enquired, catching up from the path behind with her eldest daughter Eleanor in tow.

"A snail."

Eleanor, who at the grand age of eight considered herself vastly superior in manners and worldliness to her sister and brothers, turned up her nose. "Emily is a disgusting creature, Mother. Cannot you make her be more ladylike?"

"I am trying, dear."

With a distinctly unladylike huff, Eleanor declared that she could not wait until Emily went to school and stomped away to berate her wayward sister.

"School?" Elizabeth asked her aunt dubiously.

"An idle threat that your uncle trots out whenever any of them misbehaves. And of course, Emily misbehaves thrice as often as any of the others, thus Eleanor is convinced she will be sent off as soon as she comes of age."

"Is there any truth in the threat?"

Mrs Gardiner laughed. "Not a bean! Your uncle is helplessly besotted with them all. He would never send them away. It is not a fashion for which either of us has ever much cared. If a family has the means to employ a governess, what need is there for beloved children to be sent away to school?" After a little while, she added, "I meant no comparison to you or your sisters. I hope I have not offended you."

Elizabeth looked up, frowning slightly until she comprehended her aunt's meaning. "No, not at all. We did well enough without a governess. Father ensured we had all the masters that were necessary." It was not for that reason Mrs Gardiner's remark had sent her off into her own thoughts and made her forget to reply. Rather, she had been contemplating how easy, nay, how common it would have been for Darcy to send Anna away. Not to school—not at such a young age—but to give her up entirely, to an orphanage or, as Wickham had once said, to another family. That he had chosen to keep her nearby, to provide for her, to oversee her upbringing, and to visit her regularly, showed an affection for her that she could not deny was very pleasing. Pleasing, yet unreconcilable with his disinclination to marry her mother and claim her as his own.

"You have been uncommonly distracted since you arrived, Lizzy," said Mrs Gardiner. "I hope nothing happened in Kent to upset you."

"No, nothing happened." Elizabeth looked away; she detested lying to her aunt.

"I was worried Mr Collins might have said something about your refusing to marry him."

"He did, but I did not hold it against him. He only mentioned it eight or nine times."

"There is nothing in particular that has made you so untalkative then?"

"Other than having squeezed a week's worth of visits and entertainments into the two days since I arrived in London?" she enquired with forced levity. "No, nothing." Unless one counted relentless rushes of sentiment whenever something reminded her of walking with Darcy; constant jags of pain every time she recalled that Anna was his; even occasional bouts of panic whenever she thought of her mother's response should she discover her daughter had turned down a second offer of marriage—and this one from one of the most eligible gentlemen in the country.

Her aunt grinned and bent to pick up a carved wooden soldier that one of her boys had dropped on the ground behind him. "It has been a bit of a blur has it not? Jane and I thought you might like a bit of London life after so long in leafy Kent. We might have got a little carried away with all our plans. I can cancel dinner later if you would rather."

"Indeed, I would not rather. I only meant to account for my not having said much." They were obliged to stop talking when an acquaintance of Mrs Gardiner's walked by and paused to say good morning. After she was gone, Elizabeth jumped at the chance to speak of something else. "And what of Jane? I have been gone six weeks, yet her spirits do not seem to have improved at all."

"Aye, she is still very downcast. I confess, I thought she would recover sooner from it, for she did not seem to be very much in love. But she will get the better of it eventually, Lizzy. Hearts do not remain broken forever."

Elizabeth felt unequal to responding, and with a perfunctory smile, knelt down with her cousins, preferring the simple occupation of digging in the mud to thinking about any of the weightier matters that plagued her.

DINNER WAS NOT CANCELLED, AND A PLEASANT TIME WAS had by all—or so Elizabeth thought. Yet when the carriage returned them to Gracechurch Street at gone midnight, Jane took her by the elbow, led her directly upstairs to sit on the end of her bed and began in a way that immediately let it be known the evening had not been quite such a success. "I know it is late, Lizzy, but I cannot go another moment seeing you like this without knowing what the matter is."

"Seeing me like what?"

"You know what! You barely spoke a word this evening, and I believe you only laughed twice."

"I cannot be blamed if none of Mrs Campbell's friends is particularly witty."

"Be serious, Lizzy. You have not been yourself since you returned from Kent."

"You have not been yourself since last autumn. Let us talk about that if we are to discuss anything."

"We both know what is wrong with me, I am old news. I would know what has made *you* so wretched that you were not even diverted when Mr Peters complimented Miss Rushdon on the shape of her elbows."

Elizabeth smirked. "Did he?"

"I knew you missed that. Now you will tell me what is on your mind, or I shall go and tell my uncle you let him win at cards this evening."

"You would not! You are too good."

"Desperate times call for desperate measures, Lizzy Bennet. I am not teasing!" Jane walked to the door, and with a grip on the handle, raised a warning eyebrow.

"Oh for heaven's sake, I shall tell you. I would have told you anyway when I had the chance, but I could scarcely have announced at Mrs Campbell's dinner table that Mr Darcy proposed to me." Elizabeth began the sentence in jest, diverted by her sister's tactics. She ended it with a crack in her voice and her heart thundering. Jane stared at her. She stared at Jane and let out a pathetic little laugh. "I said no. Because I could not forgive him for not marrying Miss Bingley." The turn of Jane's countenance forced more brittle laughter from Elizabeth's lips. "Anna is *his* daughter, Jane."

"What?" uttered Jane with her next exhalation.

Elizabeth hurriedly, though not very fluently, relayed all that had transpired in Kent, and groaned when her sister declared she could not believe it. "Of course you cannot, Jane. Nobody as good as you could conceive of anyone behaving so abominably, but it is true. He admitted it to me himself, and his cousin confirmed it. Indeed, Colonel Fitzwilliam spoke more than once of his pride in what Mr Darcy has done to look after the Bingleys."

"Well, it does appear that he has done a great deal to provide for them. If Mr Wickham is to be believed, then it was Mr Darcy who put them up at Netherfield Park."

"Aye, but he could have put them up at Pemberley, as his wife and family. He has not acted to provide for them. Everything he has done has been done to protect himself from having to marry Miss Bingley."

"Perhaps he felt they were not well suited for marriage."

Elizabeth laughed her first genuine laugh of the evening. "And that, I know, is as close as you will ever come to insulting her. But that is not the point, is it? If Mr Darcy did not wish to marry her, he ought not to have got her into trouble. It is not right that he should be able to walk away and live his life as he chooses, while she is left ruined and disgraced."

"But she is neither of those things, Lizzy, because he has made sure to prevent it. We must allow that he has done everything *but* marry her in his attempt to atone for his actions."

Elizabeth shook her head. "Dear Jane, you are too kind, if such a thing is possible. How can you defend him, knowing he took Mr Bingley away from you? I certainly cannot forgive him for it."

Jane tilted her head and regarded Elizabeth, a deep sigh forewarning that she must be weighing her words carefully. "I have heard your account of what he said about that, but I have not understood it in the same way as you. He advised Mr

Bingley to leave because he did not perceive that I was in love with him, and he was concerned about the family's reputation. The latter point will always be a consideration for a gentleman of his consequence, regardless of his particular circumstances. He is not alone in pursuing exemplary connexions. On the former point, Mr Bingley could have refused to go."

"But he could not!" Elizabeth objected. "Mr Darcy was paying for his house, keeping his sister and niece safe, protecting his reputation. Mr Bingley is entirely beholden to him."

"Do you truly believe Mr Darcy would have withdrawn his protection if Mr Bingley had refused to leave? Remember the argument you relayed to me at Netherfield, in which one accused the other of being too ready to yield to the persuasion of his friends. It is far more likely that Mr Bingley simply did not admire me as well as I hoped and left because his friend suggested it, than that his friend coerced him with threats into leaving."

Elizabeth's heart strained to believe Jane's defence of Darcy—as it had been straining to believe his innocence since she first learnt the truth. Yet her head forced her to say, "Mr Darcy is perfectly capable of threatening somebody into compliance. Have you forgotten the letter he holds over Mr Wickham?"

Jane twisted her mouth into a rueful acknowledgement that she could not defend him there, but then she shook her head. "It seems so unlikely to me, though. He always seemed so respectable. Certainly not the sort of man who was capable of behaving in such a disgraceful manner as this. There must be some information, some explanation for his actions of which we are ignorant, for I cannot believe this of him. I know you did not like him, Lizzy, but I never thought him as disagreeable as you seemed to."

Elizabeth's throat constricted with emotion. She looked helplessly at Jane, trying valiantly not to allow the tears that burned her eyes and nose to overwhelm her, for Darcy did not deserve them.

Jane's eyes widened. "*Did* you like him?"

Elizabeth shrugged with one shoulder and laughed awkwardly. "I had stopped despising him."

"Lizzy, do you love him?"

"I do not know!" she cried, exasperated with herself. "I thought I was utterly indifferent to him, but he was altered in Kent. More amiable, more talkative, more attentive. There was perhaps a day or two where I began to think I *could* love him before all this came to light and he proposed so abominably, and then I was sure I hated him. But I miss him, Jane. I find myself wondering what his opinion of things would be, and whether he would smile or frown at them. I miss the way he talks about things, as though everything in the world is complex and worthy of deep reflection. I miss the way he used to look at me. It is absurd!"

Jane reached to squeeze her hand. "It is not absurd, Lizzy. We cannot help with whom we fall in love."

Elizabeth clung to Jane's steadying grip and took a deep breath. In spite of all the reasons she had to despise him, regardless of all her efforts to forget him, she could not stop her heart tripping over itself each time Darcy's name was mentioned. She let out her breath with a laugh. "I never could bear to be long outdone by you. And you made heartache look so elegant."

"Oh, Lizzy. You will laugh yourself out of this soon enough, but do not punish yourself for having loved him. Nobody is all bad, and that *you* saw the parts of Mr Darcy that were worthy of admiration does not surprise me at all, even if it does you." She put her arms out and Elizabeth gratefully leant against her, savouring the comfort of her sister's embrace. By mutual agreement they talked no more of gentlemen or broken hearts after that, but of all the things they had to look forward to that would lift their spirits. When Elizabeth left to go to her own bed, she was filled with anticipation for her northern tour with Mr and Mrs Gardiner, and if thoughts of Darcy entered her head at all, it was only after she fell asleep.

25

A Flicker of Clemency

Elizabeth arrived back at Longbourn with mixed feelings. The familiarity of home gave the sort of comfort few other places could. Yet the return to all that life had been a year ago, before either Netherfield Park or Persimmon Cottage were let, left a dull echo where possibility had so briefly, yet so brightly flared. Books no longer fired her imagination; the pianoforte no longer distracted her; embroidery held even less appeal than it had before, which she would never have previously thought possible. Even her pleasure in the favourite paths of her youth was diminished by the attendant sense of solitude that had, until two months ago, been one of the great joys of her life but which now only served to remind her of other walks in better company.

Still she ventured out, though, for she was not made for inactivity. One morning, at the end of her first week back in Hertfordshire, the sun was hot, giving a true sense of summer's imminent arrival, and she walked farther than she meant to, distracted by the warmth on her face. She began, more by habit than design, to gather wildflowers as she went, paying little attention to the blooms until she picked a vivid red one and was assailed with a recollection that stopped her in her tracks: Mrs O'Neill's daughter handing her a poppy; Darcy regarding her in a way that had made her breathless then, and did so again now. Had he been forming his resolution to propose, supposing that her averred fondness of children would enable her to overlook the circumstances of Anna's birth? She felt he probably had been, and she despised his presumption as vehemently as she despaired of the palpable ache even the memory of that look aroused in her heart. She almost threw her flowers to the ground but then resolved otherwise, too stubborn to permit him to steal that happiness also. She clutched them tighter and walked on.

She paid no attention to her direction and allowed her feet to take her along whichever lanes and across whatever fields they chose. She received a jolt when the familiar chimneys of Netherfield crept high enough above the horizon to gain her notice, and she immediately altered her path away from the house. At the far side of the formal shrubbery, she came upon a narrow but well-trodden track through the trees on the outskirts of the park. Curious as to what had made the trail, she followed it, and could have kicked herself when she eventually came upon a little cottage, sitting at the edge of the woods, looking out over the lea towards Hoxley House. *Less a question of what made the path than of whom, then,* she thought wryly, picking her way through the undergrowth towards the house, just as Miss Bingley must have done.

She almost overlooked the stump at the very edge of the treeline but saw at the last moment the bunch of feathers, teasels, and old man's beard carefully wedged into a nook of the rotten trunk. She bent to pick it up and turned it over in her hands, hoping Anna had not noticed it was still there before Darcy whisked her away. On a whim, she replaced the dried, withered bouquet with her freshly gathered posy. "Just in case the fairies come looking for you, little one."

She thought better of going too close to the cottage and took a wide berth down the slope into the open field. Then she traipsed through the long grass across the lea until she reached the lane on the far side of the valley where she came upon Mrs Hanrahan leaning over her front gate.

"Who is that?" the elderly lady snapped, squinting against the sun.

"Miss Elizabeth Bennet," she replied. "From Longbourn."

"Longbourn! What are you doing this far from home, girl? Are you lost?"

"No, ma'am. I have just been walking."

"Alone? You ought not to go so far unaccompanied. Heaven knows what might befall you."

Elizabeth could not but smile at being scolded for precisely the same offence as that for which she had chided five-year old Anna. "I meant not to come this far. I took a wrong turn and ended up at Persimmon Cottage."

Mrs Hanrahan nodded sagely. "Aye, I saw you up there. I thought you might be another visitor from Netherfield until you wandered down this way. Fortunately for you, the tenants for whom *those* visitors were always after left many months ago."

Elizabeth's smile faded as she regarded Mrs Hanrahan—the tiresome gossip from Hoxley House whose new neighbours were close enough to be seen from her windows, whose regular caller while she was bedridden with a cold last autumn had been Mr Fellowes, from whom Mr Collins received the report that Miss Bingley regularly visited a child at Persimmon Cottage, which he then repeated indiscriminately, forcing the family to leave Hertfordshire, abandoning Jane, uprooting Anna, and leaving a pain behind Elizabeth's ribs that not even the most determined good sense could alleviate.

"Let us hope they have found somewhere more welcoming to live," she said with barely restrained vexation.

"I cannot imagine they will have. Nobody in their right mind would welcome a woman such as Miss Bingley into their neighbourhood."

Elizabeth would not have liked to examine whether it was for Darcy's sake or Anna's, Jane's or her own, but she could not bear to hear Mrs Hanrahan speak so blithely, as though her words had not already been ruinous to so many people, and so she contradicted her. "I know not what you have heard, Mrs Hanrahan, but the child at the cottage was not Miss Bingley's."

There was no mistaking the look she received in response: Mrs Hanrahan was clearly of the opinion that Elizabeth was a fool. "Perhaps," she said in a tone that matched her expression, "but that was not my meaning. I was not thinking of the child, but the woman, who is as unpleasant as any I ever met." She shuffled a few steps closer to Elizabeth and squinted up at her intently. "Plenty of people dislike me, Miss Bennet. They dislike me because I am old, and I talk too much. But they all suffer my company. Even your mother. Miss Bingley could not even bring herself to smile at me. She turned down my invitation to tea. She refused to sit next to me at church and told her sister loudly enough for all to hear that she thought me disagreeable, though she never talked to me long enough to form such an opinion. She ingratiated herself well enough with the rest of the neighbourhood, but she slighted me because there was no advantage to her in the acquaintance. No, I am not sorry to see her gone. Not sorry at all."

"It is a shame she was unkind to you," Elizabeth replied, less willing to defend Miss Bingley against these charges, but feeling obliged, nevertheless. "Though perhaps circumstances have shaped her character in regrettable ways."

"Poppycock. The world abounds with circumstances—nobody else is using theirs as an excuse to be mean. No, I should imagine Miss Bingley was a vainglorious self-seeker long before she fell afoul of the *circumstance* to which we both know you are alluding." Mrs Hanrahan turned around to go back indoors, but paused to say over her shoulder, with a lightness incongruous to the entire conversation, "Pray give my regards to your mother. Tell her I shall call again soon."

Elizabeth waved good-bye and continued on her way. Deep in thought, it took an icy splash on her neck for her to notice it had begun to rain, whereupon she dashed to take cover under the nearest tree. From there, she stared out across the lea to where she knew Netherfield sat beyond the trees and recalled Miss Bingley's sneering countenance the morning all the Bennet ladies had first called there. From the first moment of their acquaintance, the woman had been snide and jealous towards *her*, in whom she had perhaps recognised a rival for Darcy's affections, yet sycophantic and false towards Jane, from whose friendship she must have believed she would benefit—until that was no longer the case, whereupon she had dropped the acquaintance like a hot stone. Mrs Hanrahan was not wrong; Miss Bingley truly was a thoroughly unpleasant woman.

One to whom Jane thought it possible Darcy merely believed he was ill suited. It was with an odd feeling of warmth that Elizabeth recalled this. She shook her head, berating herself for seeking excuses for him, but the feeling grew more insistent as it occurred to her that Darcy's resistance to the alliance might not proceed from conceit, as she had thought. Mayhap he simply could not bring himself to marry a woman as cunning and unfeeling as Miss Bingley—and that perhaps his aversion was justified.

The warmth overspilled into a flood of relief as she comprehended that, despite how she had tortured herself with the idea of it, there really was no possibility that Darcy still harboured feelings for Miss Bingley. He had been impervious to her flattery and steely cold in his manner towards her while they were at Netherfield, which could only have been to avoid giving any hint of residual partiality. The recognition that they were no longer lovers lightened Elizabeth's heart as nothing else had in weeks; though it changed none of the facts, it greatly lessened the affront of his proposal. The rain passed, but the flicker of clemency these thoughts provoked did not, and it staved off the chill of her dampened clothes as she hastened home.

One of Mrs Bennet's favourite new refrains was the hope that Netherfield, being still unoccupied, might yet tempt the Bingleys back to Hertfordshire. This oft-repeated wish served chiefly to sooth her own nerves, though Elizabeth was sure she meant it to comfort Jane as well, in a misguided sort of way. Had her mother known what pain she was causing both her eldest daughters by the frequent mention of it, she might have refrained. Alas, she did not know.

"The season is nearly over," she said one afternoon during a visit to Mrs Goulding. "It is very unlikely that Mr Bingley will summer in Town. I should not be surprised if we heard in the next week or two that Netherfield is to open again."

"Mama, the season no longer ends in June," said Kitty with a snigger. "Lydia thinks their company will have the run of the beach until the end of July at least before everybody comes down from London."

Mrs Bennet was not to be deterred. "Visiting the seaside has not the same appeal for a gentleman as sport. Mr Bingley may prefer to come home to shoot some birds."

"Not in June, he won't," said one of Mrs Goulding's sons, also sniggering. His mother shushed him, but Mrs Bennet only laughed.

"Later on, then. What difference does a few weeks make?

I am assured he will return, for he told me that he considered himself quite fixed at Netherfield."

"He also told you that if he should resolve to quit it, he should be off in five minutes, which proved to be a very truthful account of his own precipitance," Elizabeth said impatiently. "They will not be returning, Mama."

"Speaking of the seaside," Mrs Goulding said in a transparent attempt to change the subject, "I heard from Mrs Forster that all the officers' wives have been sea-bathing in Brighton."

Elizabeth worried her mother might take offence at being quieted, but Mrs Bennet was unperturbed and seized upon Mrs Goulding's remark, answering as though it had been intended for her.

"Oh yes, Lydia wrote of it, too. What a fine time it sounds as though they all had!"

Mrs Goulding pursed her lips, and Mrs Long frowned as she said, "I thought Mrs Forster said it was only the officers' wives. Can Miss Lydia really have been included?"

Mrs Bennet had just stuffed a biscuit into her mouth, but it did not prevent her from answering, with much supplementary gesturing and head shaking. "Lydia will not tolerate being left out of any fun. If there was sea-bathing to be done, she will have done it."

Elizabeth did not miss the several disparaging looks scattered about the room.

Kitty whined loudly. "It is not fair! I should have loved to go sea-bathing. Why should Lydia be allowed to go and not me?"

"Because you are not Mrs Forster's particular friend," Mrs Bennet replied.

"And Lydia was evidently not allowed, in any case," said Mary. "Mrs Goulding clearly said only the married ladies joined in the activity."

"Oh, maybe she did not go," Mrs Bennet said, waving the matter away with a waft of her hand. "But she did go to a ball last week—and was asked to dance by forty officers!"

Elizabeth abstained from rolling her eyes, and as a consequence, happened to see Mrs Robinson roll hers.

"Did Mrs Forster dance with many officers do you know?" Mrs Bennet asked Mrs Goulding.

"She did not say," that lady replied. "But then, it was her ball, and she was most likely too busy finding partners for all the *un*married ladies. I am glad she paid so much attention to your daughter. Perhaps she shares your desire to see her settled. And, with so many officers at her disposal and such an inclination for fun, it cannot be long before Miss Lydia finds herself attached to one."

Somebody cleared their throat in the way people do when they are concealing a laugh. Elizabeth stared into her teacup, mortified. She had not consciously started to pay more attention to other people's reaction to her family's behaviour, though she did not doubt what had induced her to begin, and now that she had, she was exceedingly uncomfortable with what she saw. Neither her sisters' complaining, nor her mother's boasts had ever troubled her so deeply before; she had viewed them with indulgent forbearance and assumed all their friends did likewise. Yet apparently, they did not. From Mrs Goulding's veiled slight to Mrs Robinson's ill-concealed vexation, it seemed all their neighbours were thoroughly unimpressed. And if the ordinary people of Meryton were dismayed, Elizabeth could only imagine what the opinion of fashionable society would be.

Having acknowledged that much, Elizabeth could not deny that in his endeavour to protect so many parties—even if that included himself—Darcy could scarcely be blamed for wishing to avoid a connexion with a family so conspicuously indecorous as hers.

"Are you well, Lizzy?"

Elizabeth looked up and was heartened to see that her mother had moved to the neighbouring seat and was squinting at her dubiously. "Aye, Mama. Thank you."

Mrs Bennet continued to peer at her, searching every inch of her countenance for signs of fever, as she always did whenever one of her girls did not seem themselves. It made Elizabeth smile. "I am not ill. I was just thinking about Lydia and hoping she was behaving herself."

Her mother scoffed loudly. "Lydia is perfectly well. Indeed, she is surrounded by a full company of soldiers. What danger could possibly befall her?"

Elizabeth dared not look at anybody for several minutes afterwards and instead resumed her inspection of the contents of her teacup, reflecting that Darcy was not alone in having relations, however dear, of whom it was impossible not to be ashamed.

26

A Brush with Ruin

LONGBOURN SOON RETURNED TO WHAT ELIZABETH HAD previously considered an idyllic way of life, and she was dissatisfied with every moment. No sweet little girls accosted her on her walks, pleading for help to catch figments of their childish imaginations. Nobody challenged her prepossessions with intelligent conversation or ruinous secrets. Darcy was gone, and she could neither cease blaming him nor cease missing him, and her turmoil merged with the long days and oppressive summer heat to stretch the weeks of June into an unending monotony of days.

She soon wished she had better appreciated the quietude, for July arrived, and with it, a most unwelcome dose of excitement. At twelve o'clock on an otherwise unremarkable night, there came an unholy commotion at Longbourn's front door. All the family and every servant were woken from their slumber by the arrival of an express from Colonel Forster in Brighton.

"What does it say?" cried Mrs Bennet, her countenance pallid with shock. "Oh, what has happened to my poor Lydia?"

Mr Bennet held up a hand to stay her queries while he read the letter. Elizabeth watched him anxiously as his countenance changed from being taut with worry to diffused with relief and then stiffened again with anger. "Lydia is well enough," he said brusquely. "Let us go into the parlour. Jane, Lizzy, help your mother. Hill, some coffee please." The other servants were dismissed, and the family filed into the parlour to hear Mr Bennet's explanation. He leant against the mantlepiece, rereading the letter while Mary lit more candles. He briefly ran a hand over his face before divulging, with no ceremony but a good deal of displeasure, that Lydia had attempted to elope. He got no further; Kitty gasped, Mrs Bennet erupted into hysterics, Mary discharged a feverish stream of moralising, and Jane was distracted attempting to calm all three.

Elizabeth met her father's eyes. "With whom, sir?"

"Mr Wickham."

She took a very deep breath and let it out slowly. Darcy had warned her of this! Indeed, Wickham had all but said the same of himself, but she had dismissed it because he was charming, and then forgotten it entirely upon learning of Darcy's past misdeeds—but why? Why ought one man's past stain his reputation forever while another's be forgiven? *Because you love one, and not the other, and it hurt you more that Darcy was imperfect. Foolish, foolish girl!*

"What has happened to her, Father?" Jane enquired.

"Nothing has happened to her. It appears the elopement was foiled before they left Brighton. Your sister has escaped completely unscathed."

"Well, that is good," Mrs Bennet said, sounding hopeful. "There is no harm done in that case."

"No harm done?" her husband shouted. "Are you out of your senses, Mrs Bennet? Half the militia are encamped at

Brighton. How long do you think it will remain a secret that your daughter is game for this sort of nonsense?"

"Papa," Elizabeth said quietly, glancing expressively at her younger sisters.

Mr Bennet nodded and continued more composedly, though she could easily discern that he was no less angry. "Colonel Forster writes to say that he is loath to send her home with another of his officers as an escort, for obvious reasons, and requests that I go to Brighton to collect her myself before word of her brush with ruin gets out into the camp."

"When will you leave?" Jane asked.

"On the morrow. There is no point starting early, for I shall have to impose on my brother Gardiner tomorrow night anyway, but that is just as well. Two good nights' sleep ought to give me enough time to calm down before I must set eyes on the reckless girl."

"Pray do not be hard on her!" begged Mrs Bennet. "She has already had her heart broken. Do not distress her anymore."

"How have you come to the conclusion that her heart has been broken, madam?"

"Why, because the elopement was prevented. She would hardly have thrown her lot in with Mr Wickham if she were not in love with him, would she? Oh, my dear, sweet child, what she must have been through!"

Mr Bennet's expression darkened to a shade Elizabeth had rarely perceived. "I shall come with you," she said.

Her father began to object until Jane added her voice to the idea. "Do take Lizzy, Papa. She has ever been the best at talking sense into Lydia. I can look after things here." A glance at her mother confirmed what things might require that an eye be kept on them. Mr Bennet exhaled and nodded once in reluctant concession.

"Cannot I come?" moaned Kitty. "I should dearly love to see the sea, and *I* should not run away with any of the soldiers."

Mr Bennet's response to this evidently did not align with Kitty's hopes, and tears and further remonstrations ensued that persisted until everybody was persuaded to return to their beds to get what sleep they could before they must begin to unpick Lydia's mess the next day.

The two travellers arrived at Gracechurch Street an hour before dinner, and Mr and Mrs Gardiner, after being apprised of the reason for the unannounced visit, were good enough not to require Mr Bennet to be very social. He ate little, spoke less, and went to bed early. Elizabeth stayed up a little later talking to her aunt and uncle, although she was unable to assuage their curiosity and alarm much more than her father had managed to, for Colonel Forster had been short on details in his letter.

She also made no mention of Wickham's past behaviour, for she realised that, in truth, she knew very little about it—only that both he and Darcy considered it discreditable. Rather than dwell on the vanity that had allowed her to be charmed into overlooking such a glaring omission in his history, she lamented her sister's flirtatious behaviour. Mr and Mrs Gardiner agreed and went further still, bemoaning the leniency with which Lydia had been brought up that had resulted in her acting thus. Elizabeth listened in shame, thinking of how poorly she had received the same observation from Darcy, for though he had phrased it very ill, he had not been wrong in his censure.

In the morning, Elizabeth was given yet another reason to be vexed with the would-be elopers. She could tell by the expressions on the faces of her relations when she joined them at the breakfast table that she was about to receive disagreeable news.

"Your aunt and I have been talking, Lizzy," Mr Gardiner began. "There are but a few weeks until we depart on our tour of the north. There is no way of knowing how long you and your father will be in Brighton, or what state Lydia will be in when she is brought home. We cannot justify taking you away from Longbourn at such a delicate time."

Elizabeth's heart sank. "I understand. Perhaps I might be able to join you on another trip in the future."

"You mistake us, Lizzy," said her aunt. "We are not proposing to go without you. That would be the cruellest thing. No, we propose delaying our departure until things are more settled at Longbourn. It would mean we would have to give up the Lakes, for your uncle must be in London again by mid-August and that would leave too short a period to see as much as we had planned. We would have to content ourselves with a more contracted tour and go no farther than Derbyshire."

Elizabeth sat very still, determined nobody should perceive that her heart had begun to race, but it was impossible to hear that word without thinking of Pemberley and its owner. She schooled herself to composure, reasoning that in such a large county, an encounter with one individual in particular must be highly unlikely.

"What say you to the idea, Lizzy? You are a sensible girl. I know you will see the benefit to delaying."

"Indeed, I do," she replied. "And you are very good to suggest it, though I am heartily sorry that Lydia's selfishness has curtailed plans that we have anticipated for so long and that you have gone to such lengths to arrange."

"Worse things happen at sea, my dear," said Mr Gardiner. "Let us be thankful that Lydia was not successful in her design to run away, else our plans might have been scuppered entirely."

"And Derbyshire has plenty to occupy us," added his wife. "For a start, we can visit Lambton, where I used to live."

They then spent some time talking of the acquaintances Mrs Gardiner might renew in the area, and all the places they could now visit: Matlock, Chatsworth, Dovedale, and the Peak. When it came time for Elizabeth and her father to set out for Brighton, she felt far more sanguine about the amended plan, but for two aspects: she could not forgive Lydia for acting so selfishly, and she could not reconcile her disinclination to ever see Darcy again with the fluttering of hope she felt at the prospect of encountering him on her travels.

After an exceedingly tiring day of travel, they arrived at Colonel Forster's establishment and were shown to a parlour at the rear of the house where they were greeted by the man himself.

"Mr Bennet, I thank you for coming so promptly. And Miss Bennet—this is a surprise. You are very welcome, too. Miss Lydia is upstairs with Mrs Forster, packing her trunks. Would you like to be shown to her?"

Elizabeth pursed her lips. She had not come all this way to watch Lydia fold her linens. She would much rather hear Colonel Forster's account of events before she must hear Lydia's, for they were very unlikely to tally. "No thank you, sir," she told him.

Colonel Forster hesitated, looking at Mr Bennet in query. He received a nod and an impatient gesture to begin his explanation, thus he lowered himself onto the opposing sofa and leant forward with his hands folded together and his elbows on his knees. "I am heartily sorry this happened while

Miss Lydia was in my care, Mr Bennet. Had I any idea Mr Wickham was so little to be trusted, I should never have allowed him near my household."

"And I thank you for your intervention. This could have been a very different meeting had you not prevented their going."

"I should like to tell you it was I who discovered them, but I cannot. The first I knew of the elopement was when Mr Darcy delivered your daughter to my doorstep."

"What?"

Both gentlemen turned to look at Elizabeth in surprise.

"I beg your pardon," she said, feeling herself blush deeply. "But I…I did not know Mr Darcy was here."

"He is not," said Colonel Forster. "That is, he was, but he has left again. Allow me to explain."

"If you would," muttered Mr Bennet.

"As I understand it, Mr Darcy had written to Mr Wickham, informing him that he meant to hand over a sum of money from his late father's estate and announcing his intention of travelling to Brighton with that purpose this Tuesday just gone."

Elizabeth could scarcely contain herself. Darcy had come to give Wickham his inheritance.

"They met at the coaching inn on the turnpike road," the colonel continued. "We now know that thither went Miss Lydia also, for she and Mr Wickham planned to collect the money and go on their way directly."

Mr Bennet made a noise of disgust, part groan, part sigh. "They travelled there alone?"

Colonel Forster nodded.

"Had they taken a room?"

"No. Mr Darcy made sure to confirm that point with the landlord. They had only been there a quarter of an hour before he arrived himself and they remained in the taproom the whole time."

"That is something I suppose."

Elizabeth stared in horror at the floor. She had not realised quite how close Lydia had come to ruin. "How were they discovered?" she asked unhappily.

"By some exceedingly good fortune, madam. The two men met in a private dining room, and Miss Lydia waited for Mr Wickham in the taproom while they conducted their business. By rights, she ought never have been discovered, only Mr Darcy happened to see and recognise her as he passed the door. He questioned her being there unaccompanied, and she readily acknowledged the whole plan. She has since repeated the same to both Mrs Forster and me. It seems she saw no ill in the scheme at all."

"Oh Lydia," Elizabeth mumbled. "You poor, senseless girl."

"Mr Darcy then questioned Mr Wickham again, from whom, regrettably, he could discover no intention of marriage whatsoever."

Mr Bennet sucked in a breath through his teeth and shook his head.

"He was good enough to escort Miss Lydia back here before returning to London. Mr Wickham refused to return with them. He resigned his commission by letter and has not been seen or heard of since."

"And who knows of the affair?"

"No one but myself, my wife, and Mr Darcy. Those at the inn never learnt Miss Lydia's name. I have questioned Mr Wickham's friends among the officers and cannot discover that any of them had prior knowledge of his decision to leave—only of the considerable debts he left behind, amounting to more than a thousand pounds, which Mr Darcy has been good enough to settle."

"Is Mr Darcy to be trusted to keep this quiet?"

Elizabeth wished to tell him there were few people on whose secrecy she would have more confidently depended but that would have required her to explain Darcy's own concealments. Thus she remained quiet and allowed Colonel Forster to reply that he had no reason to suspect Darcy would reveal the incident to anyone after the personal trouble he had taken to ensure Miss Lydia's prompt return..

"I confess, his motivation there is a mystery to me," said Mr Bennet. "He never took any particular interest in our family before, other than to look down his nose at us."

"I believe he felt responsible for Mr Wickham's actions on account of the family connexion."

"Well, I shall have to write to him. He has unquestionably saved our family from ruin. Not quite so proud or unpleasant as we thought, eh, Lizzy?"

"No, indeed, Father," Elizabeth replied distractedly, mortified by the thought of Darcy reading such a letter. What vindication he must feel that her sister had succumbed to the same frailty as that for which she had so vehemently censured him!

They were interrupted by a servant, come at Mrs Forster's request to ask for Mr Bennet to go to Lydia, for she was refusing to come downstairs.

"Oh no," said he, "that is why I brought you, Lizzy. Off you go and see if you can talk any sense into the girl."

Lydia stuck her chin out in defiance when Elizabeth walked into the room, evidently ready for a fight. Her bravado crumbled when she saw that it was her sister, not her father, who was come, and she burst into tears. "Oh, Lizzy! I am ruined!"

Elizabeth rolled her eyes but nevertheless put her arms

around her youngest sister and shushed her gently. "You are not ruined, Lydia. That is the whole point."

"But I am not married!"

"Did you do anything only a married woman ought to do?"

"No—that is my meaning! I was to be Mrs George Wickham, and it has all been completely ruined thanks to that odious Mr Darcy."

"I think you have a skewed understanding of what it means to be ruined, but in any case, it is not Mr Darcy who has prevented you from being Mrs Wickham. The blame for that lies solely with *Mr* Wickham, who had absolutely no intention of marrying you."

Lydia pulled away and actually stamped her foot, which Elizabeth thought was doing it a tad too brown. "Yes, he did! We were going to Gretna Green!"

"Why?"

That blew the wind from her sails rather; she forgot her vexation and screwed her face up in confusion. "Pardon?"

"Why were you going all the way to Gretna Green? Why not marry from Longbourn?"

"Because Wickham said Papa would not give his permission."

"Again, why? If Mr Wickham really had come into money, and if he really did admire you, why would Papa have refused?"

Elizabeth wanted to hug Lydia again when she frowned at the floor in bewilderment, for she looked a decade younger than her fifteen years.

"I do not know," she answered at length.

"I do. He would not have—and Mama certainly would not have." She pushed some of Lydia's curls behind her ear with the back of her fingers. "Sweetheart, Mr Wickham did not take you to Longbourn to ask Papa for his permission because he did not want Papa to give it. He did not intend to marry you."

For the briefest moment, Elizabeth thought she had won through to her. Then indignation observably conquered whatever disappointment Lydia might have been about to express, and she puffed up in outrage. "You are only jealous, because he did not want to marry you."

Elizabeth sighed and glanced through the window at the darkening sky. "Lydia, we have to leave. We have less than an hour to get to the coaching inn at Lewes. Are you finished packing?"

Lydia snatched up her reticule from the bed and clutched it to her breast. "Since this is all I am ever likely to own, yes, I am ready."

"Do not be theatrical. That is not all you own."

"But I might have owned countless gowns and jewels if Mr Darcy had given Wickham the money he promised him. But he refused to give him a shilling, and so I have nothing."

"Mr Darcy has done you a very great service, Lydia. You would do well to remember that before you speak ill of him."

Lydia laughed a horrible, caustic laugh. "You see? You do not know everything, Lizzy. I do not suppose you know that Mr Darcy was supposed to give Wickham his money years ago, when his father died. And I doubt very much that you know he has a letter in his possession that could get Wickham hanged?"

"I did not know it could get him hanged, no. What did it contain that was so damning?"

"Oh, I do not know—and I do not care, for Wickham said it was all lies in any case."

"That is curious, since Mr Wickham wrote the letter himself."

Lydia was clearly put off her stride, but she soon recovered. "He was supposed to give it back! He wrote, promising to give the money and the silly letter *back*. I was there when Wickham received the letter, Lizzy, and he was so happy at the news he kissed me! We made so many plans!" She turned away and swiped at a bit of dust on the nightstand. Elizabeth heard in her voice that she was holding back tears when she continued, "Then that hateful man refused to keep his word and ruined everything. He would not give over the money, he would not give over the letter—all the things that would have freed Wickham to live as he pleased. He withheld them all."

"Mr Darcy held that letter only to prevent Mr Wickham revealing someone else's secret. In no way ought it to have precluded him from living his life as he chose. Unless what he chose was to ruin somebody else's reputation." She sincerely wished this epiphany had occurred to her some months earlier.

"Well he could not ruin mine now, even if I wished him to," Lydia replied heatedly, "for our family has been added to the list of those with whom he is forbidden from keeping company, or even mentioning, under pain of the letter being passed into the wrong hands!"

Elizabeth abruptly found herself fighting to repress a smile. The letter that had been so objectionable to her a few short months ago was now protecting her reputation as well, and it was suddenly far less offensive to her deplorably capricious sensibilities. "Lydia, cannot you see that Mr Darcy changed his mind about handing over the letter to protect you? If Mr Wickham was capable of persuading a girl of fifteen to leave all her friends, to elope, without any design to ever marry her, he would have no qualms in ruining her with the wrong word in the wrong ear. If Mr Darcy had not acted as he did, we could all have been disgraced."

"Oh, do not you start. That was all *he* kept telling me, too." She affected a jeering tone and parroted, "'Think of what you are doing to your sisters. Think of their reputations. I will not allow you to make a mockery of her integrity by ruining her anyway on the same charge.'" She dropped the silly voice and frowned. "What did he mean by that, do you think?"

"I have no idea," Elizabeth lied, even as surprise and pleasure warmed her cheeks. To call her rejection 'integrity' required that Darcy comprehend her reasons for refusing him—comprehend and not resent her for them. Her pleasure wilted almost immediately into shame. The conceited, selfish man she had accused him of being would have gloried in this proof of his every objection to her family, who, with behaviour such as this, would indeed have drawn unwelcome attention to his situation. Instead, the true gentleman she ought to have credited him with being had honoured her desire to protect her family and had gone out of his way to do the same.

"We must go," she told Lydia in a voice that brooked no argument—and permitted no quivering of regret to leak into it. "And do not tax Papa with any of your whining. He is not in a humour to hear you complain that you are the injured party." *And neither am I.*

Lydia complied with absolutely no grace, stomping down the stairs in sullen silence. The Forsters saw them to the door to bid them farewell, which Elizabeth fancied stemmed less from cordiality than from their impatience to have Lydia, and all trace of her near scandal, gone from their house. She turned, as she tied the ribbons of her bonnet, to thank Mrs Forster for her troubles, but stopped before the words were said, arrested by the funny little pirouette her heart performed when she caught sight of her sister. "Lydia, is that my old travelling cloak? The one I gave to you before I went to Kent?" *The one I was wearing when I was shown into the breakfast room at Netherfield.*

"Yes, it is," replied Lydia indignantly. "And I wish you had not. Just as I wish I had not borrowed your wretched bonnet, either. Had I worn something else, I might have been Mrs Wickham by now, but Mr Darcy saw me in these and thought I was you. Your stupid cloak ruined everything."

This remark undid all Elizabeth's efforts to avoid a scene between Mr Bennet and his youngest daughter, and he expressed his fury eloquently, if not very discreetly, as he ordered Lydia into the carriage. Elizabeth followed, a powerful feeling of tenderness settling in her breast at the thought that Darcy had recalled how she looked so many months ago; that he had still been desirous of talking to her despite their altercation in Kent; that beneath all the insults of his ill-considered address, had been a genuine declaration. *He loved me.*

27

The Road to Understanding

THE JOURNEY HOME FELT TO ELIZABETH AS THOUGH IT took four times as long as the journey there, for she passed the entire eight-and-forty hours mediating between her recalcitrant sister and her increasingly impatient father. Whenever she was not occupied with mollifying one or other of them, she was beset with thoughts of Darcy. What he had done for Lydia was generous, but what he had set out to do for Wickham was nothing short of astonishing. Never mind that Wickham had proved himself unworthy of the gesture, or that it had been necessary to recant the offer. That Darcy, who himself admitted being a resentful man, had even considered relinquishing Wickham's long-withheld deserts showed a degree of humility Elizabeth had not thought he possessed. That he might have done so as a consequence of her reproofs was really rather wonderful.

She glanced at Lydia where she was curled in the corner of the carriage. Assured she was still asleep, she whispered to her father, "What do you think induced Mr Wickham to do it? She has no money, no connexions—and I shall eat my hat if either of them is in love."

Mr Bennet smiled ruefully. "Regrettably, I should think your sister had a good deal more to do with the scheme than he. She is more like her mother than any of you in that respect—imprudent, shapely, and proficient at getting her way."

"You think she persuaded him to take her along?"

"Can you imagine her going quietly if it was not her wish?"

Elizabeth did not answer but turned to frown in consternation out of the window. Lydia had boasted of Wickham kissing her in excitement when he learnt he was to inherit at last. If she had used her arts, at that moment, to draw him in, to make him think an elopement was a sound idea, then she was equally to blame for him losing everything all over again!

Naturally, from there, her thoughts turned to Darcy. Hitherto, she had held him entirely accountable for Miss Bingley's fall from grace. Had she judged too hastily there as well? Mrs Hanrahan had accused Miss Bingley of being a self-seeker; Darcy had made mention of her scheming. Was it possible that she had condescended to similar arts to captivate him, and that he had been paying for one moment of weakness ever since? He did not seem the sort to be so easily taken in, but then, she had not thought herself particularly credulous either, until she met Wickham.

"Lizzy?" her father enquired. "You seem excessively distressed by this, but it is all resolved now and will blow over, just as it did when you rejected Mr Collins. Do not be downhearted."

"But it does distress me to consider what Mr Darcy must think of us."

"Since when have you cared for Mr Darcy's opinion?"

"Yes, Lizzy. Since when *have* you cared for Mr Darcy's opinion?" Lydia asked sleepily.

Elizabeth turned to look at her in disgust. "Do you still refuse to acknowledge what he has done for you?"

"Done for me? I shall tell you what he has *done* for me—he has prevented me from getting married."

"And thank God he did," said Mr Bennet severely. "Else you would have been shackled to the most worthless young man in the country for the rest of your life, all for the sake of one moment of youthful folly."

Lydia made another churlish retort to this, and Elizabeth did nothing to check her, weary of the futile endeavour of preventing her from antagonising every living thing within a two-hundred-yard radius. She reflected, instead, on how exceptionally fortunate both Lydia and Wickham were that Darcy had saved them from such an unhappy union—and how very unfortunate it was that Darcy could not escape the ghost of a similarly miserable alliance.

The quarrel between her father and sister showed no signs of abating as they neared home. Elizabeth rejoiced when she espied the cottages on the outskirts of Meryton and sat up straighter as they drove past the home farm. They pulled into Longbourn's driveway just as Lydia gave one too many insolent retorts, earning herself a facetious embargo against balls, suppers, soirees, and shopping trips until either Mr Bennet died or she turned thirty, whichever happened sooner. The carriage drew to a halt, and as soon as the door was opened, Elizabeth jumped down and marched into the house.

"Lizzy?" Jane called anxiously as she strode past. "Is everything well? Where are Lydia and Papa?"

"Still in the carriage, squabbling," she said over her shoulder. "Pray excuse me, Jane. It was a long journey." She kept walking, sick of so much folly, and took refuge in her room, that she might think with freedom. Yet all she was able to think when she got there, was that when it came to folly, hers had been greater even than Lydia's. For whereas her sister had leapt at the chance of happiness and only misjudged her jump, she had spurned what might have been her best hope of it.

Feelings that had, after the shock of discovering Darcy's past, been buried beneath abhorrence and dismay, began to surface once again. She recalled how, in the weeks and months up to that moment, his judgment and knowledge of the world had begun to be a source of extraordinary pleasure, as he frequently surprised her with liberal opinions and pithy observations. She remembered, too, the satisfaction of occasionally saying something that surprised *him* because it was cleverer than he was expecting, and the obvious pleasure he took in being outwitted. She began, in short, to comprehend that he was exactly the man, who in disposition and talents, would most suit her. And for fear of scandalising the world, whose scorn had never frightened her before, she had refused him, making her ten times the fool her sister was.

THE LETTER HER FATHER HAD COMMITTED TO WRITING WAS duly written, and Elizabeth reviled the weakness that prevented her asking to read it before it was sent. She rallied her courage enough to ask to read Darcy's reply. Comprising of only four lines, it expressed his gratification to hear that Lydia was unharmed and assurances of his secrecy. There was no mention of anything else, and neither had Elizabeth expected there to be, yet the letter was still of unexpected significance to her. He had signed it 'Fitzwilliam Darcy,' and though she knew it to be utterly foolish, such personal knowledge of him felt strangely comforting, as though it somehow made her closer to him. It was a revelation to discover how dearly she coveted the intimacy.

In all other ways, her father's prediction that the storm would quickly blow over proved largely true. The Bennets edged cautiously back into the neighbourhood's various entertainments, and though the good people of Meryton applied themselves diligently to the task of discovering the reason for

Lydia's precipitous return from Brighton and conspicuous absence from all entertainments in the neighbourhood, their interest waned as the days passed and nothing remarkable was discovered. Neither did any untoward reports of her misadventure emerge from Brighton. Of Wickham, nobody heard a thing, though of the many possible sources of scandal, that had always been of least concern to Elizabeth. The letter in Darcy's possession had kept Wickham quiet for nearly six years; she very much doubted he would break his silence now for the sake of a girl whom he evidently held in such low esteem.

Their deliverance from ruin notwithstanding, a general pall persisted over the household in the weeks that followed —something Mrs Bennet took it upon herself to broach with Elizabeth one afternoon, while they were alone in the garden.

"I am very depressed, Lizzy. I am sleeping ill, and my head aches nigh on constantly. You will not understand until you have children of your own, but I cannot bear to see any of my girls so wretched."

Elizabeth suppressed a sigh. "Lydia is quite recovered from her disappointment. I really do not think you need to be concerned."

"That is precisely my point. Lydia *is* recovered, though she was by far the closest to getting married and therefore has more right than any of her sisters to be miserable. What, then, am I to make of Jane's low spirits? Why should she be so quiet still, when Lydia's heartbreak is all done with?"

Elizabeth opened her mouth to deliver an impatient retort but swallowed it upon meeting her mother's gaze, which overflowed with unaffected concern—and genuine confusion. "I really do not think Lydia was ever heartbroken, Mama," she said gently. "For she was never in love."

"Has she told you so?"

Elizabeth admitted that she had not.

"Then what made you say as much?"

"Because she does not care about *him*. She has not once talked about what Mr Wickham must be feeling, or how their separation might have affected him. As far as I can tell, she would not be sorry if she never saw him again. That is not love. If you love someone, you care for their happiness. Indeed, if you love someone properly, their happiness becomes more important than your own."

Of this, Elizabeth was more than painfully aware. Accepting that Darcy had truly loved her, acknowledging that he harboured no feelings for Miss Bingley, understanding that he loved his daughter and desired a wife who could do the same—all these revelations had been slow in coming. Yet come they had, and only in understanding them had she comprehended what she had done to him.

Asking for her hand was not the imperious, selfish act for which she had taken it. Rather, it was something he had given his usual, meticulous attention. In her, he believed he had found a woman whom he could trust to accept him, his situation, and his past—who could love him and his daughter without blame or judgment. It was the greatest regret of her life that she had not proved worthy of his faith in her. She had been hateful, and all she could think now was how sad he must be, how lonely. And it hurt more than anything she had ever felt before.

"And you."

"Me?" she said with feigned lightness, blinking her gaze back into focus.

Mrs Bennet nodded. "Aye, you, Lizzy. Do not try to tell me that all is well. I know my girls. Jane may be sad, but she still smiles. You seem to have entirely forgotten how to laugh." She leant forward and patted Elizabeth's hand. "You regret refusing him, do you not?"

She felt herself redden and was too taken aback to think how to reply.

"I knew it!" her mother cried, taking her discomposure as confirmation. "Ever since you returned from Kent you have become more and more unhappy. You have come to comprehend what you denied yourself, have you not? It is a shame you have realised too late. I always thought he was a better prospect than you were willing to allow. Admittedly he is not a handsome man, but—"

"What?" Until that moment, Elizabeth's mortification had been escalating exponentially, but it was overridden with indignation at the merest suggestion of anybody finding Darcy unattractive. Her mind instantly provided her with an image of him, tall and strong, effortlessly catching her as she slid down the slope at the folly and collided forcibly with him, bringing her within whispering distance of his breath-taking smile. She was pleased to be already blushing, for the memory caught her thoroughly off-guard and brought with it a warmth that had nothing to do with embarrassment.

"Oh, fie, do not be missish, child. I know you thought the same. But if Charlotte can tolerate him, I do not see why you could not have."

Elizabeth let out a brittle, almost hysterical laugh. *She means my cousin!* "Charlotte has a far stronger constitution than I, Mama. I assure you, my time in Kent only made me more certain how terribly unhappy I should have been had I married Mr Collins."

"You are unhappy anyway," her mother replied, pouting. She soon rallied, smiling slyly as she said, "Perhaps you will meet somebody on your travels. I shall ask my brother to make sure he introduces you to as many gentlemen as he can."

. . .

This request was indeed put, repeatedly and vociferously, to Mr Gardiner when he arrived towards the end of the month with his wife and four children. He mollified his sister in a way that only he seemed able to do, whilst assuring his niece with a wink that they would be imposing no such introductions on her. The Gardiners stayed only one night at Longbourn, and Elizabeth passed as much of the afternoon and next morning as she could playing with her cousins. The reason she gave her relations was that the children were to stay behind, under Jane's particular care, and she meant to enjoy what she could of their company before departing. To herself, she did not even pretend that Anna and Darcy were not at the forefront of her mind, though she chose not to examine too closely what she hoped to achieve by torturing herself with such futile daydreams.

They set off the next day beneath a pure blue sky and a hot sun, the promise of weeks of adventure and amusement in the excellent company of her aunt and uncle greatly improving Elizabeth's spirits. They journeyed leisurely through Oxford, Blenheim, Warwick, Kenilworth and Birmingham, reaching Derbyshire after almost two weeks. Their first stop in that county was at an inn just south of Derby, whose owner was known to Mr Gardiner through a business connexion, and who, upon recognising the acquaintance, gave their party the best rooms in his establishment.

"This is a turn up for the books, is it not?" said Mr Gardiner, as he strode about their private drawing room, inspecting every nook with interest.

"It certainly is," replied his wife. "Perhaps we could stay here an extra few nights and miss out one of the other stops."

"Perhaps," he replied, "but which one? It would be a

shame not to see Matlock, and I know you will not suffer us passing Lambton without seeing Mrs Norris."

"No, indeed. Though perhaps we do not need to stay there for quite as long. What do you think, Lizzy?"

"What is there that we would miss?" Elizabeth enquired from her perch in the window seat, whence she watched the bustle and colour of life in the street below.

"We could probably do without visiting the milliners. Or the well—I should think we will have had our fill of those in Matlock by then, so we shall not miss one more."

"And there is Pemberley, of course."

Elizabeth whipped around to look at her uncle. "Pemberley?"

"Yes. It is only five miles from Lambton and reputedly quite beautiful."

"It is," Mrs Gardiner confirmed, "but we can hardly go there now, can we?"

"Why ever not?" asked Mr Gardiner.

"Come, sir. We could not show our faces within a mile of it after what has just happened with Lydia!"

"I would have thought that was an excellent reason to go. I should be very pleased for the opportunity to thank Mr Darcy in person for what he did for my niece."

"But would he be so pleased to see us? The family of a girl who has shown herself to be completely without propriety or common sense, whom he rescued from the clutches of a man he despises? How can you think he would welcome a visit from us? What nonsense."

"You exaggerate, my dear, I am sure, but if you feel this strongly about it then we shall not go. I hope you will not mind, Lizzy."

"No, not at all," Elizabeth murmured. She had watched the exchange between her aunt and uncle with mounting confusion, alarmed that her uncle's enthusiasm might force her to go to Pemberley, and distraught that her aunt's disinclination might prevent it. There could be few people in the world Darcy wished to see less, for all the reasons her aunt extolled and more, except he had still approached to address her at the inn at Brighton, before he realised it was not her. Moreover, there were few men of Elizabeth's acquaintance with whom it would be more imprudent to pursue an acquaintance, yet she could not erase the mark he had left on her heart, which the fleeting prospect of seeing him again had searingly reignited.

The decision was made, however; they would not go. Elizabeth turned back to the window and schooled herself to be content. It was undoubtedly for the best, and there were plenty of other places to see that must be of equal interest to travellers. She repeated this refrain many times over the next few days as they trawled around the delights of Derby, finally agreeing on Saturday they had exhausted the town of its novelty, and that on Monday, they would move on to Matlock.

28

Hidden Treasures in The Peaks

The petrifying well at the heart of Matlock Bath fascinated Elizabeth and her uncle. Much to Mrs Gardiner's displeasure, they spent almost two hours watching the spring waters drip and splash on the multifarious items left out to be turned to stone. Elizabeth spotted what could have been a bird's nest or a wig; Mr Gardiner was convinced he could see a fishing rod, but she thought it was only a broom. When they left there, they spent another hour meandering along the river's edge. Elizabeth set her sights on walking to the top of High Tor, but her aunt was disinclined after standing about all morning and teased her niece and husband for having wasted valuable exploring time staring at crusty knick-knacks. "Do not concern yourself, though, Lizzy," she added, "for there are cliffs and crevices enough to satisfy even you at Kelstedge Abbey." Thus, they returned to their lodgings and enjoyed an exceedingly good evening meal and early night, all anticipation for their outing the next day to the home of Lord and Lady Matlock.

It was a grand house, and somewhat ostentatious in its design, though it mattered not for they did not long remain indoors. After they were shown around those few rooms that were open for public viewing, they were handed into the care of a gardener, whose pride was obvious as he explained to Elizabeth that the finest parts of the estate, in his opinion, were the more rugged ones, beyond the formal gardens. There was even a small dripping well, apparently—much smaller than the one in Matlock Bath, but still a delight to see. Elizabeth, and then her uncle, looked pleadingly at Mrs Gardiner, who sighed dramatically.

"Have not you two had your fill of clambering about in caves?" When they both answered in the negative, she relented and said to the gardener, "You had better point us in the right direction, sir, or I shall never hear the end of it."

Her intentions were good, but her capabilities less complying; they had not reached the well before Mrs Gardiner complained of being too fatigued after their exertions the day before to manage the increasingly uneven and overgrown path.

"Come, my dear, we are nearly there," Mr Gardiner urged, though at an expressive look from his wife, he hastily changed his tune. "You go on, Lizzy. The gardener said it was only at the end of this trail. We shall go back and walk about the lake instead. Let us meet at the carriage in half an hour. Be careful not to fall off anything. Your mother might weather the loss, but your father would never forgive me."

Elizabeth thanked them and continued in the direction the gardener had described. She was exceedingly glad she had when she reached an opening in the trees, for the view across the vale was breath-taking. A memory flashed into her mind of Darcy, at Rosings' folly, remarking that Derbyshire was not as flat as Kent, and she laughed to herself at his typically phlegmatic understatement. She stayed for another minute or two, wondering which, if any, of the dips or peaks she could see from here concealed Pemberley behind it. Before long, however, curiosity got the better of her, and she continued along the path in search of the well.

She laughed when she reached it, for the gardener had not been wrong when he said it was small. It was less a cave, and more of a recess in the rock face, with water dripping over the top ledge into a pool next to the path. Still, somebody had suspended several objects from the lip, and sure enough, they were in various stages of petrification. She watched them swinging and twirling on their strings, mesmerised, until she was startled from her reveries by the sound of someone calling her name. She began to turn then cried out as a blur of petticoats, ribbons and curls collided with her, a pair of arms encircling her hips and squeezing tightly.

"It *is* you!"

"Anna?" she exclaimed. When her attempts to pry the child far enough away that she could see her face failed, she relented and returned the hug. "Anna, what on earth are you doing here?"

The girl looked up then, and the similarity between her proud expression and Darcy's stole Elizabeth's breath away.

"I have run away."

She ought to have guessed. "You promised me you would never do that again."

Her face fell. "But Miss Paxton fell asleep under a big tree."

"Miss Paxton ought to know better by now." Elizabeth wondered whether Darcy knew the woman he employed to look after his daughter had such little regard for her charge. "It is exceedingly unwise to run around here alone, Anna. Nay, do not smile, I am serious. This is not Hertfordshire, where you can run and run and never come across anything worse than a steep slope. These rocks can be dangerous." Anna's bottom lip began to tremble, and Elizabeth softened her tone. "No harm done, but you must promise me you will be careful in future. Come, let me take you back to Miss Paxton. Where are you staying?"

"At the big house."

"Which one?" Elizabeth tried to picture all the houses in the village, and all those they had passed en route that morning.

"That one," Anna replied, pointing at the uppermost tip of a gable that could just be seen over the tops of the trees.

Elizabeth smiled indulgently. "Anna, that is Kelstedge Abbey."

"I know. It belongs to my father's family. It is bigger than a whole village inside. Lady Matlock gave Miss Paxton and me three rooms between us, and each one is larger than Persimmon Cottage!"

Elizabeth schooled herself to remain composed, though it was exceedingly difficult, for she distinctly recalled—somewhat belatedly—Lady Catherine explaining that Colonel Fitzwilliam was the younger son of her brother, the Earl of Matlock. *How could I have forgotten?* "Are your mother or father here with you?" She did not know whether it was relief or disappointment that made her exhale all her breath in one sharp sigh when Anna shook her head.

"My mother is in Halifax buying things for her to sew. I am staying here with Miss Paxton until she returns. Then we are all going to Leeds."

Shopping for her own needlework paraphernalia did not seem like something to which Miss Bingley would condescend, but Elizabeth did not argue, and in any case, Anna had other things on her mind.

"There is a much better well than this one over that way," she announced, pointing along the path. She grabbed Elizabeth's arm and began tugging on it. "Should you like to see it?"

"No, Anna, you really must go back to Miss Paxton."

"But she is asleep. And she never lets me explore. Pray come, 'tis not far."

Elizabeth hesitated; in truth she had little inclination to go anywhere near the Abbey for fear of encountering a member of Darcy's family, and she did have another quarter of an hour before her aunt and uncle expected her. All hope of refusing evaporated anyway when Anna informed her, wide-eyed, that she was certain there were fairies at the other well.

"Do you promise to return to the house as soon as you have shown me?"

"I do."

"Very well then. Lead the way."

The well turned out to be much farther away than Anna had intimated, and not on the path, either. Twice Elizabeth suggested they turn back, and twice she allowed herself to be convinced that they were almost there, only to be told to clamber over one more rocky outcropping. They went so far that she could see the gatehouse at the entrance of the driveway farther down the slope. She had to admit, when they arrived, that it was worth seeing. A lighter but faster flow of water trickled from a greater height, into a much deeper hole than the well up on the path. The gossamer curtain of water cast a rainbow as it fell, and each drop echoed into a pool at the bottom, making a magical, tinkling sound.

"Can you hear them talking to each other?" Anna whispered, leaning over the gully.

"I can, but pray, come away from that hole. The edge will be slippery from the spray, and you have no idea how deep it goes. Sit with me over here." They perched on a jut of rock, and Elizabeth watched Anna as she waited in silence for a fairy to show itself. She was such a precious little thing, with her notions of magic and fairy tales, and her love of solitary explorations so like Elizabeth's own. Something like regret crept over her for having refused to accept such a dear, innocent creature into her world.

"Have you any food, Lizzy?"

"No, why? Do you think it would entice the fairies out?"

"I do not know. I am just hungry."

Elizabeth laughed in happy surprise. "You remind me of my sister, Kitty. She is always hungry, too. Come, let us get you home."

"I thought your sister's name was Jane," Anna remarked once they were back on the path and walking side by side.

"One of them is. I have four."

This news seemed to impress Anna almost as much as her three rooms at Kelstedge, and Elizabeth passed the rest of the walk back being interrogated about life at Longbourn. Delightful though the conversation was, it made her sad; chiefly at the thought of how lonely Anna's childhood must have been thus far, but partly for the knowledge that, had she accepted Darcy's proposal, she might have provided Anna her much longed-for siblings.

They were joined before they reached the house by Miss Paxton, who appeared to be roaming about rather aimlessly in the shrubbery at the edge of the formal lawn. "Miss Dunn, where have you been!" she cried upon seeing them.

Anna gripped Elizabeth's hand a little more tightly and pressed up against her leg.

Elizabeth curtseyed and introduced herself. "I managed to get myself turned about in the shrubbery, and this delightful young lady showed me the way back." She nudged Anna forward, propelling her gently back to her governess. "She has been invaluable. You must be exceedingly proud of her."

"Yes, ma'am, thank you," Miss Paxton replied. "Pardon me, are you staying at the house?"

"No, I am just touring the grounds. Indeed, my travelling companions will be waiting for me. I must be going."

Miss Paxton, and then Anna, curtseyed and walked away towards the house, Anna looking over her shoulder every few steps to wave good-bye. Elizabeth, feeling exceptionally melancholy, watched until they went into the house then set off in search of her relations. She had almost reached the road that led behind the house to the stables when the door through which Anna had disappeared was thrown open again, and Darcy himself hastened out onto the lawn.

They were within twenty yards of each other, and so abrupt was his appearance that it was impossible to avoid his sight, though it very quickly became clear that avoiding her was not Darcy's intention. No sooner had their eyes met than he strode directly towards her.

"Miss Bennet! Anna said you were here, but I could not quite believe it. I did not know you were in this part of the country."

"Nor I you," Elizabeth replied with an embarrassment impossible to overcome. "I am travelling with my aunt and uncle and they wished to see Kelstedge, but I did not make the connexion—I had no idea you would be here."

"I am not, usually," he replied, rather more awkwardly. "My family are helping me with a matter of some importance."

She scarcely dared lift her eyes to his face, but each time she did, she blushed a little deeper, for despite all her more edifying reflections of late, he was even more handsome than her memory had allowed.

"Are you staying nearby?" he added when she did not reply.

"Yes, at The Rose and Crown."

"Do you plan to stay long?"

"A few days. We arrived only yesterday."

"Have you been travelling long? When did you leave Longbourn?"

"About three weeks ago."

He nodded, and seemed to have run out of things to say, but then enquired, with none of his usual sedateness, "Would you care for some refreshments?"

Elizabeth stared, unable to believe he meant for her to walk into the house. The pause stretched long as she struggled to decide how she ought to answer, and she was inordinately grateful for the reprieve afforded when her aunt and uncle walked around the side of the house.

"There you are, Lizzy," Mr Gardiner called. "We have been waiting for you for an age. Your aunt is positively wilting." He stopped berating her upon noticing Darcy. "My apologies, sir."

"This is my aunt and uncle, Mr and Mrs Gardiner." Elizabeth watched Darcy to see how he bore the degradation of such an introduction, but so far was he from appearing repulsed that he repeated his request that they go into the house. Elizabeth was beyond astonishment.

Mrs Gardiner was apparently beyond the walk back to the carriage, and she accepted Darcy's offer with alacrity. Thus, having told herself all week that it would be better if she did not see Darcy at Pemberley, Elizabeth walked with him, equal parts mortified and elated, into Kelstedge Abbey instead.

Unexampled Kindness

Darcy led them into a different part of the house than Elizabeth and the Gardiners had seen before, though it was no less opulent. She wondered whether Pemberley was as ostentatious but thought, if owners were any reflection of their houses, it was unlikely. She was too uncomfortable to say much as they walked. Though her feelings about Darcy's situation had undergone a significant change, he knew only of her vehement objections to it. She would have expected him to remain indoors and wait for her to leave, never to be seen again. Yet with no reasonable expectation of a good reception, he had sought her out and extended an invitation that would keep her there for longer, and she was amazed by his civility.

His attention to her relations was even more astonishing. In the absence of any conversation from her, Darcy spoke to Mr Gardiner about their travels thus far and answered all Mrs Gardiner's questions about the house as they walked through it, showing no sign of the contempt he had previously owned. Elizabeth might have been persuaded that he meant to prove he no longer thought ill of her connexions, but she could not believe that was possible after Lydia's shameful misadventure. *Yet if he has been irrevocably repulsed by my family's failings, I wonder that he is taking so much trouble to give me a glass of lemonade!*

By the time they had walked the entire length of the house and gone up two sets of stairs and down another, Elizabeth had convinced herself that Darcy's generosity could only be explained by the diminution of his affections for her. She no longer had any power over him; he cared nothing for her esteem, and his demeanour towards her was therefore incidental. The hope that his attention might proceed from his still loving her was a forlorn one, buried too deeply beneath regret and confusion to be of any use to her.

Preoccupied with these thoughts, Elizabeth blindly entered the parlour to which Darcy led them and came up short. For some inexplicable reason, she had not anticipated there would be anybody else taking refreshments with them and was surprised to discover that four people occupied the room, at least one to her knowledge—and therefore likely all—related to Darcy. She wondered whether only Colonel Fitzwilliam, or every person present, knew she had rejected an offer of marriage that would have seen her join their ranks.

"This is Miss Elizabeth Bennet," Darcy said, and she did not miss the woman on the sofa raise an eyebrow. "And her aunt and uncle, Mr and Mrs Gardiner." He then introduced his own aunt and uncle, the Earl and Countess of Matlock, and his cousins, Viscount Sutcliffe and, for the Gardiners' benefit, Colonel Fitzwilliam.

"Good afternoon to you all," said Lady Matlock in a voice unlike any Elizabeth had ever heard—velvety, unhurried, and just quiet enough that one had to pay exceedingly close attention to catch every word. "Pray, make yourselves comfortable. Franks, see to the drinks." She waved a footman towards the refreshments on the table, which were duly distributed amongst the new arrivals.

"This is an unexpected pleasure," Colonel Fitzwilliam said to Elizabeth once they were all settled.

"For us, too," she replied, intensely aware of the way both Darcy and Lady Matlock were watching her but resolving to be flustered by neither. "We had no intention of imposing on your family."

"Pish posh," he replied. "We were all at a loss as to what to do with ourselves for the afternoon anyway. And I daresay you have saved us from the game of hide and seek that Darcy would undoubtedly have suggested next—it is his favourite pastime, you know."

Elizabeth looked at Darcy, predicting this would vex him, and sure enough, caught the tail end of a well-concealed sigh and miniscule shake of his head as he despaired of his cousin's nonsense. She smiled, and to Fitzwilliam said, "Better that than shooting. Your brother only has so many ears to spare."

Lord Sutcliffe shuffled forward on his seat and peered around Colonel Fitzwilliam to better see Elizabeth. "What is this? Has my little brother finally admitted to almost beheading me? I have never heard him confess to it before."

"And neither will you now," Colonel Fitzwilliam replied. "It was Darcy who blabbed that snippet."

They both looked at Darcy, whose implacable expression showed not a hint of amusement. "You ought to be thankful I did not divulge that your second bullet hit the Fitzwilliam tapestry."

"Dash it, Darcy! Four-and-twenty years I have kept that a secret from my mother!"

"No, you have not," said Lady Matlock pityingly before addressing Elizabeth and Mrs Gardiner. "How do you like Kelstedge, ladies? Have you enjoyed discovering all its secrets?" She ended her question by fixing her unwavering gaze upon Elizabeth, who took her meaning but did not have time to formulate an answer before Mrs Gardiner replied.

"It is a delightful house, madam. My husband and I were particularly taken with the staircase in the grand hall."

"Ah yes—Breccia Medicea," said Mr Gardiner. "You can tell it apart from other marbles by the purple veining."

"You know a lot about marble, do you?" Lord Matlock enquired.

"I import it, sir, so I ought to."

"Well, well, Darcy," said his lordship, sitting up a little straighter. "It seems you have brought me just the man."

The chasm between the ranks of both parties abruptly lost all its awkwardness and became a source of vast mutual convenience as the conversation turned to Lord Matlock's years-long search for a rare marble with which to make some repairs to another part of the house.

Elizabeth leant closer to Lady Matlock, that she could speak quietly. "My aunt and uncle did not explore all the same parts of the garden as I. Kelstedge has plenty of secrets they have yet to discover."

Lady Matlock inclined her head. "Thank you, Miss Bennet." She sat back and smiled, though Elizabeth still felt as though she were being scrutinised. "It is most fortunate for me that you chose to visit my house over and above any other stately home hereabouts. It has been my wish to meet you for some time, and now here you are, in my drawing room."

"You wished to meet me?"

"Why, yes. I have heard so much about you, I had begun to wonder whether any of it could be true. Now I can at least confirm two of the reports."

"Might I be so bold as to enquire which two?"

"I hoped you would. My husband's sister wrote to me at Easter, complaining that you were impertinent and plain—which of course I took immediately to mean that you were witty and handsome. And it turns out she was accurate on both counts, which ought not to surprise me, for Lady Catherine despises being wrong."

Assured that Lady Matlock had heard far worse reports about her, Elizabeth smiled with gratitude that she had chosen to mention two such innocuous ones. "Then I shall endeavour not to behave in any way that might contradict her judgment."

Lady Matlock chuckled, and her laugh was as honeyed as her voice. "Very wise, my dear. The only thing she likes less than being wrong is being *proved* wrong by somebody who knows better. We have never got along."

She allowed Elizabeth a moment to appreciate the joke before drawing Mrs Gardiner back into the conversation by enquiring how long they intended to remain in Matlock. That topic advanced to a discussion of the places they had yet to visit, and the rest of the party joined in when Mrs Gardiner's association with Lambton was mentioned—and, briefly, its proximity to Pemberley. Elizabeth could see that Darcy was toying with the idea of saying something, for he almost spoke several times, but on each occasion, glanced at her and appeared to have a change of heart. She wondered whether he felt obliged to invite them to Pemberley and did not blame him for preferring not to. Offering her refreshments at his aunt's house was one thing; inviting her into his home—the home he had wished to share with her—was quite another.

His reluctance was sobering, though, and returned her to all the shame and embarrassment she had felt upon first seeing him on the lawn. She longed to speak to him, to return the compliment of his civility, but they were not seated near each other, and she was required to speak to her immediate neighbours often enough as left her little opportunity to engage him. She tried, once, to smile at him, but her uncle addressed him as she did so, and she did not think he saw.

Either he was similarly beset or her first conjecture was correct, and he had no particular desire to speak to her.

Convinced he must now be regretting his condescension, she could not conceal her surprise when, after Mr Gardiner announced they would go, Darcy came forward to escort her to the awaiting carriage. That he then reverted to his usual silence was of no concern to her; she was perfectly comfortable with his brooding company. Indeed, she had missed it dearly. She felt compelled to break it, though, for there was one matter that could not go unmentioned if this was to be the last time they ever saw each other.

When they reached the carriage, and before the others caught up, she said in a low voice, "Mr Darcy, before I go, please allow me to thank you for your unexampled kindness to my sister. I know my father has written to you, and my uncle would thank you himself if he had the chance of a private word. But please, allow me to thank you, on behalf of all my family, and for myself most of all, for saving Lydia from making such a grievous mistake." She wished her words unsaid as soon as they left her tongue, for she fancied that calling Lydia's mistake 'grievous' could only be seen by him as yet another insult to his own history. She felt herself colour and was grateful that the others reached them before Darcy was able to respond.

Mortification compounded mortification as she waited for everybody to say their farewells; the disaster of Lydia's misadventure in Brighton, painful memories of her altercation with Darcy in Kent, the impropriety of being caught at his uncle's home, and the hopelessness of his situation all mingled with the permanent ache in her breast that grew worse every second she came closer to leaving, until she could scarcely bear to meet his eye. Yet she did not need to look up at him to see him reach for her hand or feel the gentleness with which he helped her up into the carriage. Her heart fluttered about preposterously, and she laughed at her own missishness. His grip tightened, bringing her gaze up involuntarily, and the intensity of his expression weakened her knees. She sat down heavily and barely managed to murmur a reply to his good-bye.

When the carriage drove off, Elizabeth saw Darcy walking slowly towards the house with his relatives and wished with all her heart that he would look back, but her aunt and uncle's observations of the unexpected turn of events began and obliged her to turn her attention to them. If Darcy had turned to watch her go, she would never know it. But she chose to imagine that he had.

30

A Fly in The Ointment

HAVING TAKEN THREE LONG MONTHS TO RECONCILE herself to the insuperable regard she held for a man she should not, could not, and had not accepted, Elizabeth was somewhat indignant that her spirits had been thrown back into disarray by the unexpected meeting. To see and talk to Darcy again had, notwithstanding all the attendant awkwardness, felt wonderful. To have to say good-bye to him again had been exceedingly difficult. The seed of hope that his parting look had planted in her mind left her battling between laughing at her own whimsy and despairing of her own happiness.

This infuriating state of perturbation was vastly relieved by the arrival the next morning of a letter from Jane. They had just been preparing to pay a visit to Mrs Gardiner's friend as the letter came in, and her uncle and aunt, leaving her to enjoy it in quiet, set off by themselves. Elizabeth sat at the table and devoured the letter in the hope that news from home would distract her from thinking about Darcy. The beginning, filled with news of her young cousins' antics and sisters' comings and goings, did a creditable job. The latter part, which was dated a day later and written in evident agitation, proved a less successful diversion.

Since writing the above, something has occurred of a most unexpected nature. Mr Bingley is come back. We knew nothing of it until yesterday, when my mother heard from Mrs Hanrahan that Netherfield was open again. Even then, I thought it must be a new tenant, for you know as well as I how unlikely it was to be the previous one. My mother appealed to my father to call, but he absolutely refused. Yet this morning, Mr Bingley has called at Longbourn, and now I am more conflicted than ever I have felt before. You will recall that, when he first left, I expressed a wish for him never to return, for I would rather not choose between my sisters' happiness and my own. In that respect at least, it seems I may now have less cause for concern. In others, I am more distressed than ever.

Mr Bingley's situation is about to change for the better: his sister is engaged to be married. I know no more than that, for he told me very discreetly, and only then because he must go to Leeds soon for the wedding and wished to assure me that he would return again afterwards. He asked that I keep the information to myself for now, for I understand the arrangements are not all finalised. I am grateful that he took the trouble to tell me at all, for it can only mean that he wishes me to be aware of his altered circumstances, and that has taught me to hope as I have scarcely ever allowed myself to hope before. I know you will comprehend the implications too, Lizzy. If Mr Bingley were ever to renew his attentions to me, I should have considerably less cause to worry that any of my sisters might be tainted by association. I cannot pretend that I do not still admire him. The pleasure I received just from seeing him again was beyond anything I expected. The freedom to enjoy his company without fear of an entanglement, the like of which our family could ill afford, is most welcome. But I cannot enjoy it—not while I know how it will pain you.

It grieves me deeply that this news comes too late to be of any use to you, dearest Lizzy. I wish, with all my heart that Miss Bingley had found her suitor before Mr Darcy proposed to you, for then you might not have felt obliged to refuse him. I know you had other objections, and that his situation is more complicated than his friend's, but Miss Bingley's marriage will liberate them both equally. For both our sakes, therefore, I shall not give up hope. If Mr Bingley is returned, there is a chance that his friend might also. Mr Bingley has accepted an invitation to dine with us tomorrow, and I shall endeavour to find a private moment to ask him if that is Mr Darcy's intention.

Elizabeth refolded the letter and stared at it, unsure what to think or how to feel. A moment later, she began to laugh. "My mother is buying things for her to sew. Oh, Anna!" A *trousseau* seemed much more like something Miss Bingley would trouble herself to shop for. With an affectionate shake of her head, she pushed her chair back and walked to her bedroom. She could not imagine what had brought the marriage about, but it scarcely mattered. She rummaged in her belongings for her writing case and took it back to the table. What signified was that Bingley could now marry whomever he chose with impunity. That the same was true of Darcy was something with which she refused to torment herself. Instead, she took out a sheet of paper and opened the ink well. She would write and insist that Jane accept Bingley's attentions without another thought to her or Darcy. That situation was, indeed, more complicated, but it would only become more so if it were allowed to ruin Jane's happiness. She dipped her pen in the ink and had written only the date when a wide-eyed servant opened the door and showed in Lady Matlock.

"Good day, Miss Bennet," she said, coming into the room. "No, no, do not get up. I apologise if I am interrupting your correspondence—unpardonably rude of me. But I did wish to speak to you." She pointed to one of the other seats at the table. "Do you mind?" They both knew Elizabeth would not object, but still she waited for her to say so before she pulled the chair out and sat down. She politely refused the offer of refreshments and fixed Elizabeth with an open but unwavering look. "You must be wondering why I have called."

Elizabeth fancied it must have something to do with Anna but thought it safer to let her ladyship broach the topic and so merely agreed that she could not account for it.

"Ostensibly, I am here to invite you all to join the dinner party we are having tomorrow evening. But assuming you would say yes to that, I shall waste no more time in getting to my real purpose, which is to thank you."

The surprise of the first pronouncement was yet to wear off before the second was made, and Elizabeth was momentarily lost for words as she wondered what she had done to deserve the honour of either. "If I have been of service to your ladyship in any way then I am glad of it, but I must confess it was not consciously done."

"Nevertheless, you *have* been of immense service, for you have talked sense into my nephew where apparently none had permeated before. I do not know precisely what you said to Darcy in Kent—he has not elaborated—but whatever it was, he credits you with inducing him to inform us of his...predicament. Until two months ago, Lord Matlock and I were completely unaware of Miss Darcy's existence."

Elizabeth tried to think what part of her speech in Kent

might have had such an effect but could only recall telling Darcy that he was arrogant and conceited. "I hope the discovery has not been too distressing," she said warily.

"Only in as much as I do not like that he kept it a secret from us. He had his reasons—and men always have complete faith in their own reasoning, poor things—but he ought to have involved us at the beginning. In every other way, the discovery has been rather wonderful. My sons have shown little inclination to provide me with grandchildren. I shall do very well with Miss Darcy until one of them obliges me."

"I am delighted that my words have had such a happy consequence."

"I detect a note of surprise in your tone, Miss Bennet." It was not a question, but she said no more, thus Elizabeth felt obliged to reply, and did so candidly, for it seemed apt.

"I confess, I am pleased that you have been so liberally-minded."

Lady Matlock smiled faintly. "This many years after the fact, there is little point getting upset. Miss Darcy is here, and that is all there is to it. One has to either accept the situation and make the best of it or renounce it and close a good number of doors upon the matter." She finished with another of her penetrating looks. Elizabeth baulked at the idea that this was somehow meant for her and was pleased when her ladyship continued talking, for she knew not how to respond. "Still, it had the potential to be a disaster. I will say this for my nephew, he has done an exceedingly good job of keeping all talk at bay. And now, thanks to your urging, it will be properly resolved as it ought to have been from the start."

Jane's report had forewarned Elizabeth of as much, and she nodded her understanding. "I have received a letter from my sister just this morning. Mr Bingley has told her of *his* sister's good news."

Lady Matlock inclined her head. "The marriage will take

place in Leeds next week. Everything has been meticulously arranged to ensure it all goes off without a hitch. Indeed, you are the only fly in the ointment. Nobody accounted for your sudden appearance, yet you are come, and, let us not equivocate, you have the power to prevent the happy conclusion for which so many people have strived." Her ladyship's naturally deep voice made this sound prodigiously menacing.

This, then, is the real reason for your visit, thought Elizabeth. *Not to thank me, but to ensure I keep your secret.* "Mr Darcy's reports of me must have been severe indeed if they have made you believe I would deliberately and maliciously ruin so many reputations."

"On the contrary. It was his reports of his own conduct that made me think you owed him nothing and might therefore have little to no interest in continuing to protect his reputation."

"His conduct towards me?" Elizabeth hesitated, but only for as long as it took her to comprehend that Darcy had not told his relations what he had done for Lydia. "If you mean what passed between us in Kent, then the conduct of neither of us was irreproachable. If you only knew what Mr Darcy has done for my family since then, you would not say I owed him nothing—but I am afraid of telling you. Not for fear of censure, though it would be deserved, but because it might make it seem that my secrecy comes at the expense of his, and that is absolutely not the case. I would not expose Miss Darcy for the world."

Lady Matlock did not immediately respond. Elizabeth withstood her silent scrutiny without flinching until her ladyship abruptly broke into a stunning smile and came to her feet. "I believe we are done here, Miss Bennet. Shall I have the pleasure of seeing you at Kelstedge tomorrow?"

Her change of tone was so sudden, Elizabeth could not help but laugh a little. Then, the possibility of Darcy also being at dinner, of their farewell yesterday not being their last, began to form in her mind, and she answered with more hope than assurance that her aunt and uncle would not mind her engaging them for attendance.

"Very good." Lady Matlock opened the door and beckoned to the servant. "You may tell the rest of my party they may come up now." Over her shoulder, she said to Elizabeth, "I hope you will excuse me. I have another engagement. I might trouble you to delay writing your letter a little longer, though. There are a number of people waiting downstairs to speak to you."

31

Every Reproof

INSTEAD OF WAITING UNTIL THE NEXT EVENING TO LEARN whether she would ever see Darcy again, Elizabeth had only to wait two or three minutes. Lady Matlock's party consisted of her two sons and her nephew, and they arrived upstairs with Mr and Mrs Gardiner, who had returned from their visit and been more than happy to talk to their new acquaintances downstairs until her ladyship completed her business with Elizabeth. It soon became obvious the little parlour was too small for so many people, and Colonel Fitzwilliam proposed their all walking out. It was agreed to, and to Elizabeth's particular delight, settled that they would head towards, and possibly some of the way up, High Tor.

Less pleasing to her was the manner in which the walkers arranged themselves. Though Darcy had met her eye with a look that made her mouth dry immediately upon coming into the parlour, he was very quickly caught up in the merry-go-round of conversation, and Elizabeth had little opportunity to speak to him without one of his relatives or hers interrupting. She was no less an object of interest herself and was engaged on all manner of subjects as the company circulated and swapped companions all the way to the foot of the Tor, by which point she was convinced she had been mistaken about his looking at her before.

She grew angry at herself for seeing partiality in his every gesture. A man who had been once refused, and for a situation it was not in his power to alter, would never condescend to expose himself to a repeat of her abuse. The very notion must be abhorrent to someone as proud as he. It was foolish to expect a renewal of his love—but not, she was ever more certain, reckless to wish for it. With matters 'resolved'—as Lady Matlock phrased it—Darcy would no longer pose a threat to her reputation, and the mortifications attached to his history with Miss Bingley would be more easily forgotten once she was somebody else's wife. Moreover, the happiness Elizabeth would receive from being always at Darcy's side must far outweigh any concern over one, much-repented, youthful mistake. Yet Elizabeth found it difficult to believe she had not, as her ladyship had implied, closed every possible door upon the matter when she refused him.

"You are very quiet, Lizzy," Mrs Gardiner said softly, catching up and linking arms with her.

"Sorry, I was lost in thought."

"It is well. Everybody else is being very chatty. I daresay nobody noticed except me."

Elizabeth glanced at Darcy to see whether he had noticed, but he was talking to her uncle and seemed perfectly unaware of her. She looked back to the path ahead, taking no pleasure at all in the irony of his having discovered a talent for conversing with strangers just as she became jealous of his talking to anyone but her.

"You will all have to forgive me," Mrs Gardiner said suddenly. "But I can tell you now that I am not equal to scaling that."

They had reached the foot of High Tor, and from this

approach, only the sheer rock face was visible, not any of the paths leading to the summit, as Colonel Fitzwilliam explained, but she would not be persuaded. "I shall be perfectly content to wait for you all here." She disentangled her arm from Elizabeth's and perched on the nearest mound of rock. "My husband will keep me company, will you not, sir?"

Mr Gardiner looked so dismayed that Elizabeth almost suggested none of them attempt the climb, until Lord Sutcliffe came to the rescue. "Allow me to stay with you, madam," he offered. "I have no head for heights anyway. I should much rather stay on the ground."

"We shan't go all the way to the top, my dear," said Mr Gardiner with boyish glee. "Just far enough that we can get a good view."

"Come then, sir," said Colonel Fitzwilliam. "Let us show them how it is done!" And off he marched up the rise with Mr Gardiner in hot pursuit.

"Miss Bennet, would you do me the honour?"

Elizabeth had been so busy attempting to determine the meaning of her aunt's secret smile that she had not noticed Darcy step closer until he spoke, and she was hard pressed to conceal her discomposure as she turned with him to follow her uncle up the hill. She could not immediately think what to say, and several awkward minutes of silence passed before Darcy broke the impasse.

"I hope you do not mind my coming today."

"No, not at all," she replied with some surprise, fully reconciled to it being her company that must now be objectionable to him. His look of relief made her regret her earlier absence of mind, and she wished she were brave enough to tell him what pleasure she took in his company, but she lacked the courage for anything so bold and could only repeat her assurance that she did not mind his coming in any way. It was enough to earn her an understated but sublime smile.

After another pause, he said, "I have not walked up High Tor for many years. Fitzwilliam and I used to run about in the caves at the top when we were children. It is believed they are roman lead mines, but we called them the Terror Chambers and used to try to frighten each other by shouting names into them so the sound would echo between the fissures."

Elizabeth smiled broadly, though less at the unsurprising news that Darcy had once been a boy and more at his endearing habit of inserting nuggets of his broad knowledge into even the simplest childhood tale. This was why he did not enjoy small talk, she supposed: it was too frivolous. He preferred to find the purpose in everything. It made her understand better why conversation with her mother and father had been challenging for him—one being the epitome of small-mindedness and the other a consummate tease—and glad of his having met her erudite and worldly aunt and uncle.

"We have a distinct dearth of caves in Hertfordshire. Plenty of streams, though," she said with a grin and was gratified to see from his answering smile that he, too, recalled the book they had used to joke about together at Netherfield. "Jane and I tried to take Mary out in a little rowboat on one particular brook when we were very young. We all ended up soaked through, Mary got a huge leech attached to her arm, and my father had the boat broken up for firewood. I believe that might be when my fondness for walking began."

He laughed, and not for the first time, Elizabeth was arrested by the transformation of his countenance when it was devoid of gravity. His gaze was no less piercing, but his expression was rendered less severe, allowing one to focus on his features rather than his fierceness—and his features, in their present unguarded form, were unsettlingly handsome. She looked away before he caught her staring and only just avoided tripping over a jag of rock sticking out of the ground in front of her.

After that, the trail quickly grew steeper, and more rocks jutted into their path, obliging them to go in single file for a distance. They were reduced to snatches of conversation thrown over their shoulders as the ascent grew more taxing. Upon passing a sharply inclined section that was treacherous with loose stones, Elizabeth heard the scrape of a foot slipping behind her and laughingly held out her hand to pull Darcy up. She thought only to repay him for saving her on the little hill in Kent, and not of the mortification into which such an over-familiar act would, seconds later, plunge her. He took her hand before she could retract it, though, and held it as he came up the slope, though he did not need it, for he applied no pressure at all except to gently squeeze her fingers before he let them go.

"What kept you?" came a call from up ahead. Elizabeth looked up and could see Colonel Fitzwilliam peering down at them from atop a bluff of rock.

"Until you have attempted this climb in skirts, I beg you would refrain from casting aspersions about my pace, sir," she called back, laughing.

"Why have you stopped?" Darcy called to him. "Have you given up?"

Mr Gardiner's face appeared next to Colonel Fitzwilliam's. "No, but I have!" When Elizabeth and Darcy reached the same plateau, it became clear why. From here, the path passed around the cliff edge above an exceedingly steep drop. "I do not fancy my chances, Lizzy," he explained. "And I certainly should not like you to risk it. Besides, we had better not leave your aunt for too long. Look, though," he added, nodding towards the edge. "That is a fine view, is it not?"

Elizabeth hid her disappointment as best she could but had no trouble agreeing that the view, even from this height, was spectacular. Colonel Fitzwilliam and Darcy took turns pointing out various landmarks and Elizabeth spotted Mrs

Gardiner and Lord Sutcliffe below, who eventually noticed her waving and waved back. At length, Mr Gardiner declared that they ought to return and, as before, he and Fitzwilliam led the way. Elizabeth turned for one last look across the valley, smiling to herself at the beauty of the place. She felt, rather than saw Darcy step abreast of her and stand shoulder to shoulder looking out in the same direction. Her heart rattled out three or four entirely superfluous beats.

"I did not have the opportunity to respond yesterday when you thanked me for helping your sister," he said in a subdued voice. "I am pleased to have done anything that gave you happiness, but I do not deserve your gratitude. You warned me I was injuring people in my resolve to preserve my own honour, and you were proved right in the most lamentable way. Miss Lydia would never have been endangered had not my fear of being exposed meant that I allowed Wickham's character to be so grievously misunderstood."

Elizabeth winced and looked down, unnecessarily tugging her gloves on tighter. "Mr Darcy, I have long been heartily sorry I spoke so unkindly on that subject. I have since come to comprehend that you had no choice but to conceal the truth, for I recognise that you cannot undo the past." She lifted her eyes to the horizon. "And I know it was not only yourself you were protecting by keeping Mr Wickham's letter for all those years."

Darcy made no reply. A quick glance showed that he, too, was looking into the distance, and with a pained expression.

"I also know you tried to give it back."

He looked at her, evidently surprised, then away again. "I did." The corner of his mouth twitched upwards. "You were right about that, too. It was more resentment than necessity that made me keep it for so long."

A faint call from somewhere off down the hill made them frown at each other and turn in unison to look over the same bluff from which Colonel Fitzwilliam had peered before. Mr Gardiner was farther down, gesturing for her to make haste. "For it looks like rain, Lizzy, and we ought to be getting back!"

What few clouds there were did not look particularly dark, and Elizabeth rather thought her uncle did not like her being alone with Darcy, but if *he* was offended, he was good enough to say nothing of it as they set off down the slope. The skirts that she had only jokingly bemoaned on the way up proved an actual hindrance on the way down, and she had to pick her way carefully, holding them above her boots that she could see where to put her feet. The slower pace meant they were better able to converse, though, and in a voice loud enough that Darcy, who was descending the slope behind her, could hear, she said, "I am sorry Lydia's recklessness required you to keep the letter after all the mortifications you must have borne in conceding to give it up."

"You need not apologise for that," he replied. "I was already reconsidering my intention of handing it over before I even discovered your sister was there. I had hoped to find Wickham improved, as you rightly pointed out I ought to allow, but his greed was unabated. He could have lived very comfortably on the settlement I offered him, but he thought it not enough."

"Was it less than was in your father's will?"

There was a slight pause before Darcy said, "Miss Bennet, I know not what Wickham has told you, but there *was* no money in the will. My father cut him off before he died."

Elizabeth whirled around to face him, all agitation, but her feet slipped on the same stones Darcy's had earlier, and she fell—and would have tumbled to her hands and knees had he not lunged forward and caught her elbow. He gently pulled her up, and there they remained, her heart beating wildly in her chest, confusion and dismay knotting her brows together.

"I went to give him the money not because it was his due,

but because of what you taught me." This close to her, Darcy's voice seemed to resonate in her breast. "I *have* been selfish. I have been conceited, I have been bitter—and I have been an utter fool." His gentle grip on her elbow increased slightly, and it felt as though his thumb caressed her arm, but then he let go and stepped away from her with a small shake of his head. "Would that I could undo the past, but I cannot. I am attending to all your reproofs, though, Elizabeth."

The air between them had grown so thick Elizabeth could scarcely breathe; her name on his lips stole the last of the air from her lungs. She nodded, and in an almost soundless whisper said, "I know."

He smiled the most unutterably sad smile. "I pray it has made you think better of me. The past may be unalterable, but I could bear the future infinitely better if I knew I had lessened your ill opinion."

She shook her head in abject misery to see Darcy humble himself for her, when she had shown him nothing but prepossession and scorn. "I do not think ill of you at all. Quite the contrary."

"Darcy, have you fallen off the edge? Make haste, man!"

Darcy cast only a brief look in the direction of his cousin's voice before returning his burning gaze to Elizabeth. She was almost too embarrassed to look at him but, seeing the urgency with which he searched her countenance, she forced herself to speak. "Indeed, I really think it is I who have been a fool."

With timing so unfortunate Elizabeth could not help but laugh despite the significance of the moment, Colonel Fitzwilliam appeared over the crest of the rise, breathless and red-faced from his exertions. "Darcy, get a move on. Mr Gardiner is all a-jitter wondering what you've done with his niece."

Darcy did not take his eyes off Elizabeth as he replied, "Miss Bennet lost her footing. We are coming now." He offered her his hand and, unlike in Kent, when she had resented his assistance, she took it, and welcomed his strong grip as they descended the stony escarpment. Colonel Fitzwilliam, and Mr Gardiner when they reached him, both expressed their concern for her having slipped, but she assured them she was well and together they all clambered cautiously back down to the others, Elizabeth turning to look for Darcy's support as often as he offered it.

"I am sorry we took so long," Mr Gardiner said to his wife when they were together again. "Lizzy almost took a fall."

"That is a vast exaggeration, Uncle. I merely slipped on some loose stones. It just meant I took greater care coming down. I did not realise you wished to sprint to the bottom."

"Hardly! Indeed, I think I held the Colonel up as much as anyone."

"Do not be fooled by the military connexion, sir," said Darcy with his usual impassive delivery. "The training is definitely wearing off in his dotage."

"Have at it, Darcy!" cried Colonel Fitzwilliam. "I had to climb the bally thing twice thanks to your dallying."

"Well, I should have been happy had you taken another hour," said Mrs Gardiner, smiling at them all. "Lord Sutcliffe has been entertaining me perfectly well with tales of all your past misadventures."

"Oh, Lord," Colonel Fitzwilliam groaned. "Do not believe a word of it, madam. It is all lies."

"I should not worry, sir," Elizabeth said. With her gaze fixed firmly and deliberately on Darcy, she concluded, "I have come to be of the opinion that the past is not such a great evil, as long as one is not mean enough to resent it."

There was no switching of places with anyone else in the party on the walk back to The Rose and Crown. Whilst the others mingled and chatted, Elizabeth walked in silence with Darcy. She was too distracted attempting to decipher the meaning of all that had been said between them to speak, and if she might judge from his look of concentration, his mind was not very differently engaged. Not until they parted ways did Elizabeth summon enough courage to look at him again properly. His appearance, as he expressed his anticipation to see her at dinner the next day, was too serious to be called happy, but in his eyes, Elizabeth fancied she could see a hope that mirrored her own.

32
A Manifest Reminder

MRS GARDINER WAS NOW ALMOST CERTAINLY WISE TO there being a greater familiarity between her niece and Darcy than she had previously suspected, for, over the next four-and-twenty hours, she made too many sly remarks about his looks and manners and asked too many questions about Elizabeth's time in Kent for it to be a coincidence. Elizabeth bore it as disinterestedly as she could, unwilling to arouse her aunt's hopes when her own were still so tentative. Yet she did hope, with all her heart, that she had not imagined the advancement she and Darcy seemed to have made in their understanding.

She laughed at herself for the care she took getting dressed for dinner but was nevertheless pleased when her uncle remarked how well she looked. Anticipation bloomed in her stomach as the carriage set off, and memories warmed her cheeks as they drove past High Tor. She did her best to attend to the conversation, agreeing with her relations that dining with an earl was an exceedingly exciting addition to their itinerary. It was still necessary for Mrs Gardiner to recall her from her reveries more than once in order that she answer a question or give an opinion.

They eventually arrived, and Kelstedge Abbey rose out of the landscape with majestic grandeur as they rolled along the absurdly long driveway. Elizabeth peered up at the many windows and wondered whether Miss Paxton would keep better hold of her charge this evening, or if Anna would make an unplanned appearance at dinner.

"One wonders whether any of them will object to Lady Matlock's having invited us," said Mrs Gardiner with an impish smile, gesturing towards the richly dressed ladies and gentlemen stepping down from the several other carriages arranged at the front of the house. Elizabeth and Mr Gardiner both grinned with her, none of them being unduly awed by the distinction of rank, and all of them sensible enough to believe that if Lord and Lady Matlock did not object, it was unlikely any of their guests would presume to disapprove. They were announced formally into the drawing room behind two other couples and a baron, all of whose names Elizabeth instantly forgot when, instead of Darcy, her search of the room revealed the presence of an altogether less agreeable guest.

"Lizzy? Whatever is the matter, you look as though you have seen a ghost," Mrs Gardiner whispered.

Elizabeth nodded towards the far side of the room. "The woman talking to Lord Sutcliffe is Miss Bingley."

Her aunt looked thither with evident interest, but there was no time for further discussion, for Lady Matlock then approached from a different part of the room.

"Good evening, everybody. You are very welcome. Allow me to introduce you all." This she proceeded to do, and Elizabeth smiled and nodded and curtseyed where it was required and paid no attention to anybody's names this time either, for she was too busy berating herself for being so affected by Miss Bingley's presence. A surreptitious nudge from Mrs Gardiner drew her attention to Darcy's approach. She smiled warmly, pleased and strangely comforted to see him at that moment.

"Good evening, Miss Bennet," he said, fixing her with the fervent look she had come to covet. "You look extremely well."

She thanked him and, resolved not to be troubled by it, said immediately, "I see Miss Bingley is returned."

"Yes." His smile disappeared and he looked exceedingly uncomfortable. Drawing her away from the others, he lowered his voice and said, "I hope you will forgive my not mentioning it before. She was not expected back until tomorrow."

"Halifax could not please her then?" Elizabeth replied with sanguinity she did not feel.

Darcy frowned. "I do not recall mentioning that she was in Halifax."

"You did not. Another, more diminutive member of your party mentioned it, when I was here two days ago."

"In the gardens?"

Elizabeth nodded.

"She told me she had seen you from a window."

He looked incredulous and vexed all at once, and Elizabeth laughed before she could prevent herself at a five-year old having confounded a man so unused to being disobeyed. "Pray do not be too hard on her. She is a dear girl." She meant only to save Anna a scolding but, more than chasing away Darcy's anger, she earned herself a look of intense gratitude.

"Thank you," he said with grave sincerity, a sentiment she would have enjoyed much more did it not remind her of the cold disdain with which she had responded the first time he expressed the hope that she would one day esteem Anna as he did.

Determined not to waste her evening being maudlin, she

affected a lighter tone and enquired, "Might I ask a favour of you?"

"Of course."

"Could you tell me who all these people are? Your aunt introduced them, but I confess I have forgotten most already."

He agreed readily, though, when Lady Matlock interrupted their tête-à-tête as she breezed past a few minutes later, Elizabeth realised she had paid far more attention to the shape of Darcy's mouth when he talked than to anything that had come out of it, and resigned herself to fudging her way through the evening without knowing anybody's name.

"Darcy," Lady Matlock said in her singularly compelling voice, "I believe Sutcliffe could do with some assistance." Indeed, his lordship did look to be tiring of Miss Bingley's company, and was all but hanging off the end of the sofa in his efforts to lean away from her. With an unhappy but resigned look, Darcy excused himself, and Lady Matlock turned to Elizabeth. "And how are you, Miss Bennet? I understand you fell off a mountain yesterday. You look remarkably well, considering."

Elizabeth laughed with delight. "Yes, my foot slipped on a pebble. I was fortunate to survive really."

"I am glad you did," her ladyship murmured. "Salvaging one fallen woman is inconvenience enough for me. I am grown prodigiously weary of the disruption. You will remember your promise to ensure my efforts have not been in vain, will you not?"

It chafed somewhat to be asked again, but Elizabeth supposed her ladyship had greater cause for concern with Miss Bingley in attendance. She politely repeated her assurances, which her hostess received with a nod and an enigmatic smile before drifting away to speak to another of her guests. Elizabeth turned to look for Mr and Mrs Gardiner only to discover they were now speaking to Darcy and Miss Bingley. Who had instigated the introduction she could not suppose, but for Jane's sake, she told herself she was pleased and forced herself to smile as she joined the group.

"Miss Bennet," Miss Bingley said, with the same condescending tone Elizabeth recalled from before. "I was just saying to your aunt and uncle what a surprise it was to learn you were here. You do not look a bit different to how I remember you looking all those months ago in Hertfordshire." She cast a sly glance at Darcy as she said this, and Elizabeth's gaze followed, but it was impossible to tell what he made of the remark. He was staring hard enough at the far wall to burn a hole in it, but his expression was inscrutable, and he said nothing in defence of either lady.

"Thank you," Elizabeth replied innocuously. "Jane informs us that Mr Bingley has returned to Netherfield."

"Yes, he seemed to like its country charm."

"Do you plan to join him there?" enquired Mrs Gardiner.

"No," Miss Bingley replied with an affected laugh. "I am for Nottingham tomorrow for a few days. There is a shoemaker there who has been recommended to me."

Mrs Gardiner looked rather bemused by this answer, and well she might, for it hardly explained the broader question of why an unmarried woman was gadding about the country without her brother.

"Have you visited any of the petrifying wells hereabouts, Miss Bingley?" Elizabeth enquired to change the subject.

"I have not," she replied. "They do not appeal to me in the slightest. Altogether too cold and damp."

Mrs Gardiner agreed with her, and Mr Gardiner spent several minutes amiably attempting to change both their minds. Elizabeth listened with a growing sense of sadness. She wondered whether Miss Bingley were even aware that her daughter believed in fairies, let alone that she thought they lived in the wells.

Darcy caught her eye and seemed about to speak, but Miss Bingley gave another of her loud titters, and he clamped his mouth shut on whatever it might have been. Elizabeth fancied he must be suffering the same agonies as she, for a more manifest reminder of the past they had both talked of overcoming could not have been placed before them. She sent him a reassuring smile, which seemed to mollify him somewhat, but there was little else either could do to escape their present misery.

THE CALL TO DINNER OFFERED ELIZABETH SOME SMALL relief, though not so Darcy. Either the frenzied milling about of the other guests as they jostled for the most prestigious seats, or some exceedingly clever manoeuvring on Miss Bingley's part, saw Elizabeth seated between Colonel Fitzwilliam and a Mr Turner, and Darcy stranded two seats away and across the table with Miss Bingley. They were not so far apart as would prevent them conversing altogether, but his stormy glower was enough to persuade Elizabeth that the arrangement was not of his choosing.

"Miss Bennet, might I ask how you know Lord and Lady Matlock?" enquired Mr Turner as they all tucked into their soup. "I feel rather cheated that they have not introduced us before. Have they been keeping you to themselves by design, or is it a new acquaintance?"

"It is relatively new, sir," she replied. "I met Mr Darcy first, when he stayed at a house near my own in Hertfordshire last year. Then at Easter, I met Colonel Fitzwilliam at Rosings Park."

"Rosings?" he said with some distaste.

"Oh yes," Colonel Fitzwilliam confirmed. "Miss Bennet has had the honour of meeting Lady Catherine."

Mr Turner pulled a face. "I am not sure I would call it an honour."

"Mr Turner is not an admirer of my aunt," Colonel Fitzwilliam explained. "He proposed to Anne once and was refused."

"I never got that far, Fitzy. I only mentioned to a mutual friend that I fancied the look of the exotic trees in Rosings' orangery and thought that marrying Miss de Bourgh seemed as good a way as any to get my hands on them. But Lady Cathy was not enamoured with the idea, even though I am absurdly rich."

Elizabeth raised an eyebrow, but the colonel corroborated the claim. "'Tis true, Miss Bennet. His fortune is perfectly indecent."

"Regrettably, it seems not to count for anything these days," Mr Turner countered. "Her ladyship would rather keep it in the family." He looked pointedly at Darcy, who looked back darkly, no doubt displeased to be the subject of, but not party to, their conversation.

"You should ask her again, you know," said Colonel Fitzwilliam. "For Darcy has told her categorically now that he will not marry Anne."

"Has he?" replied Mr Turner, mirroring Elizabeth's own astonishment.

"Aye. He made a special journey for the purpose in June. I understand it did not go down at all well. You might find that your offer is more appealing these days."

Elizabeth looked back to Darcy. He was talking to Lord Sutcliffe now, thus she dared to watch him a little longer. 'I am attending to all your reproofs,' he had told her. *Every one, without fail, it would seem!* Indeed, she had never known another person more willing to attend to his mistakes on so little foundation as her judgment alone. When Darcy noticed her watching him, she did not look away, but met his gaze with a smile that she hoped resembled Anna's proud expression whenever she had run somewhere fast, for she was, genuinely, proud.

"I think I might propose to Miss Bennet instead."

"Pardon?" she said, looking at Mr Turner in surprise.

"What do you say, shall I ask you to marry me? I am frightfully rich, and devilishly handsome, after all." He winked at her for good measure.

"No, I really do not think you should."

"Why ever not?"

"I do not have an orangery, sir. I should be a perennial disappointment to you."

His loud burst of laughter made her jump.

"Careful, Miss Bennet, or you might really make him like you," said Colonel Fitzwilliam, chuckling. "And take it from me, you do not want this man pursuing you. He once chased me down from Covent Garden to Eastbourne because I owed him a pound."

"You owed me ten and stole my horse to get away!" Mr Turner replied, jabbing the table with a forefinger, at which point Elizabeth could not help but join in laughing at their silliness. She stopped again when she saw Darcy watching them with an expression that she had once been convinced was unqualified contempt, but which she now thought looked more like intense yearning.

"We were just discussing Mr Turner's fondness for exotic trees, Mr Darcy," she said in a voice loud enough to include him.

"And the lengths to which he will go to get them," added Colonel Fitzwilliam.

"I bet you have a few at Pemberley, do you not, Darcy?" said Mr Turner.

"One or two, donated by Sir Lewis. Not many."

"You do not care for the exotic?"

"Pemberley was designed to complement the Derbyshire landscape. Anything extraneous would be—" He looked at Elizabeth with a slight smile. "—over-seasoning."

"It sounds to me as though you do not care for the specimens you have," Mr Turner said.

"You must not set your heart on them, though, sir," Elizabeth told him, and answered his querying look by adding, "I do not think Mr Darcy will marry you either."

"Pray, what is so amusing?" enquired Miss Bingley, drawn from the conversation on her right by the increasing liveliness of the one on her left.

"We are talking orangeries, madam," said Mr Turner. "Have you one?"

"Not yet," she replied, "but there is a wonderful orangery at Pemberley. It has a pineapple plant that is quite the most impressive thing in the whole park."

The brief flash of incredulity that Darcy hastily quashed nevertheless drew a ripple of laughter from Elizabeth that she could not suppress. It drew his piercing gaze, as it so often did, and it occurred to her that he simply wished to know what amused her. She could scarcely explain at present that she had always been diverted by Miss Bingley's unsuccessful attempts to be an authority on his every opinion. All she could do was smile and hope they would have the opportunity to speak before the evening was done.

33

Unalterable Pasts

WHEN THE LADIES WITHDREW AFTER DINNER, LADY Matlock enquired whether any of them would oblige the party with a turn at the pianoforte. Elizabeth was vastly pleased when Miss Bingley stepped up to the instrument. She may exhibit her talents as much as she chose; they far exceeded Elizabeth's own, and her being thus occupied would spare them the awkwardness of talking to each other. She sat with Mrs Gardiner as far from the instrument as possible.

"You had a lot of fun at your end of the table, Lizzy," said her aunt. "Mr Turner seems very amusing."

"He certainly thinks he is."

"You did not like him?"

"I did not *dislike* him. He is a very good-natured gentleman. It is just, all that raillery and swagger—even if it is tongue-in-cheek—gets a little tiresome after a while. Wit is infinitely more satisfying when it is clever than when it is merely loud."

"You prefer a more dignified sort of gentleman, do you?" her aunt replied with a sly look that made Elizabeth wary of answering. She did not need to, for they were joined then by

Lady Matlock and, subsequently, each of the other ladies as they all moved around, filling and refilling their cups and taking turns at the pianoforte. Eventually, however, a conversation with Miss Bingley could no longer be avoided. They were caught together at the refreshment table and could not politely evade one another.

After indicating that they step away from the footman serving the drinks, Miss Bingley said, "I am glad to have the opportunity to speak to you privately at last," apparently not of the same mind as Elizabeth after all.

"You are?" she replied in a quiet voice.

"Yes. I wished to express my gratitude."

This is becoming a ridiculous habit. "I am quite sure I have done nothing to deserve it."

"On the contrary. I know it was you who made Darcy rethink everything. My situation will be wholly transformed after years of—well, I shall call it misery, for it was scarcely a happy time, and it is thanks to you."

They were obliged to pause while another of the ladies approached with an empty cup. Once she had passed them by, Elizabeth said, "I am not sure I take your meaning."

"My troubles began nearly six years ago," Miss Bingley said under her breath. "During that time, I have been moved from place to place, never permitted to remain longer than it took for people to begin talking, never permitted to fully enjoy the privileges that most women of my station, or with my means, are at liberty to enjoy."

Elizabeth did not consider that Miss Bingley had forfeited much in the way of privilege, but she remembered her promise to Lady Matlock and held her tongue.

"Darcy has looked after me prodigiously well," she continued, "but he has never forgiven me." Elizabeth's expression must have revealed something of her thoughts here, for Miss Bingley raised her eyebrows and said, "You must have seen how he treated me in Hertfordshire. No matter how I tried, I could never please him. He was ashamed of me—and I have been ashamed of myself. But when he came to me and explained that you had made him realise his resentment was misplaced, and that he meant to cease concealing me from the world and allow me the life I have always desired—that was the first time I, too, comprehended that I was not wholly to blame. So, you see, you have done more for me than you imagine. Were it not for you, I might have remained in obscurity forever. Now I shall have the chance to live again."

Elizabeth had not given up hope until the very last part of this speech was done that Miss Bingley might make some mention of her daughter. It saddened her beyond measure when she did not, though it did not surprise her; she knew Miss Bingley to be utterly self-absorbed. "I am pleased your marriage will enable you to enjoy the society of which you are so fond."

Miss Bingley did not seem pleased with this answer, but Elizabeth was at the end of her forbearance. She wished Miss Bingley the best and returned to the sofa, where Mrs Gardiner was talking to some of the other ladies about their plans in Lambton.

"Lambton?" enquired Miss Bingley, coming to perch next to Elizabeth.

"Yes, the next stop on our travels," Mrs Gardiner explained.

"Oh, how lovely. Are you aware it is but five miles from Mr Darcy's home?"

"Yes, we know," said Elizabeth impatiently.

"Does he know you plan to stay there? You ought to tell him, for I am sure he would not object to your visiting Pemberley in his absence."

"His absence?"

"Yes." She looked at Elizabeth strangely. "Obviously we will have gone to Leeds by then."

Seeing that the conversation had continued between the other ladies, Elizabeth leant close to Miss Bingley and whispered, "But you are going to Leeds to get married."

Her heart had already pre-empted the reply and was hammering its beat in her ears, but the way in which Miss Bingley now regarded her—as though she were a simpleton—made her feel bilious.

"Yes," Miss Bingley murmured. "I thought that was clear. It is what I have been attempting to thank you for."

Elizabeth stared, her breath caught uselessly in her throat, and could say nothing. The meaning of a dozen conversations that had previously seemed inconsequential crashed over her in a sickening wave. 'I am attending to all your reproofs, Elizabeth.' *All of them, from withholding Wickham's letter to separating Bingley and Jane, apparently.* Her stomach turned over so violently she feared she might be ill as she recalled her severest reproof of all. 'Had you only acted properly to begin with and married Miss Bingley.'

She put her cup down to stop it rattling against its saucer and folded her hands in her lap. This was the true reason he had formally released himself from any obligation to Miss de Bourgh. This explained the pain with which he had spoken yesterday of being unable to change the past, and of desiring her forgiveness to make the future more palatable. Was it also Lady Matlock's real concern? Not that Elizabeth might expose their scandalous secret before a marriage could take place, but that her unexpected arrival might remind Darcy where his heart truly lay and persuade him to change his mind altogether. No wonder her ladyship had interrupted their private talk earlier to remind her of her promise.

Tears seared her eyes, and she took several deep breaths to dispel them, for she would not make a scene; she would not break her promise. Yet, worse than the crushing mortification of having been such a fool, worse than the suffocating feeling of her heart struggling to regain its rhythm, was how desperately, inexpressibly sad she felt for Darcy. For though she knew what he was doing was absolutely right, she also knew it would make him miserable for the rest of his life. And she had so wished for the opportunity to make him happy. To love him.

When the door opened and the gentlemen filed in, she could hardly even bear to raise her eyes. She knew he would come to her and could not prevent it, but was glad, in a perverse way, of Miss Bingley's decision to sit with her. Nothing could be said while she was present. He came, and for an interminable length of time spoke with every lady in that part of the room but her, because she would not, could not, meet his eye. She felt his gaze on her but had not the courage to return it. Given half the chance, she would have run and run and never looked back. Instead, she remained where she was and listened to his voice and rued every moment of their acquaintance at which she had fallen a little more in love with him.

"Lizzy, would you be a dear and fetch me some more tea?" her aunt enquired, holding out her cup. Elizabeth took it, grateful for the excuse to walk away, though she was not really surprised when Darcy followed her.

"What has happened?" he said urgently when they were safely away from the others.

Oh, how she wished to be anywhere in the world but there! She filled her lungs and forced some semblance of a smile onto her face and told him, "Nothing."

"That will not wash, Miss Bennet." His voice was a deep, demanding whisper. "Something has clearly distressed you. Pray, tell me what it is."

Elizabeth had never felt so bereft. She was used to being

braver, had withstood challenges from enough quarters to expect a better performance, but all her courage had deserted her now, and she could not answer him. Indeed, she knew not what else to do other than continue, dazedly, to the refreshment table and hold out her aunt's cup to be refilled. She made to return to her seat, but Darcy stood in her way, his countenance intensely troubled.

He bent his head down towards hers and, in a voice so low it was almost inaudible, said, "I am sorry for the situation with Miss Bingley. If I could have arranged it any differently, please believe I would have."

A noise escaped her; she hardly knew what it signified—defeat, perhaps—and she set her aunt's cup down heavily, spilling hot tea on her hand. She winced and tucked it beneath her other arm.

"Dear God, enough is enough, Elizabeth!" Darcy hissed. "You must know I would end this nonsense this instant if you would only tell me that is what you wish."

"Stop it, please," she breathed. It was the hardest thing she had ever done not to surrender her whole life, her whole heart, to his keeping. But she would not speak against a decision that was ultimately the only right thing to do. "You are being unfair."

"Am I? What, then, was all that you said of the past not being such a great evil?"

She looked up then, and he was at once blurred beyond all recognition by the tears in her eyes, and such a comforting sight it tore at her heart. "It is not, and I truly do not resent yours. But I cannot undo it any more than you can."

She saw before he did that Miss Bingley was behind him. She watched her loop her arm through Darcy's; she recognised his disgust, and she had her countenance under far better regulation than he when Miss Bingley said, "What do I not owe this man, Miss Bennet? I could not be more grateful to him, or more hopeful for the future. Come, sir. Lady Matlock wishes that you attend her."

Elizabeth looked in that direction and her ladyship was, indeed, watching them with steely eyes. *Ready to ensure I do not break my word,* she thought wretchedly. She looked at Darcy with a small but profoundly heartfelt smile. "You had better go, sir. I wish you every happiness. Truly."

It mattered not that Darcy snatched his arm from Miss Bingley's and insisted that he would be back within minutes; Elizabeth could bear no more. She found her uncle and begged him to take her home directly. Before Darcy could extricate himself from any of the women clamouring for his attention, Elizabeth was in her carriage on her way back to The Rose and Crown, never so grateful to have left a place in her life but crumbling inside for having walked away from the best man she had ever known.

34

Running Away

The route to Lambton was particularly picturesque, though without any notable landmarks on which one might comment. Thus, they travelled mostly in appreciative silence, for which Elizabeth was prodigiously grateful. Her excuse for leaving Kelstedge Abbey in such haste had been a sudden and severe headache, though she had not truly expected anybody to believe it. Yet she had cried enough tears and lost enough hours of sleep that night to bring about a real headache the next day, and the tranquil carriage ride was soothing to the raw edges of her shattered spirits.

They had not been due to leave Matlock until Monday, but Elizabeth had been so fearful Darcy would call at the inn that she begged her aunt and uncle to leave early, claiming embarrassment for her precipitate departure from dinner as a reason for wishing to avoid an encounter with any of the family. Mr Gardiner, ever tolerant of the wishes of the women in his life, agreed, and they set off as soon as could reasonably be arranged. Now, with ten or more miles behind them, the idea of Darcy calling seemed ludicrous. As good as twice refused and condemned by this second rejection to a wretched existence as Miss Bingley's husband, Elizabeth could not imagine his ever wishing to set eyes on her again.

She ached with sorrow to think of the anger in his tone and the pain in his eyes as he challenged her remarks about the evils of the past. She would never have said such a thing, never given him such false hope, had she known of his intention to marry Miss Bingley. Yet, she ought to have known. It must have been why he asked her, on the walk to High Tor, whether she objected to his having come. He had been reconciled to his fate, had told her he wished to secure her forgiveness before he submitted to it, and had only been anxious that she would not be so accepting. Except she had done more than offer her forgiveness. She had, as Lady Matlock predicted she might, thrown all Darcy's good intentions into question when she avowed that she no longer considered his past—the very reason she had rejected his proposal—an evil. It was the cruellest twist of fate that she should have raised his hopes in all innocence, only to dash them again upon finally comprehending the truth.

It pained her beyond anything to think how he must now hate her. Would that they had parted on better terms, Darcy assured not only of her forgiveness but also her esteem. Though, he could not have gleaned that from her petulant and acrimonious refusal in Kent. And try as she might, she could not recall that while they were on High Tor she had said anything more affectionate than that she did not think ill of him. And there certainly had not been any opportunity to make her feelings known yesterday.

Elizabeth thought she had cried all her tears the night before, but it seemed she was mistaken. More welled in her eyes, and regret squeezed her heart so tightly it bent her forward in her seat when she realised that she had never actually told Darcy she loved him.

"There, look," said Mr Gardiner. "I can see Lambton

tucked down in that next valley. We ought to be there in the next quarter of an hour. What say you two explore the town a little while I sort out our lodgings, eh?"

Elizabeth forced herself to smile, but as she turned to accede to the idea with a nod, she observed the look her aunt and uncle were giving each other. Their concern shamed her, for they did not deserve to have their trip spoiled by her maudlin foolishness. She forced her smile wider and blinked her eyes clear. "I should like to see the medieval bridge you told me about. Shall we walk along the river?"

"A fine idea, Lizzy," Mrs Gardiner replied gently. "And if the little confectioners is still there, I shall buy us both a treat."

It was not, as it turned out, but it did not matter. The sun was hot, the air balmy, and the bridge, when they reached it, treat enough, for Mrs Gardiner's reminiscences of Lambton as they stood atop it and watched the river dawdle by distracted Elizabeth from more distressing thoughts for a blessedly long time.

"There was a young man from the other end of the village who took a fancy to me one summer," Mrs Gardiner said at length. "He used to come calling with bunches of wildflowers for me and baskets of duck eggs for my mother. It was ever so sweet."

"That *is* sweet," Elizabeth replied. "Did not you welcome his attentions?"

"Aye, I did. Until they ceased. I never did find out why he stopped calling."

Elizabeth watched the water swirl and dance out of sight beneath the bridge and waited, for she could well guess why her aunt had begun this particular tale. She was not kept waiting long.

"Men can be inconstant, Lizzy. As you have seen with Mr Bingley."

"Not all men," she replied miserably, thinking of the honour that required Darcy to be constant to someone else.

"No. Not all of them." After a pause, her aunt added, "Your uncle and I have not asked you to divulge what happened yesterday, and neither shall we. But I know you well enough to suspect it is not a trifling matter. You are obviously very distressed, for I have never seen you this quiet or this distracted."

"I beg you would forgive me. I shall make every effort to be livelier. The last thing I wish is to ruin your trip."

"Hush! Do not be silly. That was not my meaning. I only wish you to know that you may talk to me, if it would help."

Elizabeth laughed nervously in a bid to stave off more tears. "Thank you, but—" She paused, unable to explain that she was not at liberty to tell her aunt even a quarter of what troubled her.

"It is well, my dear," Mrs Gardiner said. "You need not explain. My offer stands, but I shall not be offended if you choose not to take me up on it. And pray do not waste another moment worrying about our trip. We shall enjoy your company no less for it being a little quieter than usual. Indeed, I expect your mother would argue it is a marked improvement."

Elizabeth laughed more genuinely, prompting her aunt to grin and tell her, "That is more like it," but the kindness drew forth the tears she had been so desperately trying to contain. Mrs Gardiner reached to squeeze her hand. "Oh, my dear girl. Would there were something I could do to make it easier for you."

"There is," Elizabeth replied with a wry laugh as she wiped her eyes with the heel of her palm. "Do not make me go to Pemberley." They had previously agreed not to, but that was before Mr and Mrs Gardiner had been introduced to Darcy; before the former had declared him to be polite, unassuming, and extraordinarily generous; before the latter had complimented him on being attentive, dignified, and uncommonly handsome. Elizabeth feared they might now consider a visit more reasonable. A request to avoid one was as close as she would come to acknowledging that her distress pertained in some way to Darcy, but it was enough for her aunt, who patted her hand reassuringly.

"I would not dream of it. The grounds are overrated anyway. I do not think you would like them at all."

WITH PERMISSION FROM HER RELATIONS TO BE SAD without disguise, Elizabeth excused herself to bed very soon after dinner and made no pretence of the fact that she was too heartsore and too tired to partake in any more conversation. This was not how she had envisioned her trip would go, however, and she resolved that, after allowing herself one more evening of self-pity, she would begin the next day more sanguine.

Sanguine was not quite the word she would have chosen to describe the numbness to which she awoke after a second night of miserable reflections and desolate dreams. Still, she *had* slept, and she remembered how to laugh when she caught a glimpse of her rather pitiful reflection in the dressing mirror the next morning. She readied herself with care and joined Mr and Mrs Gardiner at the breakfast table with a small but unforced smile and her thanks for their understanding.

"You look a little better this morning," said her aunt. "Did you sleep well?"

"Aye, thank you," she lied. Draping her napkin over her lap, she enquired, "So, what adventures have we planned for today?"

Mr Gardiner took his cue and began listing options as the maid arrived with their breakfast. She was the same girl as had served them dinner before but last night she had appeared to be a chirpy, talkative soul, full of joy and running on in a way that would have horrified even Mrs Bennet. This morning she seemed distracted and went about the business of serving them in a hurried, careless manner.. When she dropped a dish of butter in her haste, Mr Gardiner drew a line.

"Have a care, now. This will not do."

"Beggin' yer pardon, sir. Only all's been in up'eaval downstairs, what with the search party going off, and I'm under strict instructions to make up time now they've all left."

"Heavens, that sounds serious," cried Mrs Gardiner, "For what is everyone searching?"

"A little girl, ma'am." All three of the party simultaneously expressed their dismay, and buoyed by the sympathetic response, the maid added, "She is but five years old."

"Is there anything we can do?" said Mr Gardiner, who Elizabeth suspected was thinking of his own young children, for he had come over exceptionally sombre.

The maid shook her head. "I don't 'xpect so, sir. She's gone missing from Kelstedge Abbey, all the way over at Matlock Bath. Only, Lord Matlock is Mr Darcy's uncle, and Mr Darcy sent for some of his men from Pemberley to join the search."

"A five-year old? From Kelstedge?" said Mrs Gardiner in confusion, at the same time as Elizabeth cried, "I think I know where she might be!"

She had no time to care how strangely everybody regarded her. If it was Anna who was missing—and there was cause aplenty to suspect that it was—then she had a very good idea where she might be found. She leapt from her chair, sending it scraping backwards across the floorboards. "Oh, where is my writing case? I must write a letter. We can send it express. I know exactly the place!"

"Lizzy? Lizzy! What on earth is going on? You are going to have to explain, or we shall not know what to do for the best!"

The maid was dismissed, and Elizabeth obliged to sit with her uncle while Mrs Gardiner fetched some paper and a pen. "Now tell me, girl, what do you know?"

She took a deep breath, frantically attempting to collect her thoughts, to gauge what she could and could not, ought and ought not to reveal. "I met a young girl in the grounds at Kelstedge last week, while I was exploring the dripping well."

"You did not mention it at the time."

"No. I was distracted by Mr Darcy's appearance." It was true in a roundabout way; it would have to do. "She showed me a place farther off the path, where she was convinced fairies lived. It is not terribly far from the house, and they might very well have looked there already—only there was a deep hole in the rock that anyone might slip into, and I cannot help but think she might have returned there. Pray, let me write a letter and send it express, or with a servant, for it cannot harm the search, can it?" Her words tumbled out in a rush that matched the galloping of her heart, but if Anna had gone missing yesterday, and if she *was* in the well, as she suspected, then the poor child had been exposed to the elements all night. Elizabeth felt nauseous to think of her fright, and her heart broke to imagine what Darcy must be suffering.

Her uncle agreed it was imperative that she send word, and he and Mrs Gardiner waited nearby as she tried, and tried again to put into words how one tiny crevice in the Derbyshire landscape might be distinguished from the countless others in the area.

"But who is she, that Mr Darcy is so concerned about her?" Mrs Gardiner said. "She must be *somebody* for him to send for his own men to join the search."

Elizabeth attended assiduously to her letter and pretended not to be listening.

"Oh, I do not know," Mr Gardiner demurred. "He helped

Lydia when he had scarcely any connexion to us. It is not such a great leap of faith to think he might help another family in need. He seems to me to just be a very noble young man."

Everything they said increased Elizabeth's sympathy for Darcy. As though fearing for the safety of his daughter were not enough, he must also be despairing that after all these years struggling to keep her away from the world's notice, such a furore around her disappearance meant the ignominy of her birth might now be discovered mere days before he made her legitimate.

She finished her letter and passed it to her uncle to check. He screwed up his face as he read it.

"I know—it is messy," she said, coming to her feet and anxiously shifting her weight from one foot to the other. "I wrote it too quickly. But it is not illegible is it?"

"No, it is not illegible, Lizzy. But it is unintelligible." Mr Gardiner passed it to his wife for a second opinion. "I do not think they could find the end of the garden from this description."

Mrs Gardiner looked up from the letter with an apologetic grimace that showed she was of the same opinion.

"What am I to write?" Elizabeth cried, wringing her hands together. "I can picture it—the exact spot—but how does one differentiate one big grey rock from another?"

"For heaven's sake, calm yourself," said Mr Gardiner. "Anyone would think the girl was of particular importance to you."

Elizabeth knew not what to say. She could think only of Anna's terror and Darcy's anguish, and after what felt like an interminable length of time withstanding her relations' searching gazes, she whispered, "She is."

"Then why did not you say so?" her uncle exclaimed, coming to his feet. "Never mind writing a paltry letter. Let us go back and help with the search ourselves. We can be there by noon if we leave now."

"Would you?" Elizabeth cried with more feeling than good sense, but she soon remembered herself. "I have imposed enough on your plans already. It would be too great an expense."

"The expense can be spared, my dear. If you wish to go, we shall go. Indeed, I have decided that we ought to go whether you wish it or not, for it would do a darned sight more to ruin our trip if a child came to harm because we chose to enjoy our breakfast at leisure instead of going to help look for her."

"Lizzy," Mrs Gardiner said, coming forward to place a hand on her arm and look at her searchingly. "Your uncle's intentions are good, but you must not feel obliged to return if it would be too difficult."

"Thank you, Aunt, but this is too important for my sensibilities to be of any moment. Please, if it is acceptable to you both, let us go, and as soon as may be."

Thus it was agreed; Mr Gardiner settled his account at the inn, and less than four-and-twenty hours after she had fled the place, Elizabeth found herself seated in the carriage and on the road back to Matlock, all the tiny fragments of her heart held together for now by the urgency of their mission. She would have time again for heartbreak once Anna was found.

35

Turned to Stone

"THERE! I THINK THAT IS IT, CAN YOU SEE IT?"

"I see nothing but rocks and ferns, Lizzy."

"Can we stop the carriage before I lose sight of it?"

Mr Gardiner banged on the roof and called for the driver to wait. They had been driving all morning and were not quite at Kelstedge Abbey itself, but Elizabeth recalled that Anna had taken her to a place within sight of the gatehouse, and she could see that less than quarter of a mile ahead.

"We could get to it from here, do not you think?"

"Do not be absurd," said Mrs Gardiner. "We must go to the house and explain the situation to Lord and Lady Matlock. Nobody will expect you to go clambering about to get to this place yourself."

"I should have to go clambering about to get to it in any case, for you have said yourself how ill I can describe where it is. It is not like the path on High Tor, anyway—it is much easier to get to and not nearly so precipitous. I got to it before without any great difficulty. Please, we are wasting time. She could be hurt."

Mr and Mrs Gardiner exchanged another look of the

variety that had been passing between them all the way from Lambton; the same mix of displeasure, impatience, and worry with which they had received all Elizabeth's equivocations around Anna's identity. That their second eldest niece was one of their most sensible was perhaps her only saving grace, though she knew this latest request was testing the bounds of their forbearance. She could not help but think, though, that if it turned out Anna was not in this place, then they could simply drive away again, without anyone ever knowing they had come.

A chorus of distant shouts bade all of them look up the hill and sent a tremor of dismay through Elizabeth. "They are still looking for her."

"Come then, Lizzy," said Mr Gardiner decisively. "Let us have a closer look at the way up. If it is passable then we shall both go and look." To his wife he said, "Will you be happy to wait here?"

"More than happy," she replied. "Take care, both of you!"

After a brief word with the driver to ensure he remained vigilant, Mr Gardiner indicated to Elizabeth that she should lead the way, and they began the ascent. It was a steep bank, thick with undergrowth, trickier to go up than it looked, yet in less than ten minutes they reached the shelf she had thought she could see from the road. She lost her bearings briefly and thought she had walked too high, but her aunt, who had stepped down from the coach to watch, began gesturing for them to move farther along to the left and after skirting around two more rocky outcroppings, the dripping well was directly in front of them.

Elizabeth ran to the edge and dropped to her knees to peer over the edge, but it was pitch black within. "Anna? Anna, are you in there?"

Her uncle skidded up to her side and joined her in listening for a response. For the longest moment there was nothing but the constant drip, drip of water. Then something moved in the darkness, tilted, and took form—and Anna's dear little face appeared.

"Lizzy?"

"Anna! Oh, Anna, we have found you!" As her uncle turned to shout down to Mrs Gardiner that they had been successful, Elizabeth leant farther into the crevice. "Are you hurt?"

"No, but I am hungry."

Elizabeth smiled with pride and delight to hear that however frightened she may have been, Anna's spirit was far from broken. "Then it is about time we got you out and fed you some breakfast. How high can you reach your arms?"

Anna lifted them above her head, and Elizabeth reached hers down, but there were a dozen inches at least between their outstretched fingers. She lay down on her stomach and tried again, and Mr Gardiner did likewise, with no success. Attempts to direct Anna to different places to find higher ground only confused her. Mr Gardiner took his jacket off and dangled it down for Anna to grab, but she had not the strength to hold on while they pulled it up, and they stopped trying when she began to cry. It was quickly agreed that Mr Gardiner would return to the carriage and go with Mrs Gardiner to the house for help. Elizabeth would remain with Anna.

"Wrap my uncle's coat around you, Anna. Good girl. How deep is the water?"

"At my ankles," she replied. "But there is a bit at the back that is dry. I slept there."

"Have you been here all night?"

"I think so. It got dark, and I could see the stars." She let out a little whimper. "Mr Gardiner's coat is getting wet. Will I be in trouble?"

"Oh, no! Not at all! You must keep it wrapped tightly about you, do you hear? You must not get cold."

"I am not cold, Lizzy." Indeed, the sun was so hot on Elizabeth's back that the cool within the crevice was almost appealing. "I was cold in the night, though," Anna continued more quietly. "I thought the magic water had turned me to stone, like it does everything else." Elizabeth heard a tremble in her voice and that decided her; if Anna could not get out of the well, then she would get in.

"Stand back, Anna. I am going to climb down." It was more of a slippery tumble, but she landed safely on both feet, bracing herself on the opposite rock face to keep from falling. The water was cool, though not icy, and it filled her boots and dragged her skirts down heavily within moments. She had barely found her balance and lowered her arms before Anna fell into them, clinging on tenaciously, her face buried from sight. Elizabeth crouched down, ignoring the water soaking into her stockings and petticoat, and hugged her tightly. "You are safe now. We shall get you out." Then, thinking it best to keep her spirits up, she leant back, lifted Anna's chin with a forefinger, and said more cheerfully, "You have been ever so brave!"

Anna nodded, in her sweet, immodest way. "I was a bit frightened at first, because I could not get out, and nobody answered when I called for help. But then I remembered there were fairies here and that made me not frightened anymore. And I remembered that you said you had to be very quiet to see a fairy, so I stopped shouting, and listened to them talking."

Oh Lord! No wonder they could not find her! "What did they say?"

"I do not know. I do not speak Fairy."

Elizabeth laughed, charmed by her matter-of-fact manner, so like Darcy's. "But tell me seriously, Anna. Did you run away from Miss Paxton again?"

She nodded guiltily.

"Will you heed me now, when I say that running away is dangerous? Everybody has been very worried about you."

"But you ran away."

Childlike frankness was not infinitely endearing. "I did not run away, Anna. I left. It is different."

"But nobody knew where you had gone so that is running away. And everyone was sad that you had left."

"I am sorry to hear that," Elizabeth said quietly.

"Lady Matlock said you were not coming back. I told them all that you would, because you always come to me when I wish for you hard enough, but they did not believe me."

Elizabeth's heart swelled with tenderness—and relief that providence had thrown the news of Darcy's search into their path, for she would never have come back otherwise, and she would not have liked Anna to lose faith in her. "But everybody has been even more sad that *you* ran away. Shall we not see if we can get you out of here, so they can all stop being sad?" She began feeling about on the walls for ledges on which they might stand to pull themselves out.

"My mother will not be sad," Anna said, "For she cannot know I fell in a well. She is in Notting-um buying shoes for her wedding."

"Well, that is as may be," Elizabeth replied, thinking uncharitably how fortunate it was for Miss Bingley that she should have been spared any of the inconvenience of Anna's misadventure. "But Mr Darcy was so worried he sent for men from Pemberley to come and help look for you." Her fingers found a protrusion of rock she thought might work. She put a foot on it and gripped the wall above to test whether it would take her weight.

"He was the saddest of all."

Her foot slipped and crashed back into the water with a loud splash. "Was he?"

"Yes. I heard him tell Colonel Fitzwilliam that he wished to marry you."

"Anna—" She meant to tell her she ought not to eavesdrop on other people's conversations but could not bring herself to say the words while there were still overhearings that might be relayed. She stood still and waited to see whether any more would be forthcoming.

"Should you like to marry him, Lizzy?"

She twisted her mouth into a rueful smile, both diverted and mortified by the direct question, and by the answer that could not make anybody happy. "I should like to get you out of this hole. Do you think, if you stood on my shoulders, you could climb out?"

With surprisingly little trouble but a good deal of silliness, they discovered that she could. Anna then giggled merrily at Elizabeth's several failed attempts to pull herself out using the little ledge she had found, and *she* laughed so much that her arms grew weak, seriously hampering her efforts. Eventually, her perseverance paid off, and she hauled herself over the ledge into the gloriously hot sunshine. After a moment to catch her breath and a hasty inspection to ensure Anna had no serious injuries, Elizabeth took hold of her hand and together they began to make their way back towards the house.

"It does not matter if you do not love him," Anna said without warning.

"Pardon?"

"Mother told me that she is not in love, but that it does not matter, for you do not have to be in love to get married."

Elizabeth knew not for whom that made her feel sorrier: Darcy, Miss Bingley, or Anna. "It is much better if you are, though," she said. She might have elaborated on her own feelings for Darcy, but she halted mid-thought and mid-stride when a voice that was very clearly his abruptly called Anna's name from startlingly close by.

"That is him!" Anna cried excitedly.

"Over here! I have found her!" Elizabeth called and then smiled to herself at the uncommonly long pause that followed before she heard him move towards them. He emerged around a sheer crag slightly higher up the slope and the sight of him took Elizabeth's breath away. He had evidently been searching for some time, for he looked almost as dishevelled as she, though it was doing him far less disservice than it was her. His skin had the sheen and colour of someone who had been out in the summer heat all day. He wore no hat or coat, his waistcoat was unbuttoned, and he had discarded his cravat. Indeed, he looked so wild he could have been a spirit of the very rocks upon which he stood, more suited to this rugged terrain than any ballroom in which she had ever seen him.

"Elizabeth!" His look conveyed myriad emotions, and she felt every one of them pierce her deeply, but it lasted only a heartbeat before he noticed her companion and his entire countenance was diffused with profound relief. "Anna! Thank God!" He dashed to her, landing on his knees before her to perform the same examination for injuries that Elizabeth had. "Are you hurt?" Looking at Elizabeth he added, "Either of you?"

"No," Elizabeth answered. "Miss Darcy is only tired and hungry, I think."

Anna had other concerns. "Who is Elizabeth?"

"I meant Miss Bennet," Darcy said brusquely.

At the same time, Elizabeth said, "I am. That is what Lizzy is short for."

"Oh, that is like my name!" Anna said happily. "Anna is short for Georgiana."

"Never mind that now," said Darcy. "Where have you been? We have been looking for you everywhere."

His tone banished her smile and replaced it with a quivering lip.

"He is only worried, sweetheart," Elizabeth said gently, though Darcy's expression suggested he was a good deal angrier than he was letting on. "There is a crevice in that direction," she explained. "Miss Darcy had fallen in."

This evidently raised more questions than it answered, for he frowned intensely and shook his head, but other voices calling for Anna nearby prevented her immediately relieving his confusion. Darcy came to his feet and bellowed, "Over here, Fitzwilliam. I have her!" before gathering Anna up and giving her a quick but endearingly gentle hug, his large hand pressing her little head tenderly into the safety of his shoulder. He kissed her on the forehead and whispered, "Remember the rules?"

Anna lifted her head, unwound her arms from his neck and nodded. Moments later, Colonel Fitzwilliam crashed into the clearing with two other gentlemen, and though he and Darcy exchanged a look of intense relief, all show of familial attachment between any of them was vanished. "Good show, Darcy. Where did you find her?"

"Miss Bennet found her."

Colonel Fitzwilliam noticed Elizabeth for the first time and his shock was equal to Darcy's. "Good grief, Miss Bennet! You look as though you have been through the wars."

Darcy did not allow him to say more. He handed Anna to him. "You had better take her back to the house. Ask Lady Matlock to inform the family she has been found. And call off the search. Thank you, Jones, Proctor." He nodded his gratitude to the other men. To his cousin, he said in a hushed voice, "I shall catch you up."

With a curious glance at Elizabeth and a nod to Darcy, Colonel Fitzwilliam left with Anna in his arms.

Elizabeth's heart raced as Darcy turned to face her—and fell when his eyes met hers. She wished fervently then that she had not come, for he did not look pleased to see her and glared at her with ferocious contempt. Yet he did not look away or speak any words of anger. Indeed, he did not say anything at all, and the longer he stared at her, the more familiar his expression became, until she recognised it as the way he had used to look at her in Hertfordshire. And then, she now knew, he had been fighting with every ounce of his strength not to love her.

"Thank you," he said gruffly. "I was beginning to fear the worst."

"I am just glad she was unharmed." She stopped, and bit her lips together, unsure what else to say.

"What are you doing here?" he asked in a tone so bewildered it made her wish to hug him as tenderly as he had his daughter.

"When I saw Anna here last week, it was at that same place. I told her at the time to be careful not to fall in. When we heard this morning that she was missing, I thought that might be where she was, and I had to let someone know, only I could not explain..." She realised she was running on and stopped, laughing awkwardly at herself. "Well, anyway, we came directly."

He continued to stare at her implacably. "Why? You did not care to say good-bye to either of us before you left. I cannot comprehend why you should suddenly care enough to rush back and help find her."

"Because I do care!" she cried, hurt by his asperity. "Because she is yours, and you love her, and I—"

He stepped towards her, his resentment displaced by a different but equally intense emotion, and his breath coming fast. "You what? Elizabeth, you *what*?"

Though she knew it would gain neither of them anything but more pain, she could not miss this opportunity to rectify one of her greatest regrets. She met his gaze unwaveringly and told him what she ought to have many months ago. "I love you both."

Darcy visibly reeled; the smile that fought to claim his mouth suppressed by the incredulity that creased his brow. "Then why in God's name did you leave?"

"Because I will not be responsible for preventing you from doing what is right."

"What?"

"Darcy, what on earth are you doing keeping Miss Bennet standing about in wet clothes like this?"

They both turned to see Lady Matlock coming through the trees with Mr and Mrs Gardiner and Lord Sutcliffe hard on her heels. She looked furious, though whether it was her nephew, Elizabeth, Anna, or the general inconvenience of the entire misadventure that had vexed her was unclear. Mr and Mrs Gardiner hastened past her and gathered around their niece, their concern evident. "Lizzy, you are drenched—and filthy! What happened? Are you well?"

She assured them that she was and explained briefly what she had done, her eyes flicking constantly to Darcy, who looked on with his distinctive, inscrutable glower.

"Come, Miss Bennet," said Lady Matlock, swishing her skirts out of the way so that she could walk back in the direction of the house. "Let us get you freshened up and into something dry."

"Thank you, madam, but that is not necessary. We ought to be going." From the corner of her eye, she saw Darcy angrily turn his back and walk a few steps away, shaking his head, and she felt her heart begin to crumble again.

"Lizzy, I comprehend your concerns," said Mrs Gardiner quietly. "But you are soaked through. If you really do not wish to ruin our trip, then I beg you would resist the temptation to catch your death and accept her ladyship's kind offer. We can leave as soon as you are changed."

She could not very well refuse such good sense. Reluctantly, she took Lady Matlock's proffered arm and allowed herself to be led back towards Kelstedge. She dared not look again at Darcy. Her heart was heavy enough already; she thought it might petrify completely if it were forced to bear the weight of his resentment and pain as well.

Elizabeth supposed *she* must be the object of Lady Matlock's displeasure when her ladyship insisted on personally taking her upstairs to help her into something dry and firmly encouraged Mrs Gardiner to take tea in the morning room rather than join them. She fully expected that 'helping her into something dry' would comprise mostly of a severe set down for her behaviour towards Darcy rather than any noble lending of dry gowns. She resigned herself to it; there was not much that was likely to make her feel any more wretched than she already did.

They walked an unfeasibly long way in horribly uncomfortable silence to one of the grandest bedrooms Elizabeth had ever seen. Lady Matlock closed the door behind them and crossed to the bed where Elizabeth's own trunk had been placed. "I had it brought up. I trust you will have something in here you can change into?"

"Yes," Elizabeth said, hoping that the haste with which she had thrown all her things into it that morning would not render everything she pulled out of it a crumpled mess. She opened it and began sifting through the contents for what she needed.

Lady Matlock perched on the edge of the bed, watching. "Your aunt has explained to me how you came to be the one to find Miss Darcy. I thank you for it."

Elizabeth smiled but said nothing, for there was nothing to say.

"I suppose this means that your aunt and uncle are now aware of who she is?"

"No, indeed, madam," Elizabeth said, pausing in her search.

"No? You expect me to believe that you revealed nothing at all about the girl you had them dashing about the country to rescue?"

"I told them I met her here last week, that her name is Anna, that she is five, and in a moment of alarm, I told them that she is dear to me. I did not tell them why, and they did not ask, though I am sure they would rather have known."

Lady Matlock inclined her head. "Then I thank you again for your service to this family. Would that more young ladies had the same integrity."

Elizabeth considered the wisdom of saying what was on her mind but thought she had so little to lose she might as well, and so replied, "I would never have revealed Miss Darcy's identity even had my secrecy not been explicitly requested by so many people. I certainly would not have divulged it *after* I was asked. But I cannot allow your ladyship to continue under the wholly erroneous idea that my aunt and uncle would have behaved any differently, had they been privy to the same information. They are kind, sensible, trustworthy people."

"I am sure they are, Miss Bennet. Indeed, they have more than proved themselves today. But the fewer people who know about Miss Darcy the better, for her sake as much as anyone's. The truth has a funny way of wriggling to the surface, and she will not be five forever. One day she will be a young lady looking for a husband, and it would not do to have any loose ends floating about that might trip her up then."

Elizabeth nodded. Then, vaguely diverted to realise that she was staring at the Countess of Matlock with one stocking and a corset thrown over her arm, she returned to her task.

"Could you answer me another question?" her ladyship enquired.

"If I can."

"We were all rather wondering why you ran away. None of us could work out what upset you so at dinner, and since you declined to tell anyone, we have been left to guess."

Elizabeth sighed; here it was then. *Better to get it over with*, she thought, and with a deep breath, admitted, "Miss Bingley informed me who she was marrying." She found another stocking and draped it over her arm next to the other one. "I had not realised before, which I recognise was rather foolish of me, but..." She did not bother finishing the sentence and instead tugged at the hem of a petticoat until the trunk surrendered it to her. "I am sorry to have left so precipitately, but I was excessively distressed."

"Hmm. As was my nephew. Particularly when he called at your lodgings the next day, only to discover you gone from there as well."

Elizabeth swallowed the lump in her throat, found a morning gown that would do as well as any other, and pulled it out, gathering it into her arms in a muddled bundle of cloth.

Lady Matlock leant towards her. "And, out of interest, Miss Bennet, who is it you think Miss Bingley is marrying?"

"Mr Darcy," she said warily.

Her ladyship remained still and regarded Elizabeth with

what she could only describe as a twinkle in her eye. "Well that explains a good many things."

Her tone ignited a conflagration of hope in Elizabeth's breast. She opened her mouth to enquire whether she were mistaken, but her ladyship stood abruptly and, nodding to her armful of clothes, enquired whether she had everything she needed.

"Yes, thank you. But—"

"Good." She crossed the room, saying as she went, "I shall send a waiting-woman to help you dress." She reached the door but turned at the last moment. "On the subject of wholly erroneous ideas, you really must get that one out of your head straight away. Darcy cannot possibly marry Miss Bingley. Apart from the obvious—and the fact that she is an absolutely dreadful woman and I would never allow it—she is engaged to Mr Drummond."

Elizabeth could scarcely form a coherent response but managed to stammer an enquiry as to who that might be.

Lady Matlock smiled one of her dazzling smiles. "Mr Drummond is an old acquaintance, who owes Lord Matlock an enormous sum of money, and who has decided that forming a deep and lasting attachment to Miss Bingley will be more affordable than paying his debts. He is wrong, I am sure, but there we are. Do join us downstairs as soon as you are ready."

ELIZABETH KNEW NOT WHETHER TO REJOICE OR DESPAIR. Darcy was not marrying Miss Bingley. Or Miss de Bourgh. Or *her*, for she had left! He had all but declared himself a second time and she had run away. She sank onto the bed and tried to recall exactly what Miss Bingley had said that had given her such a vastly mistaken conviction, but her head was too full of regret to remember anything. She gave a growl of frustration and, throwing her clothes aside, strode to open the window, where she spent a minute or two giving serious consideration to the likelihood of being able to escape from it, for the prospect of going downstairs and facing Darcy now was unbearable. She almost fell out of the window when the door opened, and somebody entered the room behind her.

"Miss Bennet? Lady Matlock sent me to attend you."

Elizabeth pulled her head back inside and turned around, laughing freely and feeling infinitely better for it. She preferred laughter to tears. The maid approached, stretching out the garment she had draped over her arm to show it off. It was a short-sleeved walking dress; unfussy but elegantly designed and beautifully constructed. "Her ladyship thought you might like to wear this."

With a glance at the over-spilling trunk and crumpled heap of clothes next to it on the bed, Elizabeth laughed again, imagining what Lady Matlock must have thought as she dragged her things out before. She thanked the maid and marvelled at her ladyship's generosity. At least, if she must face Darcy, she could now do so in a vaguely presentable state. Indeed, by the time she was ready, she was more than presentable, for the maid also provided her with hot water to wash her face—which she had not realised before was streaked with grime from the well—and dressed her hair handsomely.

Until the moment came to go downstairs, Elizabeth was convinced she had mastered herself to the extent that she would be able to conduct the inevitably painful interview with dignity and composure. When she reached the top of the stairs and saw Darcy waiting at the bottom, all her courage fled. He was similarly refreshed and pristinely turned out, as she was more used to seeing him, though now she had seen the wildness in him, she could not unsee it; it was in his eyes as he watched her come down the stairs.

He bowed slightly. "Miss Bennet, will you do me the honour of walking in the garden with me?"

She hesitated, but only to allow her heart time to cease banging painfully against her ribs so that she could speak. It was too long for Darcy.

"For God's sake, just come with me," he said impatiently, though not angrily. "I must talk to you, and I would do so in private. And before you or anyone else runs away again."

He could not know how much she loved him for making her laugh at that moment, or how willing she would be to go anywhere with him that he asked. "Very well, sir," she said, smiling despite her trepidation as she walked out of the house with him.

He took her to a different part of the garden, at another corner of the house. There were no formal flower beds and no great expanse of lawn, only a path that led to a bare expanse of rock that dropped off over a sheer cliff. The bright sun glinted off the river that wound lazily along the foot of the valley below—a very long way below. "Thank heavens Anna did not decide the fairies lived on this side of the estate. I should not fancy climbing down there to find her."

When Darcy did not answer, she turned to look at him and was rather abashed to find him smiling proudly and shaking his head at her.

"It is incredible to me that you climbed down anywhere to find her. I did not properly express my gratitude before. You are remarkable."

"It was only good fortune that I had seen her at that spot before."

His expression grew more serious. "Fortune will not have the credit for this. Lady Matlock has informed me you left here because you believed I was engaged to Miss Bingley. It was not *fortune* that made you return despite still believing that to be the case. That was an act of selflessness unlike any I have seen."

Elizabeth made no reply. She had already told him why she came back; she was not brave enough to repeat it.

He stepped towards her. "Miss Bennet, I must know. What made you think I was engaged to her?"

"I beg you would not plague me," she replied miserably. "I feel foolish enough already."

"Believe me, it is not my intention to plague you. I have good reason for wishing to know. Pray, tell me what made you think I meant to marry her?"

She took a deep breath that turned into a shrug. "I do not know. I cannot recall the exact words that laid the foundation. Perhaps it was when she told Mr Turner that she was about to gain possession of Pemberley's orangery."

Darcy's brow furrowed, but he eventually recalled the conversation. "Did not she say that she did not have an orangery *yet*? Which she probably said because she will have, when she marries Mr Drummond. I believe she only mentioned mine because she was not at liberty to talk about his. But you cannot have convinced yourself I was marrying her based on such a trifling remark."

"Well it did not help that you told me you were attending to all my reproofs."

"Yet I hope I have."

"Yes, but one of them was that you had not married Miss Bingley."

"I thought I told you that was not possible."

"You did, and so did your aunt, and I understand that she is ghastly and would make you miserable—but that is why I was so sad for you. I thought you were marrying her anyway because it was the right thing to do. And then," she added, growing increasingly agitated as she recalled more of the things that had convinced her to begin with, "she told me you would not be at Pemberley next week because you would be in Leeds with her, and it seemed certain, for I knew she was going there to get married."

"Why would I go all the way to Leeds to marry her?" Darcy said, squinting at the absurdity. "I am attending the wedding, not partaking in it. As is Bingley, which I thought you knew."

"Yes, but he is Miss Bingley's brother. You are the father of her child!"

He leant back slightly and stared at her, though he did not seem angry. Indeed, he looked positively triumphant. "That *is* it, then? What you said before, that Anna was mine, that *is* what you meant?"

"Yes."

"But you only left when Miss Bingley managed to make you think I was marrying her?"

"Yes, but you confirmed it. You apologised for the situation and said if you could have arranged it any differently that I ought to believe you would have."

"Good God, I was talking about the seating arrangements at the dinner table! I wished to sit with you, and instead she attached herself to me and rhapsodised about my blasted pineapple plant all evening."

Elizabeth could not help but laugh again but bit it back hastily, for it really was not a laughing matter. Though hope *was* trying exceedingly hard to find ingress into her heart, and Darcy *was* smiling as he took another step closer to her.

"You bore that entire ridiculous performance and still only left when you thought you had discovered I was marrying her?"

"Well...yes."

"Dare I surmise then, that until that point, you would have accepted another offer from me?"

Elizabeth did not think she could blush any deeper, but

she forced herself to hold his gaze. "If you had been inclined to make one."

"Despite believing I was the father of her child?"

"Oh, I had long overcome my scruples there, but—" She stopped, for Darcy was looking at her with such powerful intensity, and his small smile was so affecting, it made her forget what her 'but' was going to be.

"You are the most amazing woman I have ever met, but I would never ask such a thing of you."

Oh. She was rather glad she had so obstinately resisted all hope in that case. She turned away to focus on the glittering river. "I see."

"No, you very clearly do not." Darcy came to stand in front of her and with the thumb of one hand, gently brought her head back to face him. He fleetingly caressed her cheek before lowering his hand. "Elizabeth, Anna is not my daughter. She is my sister."

Astonishment knocked her two steps backwards, and she stared at him, her mind racing but comprehension eluding her entirely. "What?" It came out a little shakily, making her aware that her hands were shaking, too. She clutched one in the other to stop them.

"It is a long and not particularly happy story, and I will tell you the whole of it another time, when I do not have something far more pressing to say to you." He closed the gap between them and gently pulled her hands apart to hold them in his instead. "For now, just know this—Anna is not my child. Miss Bingley has never been anything to me but a bane on my existence." He dipped his head closer to hers. "Whereas I have never felt about anybody the way I feel about you." He brought her hands to his lips and kissed her fingers, his eyes never leaving hers. "Let there be no more misunderstandings between us. I am hopelessly in love with you. I have it on excellent authority that you love me—and my incorrigibly disobedient sister. I beg you, Elizabeth, before anyone throws up any other impediment to the idea, say you will marry me."

She could not contain her delight to see him deploy both the wit and the passion she had so often glimpsed, this time without any disguise, and she laughed for sheer joy as she assured him of her affections and wishes. Breathlessness forced her laughter into abeyance when Darcy tenderly took her face in both his hands and fixed her with such a look as she felt would unravel her heart.

"You cannot know how that laugh has tortured me. So many times I have seen you try to stifle it—and loved you more for it—but I would no longer be a bystander. I would know what makes you laugh. I would laugh with you."

"Nothing would make me happier. Though, I ought to warn you, you may occasionally find yourself the object of ridicule."

His lips twitched. "Laugh at whatever you choose, as long as you know that whenever you do, I am likely to do this."

So rocky had their journey to an understanding been that Elizabeth had not allowed herself to reflect overlong on what pleasures might await the wife of Mr Darcy. His kiss, and his caveat, more than satisfied her that theirs would be an exceedingly happy marriage with more than its share of laughter.

37
A Little Too Adventurous

"THERE YOU ARE, DARCY. I WAS JUST COMING TO FIND YOU, for we had begun to despair," Lady Matlock said when Darcy showed Elizabeth back into the house. "Has everything been resolved?"

"Not everything," he replied. "But enough of the essentials to be going on with."

Elizabeth bit the insides of her cheeks and wished she would not blush at the memory of those essentials, though she fancied Lady Matlock could guess at their nature anyway when she smiled knowingly and said, in her inimitable velvety tone, that she was delighted to hear it. "You may like to know that Mr Gardiner is in Lord Matlock's library."

They had agreed before returning to the house that Darcy would seek consent from Elizabeth's uncle in lieu of her father. She had no doubt that either would give it, particularly considering what Darcy had done for Lydia, but still she felt a tremble of apprehension as he left in search of Mr Gardiner. She worried for Jane, who had yet to reconcile with Bingley; she could not help but harbour some lingering trepidation about such a secret as her new family was harbouring, and about which she was still largely in the dark; but chiefly, she was hesitant to believe that, having awoken that morning utterly broken-hearted, it was feasible that she should end the day feeling happiness such as she had never felt before.

Lady Matlock looped her arm through Elizabeth's. "You had better come with me, Miss Bennet. Your Aunt has been understandably anxious." As she steered them towards the front of the house, she added, "You must not worry that your uncle will refuse him. I have never met anybody more proficient at getting his way than my nephew. Indeed, you are the only person I know to have made him work this hard for it." She gave Elizabeth's arm a quick squeeze. "Well done."

Elizabeth smiled vaguely, disinclined to take any pleasure in Darcy's suffering. "How is Miss Darcy?" she enquired instead.

"Sleeping. The poor dear was exhausted. The physician has given her a clean bill of health, though he warned us that she may suffer some night terrors in the coming days."

"I hope she does not. But she is a fearless little thing. I should not be at all surprised if she wishes to go out exploring again tomorrow."

"Well, one thing is for certain, she would not be as well as she is were it not for you. You have my sincere thanks. When I asked you to ensure a happy conclusion to the affair, I did not have in mind that you would have to hurl yourself into a ravine to bring it about."

"Might I ask what you did have in mind?"

"What is your meaning?"

"Well, I thought at first, when you said I had the power to prevent Miss Bingley's marriage, it was only because I knew Miss Darcy's true identity. But afterwards, I convinced myself your real concern was that my presence might persuade Mr Darcy to break his engagement and renew his addresses to me instead."

The glimmer returned to Lady Matlock's eyes. "You were right the first time. We have concocted quite an elaborate story to explain the sudden appearance of a five-year-old child to Mr Drummond's acquaintances. It would be exceedingly vexing if our plans were unravelled by a stray rumour at this stage. Besides," she added, lowering her voice as they approached a door and waited for a footman to open it for them, "I do not see how I could have expected my nephew to renew his addresses to you when I was unaware that he had made them once already."

Elizabeth winced in mortification, yet there was nothing to be done about it now, and when Lady Matlock raised an eyebrow and smirked at her, she settled for laughing at herself instead. Mrs Gardiner looked up uneasily when they entered the saloon in which she waited, though upon seeing both ladies enter laughing, she visibly relaxed. "Well, Lizzy. Lady Matlock has done us the very great honour of inviting us to stay at Kelstedge Abbey tonight. So tell me, am I to accept, or do you require that we spirit you away again?"

"I should be very happy if you accepted."

"That is good news," she said with a broadening grin. "For Lord Sutcliffe and Colonel Fitzwilliam have offered to take your uncle fishing down at the river, and we should never have heard the end of it had he missed out."

"And I should be very happy if you would accompany me on a ride around the park in my phaeton, Mrs Gardiner," said Lady Matlock. "Mr Darcy is presently speaking to your husband, and unless something goes horribly awry, I expect that you and I shall soon share the honour of being aunt to this young lady. It behoves us to get better acquainted, do not you agree?"

Mrs Gardiner did not look overly surprised, but she did look exceptionally pleased as she took Elizabeth's hands in her own and gave her heartiest congratulations. "I dared not hope after our conversation yesterday, but I could not be happier for you, Lizzy. Of course your uncle will give his consent—as will your father. Oh, come here!" She gathered her into a hug and whispered in her ear, "I knew he loved you. No man looks at a woman in that way unless he is in love with her."

One hour later, after a host of letters had been written and sent by express to Longbourn, and Darcy's relatives had been the ones to spirit away Elizabeth's, they found themselves alone once more. At his request, she agreed to show him the dripping well where she had found Anna, ostensibly lest he ever need to look for her there again, though Elizabeth suspected it was really to give her some activity to distract from the embarrassment that had crept back over her since they parted ways.

He did not seem the slightest bit embarrassed and watched her with a smile that made it impossible to mistake his happiness. "How did you ever come to think she was mine?" he asked as they walked.

"Why did you never tell me she was not?" Elizabeth replied, laughing with exasperation.

"I did not know that was what you thought. You told me you knew my secret, and I assumed you knew the truth."

"As did I." She puffed out her cheeks, trying to recall the order of events. "I heard so many differing accounts, it was impossible to know what to believe—and I did not believe *that* for a long time, for it seemed so out of character. Indeed, I did not believe it right up until the morning of the very day you proposed, when your cousin told me her name was Miss Darcy—for I knew her only as Anna Dunn until then—that your part in it was regrettable, and that you were obliged by honour and affection to provide for her. Then, the fact that

Anna had told me her father refused to marry her mother seemed to reconcile with your obvious disdain for Miss Bingley, and after that, nothing happened that did not seem to confirm it."

"I may have to run Fitzwilliam through."

"Pray, do not, for he has done as much to help you as to hamper you. His teasing you for being silent at Hunsford was one of the things that made me love you most."

Darcy stopped walking. "You loved me then?"

Elizabeth nodded. "That was why it pained me so much to discover, or think I had discovered, Anna was yours."

Darcy made a choking noise and shook his head at the sky. "Would that I had written you the letter I wished to write that night, explaining it all."

"Why did you not?"

"I convinced myself there was no point." He took her hand and pulled her back into motion. "Nothing I could have said would have explained Anna away, and her existence was your main objection—though I recognise there were others."

Elizabeth indicated that they needed to scale an outcropping of rock and let go of his hand to climb over it. "Why did you think I objected so vehemently if you thought I knew she was only your sister?"

"That remark just proves what an astonishing woman you are." He jumped down next to her and indicated that they should continue walking. "Most people would have objected on that basis alone. It is still a scandalous secret. One from which I have been running these past six years. Your wish not to be tainted by association was not a surprise to me. It only made me miserable."

"I am so sorry. I have been wretched knowing how that must have pained you. Your words to me then—that you thought, in me, you had found someone who would not blame you—have plagued me ever since. I used to pride myself on being an impartial studier of character, but I was no less prejudiced than I accused you of being. I have long been heartily ashamed of how unfairly I judged you."

He shook his head and grimaced wryly. "In the context of believing that I was asking you to accept an illegitimate child of my own, your concerns were wholly justified. But, even in the correct context, most of your reproofs still applied." Elizabeth went ahead of him to lead him over another bluff, and he said behind her, "Except, of course, the one in which you upbraided me for not marrying the mother of my own sister. I never could understand that one."

Elizabeth would have enjoyed his teasing more had it not been such a painful subject. "I thought, when you said it was impossible, it was because you did not consider Miss Bingley worthy of you. And really, given that you had, moments before, given the same explanation as to why you had fought so hard against your feelings for me, it did not seem an unreasonable conclusion."

She felt Darcy grasp her hand; he encouraged her, with a gentle tug, to face him. Their relative positions on the rocky ground put them at a height with each other, thus there was no mistaking the gravity in his expression as he looked directly at her. "I beg you would forgive me—for thinking it, for saying it, for being so egregiously wrong about it. Never has there been a woman more worthy of being loved than you. You are fearless. You are impervious to melancholy. You are intelligent, and compassionate, and distractingly beautiful." He pulled the ribbon beneath her chin loose and lifted her bonnet off, so it hung down her back. Then he brushed her curls aside with the back of his fingers and spread his hand to cradle her face, his fingertips in her hair and his thumb stroking her cheek. "Elizabeth, there is nothing I do not love about you. It is abhorrent to me that I ever considered you unworthy."

"We are both guilty of underestimating each other. But I like your way of apologising better than mine." She liked, also, the effect her remark had on his expression, which reverted instantly to the untamed fierceness she had glimpsed in him earlier.

"That is fortunate," he said, sliding his free hand around her waist and pulling her tightly against him. "For a man with as many faults as you have discovered in me is likely to be often apologising to his wife."

"Aye. Fortunate indeed." She could think of nothing else to say, though she soon discovered that mattered not, for Darcy spent the next several minutes thoroughly convincing her of his contrition without uttering a single word. It pleased her more than she would have liked to admit but did little to diminish her embarrassment, which returned in force when they eventually continued on their way. She was relieved to espy the dripping well ahead of them shortly afterwards and hoped speaking of that might make her think less of Darcy's touch, thereby lessening the flush that yet burned her cheeks. "There it is," she said, pointing. "Just beneath that overhang."

Darcy looked at it, then all around them, shaking his head. "We must have come past this place at least three times, looking." He walked to the edge and looked down into the well. "You climbed down there?"

"I did."

"How deep does it go?"

"Imagine me, with Anna stood on my shoulders. 'Tis a fraction shallower than that." When he looked askance at her she added, "That is how we got back out. She climbed on my shoulders."

Oblivious to—nay, she corrected herself—regardless of her embarrassment, Darcy kissed her again. She suspected he meant to keep doing so until it no longer made her blush. If that was his design, she found she was not averse to it. He rested his forehead against hers afterwards, so close she could only see his smile in his eyes. "My magnificent, intrepid wife."

"I am not the only intrepid one," she replied. "Anna is a little too adventurous for a five-year old. Do you know how often she ran away in Hertfordshire?"

"I knew she had done it once or twice."

"Oh yes—I saw you rescue her they day she tripped over in the driveway at Netherfield. You made her laugh and tapped her on the nose. It was quite the revelation."

Darcy's surprise was evident, though he was grave when he answered. "That cannot have helped when you were faced with the possibility of her being mine."

"No, but it helped a great deal when it came to falling in love with you." She grinned happily to see how this pleased him. He could not always be the one to make her outrageously happy; she required the occasional turn at delighting him. "But seriously, I ran into her three or four, or maybe five times while I was out walking, and she was alone every time. I really think Miss Paxton ought to be spoken to."

"Miss Paxton has *been* spoken to, and Miss Paxton is now on the stagecoach back to Ramsgate."

"Ramsgate?"

"It is where she hales from, and where we first took her on as Anna's wet nurse."

"She is not really Miss Bingley's cousin then?"

"She is—a distant one. It made her easier to keep quiet, but infinitely harder to get rid of."

"Will she be discreet now, do you think?"

"Yes."

Darcy said this with such decisive authority that it made Elizabeth smile, though she dared not enquire what measures had been taken to secure such confidence. It made her think of Wickham's letter, and inevitably brought her thoughts back to weightier matters. "Will you tell me now how it is that Mr Darcy of Pemberley has a secret five-year old sister?"

Darcy inhaled deeply and nodded as he let it out. "It must be done, although—" He took out his fob watch and checked the time. "—it is a long story. I should not like to test your uncle's lenience by being gone too long with you."

"That is well," Elizabeth said, clambering to sit on the flattest, shadiest bit of rock she could find and indicating that Darcy should join her. "You may tell me in stages if necessary. We do not want for time together anymore. We have the rest of our lives to tell each other every thought that crosses our minds."

That may well have been true, but her pointing it out prompted Darcy to express his happiness in a way that left him significantly less time to tell his tale.

IT HAD BEEN MANY MONTHS SINCE ELIZABETH HAD considered Darcy less proud than her first impression, and their other encounters that day had revealed a passionate disposition that, frankly, did not surprise her overmuch. Nevertheless, none of her knowledge had rendered him, to her mind, any less stately. She was somewhat amazed, therefore, to see him reposed on the rock like a young lover, with his long legs stretched out and crossed at the ankles, and his head in her lap—as different from the superior creature who had slighted her at the Meryton Assembly as it was possible for a man to be. The gravity of their conversation required that she keep to herself her utter delight at being the woman with whom he had chosen to evermore be so thoroughly unguarded.

Yet, grave their conversation promised to be. Darcy had begun it by speaking about Bingley, and the strength and longevity of their acquaintance. It was a very different picture than Wickham had painted; far less of Darcy governing a complying Bingley, and far more of a mutually respectful, mutually dependent friendship.

"I always assumed he was younger than you," Elizabeth said.

"He is," Darcy replied. "Two years younger. That is precisely why he was still at Cambridge when I travelled to the continent."

"Now that is something you will have to tell me more about when we have the time."

"I shall, happily, though there is not as much to tell as there might have been, for I did not have the privilege of staying there long." He paused, as he had done several times, as though to order his thoughts. And, as he had done each time before, he sighed in a jaded manner before continuing. "Not long before I was due to travel, Bingley's father died very suddenly. Regrettably, his grief was compounded by the discovery that his father had been investing poorly for years and had lost a considerable part of his fortune. Not all of it—he and his sisters still had their inheritance—but the lease on their house had been signed over to another purchaser. Bingley almost gave up his studies to return home and resolve it all. I encouraged him not to and offered for his sisters to stay at Pemberley until he was able to join them at the end of the academic year."

The ultimate result of that decision was obvious, and Elizabeth pitied Darcy deeply for essentially having incited his own misfortune. Emboldened by compassion, she began to run her fingers through his hair, gently grazing his scalp, and was pleased that it seemed to have the desired effect; he closed his eyes and observably relaxed. Indeed, he was quiet for so long, she wondered whether he had fallen asleep. He had been up most of the night searching for Anna, after all. Yet, at length, he did speak, though his voice was much lower, he kept his eyes closed, and he had ceased talking about Bingley.

"You asked me, at the Netherfield ball, whether I had any

siblings growing up."

"I recall." He had left the table shortly afterwards.

"I did not lie when I answered that I did not. I was three-and-twenty when Anna was born. But I almost had a sister as a child. My mother and father had given up hope of any more children after me, but when I was ten, my mother conceived again. She used to complain at being unable to ride while she was increasing. She loved to ride. My father used to arrange little diversions for her, to keep her occupied. She was heavy with child when he arranged an afternoon of archery."

That he stopped talking *then* sent a shiver up Elizabeth's spine, for she knew from Wickham that Darcy's mother had died when he was ten. She waited in silence for him to continue and could see him clench and unclench his jaw as he searched for the right words.

"There was an accident, and my mother was injured. I was spared the details, being so young, and there was a strict embargo on the subject afterwards but, given my father's behaviour at the time and since, I have always suspected he was in some way culpable." Elizabeth held her breath as Darcy added, "My mother did not survive. They tried to deliver the child—a girl—but it was too late. They could not save her either."

Elizabeth had not expected the truth to be quite so horrific. Feeling such pity as made her wish to weep, she cupped her hand beneath his chin and bent to kiss his forehead. He opened his eyes and, this close, it felt that he stared directly into her soul. "I am so very sorry," she whispered.

Darcy reached up to briefly stroke her face and smiled sadly. "My father never forgave himself. He withdrew from society—from life, really. And from me. He did his duty and taught me what he could about Pemberley, but he never again tried to be a father to me in the true sense. He told me once that he believed he had forfeited the right."

"So you lost both parents that day."

"Effectively." He sat up abruptly, and when he next spoke, it was in an officious tone. "Mr Wickham Senior was hired as steward the following year. His son was of a livelier disposition than me—and was a lot less like my mother in appearance. My father was able to look at him without being weighed down by guilt and thus, Wickham soon became his favourite."

"That must have been difficult to bear."

"No, indeed, I encouraged it, for Wickham was the only person who brought him any solace. As we grew older, and Wickham began to show his true character, I often intervened to conceal the consequences of his idleness and dissipation from my father, lest he be disappointed."

Elizabeth thought bitterly of the time she had sat in Mrs Phillip's parlour and joined Wickham in censuring Darcy for his resentful nature. Never had she been more disappointed in herself. "I do not know what to say."

"You do not need to say anything. I am not telling you to garner sympathy—this is all in the past. I am telling you so that you comprehend how lonely and broken my father was by the time Miss Bingley came to Pemberley." As suddenly as he had sat up, he now got to his feet and held out his hand to pull Elizabeth to hers. "Let us walk back."

She complied readily, for his agitation was evident. She wished she knew how to comfort him, but every possible method seemed trivial or vulgar in the circumstances. When they had gone two or three minutes in silence, he resumed his tale.

"She was twenty, intelligent, pretty—and you would have had to be a clairvoyant to tell that her father had just passed away. While her brother grieved alone at university and her sister sobbed from dawn till dusk, Miss Bingley thought her time would be better spent flirting with me. For the month before I set sail to Calais, she did not leave me alone. No trip across the Channel has ever been undertaken so eagerly."

"You were not tempted by her attentions?"

That earned her a reproachful look. "You have met the woman. You may answer that yourself."

Elizabeth grimaced expressively and said no more. She made no objection when Darcy held out his hand to assist her, quite unnecessarily, over the rocky section they had passed on the way here. In lieu of any other ideas, allowing him to feel useful was the least she could offer him. He seemed to grow angrier with every advancement of his story, and she jumped a little at the bitterness with which he said the next part.

"About four months into my travels, I received a letter from Bingley demanding that I return home because my father had got a child on his sister."

"That must have been a terrible shock. I cannot imagine what you must have thought."

"I *thought* that, having failed to draw me in, Miss Bingley had turned her attentions to my father—which was precisely what turned out to have happened. He was a shadow of a man who had, by then, been alone for above a dozen years. I do not believe it took much effort on her part."

This time, when Darcy helped Elizabeth around a jutting promontory, he seemed to be clutching more tightly to her than the reverse. She did not let go when they cleared the obstacle; when he tried to release her hand, she squeezed his tighter and kept walking.

At length he gave a wry huff of laughter and shook his head. "It is only because of you that I have been able to accept she was not wholly to blame." He fixed her with an earnest look. "I never wished to think ill of him. But, as you rightly pointed out, Miss Bingley cannot have ended up a mother on her own. I have no doubt that she knew precisely what she was about, but she was still a guest in his house, still the sister of my closest friend. And he compounded his sins by refusing to marry her. All the outrage you directed at me at Hunsford for not doing so, ought justly to have been aimed at him."

Elizabeth did not much care for the distinction of being the person to shatter Darcy's faith in his own father, and she could not bring herself to rejoice at his revelation. "Why did he refuse to marry her?" she asked sombrely.

"For my sake," Darcy answered with equal solemnity. "He may not have been able to face me, but I was always his son and heir. If I recall correctly, his words were something to the effect of not being prepared to inflict such a woman on me after having deprived me of a real mother for most of my life."

They came out onto the lawn with this unhappy reminiscence still hanging in the air between them. Elizabeth tried to pull Darcy in another direction, but he resisted and reached to check his watch again. She put her hand over his to prevent him. "My uncle will understand. Come." She pulled him towards a path that led behind the house. When they reached a stone bench in full view of most of the windows, but far enough away to preclude being overheard, she suggested they station themselves there. "He will be able to see us here if he wishes."

Darcy nodded but did not join her in sitting down. Instead he paced back and forth in front of her, glowering at the ground.

"You need not tell me any more," she said gently. "I can live without the details. And certainly, I am not so interested in hearing them that it warrants your being this distressed telling me."

"I am not distressed, Elizabeth. I am merely attempting to work out which part of the sorry bloody mess to tell you next."

His imprecation—unconsciously uttered, Elizabeth was

convinced—rather suggested otherwise, but she did not cavil. He evidently wished to tell her everything. "What did you do after you received the letter?" she prompted softly instead.

"I returned to England. It took me three weeks to get home. By the time I arrived, so had Wickham."

Elizabeth's stomach sank. She had long since comprehended that Wickham was an unscrupulous character, but she had almost forgotten he even knew about Anna. His name cropping up at this point in the tale could not bode well, and every smirk he had ever worn while he talked about Darcy suddenly took on a different meaning.

"My father had been too ashamed to write to me and had, instead, written to his favourite, begging for help. I believe he hoped for some support in persuading Bingley to have his sister give up the child—or get rid of it. I know for a fact he hoped Wickham would ensure I never found out. He was frustrated on every score."

"Mr Wickham refuse to help?"

"No, he offered to help," he replied, laughing bitterly. "He offered to marry Miss Bingley and bring the child up as his own. In exchange for Pemberley."

"What?"

"He wanted me written out of my father's will entirely and everything to be left to him. He threatened to ruin us all by revealing what had happened if my father did not comply with his demands."

Elizabeth sucked in a deep, shaky breath. 'Some trifling squabble so minor I can scarcely recall the foundation for it', was how Wickham had described his final altercation with the late Mr Darcy. She put the back of her hand to her lips, feeling genuinely ill at how close Lydia had come to being married to such a contemptible man. She collected herself quickly, however, for her anguish was more than five years too late to benefit Darcy. "And only the letter you had in your possession prevented him?"

Darcy nodded. "That part was, in the end, the easiest to resolve. The rest was not so simple. My father did not take Wickham's betrayal well. He disinherited him directly, but his disillusionment took a heavy toll on his health. As did his shame. I impressed upon him the importance of marrying Miss Bingley, not only because honour demanded it, but to truly put pay to any scandal. He eventually conceded, but by then, Miss Bingley was in no fit state to marry anyone. She had been frightened by the prospect of being made to marry Wickham, and my father was no longer such an appealing match. He was ill, by this point, and looked more his age than I am sure he had when she set out to secure him. And I do not think it had ever truly occurred to her that a child might be the consequence of her schemes. She protested so often and so hysterically that she did not want it, Bingley began to fear she would attempt to end the pregnancy herself. We thought it best to remove her from Pemberley and took her to be looked after by her cousin in Ramsgate." He stopped pacing and ran a hand through his hair. "While we were gone, my father passed away."

Elizabeth felt as though her heart were in a vice. There was nothing she could say that would alleviate the unpleasantness of such a history. She thought of Jane and wondered whether Bingley were sharing the same details with her. She was inclined to hope not, for her sister was too convinced that all the world was good to hear a tale of such wickedness and folly without considerable distress. She glanced at the house, and when she saw nobody watching from any of the windows, reached for Darcy's wrist and pulled him towards her. She wrapped both her hands around his and kissed it, then held it under her chin and looked up at him. "I am astounded that you have found it in your heart to forgive any of them."

His countenance softened into a grateful smile. "I would not go so far as to say I have forgiven them, but certainly I hope I have let go some of my resentment. It was not doing me any good. And it nearly lost me you." With a quick tug, he pulled her to her feet and wrapped his arms around her waist. "Whose idea was it to sit where your uncle could see us?"

"I am sure I do not know. Personally, I should prefer to sit somewhere shadier."

"An excellent suggestion. We must get you out of this sunlight directly before you swoon in the heat."

She snorted, and that made Darcy chuckle, which pleased her greatly. She allowed him to lead her to a formal plantation at the farthest end of the garden, where, as soon as they were out of sight, he pulled her into his arms and held her to him tightly. She returned the embrace with equal feeling, determined that he should know he would never want for comfort from her. "You were right," she said into his shoulder. "That was a desperately unhappy story. I wish there were some way I could make it better."

"You have," he replied, loosening his hold to lean back and look at her. "I have been presiding over this fiasco for nearly six years and not until I met you did I comprehend how insufficient were all my pretensions to behaving honourably."

"No!" she cried heatedly. Bringing both her hands to rest upon his chest as though to quell the very suggestion, she said, "Was there nothing honourable in the way you protected your father from Mr Wickham's iniquity? Is there nothing honourable in the way you have protected Mr Bingley's entire family for all these years?"

"I could scarcely do less for them, in the circumstances. But I was convinced that everything I had done had been done for the best, until you forced me to acknowledge that was not the case."

"You mean when I told you that you were not the paragon

of discernment you believed yourself to be?" she enquired guiltily, resting her forehead against his chest in mortification. "I was very wrong to say that."

He hooked a finger under her chin and tilted her face back up. "No, you were not. Neither were you wrong when you accused me, at Netherfield, of being sanctimonious when I claimed I did not need to forgive people as long as I was civil to them."

Jane had been closer to the mark than Elizabeth realised when she said that criticism had hit home, then. "Truly, I do not know why you ever fell in love with me. I have done nothing but abuse you."

"Because you are not afraid to speak the truth, Elizabeth. Had not you forced me to reconsider my principles, my anger would never have begun to take a proper direction, and I would have continued indefinitely to blame everyone but my father. Such was my resolve to protect his name from disgrace, I kept Anna secret from all my family. Except for Fitzwilliam, who has been a steadfast ally throughout, I told none of them about my father's transgression, for I did not wish *them* to think ill of him any more than I wished to think it myself. But you taught me how foolish a notion that was."

"Lord and Lady Matlock certainly seem to have taken the news well."

Darcy nodded. "It would seem they understood better than I just how severely my mother's death affected my father. They knew things about his suffering that I never did—and things he did for me from afar, which I wish I had known about at the time."

"And they have found Miss Bingley a husband."

"They have. That was no small weight off my mind, I assure you."

"I wonder that you and Mr Bingley prevented her from marrying before."

"It was not by design. Finding a man willing to take on an illegitimate child is not an easy undertaking. Finding a man willing to take on Miss Bingley is even harder."

Elizabeth laughed aloud in surprise but thought that, in the scheme of things, it was a lesser insult than the woman deserved. "I am surprised—prodigiously pleased, but surprised—that Miss Bingley did not choose to give Anna up."

"It is her one saving grace, in my opinion, that once Anna was born, she would not hear of her being taken away. It was her choice to name her Georgiana, after my father. She cares for her, in her own way, though God knows she is not a natural mother. Bingley had to insist that she sat with Anna when she was unwell last autumn. She was adamant it was only a slight cold and that her sitting next to the bed and watching would do nothing to hasten her recovery."

Elizabeth grinned. "She sounds quite like my mother."

Darcy regarded her raptly. "Then I have no cause to be anxious, for look how you have turned out."

He truly had an unnerving ability to overset her sensibilities. She felt irrationally happy as she met his ardent gaze. "Thank you for telling me all this. I know it has not been easy, but I am glad I know. Not that I required any more proof of what a wonderful man you are, but now I understand better what has made you that man. I cannot express how proud I shall be to have such a husband."

Darcy, clearly moved, lowered his head towards her, but a nearby wood pigeon seemed to distract him and rather than kiss her, he glanced over her shoulder. "I believe that is our cue to go in."

"Oh, good, you heard me," said Colonel Fitzwilliam coming to meet them as they crossed the lawn. Behind him, Lord and Lady Matlock, Mr and Mrs Gardiner, and Lord

Sutcliffe were sitting at several tables set out on the terrace—and they were all watching them approach.

Darcy's lips twitched into a barely noticeable smirk and with one, almost imperceptible nod to his cousin, he kept walking. Elizabeth looked askance at him until he muttered, "I told you he was an ally."

Surmising that the wood pigeon had been about Colonel Fitzwilliam's height and a lot nearer the ground than the canopy of any tree, she whispered back, "And you were going to run him through!"

"You two look very happy," said Mrs Gardiner when Elizabeth and Darcy both arrived at the terrace laughing.

"Darcy, I declare you have spent more time missing than anyone else has today," said Lord Sutcliffe.

"We have been walking the grounds," Darcy replied. "Had I known you would pine for me so I should have walked faster."

"Did you see the amazing view down to the river, Lizzy?" Mrs Gardiner enquired.

Elizabeth gratefully accepted a glass of lemonade from a footman and had to refrain from gulping the entire glass before replying, for she had not realised how thirsty she was. "I believe we have seen as much of the park as you, Aunt—only on foot. We ought to have taken a phaeton, as you did."

"Darcy ought to have taken you in his curricle," Colonel Fitzwilliam said. "He has it parked in the stables."

"Balderdash," said Lord Matlock. "You cannot get lost in the shrubbery in a ruddy great curricle."

Elizabeth decided that drinking her entire glass of lemonade was a good idea after all. As she stared into the glass, she reflected that probably only an earl could get away with saying such a thing, and that being one would evidently not preclude Lord Matlock from being added to the list of relations who seemed determined to make her blush.

39

Holiday Souvenirs

It was agreed that Elizabeth and her relations would return to Lambton the next day. Darcy proposed all manner of preferred alternatives, each of which Elizabeth reasoned away: it would not be fair on Bingley or Anna if Darcy did not attend the wedding; she had disrupted her aunt and uncle's plans enough already and would not abandon them to go to Leeds with him; she should not like to stay at Pemberley until he returned, for she should much rather wait and see it for the first time with him. Thus, she would go to Lambton, he would go to Leeds, and they would dine together at Pemberley on the last night of her travels, before she and the Gardiners set out to return to Longbourn.

Despite her professed reasonableness on the matter, Elizabeth was loath to be parted from him for any length of time and was pleased the Gardiners did not seem in much haste to depart the next morning. The consequence of their leisurely beginning was that, before their trunks had been loaded onto the carriage, Miss Bingley arrived back at Kelstedge. Darcy excused himself to apprise her, with Lady Matlock's help, of the events of the past two days, and since Mrs Gardiner had taken Mr Gardiner to see her favourite view down to the river before they left, Elizabeth found herself alone in the morning room. She did not wish to walk out, for she would rather wait for Darcy, and with nothing to occupy her, she resorted to wandering the room, inspecting the many curios on display. It was not an activity that provided much enjoyment, and she was relieved when the door opened behind her, signalling Darcy's return.

"Thank goodness, I thought I—" She stopped upon realising it was not Darcy, but Miss Bingley who stood before her. An awkward pause ensued after they curtseyed to each other, during which neither spoke. Elizabeth held her tongue, fully anticipating a supercilious remark about her mode of dress or style of hair. The impasse was broken when, to her utter astonishment, Miss Bingley dashed forwards and hugged her. A more awkward embrace Elizabeth had never experienced, but it did not want for feeling.

"Thank you!" Miss Bingley said in a quavering voice. "Thank you and thank you again. Thank you, a thousand times." The clinch ended as suddenly as it had begun and Miss Bingley stepped back, though she took up Elizabeth's hands in her own. "I have told Anna over and again that she must not run away, but she does not listen. I cannot bear to imagine what would have happened had you not come back to find her. I do not know how I shall ever thank you enough."

Elizabeth felt rather ashamed for having assumed Miss Bingley would be unaffected by Anna's brush with disaster but was still amazed to see her display such an excess of humility. "You need not thank me at all, Miss Bingley," she said, indicating that they should sit down, chiefly so that she would let go of her hands. "I was very happy to be able to help. Anna is a charming girl. You must be very proud of her."

She thought for a moment that Miss Bingley was about to burst into tears, but instead she smiled—a bewildered, sceptical sort of smile that was accompanied by a shake of her head. "I believe you are the first person I have ever heard say that I ought to be *proud* of my daughter. I am more used to people thinking of her as an affliction. Indeed, you are the only woman beyond my own family circle ever to have found out about her and not instantly renounced my acquaintance."

"That is not strictly true, madam. Jane knows."

"Pardon?"

"You must not be anxious that anybody else does, but yes, Jane was well aware that Anna was yours when she called on you in London. Indeed, she called with the deliberate intention of making you aware that she knew and thought no less of you."

She really did think Miss Bingley would cry then, for she began to blink excessively and took three or four deep breaths before speaking again. "That means a great deal to me, Miss Bennet. Would you be so kind as to pass on my good wishes?"

"I should be happy to, although I am sure Jane would have no objection to your writing to her. She mentioned more than once that she hoped you might remain friends." *Which is why she will go to heaven, and I never shall, for I could happily never set eyes on you again.*

"I should very much like to call her my friend. That is, if I am not soon able to claim an even closer acquaintance."

Elizabeth rejoiced to hear her speak so plainly of Bingley's intentions towards Jane but dared not do more than smile, for it was not a foregone conclusion.

After a pause, Miss Bingley hesitantly continued, "Anna has very much enjoyed *your* friendship, though I confess it was some time before I realised it was you she was speaking about."

"I hope you do not think I make a habit of secretly befriending other people's children," she replied laughingly. "Only we kept bumping into each other when I was out walking. What made you guess she was talking about me?"

"It was Darcy who first suspected, actually. When you mentioned in Kent that dead leaves look like fairy wings." Elizabeth's recognition must have shown on her face, for Miss Bingley added, "It was you who gave her the leaf then?"

"I confess it was. I thought she might like it because she mentioned that she liked fairies."

"Oh!—To be young and innocent again. I remember a time when I used to believe in fairies. Charles used to pretend to catch them for me in the garden."

Elizabeth smiled, recalling a long-ago conversation. "And did not he once fall in a pond doing so?"

Miss Bingley laughed unaffectedly—such a rare sight that Elizabeth was too shocked to laugh with her. "He did! How ever did you know that?"

"He told Jane. I never connected the story to you, though. I hope you will not mind my saying that such a frivolous activity did not seem the sort of thing you would enjoy."

Miss Bingley looked into her lap. "I am aware what you must think of me, Miss Bennet. You may believe that I feel enough shame myself to render your disapprobation completely superfluous. But I would have you know my intentions were good."

"Sorry?" Elizabeth could not keep the incredulity from her voice.

"When my father died, we lost almost everything. We *did* lose the home in which we had grown up. My brother was distraught, my sister was inconsolable. All I wished was to make it better for them. I knew—at least, I believed, that if I could make Darcy love me, marry me, then we could all live at

Pemberley, and our troubles would be over. But he rejected my affections, and being freshly bereaved, it was a loss too far, and I grew rather desperate. That is when I turned to George." She cleared her throat. "His father."

Elizabeth wished Miss Bingley would cease talking, for she was saying nothing that absolved her of blame—she was only making her increasingly angry on Darcy's behalf.

"He did not look his age, you know," she went on. "And he was exceedingly handsome. I would not have you think that I pursued a grizzly old man."

"I assure you I was not thinking of that at all!"

Miss Bingley's expression clouded as her more usual disdainful poise stole back over her. "No, of course not." Her mouth stretched thin into a reluctant smile. "I hope you will be very happy with Darcy."

"He told you then."

"He did."

"Good. I am sure we shall do very well, thank you." After an uncomfortable silence, Elizabeth added, "And I am sure you will be very happy with Mr Drummond. I hear he has a very impressive orangery."

"He does! With a collection of pineapple plants to put Pemberley's to shame. He tells me it is quite the envy of Leeds society."

The door opened and, not a moment too soon, Darcy came in. Elizabeth met his eyes and whatever he saw in her countenance did something quite extraordinary to his. "If you ladies are done, I should like to steal Miss Bennet for a moment," he said in a tone that brooked no objection.

Neither lady offered any resistance, and they parted ways without expressing any desire to see each other again, though both knew they would be obliged to, and no doubt more often than either would like. Darcy said nothing as he led

Elizabeth up the main staircase and along a corridor; he only listened as she lamented Miss Bingley's unfathomable self-absorption. He remained subdued until they passed a vacant alcove, whereupon he nudged her into it and, pressing himself heavily against her, kissed her more passionately than Elizabeth had yet comprehended was possible.

"What did I do to earn that?" she enquired breathlessly as he led her along the corridor afterwards.

"I warned you I would do it every time you laughed at something." He cast her a sideways look. "What was it that amused you this time?"

"Mrs Drummond's new pineapple arboretum. Where are you taking me?"

"To visit somebody else who wishes to see you before you go. This interview will be pleasanter than your last, I promise."

He was not wrong; the hour Elizabeth then spent with Darcy and his sister in the nursery was the perfect antidote to the five minutes she had been obliged to spend with Miss Bingley. Anna's delight at the news that Elizabeth would soon be her sister was uncontainable. She shrieked with pleasure before spending ten minutes at least alternately hugging each of them, and asking them to confirm, again, the news that she was too overjoyed to fully believe. Elizabeth and Darcy then managed, between them, to excite her about the adventure of gaining a new father, convinced her that Leeds was the best place to live in the whole of England, and promised that she could visit them at Pemberley as often as she chose.

When Elizabeth's departure could be delayed no longer, Darcy saw her to her uncle's carriage and sweetened his good-bye with the promise that this would be the last time they must part before he married her, for he meant to follow her back to Hertfordshire directly when she returned.

"Lizzy, I am most put out," said her uncle as they rolled out of the driveway. "I was rather pleased with my petrified spoon, but as holiday souvenirs go, I think your mother will consider that you have outdone us all when you bring home Mr Darcy."

40
To Catch You, Should You Fall

ELIZABETH TRIED HER HARDEST TO BE ATTENTIVE AND engaging during every one of her aunt's social calls in Lambton, but both Mr and Mrs Gardiner laughed at her so frequently for being distracted that she knew she could not claim much success. The days seemed to pass in both an abstracted blur and an agonisingly slow crawl—with one, notable exception. On Thursday morning, she received two letters from home. The first was from her father and was typically sportive.

> *My dearest Lizzy,*
> *I have written to Mr Darcy to give him my consent. He is the kind of man, indeed, to whom I should never dare refuse anything that he condescended to ask. I now give it to* <u>*you,*</u> *along with my heartiest felicitations. I am not completely happy with you, however. Had I known that you meant to reward him for his services to this family by giving him your hand in marriage, I should never have troubled myself to compose a letter so full of unctuous vapidity as that which I*

sent him upon our return from Brighton. You have put me quite on the back foot with my future son, and you must, therefore, be prepared that I shall take pains to regain what ground I can in the coming months. I shall begin my search for recompense in Pemberley's library at your earliest inconvenience.

Your mother will undoubtedly send her best when she has regained the faculty of speech.

Yours, &c.
Your Father

The second was from Jane and, in typically selfless style, not until she had filled two sides of paper expressing her delight at Elizabeth's engagement did she mention her own. Bingley had wasted little time in renewing his attentions, it transpired, and as there had been considerably fewer misapprehensions for them to navigate before they reached an understanding, they had come to it far quicker than she and Darcy. The news was shared joyously with Mr and Mrs Gardiner and gave Elizabeth even more reason to be pleased when she finally arrived at Pemberley on Friday evening and was greeted by not only Darcy but Bingley, too.

"My sincerest congratulations, sir," she said to him, shaking his hands warmly. "I could not be happier for you or Jane."

"You have beaten me to it, Lizzy. I meant to congratulate you first for, from what I hear, your engagement was the harder won. I did not have to leap into any underground caverns to persuade Jane to marry me."

"No, but your forgoing a cave in lieu of Longbourn's parlour means you have had to endure my mother's raptures in close confinement. We have all had our share of difficulties to overcome." She then introduced him to her aunt and uncle and left him speaking to them while she turned her attention to Darcy. "Well—how did it go?"

"With pomp and ceremony and too much time away from you. Mr Drummond seems to have taken a shine to Anna, though. I left them looking for fairies together in the famed orangery." He lifted Elizabeth's hand to kiss her fingers. "How do you like Pemberley?"

She smiled broadly, for she had decided within about a heartbeat of her first glimpse of the handsome stone building in its naturally rugged setting that she could very quickly grow accustomed to being mistress of such a house. "It is exactly as you described—it perfectly complements the landscape. Never have I seen a place for which nature has done more. A little like its owner, in fact." She enjoyed his surprise but did not allow enough time for it to turn into complacency before adding, "Shall I ever see inside, do you think?"

His gaze, which had already been boring into her as though to make up for lost time, became positively rapacious. He offered her his arm, and when she took it, he pulled her tightly to his side and said under his breath, "God, I have missed you."

They were shown all the principle rooms, which Elizabeth agreed with her relations were well-proportioned and elegant, but Darcy reserved showing her certain parts of the house for a private tour after dinner, to which none of the other guests objected. A man showing his future wife her new home—indeed, her new life—for the first time had a right to expect some privacy.

In a small, comfortable sitting room on the second floor, she was delighted to discover a glazed door that led onto a small balcony. She went out onto it immediately to admire what she could see of the grounds in the twilight. The ridge of the hill, crowned with wood, from which they had descended to reach the house, could just be made out. The black course of the river, rendered motionless by the dark, lay corkscrewed across the lawn, and the spectral silhouettes of trees were scattered on the banks.

Darcy stepped behind her and placed his hand upon her hips. "What is your real opinion?" he said quietly with his mouth close to her ear.

"I think that if Anna is going to find a fairy anywhere, it will be here, for it is absolutely magical." She felt his lips curl into a smile.

"You think you will be happy here then?"

"I never doubted that I would be happy, but I confess I had not comprehended quite what a beautiful home it would be. It is almost a shame we must go back to Hertfordshire."

"On the contrary—the sooner we go there the better. I have waited long enough to marry you."

Elizabeth abruptly became intensely aware of the solidness of his presence behind her, the heat of his hands at her waist, and warmth of his breath on her neck. She had not yet learnt to display her affections as boldly as he so did not turn and kiss him as she would have liked, but she smiled to herself at his admission of impatience and looked forward to such a time as her courage might have risen enough that she could alleviate it.

"Speaking of marriage," she said, "Mr Bingley seems very happy."

"He is," Darcy replied. "Which is a vast relief to me. I should have been very sorry if my interference had ruined his chances of happiness."

"But be truthful—was not his return to Netherfield at least partly your doing?"

"Only in as much as, once his sister's engagement was

agreed, and all their reputations secured, I relayed to him what you had told me of Jane's feelings. I made certain to leave to him the decision of whether or not to return. I had worried that your sister's affections might have diminished in the intervening months, but I could not justify concealing them from him if there was even the smallest hope that he might succeed in regaining her esteem." He slid his arms all the way around Elizabeth's waist and rested his chin on her shoulder. "I have never been more jealous of anyone than Bingley, when he left Matlock to return to Hertfordshire. I would have given my eyeteeth for the chance to see you again. Imagine my delight when you turned up at Kelstedge a few days later."

"That was an exceedingly opportune turn of events, but not one Mr Bingley can have foreseen. I hope he appreciates that you remained in Derbyshire to arrange *his* sister's wedding while he gadded off to make love to mine."

He hugged her a little tighter. "I like this fierce defence of me, and I would have you do it as often as possible—but I offered to stay and make all the arrangements. It was important to me that I put an end to all the trouble and anguish my father caused, and it was the least I could do for Bingley after the misery I inflicted on him by persuading him to leave your sister in the first place. It was what you said to me at Hunsford about treating his happiness with contempt that made me realise—"

"I wish you would stop reminding me what I said then," she interrupted, laughing, though she was not entirely joking.

"But you were right." He released her from his embrace and came to stand beside her, leaning with his forearms on the parapet and looking out into the gathering darkness. "Both our lives were turned upside down by the actions of his sister and my father. He and I have been protecting Caroline and Anna for nearly six years now. I front most of the costs, because I have the means and because it is what my father's estate owes them, but I can at least remove to Pemberley or Town whenever I choose. Bingley must live with his sister and take the brunt of her unhappiness—and as you know, she is scarcely a grateful charge. It is a very difficult relationship."

"I had noticed that they argue frequently, which he obviously dislikes."

"Neither does he enjoy being moved from pillar to post, but it has been necessary to relocate them again and again as they are chased away by rumours and pettiness. Netherfield was the ninth lease I took for them, and we hoped it might be different, for it was the first time we had tried situating Anna in a separate house. The intention was for them to maintain a minimal presence within the neighbourhood until they had established a more robust reputation. Instead, Bingley committed us to the first assembly someone mentioned, danced with every woman there, accepted every invitation to dinner, and allowed every mother in Meryton to believe he was the rightful property of their daughters. I was furious with him. After everything I had sacrificed, all the money I laid out, all the trouble to which I had gone—even having the cottage refurbished for Anna—I took it as a betrayal that he should so flagrantly cast aside all our carefully laid plans."

"I cannot say that I blame you for feeling that way."

"But I ought to have seen—I *did* see, when you made me look—how unhappy he was. For six years he put his sister, his niece, me, my pride, my father's name, above his own wishes. In retrospect, I think he was so tired and lonely, and Hertfordshire society was so appealing, he could not resist."

Elizabeth looked surreptitiously at Darcy's profile. The same could evidently be said of him, for he had come to Hertfordshire burdened with all manner of responsibilities that required him to remain aloof, to speak as little as possible so as to deter interest, to slight anyone with whom it was even suggested he dance—only to fall in love with a woman he was convinced would jeopardise it all. "I understand now why you were so opposed to his having a ball."

Darcy scoffed derisively. "Can you conceive of a worse way of concealing a scandalous secret than to invite a hundred people into your home? Dancing with you was the only part of that evening I enjoyed. I spent the rest of it seething. Especially after Sir William announced that the entire neighbourhood expected Bingley would propose to your sister."

"Is that why you left the supper table—because you were angry with Mr Bingley?"

He turned to look at her. "No." Then he lifted a hand to caress her face. "I left the table because had I stayed a moment longer with you looking at me the way you were, I should have scandalised the whole of Meryton anyway by doing this." He kissed her with a heady mix of tenderness and urgency that left her reeling.

"Oh!" she whispered breathily, smiling because she was certain she had not blushed this time, when it was too dark for her rising bravery to be worth aught. "I thought you left because Mr Bingley mentioned your mother."

"He only said that to direct the conversation away from siblings."

"I thought that was what he had done! Only I could not work out why. And I was more used to you being the one to alter the course of a conversation. You do it very often."

He pulled a rueful face. "You would never know it, but disguise of every sort is my abhorrence. Yet, I have been forced to conceal the truth for so many years I have become disagreeably adept at it. Bingley and his sisters have not. They become flustered by the mere mention of children and draw more notice to themselves in their attempts to evade the matter than if they simply answered the question. I suppose it has become second nature for me to assist them where I can."

Elizabeth had used to think him supercilious for it. Now she merely loved him more for the prodigious care he took of all his friends. Friends to whom they really ought to return, for they had been gone for some time. This she pointed out to Darcy, but he did not immediately comply.

"I have something to show you first," he said, and taking her hand, he led her back into the sitting room and through a door to an adjoining room.

"Is this your bedroom?" Elizabeth enquired.

Darcy was rummaging through a writing desk and answered without turning to look at her that it was.

"I am almost too afraid to ask why you were in such a rage to show me in here."

He came towards her and handed her a letter. "I did not want to show you the room. I wanted to show you this."

She took it, and at a nod from him, opened it. One glance was enough to confirm what he had given her. "This is Mr Wickham's letter!"

Darcy nodded.

"May I read it?"

"I should like you to."

She leant closer to the nearest candle to more easily see the spidery scrawl.

My dear Darcy,
I trust you are well. I have not heard from you in a while, which must mean I have done nothing to disappoint you in that time—a fact I should be very grateful if you could bear in mind when you read this next.

Do you remember old Sheringham, from Trinity? Strange, pedantic little man whose eyes are too close together. I recall *that you never liked him, in which case, this might make you laugh, if indeed you can remember how. I owed him a bob or two, and since he was being a top-notch prig about it, I resolved to lift his watch from his lodgings and pawn it to pay him back with his own money. It would have been a fine joke for a most deserving fellow, had not he spotted me climbing back out the window. Turns out it was his grandfather's watch, and he is threatening to involve his father if I do not return it. I am unable to do that, however, for I had to ditch it before anyone saw me with it, and though I have scoured the place I threw it, it is yet to turn up. He cannot prove a thing, of course, for it is his word against mine, and that, he is well aware, means his word against <u>yours</u>, so there is not a hope in hell of his being believed. One has to wonder, if he is making this much fuss about a dead man's watch, what manner of hue and cry he would make if he discovered I had tupped his sister. Thank my stars he did not catch me at <u>that</u>.*

The debt is another matter, for more people know about it, and since I had to lose the watch, I could not pawn it as I planned. I was rather hoping you could settle the bill for me. I know you will, for you love nothing better than being richer and more righteous than I. You may thank me for giving you another reason to despise me next time we both dine at P.

Do give my regards to your father.
Yours, &c.
Wickham

PS The debt is £360.

Elizabeth thrust it back at Darcy in disgust. "He is vile. Absolutely vile."

Darcy nodded but did not take the letter.

"Lydia said the contents of this would get him hanged," she said as she folded it more neatly. "If you could hang a man for insolence, I could well believe it, but for stealing a watch—surely not?"

"Indeed not. He no doubt said that to impress your sister. But Sheringham's father is the Earl of Casterbury. Hanging would probably be preferable to crossing him."

"I see." She tried to give the letter back a second time, but again, Darcy refused to take it.

"I showed this to you for a reason, Elizabeth. Now that you have that in your hand, pray tell me, what would you do with it? Burn it? Give it back? Hand it to Sheringham? I am not used to indecision, but I do not mind admitting to you that I have lost a good deal of sleep attempting to decide what would be for the best."

Elizabeth looked at the letter, feeling all the considerable weight of the responsibility Darcy had born these past six years. After a few moment's consideration, she enquired, "Will I have my own room?"

Darcy was evidently taken aback by the question but confirmed that she would.

"Before I answer, may I see it?"

Frowning in puzzlement, Darcy led her back into the sitting room and through an opposite door into a very fine bedroom, but Elizabeth was too occupied looking for something specific to pay much attention. As she had hoped, there was a desk in this room, too—an exquisitely inlaid writing desk with several drawers. She opened one and put the letter in it then turned to Darcy. "There, now it is *our* burden, not yours alone. As all your burdens will be from now on."

Darcy stared, his lips slightly parted as though he wished to speak but did not know what to say, the turn of his countenance leaving her in no doubt that he was deeply moved. In that moment, Elizabeth found she had no need of courage.

Showing him how dearly she loved him was as easy as falling into his arms; and once there, she knew, unequivocally, that they would always catch each other if ever it seemed that either of them would fall.

The End

ACKNOWLEDGMENTS

Fallen was begun in a time when things were normal. Then the Coronavirus Pandemic struck, and the entire world was plunged into chaos. As a result, *Fallen* was finished during the strangest of circumstances: a global lockdown. My first thanks, therefore, go to my family. My husband, who, compelled to work from home, set up his temporary desk in the tiny little bedroom at the farthest corner of our house so his Zoom meeting wouldn't disturb me as I wrote. My children, who, consigned to home learning and banished from playing with their friends, tiptoed around our house during my working hours, interrupting me only in the direst emergencies (needing a snack, being bored, fraternal in-fighting and the like). My parents, who spent hours a day Skyping my children to give them some much-needed human interaction and preventing them from turning completely feral while I scribbled away at my desk and my husband hid, whispering, behind his. Without all their significant compromises, *Fallen* would still be in my head and these pages would be blank. Particular thanks go to my mum, who shares the journey of every story I write from inception to completion, and whose insights and enthusiasm keep writing fun, even when it's tortuous.

Thank you, as well, to everyone at Quills & Quartos for their continued faith in me as a writer. To Amy D'Orazio, who has the vision to sort the wheat from the chaff of my writing, leaving only the best words behind. To Kristi Rawley, who helps me, again and again, to polish my words into finished stories. And to Susan Adriani, for creating the most beautiful cover for this story to live in.

Most importantly of all, thank you to Jane Austen. For your razor wit, stunning turns of phrase and captivating characters; for the privilege of spending more time with your Darcy and Elizabeth; for the honour of incorporating some of your inimitable writing into this alternative journey for them; and for inspiring me to write, I thank you.

ABOUT THE AUTHOR

Jessie Lewis enjoys words far too much for her own good and was forced to take up writing them down in order to save her family and friends from having to listen to her saying so many of them. She dabbled in poetry during her teenage years, though it was her studies in Literature and Philosophy at university that firmly established her admiration for the potency of the English language. She has always been particularly in awe of Jane Austen's literary cunning and has delighted in exploring Austen's regency world in her own historical fiction writing. It is of no relevance whatsoever to her ability to string words together coherently that she lives in Hertfordshire with two tame cats, two feral children and a pet husband. She is also quite tall, in case you were wondering.

Jessie is also the author of *Mistaken, Speechless*, and *The Edification of Lady Susan*. *Fallen* is Jessie's third novel.

You can check out her musings on the absurdities of language and life on her blog, **LifeinWords.blog**.

Subscribers to the Quills & Quartos Mailing list receive bonus content, advance notice of sales and alerts to new releases by Jessie Lewis and other great authors.
Join our mailing list today at
www.QuillsandQuartos.com

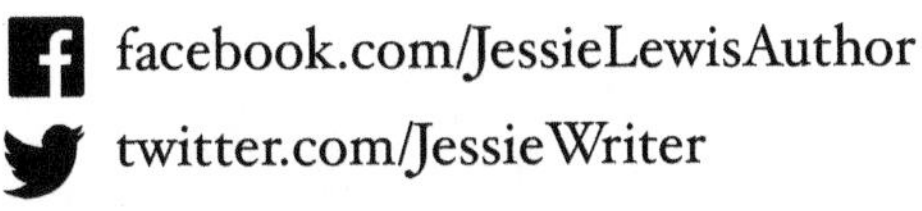

ALSO BY JESSIE LEWIS

Speechless

Voted Austenesque Reviews Readers' Favourite 2019 and From Pemberley to Milton Favourite Book 2019

Could anything be worse than to be trapped in a confined space with the woman you love?

Fitzwilliam Darcy knows his duty, and it does not involve succumbing to his fascination for a dark-eyed beauty from an unheard of family in Hertfordshire. He has run away from her once already. Yet fate has a wicked sense of humour and deals him a blow that not only throws him back into her path but quite literally puts him at Elizabeth Bennet's mercy. Stranded with her at a remote inn and seriously hampered by injury, Darcy very quickly loses the battle to conquer his feelings, but can he win the war to make himself better understood without the ability to speak?

Thus begins an intense journey to love and understanding that is at times harrowing, sometimes hilarious and at all times heartwarming.

Mistaken

Voted Austenesque Reviews Readers' Favourite 2017 and Austenesque Reviews Favourite 2018

A tempestuous acquaintance and disastrous marriage proposal make it unlikely Mr Darcy and Elizabeth Bennet will ever reconcile. Despairing of their own reunion, they attend with great energy to salvaging that of Darcy's friend Mr Bingley and Elizabeth's sister Jane. People are rarely so easily manoeuvred in and out of love, however, and there follows a series of misunderstandings, both wilful and unwitting, that complicates the path to happiness for all four star-crossed lovers more than ever before.

A witty and romantic novel that delights in the folly of human nature, Mistaken honours Jane Austen's original *Pride & Prejudice* and holds appeal for readers of all genres.

Rational Creatures: Stirrings of Feminism in the Hearts of Jane Austen's Fine Ladies (The Quill Collective)

Jane Austen: True romantic or rational creature? Her novels transport us back to the Regency, a time when well-mannered gentlemen and finely-bred ladies fell in love as they danced at balls and rode in carriages. Yet her heroines, such as Elizabeth Bennet, Anne Elliot, and Elinor Dashwood, were no swooning, fainthearted damsels in distress. Austen's novels have become timeless classics because of their biting wit, honest social commentary, and because she wrote of strong women who were ahead of their day. True to their principles and beliefs, they fought through hypocrisy and broke social boundaries to find their happily-ever-after.

In the third romance anthology of The Quill Collective series, sixteen celebrated Austenesque authors write the untold histories of Austen's brave adventuresses, her shy maidens, her talkative spinsters, and her naughty matrons. Peek around the curtain and discover what made Lady Susan so wicked, Mary Crawford so capricious, and Hettie Bates so in need of Emma Woodhouse's pity.

Edited by Christina Boyd

Foreword by Devoney Looser

CPSIA information can be obtained
at www.ICGtesting.com
Printed in the USA
FSHW021927120421
80396FS